"There's a little bit of Rachael in every woman. Told with Southern charm and grit, her story is about the price we pay for love. With just the right mixture of humor and pathos, we are led through the turbulence of a passionate love affair. Travel with Rachael and Christopher from the beauty of the Smoky Mountains to the grandeur of San Francisco; you'll be glad you did!"

—Patti Speer, D.D.S.

This novel is a work of fiction. Any references to historical events; to real people, living or dead; or to real locales are intended only to give the fiction a sense of reality and authenticity. Names, characters, places, and incidents either are the product of the author's imagination or are used fictiously, and their resemblance, if any, to real-life counterparts is entirely coincidental.

All rights reserved. Printed in the United States of America. No part of this book may be used or reproduced in any manner whatsoever without written permission except in the case of brief quotations embodied in critical articles and reviews. For information address inquiries to L. A. Dydds, Inc., P. O. Box 10764, Knoxville, TN, 37939.

Book cover designed by Melinda Winters
Layout designed by J. L. Saloff
Photograph of *Euonymus americanus* (a.k.a.: Hearts-abustin'-with-love) used by permission

Fonts used: Times New Roman, Parisian BT, Century 725, Hoefler Text Ornaments

First Edition

Hunley, Nancy Melinda
   This Time Around

ISBN 0-9742830-0-2 (soft cover)
ISBN 0-9742830-3-7 (hard cover)
Copyright TXu1-096-390
        TXu-885-617

This book is dedicated to the man who held
the sparrow until her wing mended.

This Time Around

Nancy Melinda Hunley

The silken bands that bind lovers together
are only as strong as the weaker heart
and only as weak as the stronger.

—Nancy Melinda Hunley
May 1997

One

Running reconnaissance for the coming day, dawn slithered between the slats of the closed wooden blinds. After stealthily easing across the bedroom floor, its rays reached the rumpled bed to nudge lightly her limp, bare arm.

Rachael JubelleLee Taite was awake. The rest of the household was not. Her two elderly Siamese cats snored a soothing duet from either side of her body. Beatrice's contralto carried the melody while Sybyl harmonized in a slightly higher tone. Rachael listened to their familiar song while she remained motionless, face down on her bed, in a futile attempt to stop the forward progress of time.

Rachael had never liked sleeping alone, and after the sisters joined her almost sixteen years earlier, she was never again alone in her bed. Rachael felt her cats' warmth and the weight of their furry bodies nestled against the crook of her left leg and the bent elbow of her right arm. Planning to discern which cat was on which body part, she concentrated on their voices but was not quite able to distinguish the direction of the separate sounds. She might have been awake, but she certainly was not alert.

She heard the clock in the downstairs living room strike six. A few seconds of quiet followed before the clock radio on the table across the room clicked on and a sultry Tina Turner demanded, *"You better be good to me!"*

The sun had refused to halt its advance, and her Friday had begun.

Rachael's eyes snapped wide open. Maybe I should've selected that as my wedding march! flashed through her consciousness.

The cats stopped snoring as the song's barrage announced the day. Since their bedmate did not immediately move, they snuggled closer. Each cat took a deep breath that was immediately exhaled into a low purr. Relaxing back against her naked body, they offered her a share in their feline plans for a lazy morning.

"Sorry, ladies," Rachael apologized to the cats as she carefully moved over Sybyl's prone body to sit on the edge of her bed.

From the very day she had carried the kittens home, Rachael had treated her four-legged companions as hirsute toddlers who were at that stage of verbal development where they could understand language but had not yet themselves acquired the gift of speech. After years of living together, each had learned to distinguish meanings to some of the other species' vocalizations. Although Rachael was never able to speak Cat, just as the sisters never came to speak Human, that minor oversight never interfered with their mutual dialogues.

While mustering energy to stand, Rachael dangled her legs over the edge of the mattress. In the subdued early light, she focused sleep-fogged eyes on her preferred sleepwear, plain cotton socks covering her feet. For some time, she blankly stared at their ghostly white glow against the dark oak floor.

"This isn't goin' to get it!" she suddenly announced. Completing her one-sided conversation, Rachael explained to Beatrice and Sybyl, "My plate's too full today to laze about with the likes of you."

She stood, stretched and then padded across the floor and down the short hall to the upstairs bath.

Her eyes stared back.

Rachael knew she had completed her morning jog because her skin felt grainy with dried sweat; however, she could not remember how long she had been staring at her reflection in the bathroom mirror or what activities she had completed before getting herself in front of the chunky, porcelain pedestal sink. Her brain processed that white, foamy globs peeked around the black-handled toothbrush held motionless between her lips, but Rachael was quite oblivious to the steam billowing up from the tub behind her.

Not bothering to remove her toothbrush, she mumbled a proclamation to the familiar face in the mirror, "Today, I marry for the last time." Rachael briefly considered her previous marriages before invoking the ancient chant, "Third time's the charm."

No, this is our fourth time, her mind interrupted.

After that comment registered, Rachael shrugged off her inertia to continue brushing her teeth. She was accustomed to being corrected by her mind.

A loud slurp followed by gulping rales filtered into her awareness. She frowned. Rachael's attention shifted from her reflection to the steam filling the room.

"Oh, double damn!" She muttered, "Not the tub again!"

She quickly turned. The water in the deep, vintage tub was within an inch of overflowing. She stepped over to turn off the hot water. Soaking in an almost-too-hot bubble bath was one of her many indulgences, yet this particular treat would require work before she could step in without blanching her body. Rachael sighed and shook her head in disbelief. This was not the first time her mental flights had allowed a tub to fill too full and too hot. She found that fact irritating because she had been schooled in the best Southern tradition to strive for perfection, as in the perfect daughter, the perfect lady, the perfect hostess, the perfect . . . whatever. She hated looking down to find clay feet attached to her ankles.

Her hand burned as she reached under the scalding water and flipped up the lever to open the drain, making room for the necessary tempering. With the water level lowering, Rachael returned to the sink to spit out toothpaste and rinse her mouth.

"Oh, double, double damn!" she mumbled as she reached for a nearby white plastic container. She had forgotten to floss first. In exasperation, she shouted, "I don't have time for this!"

Rachael was fifty-seven years old. She knew this was not the morning for her mind to wander but wandering it was, for Rachael Taite's mind had a mind of its own. She had been blessed with that particular curse early on in her existence. When she was younger, Rachael had regarded her mind as an invisible conjoined twin that spoke when not spoken to. Hers had been, at best, an inconvenient sibling to have.

The steam fogging her bathroom did not help matters either. Its mistiness merely cleared the way for memories, and those sweet memories only made keeping Rachael's mind present in the moment a more difficult task.

Time is such a relative thing, she thought. Reaching for a dry washcloth, Rachael continued aloud, "Einstein had said so and later devised a theory to prove it."

After wiping the mirror free of condensation, her eyes once more stared back at her. Without the help of her prescription glasses, the tiny wrinkles that whispered the reality of her years were not seen, allowing Rachael to view her reflection as it had appeared many years back.

She always noticed her eyes first because she considered them to be the only features which were truly hers. Dark, teal-colored irises outlined by a narrow band of navy. That coloration had not been handed down through the generations like some piece of old family silver and, happily, she did not have to share her iris pigmentation with anyone she knew.

When Rachael was much younger, more than a few lovers had insisted her eyes were green. Rachael had always thought those fool men had balls to argue with her. She had told them she ought to know damn well what color her eyes were because she saw them every time she applied make-up. She knew them to be blue, but then she had never seen her eyes flip color from blue to green as they had.

She went on inventorying the features creating her composite face. Her short nose came to her through her father. It had been his mother's and all her people's. Her full lips smiled her mother's generous smile. The shape of her face with its high cheekbones and gently squared jaw echoed the face in the fading sepia picture of Jubelle Lee, her mother's father's mother. Her complexion, which lied about her age, came from Rachael's maternal grandmother. Although she would tease people who commented on her flawlessly youthful skin that they really would not want to see the portrait she kept hidden in a closet at home, Rachael was always secretly pleased with what they saw.

The rest of her body came from parts borrowed at random from the combined gene pools. She would never see five-two in height. From the eighth grade onward, she never wore anything smaller than a D-cup. Rachael was also burdened with the family tendency to cruise past pleasantly plump. She had small ears with smaller ear lobes that had just enough room to hold posts for the now fashionable pierced earrings. Otherwise, she would have been forced to glue ear adornment on or go without.

The Taites always commented she had her father's sense of humor. Not even the sound of her laughter belonged to her for Maurie, her mother's deceased sister, had originally owned it.

Rachael looked again at the black lashes guarding her eyes. She liked that old saying about eyes being the windows to the soul, and she was fiercely proud that hers were uniquely hers.

She pushed a lock of hair behind her right ear before leaning forward to check for telltale gray roots around her hairline. She saw none. After that aborted trip to Seattle, Rachael had taken to coloring her hair. Her once graying, brunette locks were now kept rich auburn, a tint purposely selected because there were no redheads to be found hanging from her family tree.

She was also secretly pleased that little rebellion went unnoticed, since people who did not know her well simply assumed her dye job was due to a run-of-the-mill, mid-life crisis. She had always favored minor forays against the Established Order rather than out-and-out confrontations because she believed that tiny acting-outs remained below Society's radar, greatly reducing any chance of being detected. Since Rachael never considered herself bold enough to be a cultural revolutionary, she preferred to think of her rebellious nature as simply marching to a different drummer.

Rachael Taite did not appear her age. Nor had she looked her age years earlier when her graying hair was worn in a tight, no-frills bun and the morning had been filled with preparations for that fateful Friday.

Thinking back to that pivotal day, Rachael closed her eyes and bent her head as if she were about to receive a benediction. Moments after her eyes closed, she distinctly felt a current of cool air against the nape of her neck. She sensed a familiar presence moving to stand behind her. Instantly, she felt the hairs on the back of her neck and on her arms stand up. She knew if he only stood a fraction closer, they could be touching.

"Sweet Mother," she whispered, "I didn't expect you."

She heard him say, "You're the icing on my cake. Where else would I be today?"

With the treasured timbre of his beloved voice easing the shock of his surprising arrival, she relaxed into the pleasure of having him near once again. With eyes still closed, Rachael thought she felt fingers brushing across her bare shoulders before moving over to trace a line down both upper arms. She smiled, laughing softly, as a delectable shiver traveled her spine. The thrill gradually increased to a strong shudder before abruptly ending and, next, she felt cold.

Had her mother been there to witness that tremor, she would have automatically commented, "Rachael, someone's walkin' on your grave!"

Rachael drew in a deep breath and slowly released it. She almost detected the faint aroma of his body in the air.

She confided in a low voice, "I'm marryin' a most wonderful man this afternoon." Her tone held such love and pride and contentment that anyone overhearing could not possibly misinterpret her words for a spiteful boast.

He responded, "I know, Rachael. Nothing in heaven or on earth could keep me away from you this day."

She felt, rather than heard, his throaty, whispered words caressing her right ear. With eyes still shut, Rachael willed herself to concentrate on his unforgettable voice and on the delicious sensations resonating through her body.

"If we hadn't met, I'd be too scared to ever try again," Rachael told the man she could not see. Her throat tightened as she spoke until she could barely utter her last few words.

For most of her life, she had foolishly thought that aching sensation was caused by fear. Wiser now, she embraced it. She did not resist the forceful emotions underlying her last statement as they spewed from her gullet to press against her vocal cords, rushing higher still until her eyeballs prickled and tears flooded her closed eyes. Rachael felt the warm, heavy liquid well up and then spill between her eyelids, tracing heat down her cheeks before falling chilled onto her naked breasts.

She would not wipe the tears away.

He could not even if he tried.

She heard his barely audible words of comfort. "Cry only happy tears, my sweet Rachael, for this is a happy time."

She felt a sensation gently brush against her right shoulder and thought it could have been his lips. She next felt warmth at her back as she sensed him moving away. Rachael opened her eyes as she quickly spun around, hoping to catch a glimpse of him before he left, but he was gone as if he had never been there at all.

Rachael raised her head. Leaving the dueling tear tracks on her body, she walked over to the tub and lowered herself into the embracing, almost-too-hot, foamy bathwater. With memories of the past pressing against the present as lightly as the bubbles resting on her body, she held up a soapy right hand to stare through the glistening suds cupped there. The massed, iridescent circles distorted her view of the bathroom as the events of that Friday in May, fifteen years ago, drifted between her and this Friday's busy agenda. Finally, relaxing against the curve of the old porcelain tub, Rachael Taite chose to do nothing at all that might interfere with the passage of retreating time.

Two

Peering deeper inside the bubbles resting on her hand, Rachael was momentarily taken aback at the ease with which those long ago events bled into the present. She had once believed those memories were safely tucked away. Stopping to briefly consider whether to continue her viewing, she almost hesitated. Then, easing her body deeper under the water until only her head remained above the mounded, fragrant bubbles, she allowed those old visions to wash over her mind unimpeded.

She had always enjoyed replaying segments of her past, a form of recreation learned by listening to her parents' conversations when she was a small girl. But oddly, whenever she revisited her personal collection of memories, she occasionally experienced scenes that her Mom and Daddy never described to her. She had fleeting visions of being crowded alongside unwashed bodies in a drafty hall awaiting a stirring saga to be told by a medieval storyteller or of sitting primly, her ankles crossed, in a parlor while viewing pictorial vignettes in a newfangled stereoscope. But most times when she played the game, Rachael felt as if she were comfortably stretched out on the refurbished fainting couch by her bed, ready to view a favorite home video.

Just as some tales depicted cruelties and some pictures recalled sadnesses, she, too, carried unhappy memories. However, Rachael had always fast-forwarded, quicker than a crawdad scooting backwards, right through those segments.

Relaxing within the warm bath, she recalled it was spring when they began and, appropriately enough, it was spring when they ended. In the past, if she spoke at all about that May and the events that followed, Rachael had jokingly placed full responsibility upon the unearthly powers wielded by the ancient moon illuminating the night they met. Otherwise, she reasoned, how else would a responsible man and an intelligent woman embark upon the long journey they had shared? She brooked no other explanation suggested by her listener.

She publicly proposed that unverifiable argument to justify their actions because Rachael understood that what she accepted to be the real truth would be much too farfetched for many to believe. She knew, deep in her soul, that people who have never felt the sharp pang that pierces your heart upon seeing a foal's first wobbly attempts to stand and nurse would most likely misjudge their few days together. She also firmly believed those same individuals would neither hear the crashing symphony in a thunderstorm nor the soft hymn in a misty sunrise. She felt only pity for people like that, regarding them all as being shade-blind, since they perceived only black and white while missing out on all the subtle grays.

Whenever Rachael wondered how people like that live, her fertile mind would immediately counter with the better question: Wonder if people like that truly live?

She remembered the hike that long ago Friday had started with the sameness of a ritual. Having no reason to think it would be any different from any other pleasant hike she had taken, Rachael awoke early that morning, needing no help from the clock radio she kept as backup on the other side of the room. Stretched out their full lengths, the furry sisters had slept closely on each side of her body. The three had been sharing lives and her bed after Rachael purchased the two kitties when they were six weeks old. Still lying on her king-sized bed sandwiched between their soft, warm cat bodies, she had mentally listed the preparations required for another trip via her favorite trail up the mountain to stay one more time at the Lodge.

After countless hikes, the list had acquired a methodical familiarity: wake the cats, feed the cats, feed herself, pack for the two-day hike, get Mom, drive to the mountains and park where the car would be visible from the highway, thereby lessening the chance of a break-in during the night.

Except for the addition of the cat steps, the sequences of The Ritual had been unchanged for many years. She felt it anchored her life to some larger, intangible force. Rachael found that repetition comforting, almost like praying with a rosary.

Alum Bluff was not the only trail to the Lodge or, in fact, the only trail she hiked, but this particular path was knitted into important events in her life. Rachael had first hiked it during the days of uncertainty following separation from husband number one. Although she usually invited various friends to walk along with her, when it became time to work out tangles in her life, Rachael wanted just this trail and the company of her mother. Through the years, the hike had come to represent a time and place for rethinking her future, for starting off in new directions. She used the time on the trail, instead of those at year's end, to make new resolutions. But mainly, she had come to realize those few hours were simply a chance to have her mother's undivided attention.

Even with small alterations which are inevitable with the passage of time, Rachael found the overall sameness along Alum Bluff Trail life-affirming: a tree could be overturned with its great tangled knot of roots at right angles to the ground, revealing the absence of an anchoring taproot that the young Rachael had been taught all trees were supposed to have; a new rockslide could expose barren, slate-blue stones, leaving a mountain wound that later haired over with tenacious ferns and delicate saxifrages; new drainage cuts could be carved by work crews into the rocky soil since her last visit; even the change of seasons affected the feel of the treks. Each hike was different yet wondrously the same.

This particular one started on the third Friday in May 1989. The mountains had received a hard rain the day before, and water was audibly percolating through the leaf litter down into the loamy soil. Spring was showing in shy glory. Painted trilliums looked like fallen stars. Jacks-in-the-pulpit hid along the trail's edge. Ferns made fiddleheads. A golden glow filtered through newly green foliage as piercing shafts of sunlight knifed through gaps in the leafy canopy, dappling the path ahead and the woods all around. Water bounced and roared down jumbled boulders in nearby creek beds. Insects hummed. Crows occasionally cawed. Juncos sang as they flitted about. The rich aromas of the mature forest permeated the air with more than enough scents to stimulate all scent receptacles in every available nostril. Soaking up the abundance of the mountain's opulence, Rachael felt that this day was picture perfect for detailing changes for the coming months.

Rachael and her mother walked a leisurely pace. Both women held the philosophy that hiking was comparable to life, in that it was never the destination but the journey that made either one a pleasure. Their conversations ran the gauntlet from work to friends to family to their surroundings.

"Volume was up fifteen per cent over last year," I told Mom.

"Good for you!" she replied before changing the subject. "How do you think Margaret will do this weekend without you?"

"Just fine. She's been there two weeks." I grew thoughtful as I considered Mom's words before adding, "Besides, Liz will keep her goin' in the right direction."

"Do you think she'll ever find a man to marry who has a good heart?" Mom always had believed, right down to her painted toenails, that a woman's life was worthless without a husband to share it.

I chuckled. "Well, she did move to Knoxville after that third one died. Maybe a new venue will help. But don't worry about Margaret, Mom. This one remembered her in his will, too. She's better off financially than I'll ever be."

Six months earlier a tearful Margaret DuBose Millirons had phoned from South Carolina with the news that Regions Gallyon had died and that she did not think any other man in McKibben County would ever be brave enough to ask her out again. Now having gone through the top available candidates, I knew there were few single men left in that county who Margaret considered financially able to afford her. Because I had liked this one, I tried my damnedest not to make light of the man's death but seeing how this was Margaret's third fiancé to die from a heart attack, being engaged to her had become a horrible, black joke.

Only the week before his death, Margaret had called to describe the bitch of a time she was having selecting a suitable wedding gown and had added that, as a last resort, an exasperated Regions had finally sent her to a Charleston dressmaker.

After the whirl of her fiancé's funeral activities was over and before I left the community of North, South Carolina, to drive back over the mountain to Tennessee, I had casually asked my grieving friend to come visit. Much to my surprise, three weekends ago Margaret showed up, announcing that she was moving to Knoxville and would be coming to work at my restaurant. I knew Margaret did not need the money; she merely wanted something interesting to occupy her time while she shepherded her financial windfalls through the stock market.

"I'll tell all the men to schedule a treadmill test," I assured my mother, "should they decide to ask her for a second date."

Having my former college roommate nearby felt like the good old times. When Margaret and I were younger, my world seemed to swirl with more exciting possibilities whenever we got together. Back in our late teens and early twenties, I had never known what kind of mischief we would fall into, a fact both sets of parents had found unsettling.

Even now, despite being in my forties, I was aware of a vague twinge, like the sudden lone, stiff breeze whispering the announcement of a coming storm, hinting of future excitements. That teasing, tingling sensation had been missing from my life for too many years, but it returned when Margaret waltzed into Knoxville. Although the charged atmosphere hinted of unforeseen doors waiting to be opened, Margaret's presence at the restaurant eased some of the pressure on Liz and me.

With her questions about Margaret answered, Mom shifted to a different subject. She cleared her throat, signaling she was about to share a great secret. "Do you know what I heard Liz say yesterday?" she asked in a low, conspiratorial tone.

Playing the straight man in a comedic skit, I fed her my line, "No, Mom, what did Liz say yesterday?"

Mom drew a deep breath before confiding, "Liz dropped a plate of lemon squares in the back, and she said the f-word." According to my mother, it was permissible for a lady to do the f-word, but no lady ever said the f-word.

I laughed aloud for, as far as I knew, Liz — nee Elizabeth Aiken McNabb — did not do the f-word. She was an innocent who was committed to waiting for the right man to come into her life. Whenever I thought of towheaded, blue-eyed Liz, a pristine field of daisies waving under a blue sky dotted with lazy, powder-puff clouds came to mind. How Liz had remained a close friend for the past sixteen years was beyond my understanding, because I was no angel and that expletive was one of my favorites. We were as different as *crème brûlée* and old-fashioned, blackberry cobbler. Like Mom, I found it incongruous that my sweet, soft-spoken Liz would say the f-word. One blasphemed when using that word and 'Liz' in the same sentence.

"Well, I am surprised," I replied. "I didn't know she even knew the f-word."

I learned long ago it was more expedient to use Mom's euphemism than to say 'fuck' and have to listen to her lecture. Most times, I appreciated the rules that a woman raised in the South must juggle. Other times, they were as inconvenient as dead weights crammed into a poorly balanced backpack I was made to shoulder. Still, I could not imagine anywhere else I would rather live, because here I knew the lay of the land. It was as familiar as this trail I climbed.

As we continued up the mountain's slope, Mom and I pointed out signs heralding spring's emergence, each not wanting the other to miss any part of the beauty about us. Specific areas along the trail brought to mind past hikes, and discussing previous hikes was another important step in The Ritual.

When Mom stepped off the footbridge that park rangers had created from a fallen tree, she stared up at the steep, crudely hewn stone stairs set under the massive natural formation known as Arch Rock. Placing her boot on the first tread, she asked, "Wasn't it here that your father turned back because it started sprinklin' and he didn't want to get wet?" Her thoughts were posed as a question, but they were not really a question, she knew she was right.

"Yep, Daddy was afraid he'd melt," I answered.

Remembering that trip when my father stopped hiking, I recalled his physical health had started declining about the same time. In reality, he had never experienced the same feeling of spiritual renewal that hiking up Mount LeConte gave Mom and me. Preferring the comforts of home, Daddy's idea of roughing it had always been a motel with towels that did not match in pile thickness. Later, he had supported our female bonding, as he called our many treks to the Lodge, by driving us to whatever trail head we planned to ascend and picking us up at whichever trail we chose to descend. That arrangement had carried on well for many years until his health bottomed out and Daddy could no longer walk from the parking area to meet us.

Even now, too many months after his death, I still found myself looking for him to greet me whenever Mom and I strolled back to my waiting car. I missed him. Daddy had been a man who placed no chains on me, who made no demands that I must fit into a certain mold. There had been a scarcity of males like that in my life.

He had been a sweet man and a good provider, and I had adored him, but growing up I was never quite certain if I measured up to his expectations. I remembered being nine years old and seeing little Brenda Lee performing on television. I had wanted to be her on that stage, being introduced by Red Foley, showing Daddy that I was good at something and that he could be proud of me.

After our brief reference to his last hike, we waited to speak until after climbing the uneven steps. When Mom reached the last rock in the rustic stairs, she continued with a great sense of accomplishment in her voice, "And we put everything in one pack and headed the rest of the way up in the drivin' rain."

"Boy, that pack was heavy." I quoted one of Granddaddy Taite's favorite sayings, "As someone famous once said, 'Tis better to have it and not need it, than to need it and not have it.' Back then we packed way too much stuff." I reminded Mom, "Remember how we would carry up makeup so we could present proper faces to our table companions?"

How silly we had been. How heavy our packs had been back then.

After slipping my lightly weighted daypack off my shoulders, I located a canteen of cold water to share. Removing her pack, Mom propped herself against nearby boulders. The hike's steep elevation gain began here, and years back, this was the rest stop where I allowed myself the first of many cigarettes. I always sat to enjoy that activity because I had been taught ladies did not walk and smoke at the same time. Only women of ill breeding walked and smoked, even on isolated mountain trails.

My errant mind interrupted, *And who said real ladies smoked?*

Since there were just too many restrictions for me to keep track of in the southern edition of The Manual, I had long since given up any hope of becoming The Lady my mother envisioned. As a girl child born and reared in the South, I had been exposed to a myriad of inane social rules and had adopted them without question. That hike, when Daddy had beaten a hasty retreat and our mother-daughter duo had trudged onward through the light mist that quickly became a blinding downpour, had occurred in the early 1970s when it was unusual to see women hiking in the Smokies without benefit of a male escort. That sodden day had marked my conscious awakening to what real women could and could not do.

At the time I graduated from high school in the 1960s, the South gave nice girls two career choices: you either graduated from high school, got married, raised a family and lived happy ever after or you went on to college, majored in home ec, married a doctor, raised a family and lived happily ever after. Since not marrying was never an option in the South at that time, spinsterhood was considered a choice only by default.

As my mind, playing the devil's advocate, would say, *And de fault was de girl's*.

Those two choices never worked for me. I got through high school without getting married. In college, I eked out a 2.19 overall grade point in home ec without snaring a pre-med student. During one quarter I did date a pre-dental student named Joe Bill Everhart, allowing my Southern-born mother to hope a college education was not being wasted on me.

When we reached the dusty climb at Alum Bluff, Mom asked, "Remember that time we had lunch under here and it was so foggy we could hardly see ten feet in front of us? Wasn't that when a hawk flew in, hovered and then swooshed back into the fog?"

"Yes, Mom, I believe it was."

I could have sworn that hawk had screamed a curse when he saw us under the rocky ledge. If hiking was like living, then that day we were blindly going through life, wondering if we would ever meet another soul and having no guideposts along the way to mark our progress. All I remembered seeing, besides that startled bird, were ghostly trees leering through the vapor shrouds that hung within five feet on either side of the path. No vistas were available but I could bank on a cup of hot chocolate when we arrived at the top of the mountain. In real life, one never knows what will be poured into the cup one holds out.

I broached a new subject. "I think it's time to make some changes to the restaurant." I looked up the trail, took a deep breath and began the steep grade. "I want to enlarge. What do you think about changin' the color scheme at the same time? I've read that mauve and teal are the comin' new trends."

When feminism began filtering down to the South in the early 1970s, I had already gone through one disappointing marriage and divorce and was mired in a dead-end job. After they realized how miserable I was, my parents had an epiphany and called a family conference. In reality, we went for my first hike up the mountain, which resulted in my heading back to the university on their nickel. Sitting through my first physics lecture, I vowed that never would a man hold power over my paycheck and back me into a corner to press his unwanted body against mine. No male, I promised myself that day, would do that ever again and live.

Studying for the first time in my life, I went after a degree in engineering, graduating with a 3.98. During that second bout with higher education, I learned that I was not just another pretty face. Unfortunately, the South in the early '80s had not changed as much as the rest of the nation. I soon grew disenchanted with being the token female. I also became frustrated having to deal with the pervasive, only-men-know-best attitude and being the one employee who always made coffee. I was ready to drop out after less than five years, just worn down by the system in which I had been reared.

Then came the unfortunate afternoon when I arrived home early to find, like the three bears, that a stranger had been sleeping in my bed with Mackey, husband number two. This time, I experienced the epiphany and initiated my second divorce. I put away my sheepskins and started a small restaurant with the money from my half of our savings account. I called it Rachael's For Lunch.

During those first starving months following the opening, the assistance my parents gave was unwavering. Mom helped by charming the customers and mopping the floors. I can still see Daddy meticulously chopping meat for the chicken salad. Even now, it hurts my heart when I recall all they did to help get my business started. After Liz McNabb came on board, my parents went back to enjoying their retirement, showing up at the restaurant only when they were ready to break for their midday meal. With friends and other residents of Knoxville being very supportive, my restaurant took off. After a few years, business became too good and my accountant declared I had extra money I needed to spend.

"Rachael, remember that day in May when we hiked up in all that snow?" Mom called up to me as the rugged ridge, on which Bullhead Trail snaked across, came into view. We were passing under the crags of Cliff Top, about a mile from our destination.

"Won't have to worry about that today, Mom." I answered.

Wiping the sweat from my brow and pushing my glasses back on my nose, I recalled that experience all too well. For every two steps we plowed forward that May, we seemed to slide one step back. That long afternoon had been one miserable ordeal I never wish to repeat. In order to stay as warm as possible, Mom and I had stopped to put on all the clothes that we had packed to wear the next day. I remembered looking back to check her progress, noticing that she was carefully stepping in my boot prints. After I told her that children were supposed to follow in their parents' footsteps, not vice versa, we had laughingly trudged onward.

May had proven to be a fickle month for hiking. Humidity could be so dense that my body would nearly drown with each intake of air, or the trail could be covered with ten inches of snow dusted with green fir needles, or somewhere in between those two extremes. I never knew to which season we would be exposed but, as long as we stayed on the trail,

LeConte was a safe undertaking. Getting off the beaten path laid out by the National Park Service, however, was quite another story. That was when a hiker would become like Hester Prynne bucking the system.

Upon introduction to poor Hester during American literature class in high school, my heart had gone out to her. I was aware, deep in my bones, of the oppressive confinement that woman had faced. I knew, without being able to say how, the existence of a greater array of rules governing her life than even the author spelled out. Because the writer was just a man, I understood he could never have had knowledge of the entire Feminine Manual. I also felt I would have colored outside the lines had I lived back then.

According to an addendum somewhere in the unwritten rules for Southern womanhood, getting caught like Miss Hester would have been none too lady-like. However, had I gotten found out, I doubted I could have been so bold wearing my scarlet letter. Although, as I learned years later when I had my color chart done, I was a 'winter' and true red would have been a most becoming hue for me to wear.

The dangling carrot for my LeConte hikes was the overnight accommodations waiting on top of the mountain. The Lodge was my idea of civilized roughing it. Its rustic cabins were watertight, not necessarily mousetight. The on-site staff provided clean bed linens, lit each cabin's kerosene stove and served up supper and breakfast. Coffee and hot chocolate were freely available for those lucky hikers with overnight reservations. Flushable necessary houses, with doors that securely locked, were located within a short distance of the cabins. Being my father's daughter, I packed in my own matching, thick hand towel and face cloth. So, what more could I want in a true back-to-nature experience?

The Lodge was an oxymoronic environment that I found endearing, as would any female schooled in Southern womanhood-ness for we truly understood absurdity. It is the very glue of our lives, a constant in an inconstant world, but we females who breathed our first breaths after the Second World War received a double dose. Like our mothers before us, my generation of girl babies birthed in the 1940s, reared through the '50s and into the '60s by a changeling South, accepted phases like 'non-working mother,' 'friendly fire,' 'emancipated slave,' 'congressional ethics,' 'cruel pleasures' and 'married men' without blinking our pretty little eyes. Contradictory terms mingled freely with the air we breathed and were intertwined alongside RNA and DNA in the double helix of our genes. That first batch of post-war boomers like me, however, had mothers who, unlike the women who had instructed them, had gotten a taste of life-off-the-farm before training daughters of their own.

My own mother, for example, had been a teenaged war bride and followed Daddy from army base to army base before he was sent overseas. When Daddy was stationed up North, Mom supplemented their income by pouring bombs in a converted cereal factory located near his base. Creating instruments for death and destruction in a place that had been built originally to manufacture food for sustenance and life seemed to her a reasonable enough activity. Later in the '50s when I headed to grammar school, she sought employment outside her home. Even though she had felt stifled being tied to a house by her apron strings, my mother lectured that my life could never be complete until I belonged to a man.

Having cut my teeth on oxymora, I had no trouble accepting inconsistencies as I grew up, for I was a product of my raising. A tidy bundle of contradictions, as my dear Daddy would describe me, neatly wrapped in plain, brown paper and tied with a fanciful bow of pink satin ribbon.

After Rachael's opened, LeConte Lodge's mundane pleasures had assumed the status of luxuries because I never had to cook food or greet patrons or wash dishes. Neither was I called upon to step on any spiders. I was not responsible for anything those thirty-six hours except getting me up the mountain one day and getting me down the next.

In recent years while Mom and I went tromping through the wilderness, Liz and Daddy had guarded the homefront. Beginning with the weekend in 1989, Margaret would assist Liz at the restaurant and Liz would replace Daddy at tending to my four-legged girls at the house.

With the Lodge maintaining a strict meal schedule, Mom and I always allowed plenty of time to get up the mountain for our enticing allotment of smoking-hot chocolate before the kitchen closed at 5 p.m. That deadline was firm because it enabled the staff to complete their supper before serving guests promptly at 6 p.m. As long as we were up the mountain by four-thirty with no bears impeding our progress, we considered it an utterly successful hike.

Just another step in The Ritual, another bead in the rosary, but Fate unexpectedly slipped in a new bead at supper that Friday. And my rote was never the same again.

Three

After downing our usual two cups each of hot chocolate, Mom and I returned to cabin number four. While making reservations for our second stay atop the mountain so many years earlier, we began requesting that particular cabin because it was located closest to the Lodge's main building where hikers signed in. Even though we had driven to the National Park to hike, we saw no good reason to walk any farther than we had to after arriving at the clearing for the Lodge.

Like the other single-party dwellings, our favored cabin was constructed of wood planks set on stacked stone footers with split-wood shingles for its roof. Number four was the smallest one available for guests and barely had room for its sparse contents: a handmade, double-bed-sized bunk bed that took up better than half of the floor space; a small, square wooden table to the right of the doorway and a single chair with a wooden slat seat against the left wall near the foot of the bed.

A rectangular mirror, big enough to reflect one face at a time and framed in mitered wood, was securely attached to the wall above the chair. Hand-loomed linen curtains hung at quaintly designed windows positioned for cross ventilation in the opposing long walls. The wall behind the bed was without windows and faced the wall with the door. These two walls were much shorter in length. Crude hooks, fashioned from forks of small branches, were nailed high on three walls.

The table held an ashtray; a box of wooden matches; a clear glass kerosene lamp; a paper-wrapped, motel-size bar of soap and four dull-green, plastic coffee cups with two, resting unused and upside down, and two, which now contained our fresh chocolate dregs, sitting upright. Over the table, an aluminum wash pan hung on one hook and a water kettle from another, their metallic skins dulled and dented from long use. A compact, woven willow wastebasket sat on the floor between the table and the short wall to the right of the door. Nearby, a hand-lettered sign tacked to the wall requested that guests pack out the trash they packed in. Before walking down to the dining room for chocolate, I had placed a water pail, handed to me earlier when Mom and I registered, on the floor by the heater.

The cabin's interior was entirely of vertical wood planks except for the rectangular, gray firewalls guarding two sides of a heavily kerosene-scented, squat heater whose shiny, robotic design was grossly out of place with the cabin's other handmade furnishings. I fully expected the thing to whirl in circles announcing in a pre-programmed, mechanical voice "Warning! Warning!" whenever a black bear approached the cabin. I thought the cozy interior had smelled nicer and earthier when the Lodge was permitted to burn wood but, despite that change, the cabin remained a cherished home away from home.

Having pulled off our boots, Mom and I snuggled under the colorful Hudson Bay blankets on the lower bunk to catch a short power-nap before supper. She soon fell asleep and almost purred a gentle snore with each exhale. Her soft sounds were like having one of my cats in bed beside me. My mother, however, never would agree that she snored. Mom only admitted to breathing hard when she slept because no lady ever snored.

After our last stay on the mountain, when I actually had to call down to Mom for a third time complaining that her snores were keeping me awake, I threatened to record her sleeping on some future hike for audible proof that she was no lady. Of course, I have never snored in my life although I have snorted myself awake a few times.

From outside the thin, wooden walls, I heard footsteps and voices of unseen guests as they tramped about the camp. Noises faded in and out, reminding me of the first demo record for stereophonic sounds I had heard as a teenager. Mom and I had explored like them, years ago when the mountain and its views had been new to us. Now opting for comfort, we rested our tired muscles in the quiet cabin's subdued light.

I stared at the names that previous guests had carved on slats of the bunk above me. Someday, I might leave my name there and then again, maybe not. I considered it more refined to sign registration sheets than to deface wood. Besides, The Manual makes some reference to fools' names and public places.

Lying there under the weight of a scratchy, wool blanket with Mom asleep beside me, I envisioned myself as a child: eyes closed in a pretend sleep, resting on my mother's lap with her loving arms loosely around me, feeling that womanly-cushioned, warm chest rise and fall beneath my shoulder, hearing other adults as they discussed things that seemed important to them at the time while heeding only my mother's regular breathing.

I must have fallen asleep because I jumped upon hearing the familiar harsh clamor of a metal triangle being struck by a metal rod. That annoying noise, which served as the Lodge's dinner bell, clanged through the thin mountain air signaling six o'clock and announcing the dining room was open for service.

Another nicety associated with the Lodge was that guests did not have to rush the door in order to grab seats together. An employee positioned just inside the dining room would direct parties to their assigned table. Someone, somewhere, had already determined at which table each person would sit, thus insuring eight guests to a table and no squabbling amongst strangers.

I welcomed the treat of having decisions, no matter how minor, made for me during these short hours atop the mountain.

After Mom and I were pointed in the direction of the last table on the far right, she walked ahead of me down the center aisle between two rows of rectangular tables. With only light from a few windows and a single set of French doors available to illuminate its paneled dark walls, the large dining area was initially dim in comparison to the outdoors. The naturally aged, wooden walls had been further darkened for too many years by lampblack from the oil lamps. Since each and every item had to be helicoptered up or packed in by llamas, the frugal management was not about to cut into profits by wasting kerosene when perfectly good sunlight was still available.

Following Mom into the room, my eyes soon adjusted to the reduced light. After she sat and no longer blocked my view of our assigned table, my mental twin announced, *Well, now, that certainly looks queer!*

Six chairs for our table were momentarily vacant while two men sat knee-to-knee, hip-to-hip and elbow-to-elbow on two chairs that had been pulled together at the far end. Mom had chosen to sit sharing the table's corner beside them, facing the windows across the rear of the dining room, with her back to the front door. I would have picked seats at the other short end had I led Mom to our table.

I pulled back a chair and sat on her left before giving a barely audible "Hey" in greeting because I found it just too strange for grown men with graying hair to be sitting that close together. I knew, without being told, the two definitely were not from around here.

Friday night's dinner was the usual LeConte fare served in its time-honored, family-style tradition: half a canned peach for starters; then came crumbly cornbread that could not hold together even if it wanted to, served alongside a transparent, beef-based broth with floating, not-quite-rehydrated vegetables; quickly followed by generous bowls of steamy hot, canned stew beef with gravy, canned green beans, good instant mashed potatoes and the best cinnamon-flavored stewed apples anybody could ever wish for and, finally, one generous chocolate chip cookie per guest for dessert.

During the meal, servers periodically wove between the red-checked oilcloth covered tables, pouring either steaming chocolate or coffee from squat, metal pitchers. Although none of the Lodge's other guests present opted for wine by the glass, those two men sitting at the end of our table did.

During my conversation with the five people seated at my end of the table, I learned they were part of a Baptist Church group from Georgia, making up the remainder of the guests at the Lodge for the night. Since Mom and I preferred hot chocolate, I knew that being Southern Baptists explained why no one at dinner, except the two outsiders at our table, drank wine. I listened as the Georgians described their experiences coming up the mountain and which trails they had used and how many times they had made the trip and which trails they were taking down in the morning. Mom spent her time talking with the obviously fascinating odd couple.

Later into our meal, she touched my arm to get my attention. When I looked in her direction, Mom exclaimed delightedly, "They're from San Francisco!"

I knew it was her favorite city and one that she had not yet visited. Although she and Dad had always planned on going there eventually, they had not gotten any farther west than New Orleans in their travels. The money they had put aside for that long-dreamed-of vacation had generously been used instead to finance my second college education.

Uninterested, I automatically commented, "How nice." While simultaneously assuming the two enjoyed an alternative life style, I presumed an explanation to justify why they sat so intimately.

Since my mother had found them engaging, I examined the men with more interest. One had dark, graying hair, thick and slightly curly, and he appeared shorter than his companion who was sitting next to Mom. That man had lighter hair, trimmed close to his head, with silvery gray at his temples. I could not decide if the shorter man was truly shorter or if he was merely sitting in a chair assembled with its seat lower to the floor, or perhaps the taller one was really not taller but had a longer torso than his friend and, therefore, appeared taller. Since those possibilities were more complex than I wished to consider and since I really did not care to know, I soon returned to the conversation on my left while Mom continued hers with the visitors from California.

As the meal came to an end, the Baptists gradually drifted outside in small groups to make preparations for the night's entertainment. While I waited, Mom slowly enjoyed the remainder of her dinner and chatted with her newly found acquaintances.

Since she always won the race for being the last to finish a meal, I knew better than to hurry Mom along. Besides, the top of the mountain did not have much to offer after supper. Having no television, no radio and no electric lights were all part of its enduring, luring simplicity. The main event for an evening at the Lodge, for those whose legs still worked, was climbing up to Cliff Top to see if a sunset would be awarded those who had ascended the mountain that day.

Now, up here, the regular occurrence of a golden sunset was definitely not like manna from Heaven given daily to those hordes following Moses. Although each day has its setting sun, when you are on top of this mountain, rain or clouds could quickly obscure the view. The Lodge, after all, was located in the Great Smoky Mountains National Park, an area considered to be one of the few temperate rain forests in the world.

I had gleaned that tidbit of information while sitting through a non-credit, wildflower identification class about five years back.

I was ready to leave for the stroll to sunset, but Mom still conversed with those two strangers, charming them with her soft Southern drawl. That woman's voice had captivated men and women for years. Before she finally retired, Mom had been employed by the law firm of Childs, Sullins and Childs, and in the course of her days there had talked to people from all over the country. After they had completed their official business, most of the male clients coming to Knoxville for the first time would discreetly ask old Mr. Childs' secretary for directions to Mom's office. Those men, a box of chocolates in hand, would drop by Mom's desk just to put a face with the wonderful voice that had guided them through some tangled legality.

Daddy and I sure did enjoy plenty of candy before Mom left the firm. Clients of long standing, whose problems Mom had spent time smoothing out, were generous with little nothings, too. Each year after the annual Christmas party, Daddy would come home teasing Mom about old Mr. Childs calling her his silver-tongued charmer and remarking that it was the only reason he kept her on the payroll. Old Mr. Childs always said Mom made him money because she never cost him clients.

My mother could charm the life jacket off a drowning man. Not that she would, mind you, but she could.

I had called her The Velvet Hammer behind her back while I was growing up. I knew well her awesome power. Mom had managed me too many times into too many situations that I had no desire to be in, and I never saw it coming. Too, too often I had found myself doing what she wanted me to do, not what I wanted me to do. Thank God, she only wanted what she thought would be best for me.

Since they were not from around here, the men occupying the end of our table had little experience in dealing with anyone like her. Like hapless cannon fodder, those ill-prepared dinner companions did not stand a chance, and I was not the least surprised that Mom had them under her spell.

We sat in the emptied dining room well after the staff had cleared away supper and had centered kerosene lamps on each table in preparation for tomorrow's breakfast. At last, my charming mother issued them an invitation.

"Why don't y'all join my daughter and me on the walk up to sunset? We take a different path from the one the staff recommends. We go the old way. It's longer, but the scenery is just too beautiful."

Both men turned to look at each other while deciding how to answer. The taller-appearing one shrugged his shoulder and said, "Why not? We'll never be here again."

The one with darker hair replied, "OK. Why not?"

"It's settled then." Mom sealed their verdicts with her smile. "We'll meet y'all at the trail above the cabins in about ten minutes."

As we stood to walk out of the dining room, I saw that the man with the darker hair was taller by three inches than his companion, answering my earlier question as to which one was taller. Since both their bodies were well proportioned, their chairs had caused the height difference.

At the top of the steps outside the dining room, we parted company. The men walked toward their cabin on the left of the central passageway as Mom and I headed for the necessary houses on the right.

⚜

Back inside our little cabin, I realized I could not remember if I had been told the guys' names. Helping Mom with her jacket, I asked, "Mom, tell me their names."

"Christopher and Carl," she answered. Mom always remembered names. That was part of her allure.

Unfortunately, that ability had been left out of my bag of tricks. I easily remembered identifying circumstances surrounding people, and that was my strong point. I silently repeated, Christopher and Carl, Christopher and Carl, Christopher and Carl.

I asked next, "Which one's which?"

"The shorter one is Christopher," Mom replied, stepping outside.

"Thanks," I responded. Quickly recalling the mnemonic for the leaf differentiation between laurel and rhododendron, I reversed and modified the phrase to specifically apply to the men. No trouble to keep separate. Short name, long man; long name, short man.

⚜

I led our party to the cut-off for the lesser traveled path to Cliff Top. On the way, we passed through the small growth of Frazier firs that covered most of the saddle between the mountain's double peaks. Embracing us with the rich, heavy fragrance of living Christmas trees, the dense growth towered around us and reached overhead where we walked. Mom was in line between the two men, and I overheard her telling about the original encampment, located downhill from the saddle, which was built to convince the moneyed national movers and shakers brought in by regional VIPs of the splendid national park these mountains could make. That first camp was the forerunner of the present-day Lodge. She told them how, during the Depression, she and other grammar school children around Knoxville had gathered up their loose change to help raise money to purchase the needed land from the giant lumber mills.

Where the trees ended and a flat grassy area began, I took the right fork in the trail leading to the brief ascent toward the lower of the mountain's two peaks. My entourage stepped closely behind with the men remaining engrossed in my mother's seductive, siren voice. I stopped when, a few yards ahead, I spotted a doe grazing on the tender, new grasses. Carl ran into me and began to apologize but I quickly shushed him by pointing to the deer.

She was so close that I could see the gentle rise and fall of her ribs. The doe turned one ear in our direction, pretending to be unconcerned with our intrusion upon her evening meal. Quietly, we watched her dine. After a few moments, I continued because the sun would not delay its setting for us to admire a mere deer. As soon as we broached her comfort zone, the doe flipped her white flag of a tail at our impertinence and, gliding ghost-like into a small copse of fir, disappeared from sight.

From that stop onward, I allowed the men to walk ahead of us on the narrow trail to Cliff Top because, while watching the deer, a frightening thought dawned on me. I did not know these men from Adam. For all I knew, they could have been axe-toting, murdering rapists on the run from California. To be nice, however, I told them I wanted them to go ahead of Mom and me so that they would have an unobstructed view of this beautiful trail. The reality was that I would be better prepared to scream for help if I could see them pull out their axes. I did not trust them enough to give them my vulnerable back.

Beginning with the 1970s, no one had taken the time to clear this older route after storms. By the late '80s, it had become as tangled as an unkempt man-way. With the narrow path often blocked by leaning or downed trees, we continued slowly in the direction of the sunset place, stepping over what trees we could and squatting down to pass under the ones we could not.

Mimicking haughty, well-practiced waiters supporting huge serving trays atop braced fingertips, the remaining trees extended their needled branches on which the deepening blue-to-mauve sky rested. With each step we took, our boots clinked against loose pebbles. Thick pads of new-money-green mosses were strewn about the ground, like so many discarded carpet samples. Scattered, dense colonies of blue-bead lilies peeked up through the rocky soil next to the stony path, their leaves still balled into tight fists needed for the forced, dark journey from the bulb underground to the light above. Young buds on the clumps of surrounding rhododendron gave no hint to their future color. The golden sun's dying glow backlit each individual leaf on the vegetation along our way, lending the forest an enchantment that Disney animators would have coveted.

I had always felt I strolled through a storybook forest each time I took this path to the sunset. I would not have been surprised in the least to see a unicorn picking his way through the undergrowth to the same destination, but after over two decades I had only seen white-tailed deer.

"Rachael, do you think we'll have a good sunset?" Mom asked, bringing me back from my magical forest to reality.

"I sure hope so." I explained to the men the reasoning behind her question, "A seasoned hiker always walks out for the sunset, no matter what the weather, because clouds can suddenly part to expose a breathtakin' sky painted with a heavenly palette of colors."

Not waiting until I reached him, Carl held out his hand in anticipation of helping me step down a steep break in the trail. Mom and I had forgotten our hiking sticks back in the cabin and occasionally needed the men's assistance along the way. We also could have used the sticks to beat them about their heads had that been required, but so far the strangers had been gentlemanly, aiding us over fallen trees and off high rocks.

Nice manners, I thought, even if they aren't from around here.

"Back one fall, I was up here with this guy, and we tried walkin' to sunset as remnants from a hurricane blew through. The storm that evenin' whipped through the trees with such fury that the ground undulated." Before reaching for Carl's out-stretched hand, I demonstrated with my hands the tidal movement of the ground I had witnessed. "Just like ocean waves from the movement of the interlockin' root systems lyin' in this shallow soil. The wind screamed up the ridge from North Carolina so strong that Joe Bill and I couldn't stand against it to get within even twenty feet of the mountain's edge. Wasn't any sunset that night, for sure!"

"Joe Bill!" snorted Carl, amused by the Southern penchant for double names. "What's his middle name? Freddie Wayne?"

"Play pretty!" I quickly shot back. "No, Freddie Wayne isn't his middle name. It's William." Patiently, I detailed the reasoning behind my friend's name. "His granddaddy is Big Bill, his daddy is Little Bill and so everybody calls him Joe Bill. That way everyone knows which Bill they're talkin' about."

"Play pretty," he repeated to Christopher. "This woman uses the same words, but she certainly doesn't speak the same language we do."

"Regional differences, that's all it is," I hastened to explain. There was laughter in my voice because I, too, had been having difficulty understanding their side of our conversation. They talked faster and in a different cadence from what I was accustomed to hearing. I was amused that the men were having the same trouble. "Did you know y'all talk too fast?" I teased.

Christopher looked overhead at the gathering clouds and asked much slower than he had spoken earlier, "Do you think . . . the clouds . . . will roll in . . . tonight?"

Irritated by the man's condescending attitude, I replied quickly, "I don't know. Hope not." I was under-amused by the overly solicitous pauses in his question.

Walking through the softening light, we picked up speed, hurrying to join our fellow guests sitting on the rocky pinnacle among the wind-sculptured shrubs at Cliff Top. The beckoning foundation of naked, gray rocks created a rustic, natural balcony for those undertaking the final climb to the mountain's shorter peak. That portion of Mount LeConte, best known for sunsets, extended like a rocky elbow bent out over a curve near the end of the Alum Bluff trail. The slope underneath the out-cropping was not the greatest angle of ascent along that trail, however, after hiking almost five miles uphill, it always seemed to be the steepest to my tired legs.

Cliff Top consisted of huge rock slabs pushed up haphazardly on their sides with massive, hip-high clumps of dense Huger's sand myrtle hunkering over what thin soil their roots could find. Misshapen, hardy firs fenced in the area. As the stubborn evergreens had matured, harsh winds coming over the cliffs had pushed growing branches away from that side. When viewed from certain angles, the trees appeared like solid, green flags permanently caught in a brisk breeze. Beyond Cliff Top, the surrounding mountain ranges spread across the panoramic view like wrinkled, smoky-gray sheets on a bed that had been hastily exited.

By the time we arrived, the exposed rocks were crowded with most of the Baptist hikers staying at the Lodge. They sat scattered about in huddles, seeking protection from the ever-present wind. Mom and I stood while Carl and Christopher scouted for an available spot for four to sit together. When the men first suggested dangling our legs off into that vast, empty space at the mountain's edge, neither Mom nor I cared to join them. After spotting a location we found more suitable, Mom plopped down, facing the direction of the sinking sun.

I was in the process of sitting, too, when Christopher asked, pointing to an overgrown path that snuck into the firs, "What's over there?"

I straightened up. "Beats me. Do you want to go back in there?"

"Yes, I'd like to," he answered. "We won't be here again and," he squinted in the sun's direction, "it looks like we have about ten more minutes before the sunset."

Mom did not make any effort to rise. She said, almost too quickly, "I'll stay here and save our seats."

Based on the face value of her comment, I thought she really wanted to save our places.

The men and I pushed through the thick undergrowth as we explored the hidden trails around Cliff Top. Although I had never walked in there before, I had always wanted to but had never been with anyone adventuresome enough to speak up in favor of this mini side trip. When we returned as the first rays of the sun sank behind the distant deepening purple ridges, my mother's face had an unmistakable look of relief that I thought strange at the time.

As the sky's molten colors faded to grays, we each removed packets from our pockets. At supper, Mom had convinced the men to save their desserts to enjoy later. Sitting on hard, cold rocks, pinching off small pieces of chocolate chip cookies to chew slowly, making each mouthful last as long as possible, while the day died into night was just another step in The Ritual. We lingered at Cliff Top long after the other guests had returned to the cabins, our treats lasting until the moon appeared and the clouds blew over towards Knoxville.

While the rising moon crept overhead, Mom related more of the Lodge's lore. She spoke of the dog, Cumberland Jack, who long ago padded down alone to the only grocery then in Gatlinburg with a shopping list tucked into his custom-made backpack and patiently waited for the order to be filled before heading back to his young master at the base camp below the saddle; of Bear Cat, the only domesticated feline ever allowed at the Lodge, who went courting down the mountain one night and returned alone an unwed mother and who later fluffed herself up like a big cat to chase away a threatening bear who came too close to her kittens; and of the lanky man, who so dearly loved his mother that, when she desired to see her beloved mountaintop one last time before she died, strapped a ladder-back chair to his thin shoulders and carried her, comfortably seated, all the way up LeConte.

Next, I told them some of what we had learned from Jack Sharp, *professor emeritus* of biology at The University of Tennessee/Knoxville. Old Dr. Jack taught us how these ancient mountains were the depository of all plant life in this region when most of this part of the world was under the ocean, how some of the plants native to this area have their closest cousins growing in Japan and how the changes in vegetation one sees while hiking from Gatlinburg to the top of LeConte mimic the changes seen while driving from Tennessee to Canada.

When Christopher and Carl began talking about San Francisco, I could almost see my mother creating mental pictures of their descriptions, using their words for paint. She wanted to hear about the cable cars and how it felt to ride them. She wanted to know about the sounds and smells of China Town. Mom pulled descriptions of the famous fogs out of their memories. She wanted to see the views from Top of the Mark taken from their experiences there. Despite having an inexhaustible audience, both men happily shared.

None of us had carried up flashlights but with that huge, crater-scarred, full moon gloriously brilliant and the navy-blue sky now free of clouds, we had no need for artificial lighting to illuminate our surroundings when we decided to return to the Lodge. While slowly inching down a steep rocky descent, which was not the path we had followed on the way up, Christopher related how they happened to be on the mountain this particular Friday night.

"Carl and I have a conference in Nashville next week. Since neither of us had ever been to Tennessee, we thought we'd do some traveling before the meetings started. We both like to hike and, as I was reading about the National Park, I ran across literature on La Contee Lodge—"

"That's 'lee-CONT'," I interrupted to correct his pronunciation.

"Leigh Count Lodge, whatever." Unperturbed, he continued, "I called for reservations and learned the only night in our time frame, when the Lodge had space, was tonight and that was because some church group had a cancellation. But, for some crazy reason about the count they have to maintain for the Park Service, we have to sit on two chairs in one spot at the table so they could count us as a party of one."

"Oh, yeah," adding to their store of information, I interjected, "I think they have to average no more than forty-two visitors a night."

The other commented, *So that explains why they were sitting so cozily at supper. So much for first impressions. Maybe they aren't queer for each other after all.*

Silently, I told the ever-present twin in my head, Thanks for sharing.

Following the sun's descent behind the distant ridges, I had found every aspect about being on top of my dear mountain intoxicating. I knew the summit must have been charmed when I was not looking. I felt so energized that my skin actually tingled as if I had crossed over a force field into a different dimension. Maybe the others felt that way, too. I did not dare ask if they had noticed the sorcery. What if they had not? Then, again, what if they had and what if, as I mentioned the enchantment, the magical feelings disappeared? In any case, I did not know how to pose such a question without seeming to be much too New Age. Had I asked, perhaps our West Coast companions would think I had secretly smoked some dope. Maybe the breeze coming up from North Carolina was simply laden with faerie dust designed to make us mortals incapable of rational decisions, and maybe Puck was chuckling behind a nearby rhododendron. Whatever the true cause, I felt strangely at ease being inside my skin, and I had not felt that comfortable in a long, long time. If ever.

Everything associated with those first hours after sunset remained otherworldly. The full moon stayed intensely bright and seemingly hovered so low that I could almost put a hand on its rough surface. Caught in the glare of that solitary, lunar spotlight, I felt we could have been actors strolling across a surreal theater set designed by Salvador Dali, casting velvety black shadows upon a dun-colored stage floor. The mountainside was just too ethereal in the moon's shimmering, silvery-blue glow and the company too engaging to call it an evening so soon after sundown. I noticed, also, that the evening's temperature remained uncharacteristically warm despite the sun's absence. Occasionally, a slow breeze teased through all the loose hairs that I have never been quite able to catch up into a tidy bun, and they became tiny fingers tickling my neck and face. As the air brushed against my skin, its molecules were heavy with the weight of sweet, dense, woodsy fragrances.

With all my sensory nerve fibers vibrating, feelings I remembered feeling when I was much younger and much newer to the world coursed through my veins as if I were some young, wild creature kicking up her heels, playing tag with a gang of flashing fireflies, during the bounty that is spring. Without being able to explain my line of reasoning, I fully understood how I could live forever.

Just as we had done as first-time guests, Mom and I plundered over the mountaintop near the Lodge with our new acquaintances as church songs, rising from the direction of the cabins, eerily drifted on the playful breezes. As former Baptists, Mom and I recognized the old hymns by their melodies even though we were too far away to distinguish lyrics.

When the men asked if they might be quaint mountain tunes from long ago, I decided our new friends must have raised a different, joyful noise to God when attending church in California.

We first guided them partially up Mount LeConte's higher peak along the trail that would take them to Myrtle Point, should they decide to make sunrise in the morning. Christopher walked nearer to Mom. I overheard them discussing his wife and two children while Carl and I were some feet behind, talking about our work after having established we were both divorced with no children. Not surprisingly, the subject of regional differences came up again when I tried to explain the difficulties women of the South have in the workplace.

"Hey, Christopher! Listen to this," Carl called to his friend to come to where we stood looking into the valleys of North Carolina. "You tell him what you told me, Rachael."

When Christopher came near, I started my story again. "I was just tellin' Carl how it was when I worked for the state unemployment office. I won't go into all the gory details again, but I left there because the director would back me into a corner to kiss me or have me sit on his lap before he would give me my paycheck."

"No," Christopher exclaimed, "I can't believe that! That would never have happened in California, not with the sexual harassment laws we have in place."

"Well, it happened to me in Tennessee back in the '70s," I insisted, more than a bit put out that neither man sounded as if he believed me.

Christopher questioned, "Didn't you go to your supervisor?"

"No." Casually, I added, "She was havin' trouble with him, too. In fact, just about every other young woman in the office had to run that gauntlet. Besides, nobody would have paid any attention to what we said. It would just have been our word against his. And because we were women, ours didn't count."

"That could never happen in this day and age." Christopher waited only seconds before asking, "Whatever happened to the old goat?"

Encouraged to hear some contempt for my former director creep into his voice, I replied, "Don't know. I quit before too long. He started gettin' mean and roughed up a few of the girls he 'had lunch' with." I went on, adding sarcastically, "Glad I was always on a diet and never went to lunch with the jerk. I heard he died not long ago. Hope it was long and painful."

Turning towards my mother, Christopher asked, "Do you believe that actually happened?"

Mom nodded her head.

For some working women in the South, toiling for the almighty dollar had not been for the faint of heart. We both had experienced it. Mom had been the one who had advised me to quit my state job before things got any worse and to go back to school. I knew what mother had gone through before she found that dear Mr. Childs. Her previous employer had called her into his office for dictation while his pants were unzipped and his hands were not playing with coins in his pockets. She had immediately walked out. Since Mom had elected not to take his dictation, she had been promptly fired for poor performance on the job.

"Well, it couldn't have been that bad," Christopher said dismissively, not really believing the events that I had recounted.

Mom smiled sweetly. "Oh, yes, indeed," she said, "occurrences like that happened all the time."

I heard the approaching, veiled vagueness in her voice. I saw the woman who was my mother disappear behind a familiar, vacant smile. At the same time, I realized these men from California had no idea of what had just occurred, neither by her demeanor nor the tone of her voice.

Mom offered no additional information, and I did not bother to expound further on the inequities. 'You can lead a horse to water,' as Granddaddy used to say. Because they were just men, I knew neither would ever understand what we had tolerated while trying to earn a living. Our entire conversation on this particular subject had been a waste of Mom's and my breath.

"Let's head back," I said, trying to disguise my dismissive tone. "I could sit for a spell. My feet hurt."

While turning in the direction of the cabins, Carl reminded Christopher, "Don't forget to get the staff to light our kerosene lamp."

"I can do that for you." I volunteered my services, yet I was a bit surprised that men, who hiked as much as they professed to hike, could not light a little old lamp. I kept that thought to myself. For as a Southern woman, I had been taught not to make light of a man's lack of knowledge, bless his heart. At least, not to the man's face. That would be rude and, here in the South, mothers had always taught their daughters that ladies must not appear to be rude.

As I brought the match's flame to the burnt edge of the woven wick and adjusted its length back to reduce the smoke, I noticed the bodies of all the dead, wooden matches strewn about the table, evidence of numerous failed attempts to light the lamp. The men had certainly not lied, I thought as I placed the glass globe securely inside the prongs of its metal base.

Now aware on some level that I could not allow the evening to end, I opened a new avenue of conversation by revealing the number one rule surrounding breakfast. "You'll need to get back from sunrise by eight. That's when they ring for breakfast. Do you want to borrow our alarm?"

Even though we quit going out to Myrtle Point many trips ago, Mom continued to pack up a clock in case we ever needed it. Old habits died hard.

"How far is it to the Point?" Carl asked.

"Oh, about a mile and a half each way, I guess." I no longer remembered that tidbit of information because I never walked there any more.

A burst of loud laughter welled up from the direction of the largest building where the church members remained gathered.

"If you ladies aren't too tired," Christopher tentatively suggested, "we could go over to that meeting room." He looked from Mom to me. "You could sit on those rockers outside on the porch, Rachael, and we could talk more."

Although unable to explain why we did not want to say 'Good night,' I was secretly pleased that neither was Christopher ready for the evening to end. I guessed on some level, maybe, we were kindred souls. Whatever the reasoning, Mom and I followed them to the deck outside the main building.

Before we sat, I gave the men a brief, local geography lesson. Standing against the protective banister, I pointed out the liquid darkness in the valley that was Douglas Lake. I identified the scattered clusters of sparkles as the individual towns of Sevierville, Dandridge and Newport. I had the men lean out over the railing to the far left where they could see the streetlights of Pigeon Forge. The lights twinkling in the valley were as numerous as the stars twinkling above our heads. After we settled onto the rocking chairs, we leaned back, searching the sky for constellations we had learned as children.

I felt safe talking to the men on the deck while being guarded by the Baptists congregated on the other side of the wall. Red danger signals would have immediately gone off in my head had Christopher asked us to stay in their cabin to chat. If that had been his suggestion, I would have quickly responded that we would see them at breakfast, unless Mom had already beaten me to it.

We rocked and talked. We stopped talking but kept rocking. No one was ready for the dreaded parting words. We created our own music with the curved rockers bumping rhythmically over the rough plank decking.

Inside, the church group, with their vespers completed, joked and sang secular songs as someone picked melodies on a slightly out-of-tune guitar. We listened to Beatle songs and Kingston Trio songs and John Denver songs. When a lone male voice started Otis Redding's "Dock of the Bay," Carl, Christopher and I joined in the singing. Being from another generation, Mom could only listen because she did not know the lyrics. After the song came to an end, I became aware that the evening air had cooled.

Carl stood up, saying, "Let's go inside. I'm cold."

We all stood to march single file behind him into the lamp-yellowed, body-warmed room. Most of the people were sitting around a large oval table at our left playing *Trivial Pursuit*. Behind them against the far wall, the guitarist was perched on the arm of an oversized, faux leather couch. Others sat in rocking chairs circled about the unlit stove in the center of the room. On the same side of the room as the couch, a massive wooden loom crouched in front of a bank of windows. Four children worked a puzzle on a smaller round table on our right near the windows overlooking the valley far below. The chair behind the big desk that served as the Lodge's office when guests checked in was vacant.

A male voice called for us to join the game, arbitrarily placing Carl and me on one team and Mom and Christopher on the other. I went to a free rocker in the circle of chairs facing the stove while Mom circled the room with the men, discussing newspaper clippings and pictures on the walls that detailed its history and the people associated with the Lodge.

With their tour completed, Christopher pulled an empty rocker next to mine. Paying scant attention to the game, I waited until he had settled into the chair before asking, "Did Mom tell you the curtains in your cabin were woven on that loom?" After he shook his head in the negative, I continued, "It belongs to the wife of the last manager. I saw it helicoptered up their first season here. She made all the curtains that hang at each window of every cabin. She and her husband have long since gone on to different employment, but her loom remains because no one has had any desire to pay good money to get that heavy contraption down the mountain." I looked about the room before commenting, "Don't you just love the rustic feel of this place?"

He nodded in agreement. Resting his head against the high back of the rocker, Christopher closed his eyes.

After waiting four complete rocking cycles, I said, "I especially like the red exit sign glowin' above the only door out of this room."

He opened his eyes before turning his head towards the door. "OSHA?" he asked.

"OSHA." I quoted from a favorite old joke, "Washington's way of sayin' that I'm from your government and I'm here to help you. I'm sure that agency must do some good, but what a pain in the butt it is when you own a small business." I rocked a bit more before adding, "You can't believe all I have to do at the restaurant because of them."

We were well into that discussion when I heard a definition directed to his team. Since I did not have a dog in the fight, I leaned over to whisper, "The answer is ballistics."

"Are you sure?" he whispered back. No one on his side had yet come up with an answer.

"Of course," I assured him, "I remember that one from physics."

Christopher yelled out authoritatively, "Ballistics!"

With no discussion amongst themselves, his team members readily accepted my answer. After his team won the point, we resumed talking about my restaurant. Later, I heard pieces of a question dealing with a Walter Matthau movie but did not know the answer.

He leaned over and whispered conspiratorially, "I saw that movie last week on television. It's *Fortune Cookie*."

"Are you certain?" I whispered back.

He nodded.

I shouted, "*Fortune Cookie!*"

A male voice on the far side of the room suggested the movie in question was *Cactus Flower*. My team members entered into a lively debate on the merits of the two movies before unanimously voting on *Cactus Flower*. I did not vote for I saw no reason to do so. The correct answer was *Fortune Cookie,* and no point was awarded my team.

Christopher leaned forward, effectively stopping his chair. He took my hand in his and looked into my eyes before saying quietly, "Rachael, I understand now what you meant earlier."

Dumbstruck, I stopped rocking. The cold, prickling cloak of instant recognition draped itself over me. Had he shouted his words, I would not have been any more stunned. Here sat a man who now comprehended what I had tried to explain earlier about a woman's treatment in the South. By his solemn, controlled reaction, I immediately understood that the distant world Christopher inhabited valued a woman for her abilities, not for her drop-dead gorgeous looks and passive sweet smiles of resignation, and that was the reason he could not believe the harassment I had endured.

Sweet Jesus, men like that actually exist! We've been talking with one most of this evening and didn't know it.

Unable to formulate a reply to his comment that had so shaken my world, I began rocking in silence. Being without any quick retort was most unlike me.

After the game ended near midnight, the Baptists left for their cabins. I never knew which team won and did not much care to find out. Our foursome had run out of excuses to stall for time, keeping us from saying 'Good night and sweet dreams.' An enchanted evening quietly ended. One that I instinctively knew Mom and I would be discussing on future hikes when we played our game of Remember When.

◈

With our final visit to the necessary houses before bed completed, I followed Mom back to our cabin, our steps lit by brilliant moonlight. She casually mentioned over her shoulder, "You know, Rachael, I was afraid that those men would carry you off into the woods and have their way with you before the sun set. I was absolutely miserable until I saw you come back."

Because her alarming statement was so unexpected, a frightened chill knifed through my body. Stopping in my tracks, I stared at her back.

"Mother!" I cried out in astonishment.

She continued calmly, her boots clicking against the rocks on the worn path beside the main lodge. "Darlin', I felt I needed to stay behind on the rocks so that I could give, if necessary, an accurate description of your assailants to the proper authorities. Besides," she waited two beats before adding wryly, "my feet were tired."

With her final remark, I realized I had just been zinged, and my budding fear abruptly became a low chuckle. I called to her, "You've spent too many years around my Daddy!"

Back in our cabin, I turned down the lamp's wick before climbing the ladder to the top bunk. As we rustled about, making nests under the covers in our respective beds, Mom asked, "Wonder which trail they're takin' down?"

In the enveloping darkness, I yawned back my answer, "Don't know."

"We ought to ask them to walk down with us," she declared seconds before she drifted off to sleep.

Four

The next morning as we walked into the dining room, I noticed that Christopher and Carl again shared the foot of the table, their backs to the window. Mom reclaimed the chair on Christopher's left, her back to the room. I settled onto the chair to her left.

Scooting my seat closer to the table, I leaned over Mom to ask the men about their morning. "So, how was sunrise?"

"Didn't make it," Carl mumbled, his voice drugged by sleep.

"Too bad. Y'all have to do it next time," I replied, despite knowing there would be no next time because these men would never again be in East Tennessee. "We didn't go either. I'll walk up for sunsets, but sunrises just aren't special enough for me to want to crawl out of a warm bed." I further explained, "When you've seen one sunrise, you've seen them all."

Assuming the mindless gait of the living dead, others who had spent the night at the Lodge silently shuffled in. Our table gradually resumed last evening's seating arrangement.

From past experience, I had found the mood at breakfast to be more subdued than at supper. At night, everyone would be talkative, invigorated by the hike up and by the sights seen along the trail. By morning, however, bodies and tongues never moved as easily as they had the evening before because, after that passage of time, muscles had stiffened. In addition, the hours spent abed had to be factored in as well. Either your sleep time was wonderful with morning coming too soon and you were not firing on all six cylinders, or while everyone else slept, you lay awake listening to mountain mice rummage through your possessions and you were suffering from sleep deprivation.

Pick a reason. It did not matter which. Breakfast was always quieter.

I noticed everyone about me sat mute with shoulders hunched slightly forward and glazed-over eyes fixed on empty, dull green plastic plates. Within minutes after the entire dining room had assembled, staff members rushed to each table carrying matching green plastic platters stacked with enough smoking-hot pancakes, allowing every guest two large pancakes each. Like the others seated at my table, I reached down deep within myself to draw upon just enough strength to raise my arms to help my plate before passing the platter along.

As Christopher poured maple syrup over his pancakes, he asked pitifully, "Is this all there is?"

Reaching for the basket in front of her, Mom unfolded the large red bandana, which had covered cookies last night, to pick up a lightly browned biscuit.

"No," she reassured him, "there'll be eggs and Canadian bacon." She handed the basket to him as the same staff person who brought the pancakes to our table returned to whisk away the now empty platter.

"And good ol' grits," I added.

The men made faces when I mentioned grits.

I could not blame them. Having been exposed on too many occasions to plain, unseasoned grits prepared by the culinary uninitiated, I easily recognized the experience their faces conjured up.

Sharing my version for what Daddy had always referred to as Georgia ice cream, I said, "If the cook would just add some cheese and a little garlic powder and cook them in half milk and half water, these grits could be right tasty but you gotta have the liquid boilin' before you add the grits. Unfortunately, nothin' boils too good at this elevation. She does add enough butter, however, to give them a little flavor. You'll have to try them this mornin', in any case, if only to say you did when you get home."

On an earlier visit to the Lodge, the breakfast presentation had been quite bizarre. Since retelling that morning's meal always brought a smile to an otherwise silent table, I shared my story with Carl, Christopher and the rest.

"One Easter, years ago, when Mom and I were up here, the staff got creative and dyed the scrambled eggs. Each table got a platter with a different color. There were red eggs and blue eggs. Our table got the platter with green eggs and ham. I felt like Sam-I-Am. That was the first time we ever sat at a table that didn't eat up every speck of their eggs."

As I finished the last of my story, our platter was returned piled high with a generous, steaming mound of scrambled eggs, in the appropriate golden color, and covered with nine large circles of Canadian bacon. After everyone heartily agreed they were grateful that today was not that Easter morning, we continued eating with only sporadic snippets of conversation.

Before I scooted my chair back from the table, Mom touched my arm. "Ask them," she reminded me.

All morning, I had halfway hoped Mom would forget what she wanted me to ask the men. Since she had not, I reluctantly complied. "Which trail are y'all takin' down?"

Christopher thought for a moment before answering. He spoke slowly, as he dragged the correct trail names up from memory. "We came up . . . Trillium. Guess we'll go back . . . Bullhead. Then take that short spur over to our car at . . . Grotto Falls."

Carl nodded in agreement.

I completed Mom's request. "Why don't y'all walk down with us? I'll carry you back to your car."

Carl looked at me in total amazement. He snorted. "Carry? I don't think you can carry us anywhere!"

Puzzled by his outburst, I frowned hard at him before it occurred to me that, during my sleep, I had forgotten that my Southern idioms were unfamiliar to him. "Yes, carry." Patiently, I explained to the foreigners, "I'll carry you back to your car in my car." Regional differences, again, I thought. "Alum Bluff is 'bout four miles shorter than your way."

Christopher asked, "Will your car hold all of us?"

"I think so," I replied.

I owned a 1985 Sedan de Ville that had always held everything I ever wanted to haul. Surely, I thought, they couldn't have carried up that much gear in their packs.

"Do join us," Mom urged. "The views along Alum Bluff are spectacular. If y'all never get back to the Lodge, it would be a shame to miss out on this one trail."

Who could refuse my mother anything? I knew it was a done deal from the expressions on their faces.

She paused before applying the *coup de grâce*. "It won't be any trouble at all."

"No trouble at all," I chimed in, on cue.

In the South, that phase means it will be out of the way or out of the ordinary but I will do whatever-it-is for you because you-are-who-you-are. It would be about a ninety-minute drive out of the way for me but no trouble at all for my mother. She did not drive. Since they would not be in the area again and since we had said it was no trouble at all, the men agreed to a change of trails.

We met at the same spot above the Lodge where we had gathered the night before. The new morning was crisp and clean. The nippy air was rich with the now familiar sharp, clean scent of fresh balsams. The sky matched the cheerful blue of a patch of prim Quaker ladies in bloom. Puffy, white clouds floated overhead. Juncos sang arias, and boomer squirrels chattered insults to one and all.

After we started down the trail, we found the men walked much faster than either Mom or I had anticipated they would. We trotted along behind them for about a half-mile until we reached the beginning of the steep decline under Cliff Top. This was not exactly the hike down my mother had envisioned, and she told me so in no uncertain terms when she stopped to catch her breath.

After listening to Mom's terse remarks, I called out to the men's shrinking figures far ahead of us, "Y'all can either walk with us now or wait for us at the parkin' lot later."

They stopped for us to catch up. Without further comment from anyone, we smoothly accommodated each other's hiking styles. The men slowed down some, we speeded up a bit. Still, the remainder of the morning sped by much too quickly. The views from the overlooks were every bit as breathtaking as Mom had promised, and our conversations were as lively as the evening's before. The potential awkwardness of handling the call-of-nature among strangers never became a problem. When the times came, Mom and I left the trail for a discreet thicket of rhododendron and the men simply found their own solution. Sometimes, Mom and Christopher walked together. Sometimes, Christopher and I walked together. We soon became a mercurial foursome, coming together to form a whole only to separate later into two sets, which then joined again to divide again into a different subset of two. Despite all our stops to share the scenery, I knew it was going to be a much shorter five-and-a-half-miles down than Mom and I had hiked up the previous day.

Above Alum Bluff near the site called Gracie's Pulpit, I found myself alone with Christopher. I stopped to look back for Mom and Carl. With neither in sight, I felt ill at ease.

"Let's wait up," I suggested as I reached for my canteen. Holding the container toward him, I asked, "Want some?"

"Not now." He retraced his steps to where I stood. "She'll be OK." His tone was sympathetic as if he understood my true reason to wait. He added, "Carl will look after her." Next Christopher said, "Turn around and don't look back until I tell you to."

Now, here comes that deadly axe.

Although my body stiffened with that uneasy thought, politely I asked aloud, "Whatever for?"

He answered, "I want to talk to the trees."

My twin whispered, *Must be a California thing.*

Well, I commented silently, they do hug trees out there. Maybe the man wants to get on a first name basis with a few here in Tennessee.

I turned to face the deserted trail. When we stood back to back, I heard zipper teeth move.

Christopher went on to say, "Did I tell you that I was shot when I was in Vietnam?"

"No, you didn't say anything to me about that last night," I replied, now realizing we were about to share an intimacy that a man and a woman, who had met for the first time less than twenty-four hours earlier, had no business sharing and also knowing I had no idea how what he was about to do next related to his Vietnam experience. No sooner than it took for all those thoughts to occur, I heard the sound of liquid falling to the ground.

"Yeah, I was shot up pretty bad and lost a kidney."

I still was unclear what the significance of having a single kidney had to do with us standing back to back as the man peed on the ground.

Not convinced that his was a reasonable explanation, I asked, "Are you sure you're not just markin' the territory?"

Ignoring my sarcasim, Christopher changed the subject. "Is there a place in Gatling's Burg to buy trail patches?"

I heard the sound of zipper teeth for the second time as Carl and Mom came into view. I breathed easier upon seeing Mom unruffled and realizing that Carl was not an axe murderer either.

"That's Gat-lin-burg." I corrected his pronunciation before answering in the affirmative.

For the remainder of the trip down the mountain, I kept pace with Christopher while Mom and Carl walked about forty yards behind. At the first creek crossing below Alum Bluff, Christopher stopped for another pee break. To make small talk that would drown out the sound of his activity, I told him about the origin of the creek's name.

"Some think that mountain people aren't very literate, but I don't believe that for one minute. This creek got its name because some men had to cross it to bring down a neighbor who had died. The mountain people started callin' it Styx Creek after that."

"Sticks?"

"Not s-t-i-c-k-s, but S-t-y-x," I spelled, "as in Greek mythology's river of the dead. People up here were well read. They just weren't well educated."

"Interesting," Christopher commented. "Let's move on. By the way, how do you and your mother know so much about this trail and the Lodge?"

"Oh, we studied for the exam," I teased before giving the true explanation. "One year, we started down Alum with the couple who had managed the Lodge back in the 1950s and '60s. While his wife walked with us, Mr. Brown ran on ahead to get their car. They'd come up to LeConte from Newfound Gap, and he planned to hitch a ride up the mountain to bring the car on down to her. Boy, she certainly kept us entertained with all her stories!"

"Which trail had they taken up?"

"The Boulevard off the AT. In case you don't know, that's short for the Appalachian Trail." Tired of carrying most of the conversational load, I changed the subject in order to have him talk. "Tell me about your wife and children. Did I hear last night you tellin' Mom you had a boy and a girl?"

I had my mother to thank for being well schooled in the art of maintaining polite conversation. The remainder of the time on the trail, I made appropriate sounds and asked more leading questions, but only listened with one ear to the words coming from the man in front of me because I knew there would be no pop quiz to take after we got off the mountain.

***

From the position of the sun overhead, I figured it was well after noon when we reached the parking lot. After more than twenty-four hours in the woods, sounds of passing autos and odors from their exhaust fumes insulted my senses. For the first time that morning, my feet felt hot and weary inside my boots. As I led the way across the hard pavement toward my waiting car, I knew I truly had arrived back to reality as soon as my boots made hollow sounds against the asphalt surface. Reaching my car's rear bumper, I pulled off my backpack before unlatching the trunk lid. As soon as the air reached it, the sweat-soaked patch, marking where my pack had rested, quickly chilled my back.

The men stopped a few yards behind me.

"Is this your car?" Carl asked in amazement.

"What were you expectin'," my voice arched like a defensive cat's back, "a dented pick-up truck?"

"Well, no, but I didn't expect a brand new Cadillac," he answered.

"It's not new. It's four years old and bought used." I snapped briskly, as if it were any of his business, "Bein' second hand, does that make it better?" But I must admit to a sweet twinge of mischief, knowing that I had caught them off guard with my car's appearance.

My gleaming black car looked especially grand after coming off rustic Mount LeConte. Its first owner had custom-ordered a black cherry finish that glowed a rich burgundy red wherever the paint was struck by light. Its interior was a pale camel color, and the matching leather seats were as soft to the touch as a baby's butt. I had washed the car myself late Thursday afternoon before the hike, and its outer surface looked like a new penny shining. I smiled as I watched the men carefully remove their dusty, heavy boots before slipping sock-footed into the back seat for the ride back down the mountain.

***

I stopped in Gatlinburg at the Lodge's company store where, after deciding they did not like the design for the trail patches, the men purchased official Lodge T-shirts to commemorate their hike. Afterwards, I drove us out of town on Airport Road to retrieve their rental car.

When we arrived at the parking area for Grotto Falls Trail, the one-way road was crowded on both sides with parked vehicles belonging to other park visitors. After easing the car off the pavement into the only available parking slot, we stepped out to say our good-byes as the men looked for their vehicle.

Unfortunately, Carl and Christopher had a difficult time remembering which car they had been assigned by the rental company. To speed along their search, they separated while each peered into parked autos seeking some personal item that would identify a car as theirs.

Because we had no idea what to look for, Mom and I merely leaned against my car to wait patiently, for no properly reared Southerner would drive away before learning the men had located their car and it would crank. Since our muscles had stiffened during the ride down the mountain, standing and not having to walk felt good. Silently, we watched with repressed amusement as the men walked stiffly about for some minutes before deciding theirs was a blue compact.

Still, with the time upon us at last, I could not find a stopping point on which to hang the phrase 'Good-bye,' and it seemed neither could they. We stood discussing the Lodge and the hike down. We foolishly exchanged business cards should Mom and I ever make it out to San Francisco, should they ever come back to East Tennessee. The men inquired about restaurants in the Townsend area where they were staying the remainder of the weekend. I was familiar with that small town being as my recently acquired cabin was located in a little community not far from there. Carl requested the name of a restaurant with local atmosphere that served food specific to this region.

Christopher defined his friend's request more narrowly. "I want some of that good Southern fried chicken I've heard about all my life."

I told them of a place on the river I liked. After Carl had handed it back to me for that purpose, I wrote out the directions on the back of my business card. When I returned the card, we had nothing left to discuss. In the deafening silence, we awkwardly shook hands in formal parting.

As Mom and I returned to our appropriate sides of my car, Christopher called out, "Come to Townsend tonight. We'd like to take you both out to supper as thanks for the hike down."

Carl added, "You were absolutely right, Mrs. Taite, that was a beautiful trail. Glad you insisted we join you. Wouldn't have missed it for anything."

I looked at Mom to read what her eyes said about their last minute invitation and found no negative squint.

"OK," I called back. "What time?"

"Seven," Carl answered.

"What's your room number?"

Christopher examined an object he pulled out of his pants pocket before calling out, "One-ten at The Tanglewood Inn. We'll treat you to some real Southern fried chicken."

I laughed. "That'll work," I replied as I opened my car door.

We drove off in our separate cars, finally going our separate ways. Strangely, my car and my life felt much emptier without them.

During the return to Knoxville, Mom begged out of going to supper. "Darlin'," she explained, "I'm just too tired to get cleaned up, dressed up and go out again. Besides, I'm not ready to be seen out in the company of men right yet."

As the miles and minutes away from the men added up, the idea of driving back up to the mountains for supper began to seem ludicrous to me, too, except I had enjoyed their company and, really, had nothing better to do. Just no trouble at all. Besides, I could stay at my cabin down the road in Sunshine and not face a second trip back to Knoxville later that night.

After I dropped Mom off at her condo, I drove to my house where I caught a quick power-nap with my cats curled up next to me. When my head sunk into the pillow, I suddenly realized how worn out I actually was.

***

As I slowly thumbed through the various garments hanging in my closet, I faintly heard the downstairs clock chime five. Selecting the perfect outfit and carefully applying make-up seemed silly, I decided, because it was going to be just those two men and me.

I mumbled, "What the hell was I thinkin' when I agreed to have dinner in Townsend? And what the hell will I wear? It isn't as if it's a date. It isn't as if I'll ever see them again. So what does it matter what I wear or what my face looks like?" They had already seen me in an old

T-shirt and faded scrub pants, my customary warm weather hiking apparel. They had also seen me during breakfast at my early morning worst, without benefit of powder and paint.

Because you're dining with men, it matters. And don't you forget clean, good underwear in case we wreck, my constant companion reminded me.

After donning red lacy undies, I selected black cotton slacks, pulled a loose fitting red cotton sweater over my head and slipped my sockless feet into dark brown Sebago Mariners. Thus appropriately presentable and prepared for a possible automobile mishap, I drove to Townsend, on the sleepy side of the Smokies, for this non-date with two strangers from the Left Coast.

I turned my Cadillac into a space next to their car in front of the correct motel room at seven on the dot. Being a Virgo, I was compulsive about being on time. The door to room one-ten was open but the men were nowhere to be seen. They had said seven, and I had fully expected Carl and Christopher to be dressed, outside their room and ready to go by seven. They were men, for God's sake. They have less to get ready; ergo, they're supposed to be on time.

I left my car and walked to the gaping doorway, the better to peer inside their room. I saw two untidy beds and a cluttered dresser and Carl walking about, his hips wrapped in a towel. From the far back, I heard Christopher loudly singing something in Italian, his happy voice almost drowning out the sound of running water.

When Carl noticed me standing in the doorway, he apologized. "Sorry. We took the one-way loop through that cove and got caught up in some heavy, sightseeing traffic."

"Carl, I'll just wait outside 'til y'all are ready," I responded, thinking to myself that this was not the first time punctuality had been a problem for me.

I walked away from the open door. Leaning against my car's hood, I considered that, perhaps, I had made a mistake about coming to Townsend to dine alone with two men I really did not know. For the first time since the walk to sunset the night before, I saw flashes of unpleasant scenarios involving these two strangers. Each ended with me lying naked, dead on the floor after having been brutally ravished, and my poor car burning, after having been stripped for its parts.

Man, oh, man, this is going to be a long, long evening. What the hell are we doing here?

After a few minutes, which seemed to me longer than that entire hike down the mountain earlier this morning, Carl appeared in the doorway, dressed and ready to go. He wore a red polo shirt, khaki pants and brown Mariners by Sebago, without socks.

"Where's Mom?" he asked as he donned aviator sunglasses similar to the ones I wore before strolling over to join me where I remained leaning against the car.

"She sends her regrets. Since Daddy has been gone, she doesn't feel much like goin' out at night. It'll be just us three for dinner."

Wordlessly, we checked out our matching footwear and similar choice of sunglasses and smiled. About that time Christopher appeared, smelling of generic motel soap and his hair still wet from the shower. He wore a black polo shirt over pleated khaki pants, aviator-style sunglasses, brown Mariners by Sebago and no socks.

My mind informed me, *Well, they can't be completely bad if they both wear Sebagos and aviator sunglasses, too.*

Rubbing his hands gleefully together when he reached my car, Christopher demanded, "Where's that fried chicken I've been waiting to taste all my life?"

Not wishing to give up entire control of my destiny, I quickly offered to drive my more comfortable car, suggesting that would leave the men free to enjoy the scenery. Without any discussion among them, Carl sat in front with me and Christopher rode in the back behind him.

The family-owned Townsend restaurant that I had suggested was situated a short distance from their motel beside the narrow river bisecting the quiet valley. Its wood plank exterior promised nothing, but the aroma greeting us as we walked inside its doors was enough to make the most jaded salivary glands sit up and beg.

I asked the hostess for a table next to the rear windows to give the men an opportunity to watch wild ducks floating the water. To observe my companions more closely, I sat across the table from them. The men told me about some Sierra Club outings back home that they had hiked. They commented on the beauty of Cade's Cove which they had toured earlier in the day, going on and on about the lushness and greenness that I woke up to every morning in East Tennessee.

We selected identical meals consisting of fried chicken, with them ordering white meat while I chose all dark; creamy, mashed Irish potatoes; half an ear of boiled corn; crispy coleslaw; and a basket heaped with smoking-hot White Lily biscuits and yellow corn muffins accompanied by chilled, individual pats of real butter.

Having no previous exposure to indigenous customs, Carl and Christopher used their knives and forks to get into their chicken. I managed mine with my fingers.

As supper progressed, I paid close attention to their body language and listened intently to what they revealed about themselves through the various subjects we discussed. Before dessert was served, I found myself relaxed after having assured myself again that these were, indeed, nice men and that this would be an entertaining evening, after all. To end our meal, the waitress cleared our table before carrying out three fresh forks and one generous slice of hot pecan pie, crowned by a heaping mound of homemade vanilla ice cream.

Upon leaving the restaurant, I headed the car in the direction of Newfound Gap. The men decided to check out the moon from the Gap after agreeing with me there was not much to do in Townsend.

Thankfully, the men had not suggested returning to their room to watch the televised basketball game that would determine who would play the next leg toward the championships. That would have been a red flag, and I would have ended the evening right then and there. Besides, I was not much for pro basketball. Now, that offer would have been more difficult for me to refuse, however, had it been football play-offs.

I drove alongside the rock-filled, dancing mountain river on a narrow road that had originally been constructed over an old logging railroad bed. Above Gatlinburg at the Park's visitors' center, I turned right onto Highway 441 to get up the mountain. As the roadbed snaked between steep ridges and deep valleys, its pavement clung to what little available flatness had been blasted out of the rugged mountains' flanks.

After parking the car at the Gap, we walked over to a sturdy, skillfully fitted, low rock wall built in conjunction with the site where President Roosevelt gave his speech dedicating The Great Smoky Mountains National Park. We sat soaking up the serene order of the distant smoky ranges and breathing in the rich aromas from the riotous plant life growing on the mountaintop, at the same time trying to ignore the over-heated engine smell and over-used brake stench from the recently parked cars recovering behind us. Sporadic pings rang out as metal automotive parts cooled throughout the parking lot.

We found the Newfound Gap parking area as crowded with vehicles as the rocks at Cliff Top had been crowded with hikers the night before, and the moonlight was as bright as it had been when we sat on Mount LeConte looking across to this gap. As a warm wind softly rustled up the ridges from North Carolina, every leaf within our sight shimmered in the silvery moon's diffused light. Finding words unnecessary, we looked about, silently appreciating the spectacular beauty laid out before us.

Several long minutes later, Carl finally broke our silence. "That fried chicken was better than I'd expected. By the way, what do you call where we drove by the river?"

"A gorge," I answered.

"Back home, it would be called a canyon," he offered.

Smiling, I considered his answer. Summing up the comparison, I announced, "Regional differences, again."

When I had sat long enough on that rock wall for my butt cheeks to conform to the stones beneath me, I asked my companions, "Now what?" I listed our options, "Go back to Townsend and call it a night? Check out the wild nightlife in Gatlinburg? Cruise the main drag in Pigeon Forge? Drive over to Cherokee in North Carolina? What suits your fancy?"

"How far are we from North Carolina?" Christopher asked. "I've never been there."

"Actually," I answered, "the state line is a few hundred feet over your right shoulder. Cherokee is down the mountain a bit."

When we pulled into the sprawling resort of Cherokee, the clock in my car indicated the time was a little after ten. All shops were closed. Mine was one of the few cars on the streets, and only a handful of people walked about.

Not a good choice, I thought, as I drove slowly through the town, listening to the men comment on the tourist-enticing shops.

I wandered the nearly deserted town until we came upon a large parking area where a street dance was in progress. After declaring this could be entertaining, I stopped the car. As soon as we opened the car doors, the seducing sounds of "Under The Boardwalk" beckoned us.

The night air in this deep valley was cool. Being native to the region, I was prepared for this temperature change with the long sleeves of my cotton sweater, but Christopher was not.

As he rubbed his bare arms below the short sleeves of his knit shirt, he announced, "I'm cold."

Reaching into the backseat, I pulled out my Boys Club Duck Race sweatshirt to hand him. After dragging the thick jersey over his head, he said, "This smells like you."

How would he know? When was he that close? Did we put on too much 'Poison'? The other raced ahead with too many questions for which I had no quick answers.

Arriving at the makeshift dance floor, Carl and I danced to the remainder of "Under the Boardwalk." He and I laughed at our awkward attempts to move together, as those regional differences simply would not go away. The next song was the old beach classic, "My Girl," and I danced with Christopher. I tried shagging, but since he was not familiar with that Carolina art form, we, too, stumbled through that tune. Following that second selection, the band's choice was "The Tennessee Waltz," and Christopher whirled me away before Carl could get close enough to ask for the next dance. As we executed a passable waltz through the maze of freestyle dancers, we each confessed to taking ballroom dance classes in college.

After that third song, Carl did not attempt to cut back in. The band played "Miss Grace," following with "In the Midnight Hour" and a Tom Jones-esque remake of one of my Daddy's favorite country songs, something about putting your sweet lips a little closer to the phone. Still, Carl remained nowhere to be seen.

"Where's your friend?" I asked, glancing about for the third member of our trio as the band started "When a Man Loves a Woman."

"He's all right." Christopher curtly informed me, guiding me to the far corner of the floor.

Finally the band played "Good Night, Ladies," the universal signal indicating the party was over. I had enjoyed a fun evening; however, I felt a bit like a bad hostess for not dancing with Carl after the first song.

It's all Mom's fault, I thought, she should have had real twins.

After the music stopped and the crowd thinned out, we found Carl leaning against the side of my car. For the first time this evening, Carl opened the back passenger door to sit in the rear while Christopher opened the front passenger door to sit alongside me.

Returning to Tennessee under a crisp navy blue sky, the sporadic conversation was mostly between Christopher and me. Carl did not contribute much after he commented he had never found anyone else to ask for a dance. Occasionally, I looked for him in the rearview mirror. He was not asleep. He simply looked out the window, apparently no longer feeling a part of the threesome.

We had driven halfway back up the mountain when Christopher suddenly asked, "Please explain to me the difference between 'you' and 'you all.' I know you Southerners use 'you all' as plural, but since I've been in Tennessee, I've heard people use 'you all' for one person."

I chuckled, saying, "Give me a minute." After thinking over his quandary, I finally replied, "The best answer to your question is that 'you' is always singular in the South, and sometimes it's used for the plural form, too, just like in other areas of the country. In most parts of the South, 'y'all' is the plural form of 'you.' In East Tennessee, however, oral grammar rules can get a bit odd. I think it has to do with our strong Scotch-Irish heritage because here 'you' is singular and plural; 'y'all' can be singular, but is mostly plural; and then, there's 'you'ns' which can be singular and plural, too."

Puzzled, Christopher quickly repeated, "You'ns?"

"Yes."

"You'ns," he repeated more slowly. Still perplexed, Christopher pondered my drawn-out explanation for a long time before finally commenting, "I'm sorry I bothered to ask."

We reached the deserted Gap after midnight. As I steered my car down the mountain, the pearlized moon seemed bigger and its silvery light even brighter than earlier this evening. I hardly needed headlights to illuminate the pavement. A few ghostly clouds sailed the sky as I felt, for the second night in a row, that I could live forever.

Passing the entrance for The Chimneys picnic area, I recalled other locally acceptable, grammatically correct forms for the word 'you.' "Oh, Christopher, I forgot to tell you about the plural form of 'y'all,' it's 'all y'all,' but I can't tell you at what numeric amount that form comes into use. It's not as definite as when 'you' becomes 'y'all' at two. Then there is the equally aberrant, 'you'ns-ez' for 'you'ns.'"

Taking my eyes off the curving road before me, I briefly turned my head in Christopher's direction to find him staring at me in disbelief. Proud of my convoluted efforts to purposely muddy the waters, I grinned broadly before returning my concentration to the highway and suggesting, "Now, after all that, I know y'all are really sorry you asked."

I waited until after we had crossed the park boundary at Townsend to tell my passengers about my cabin, before asking if they would like to see it. I sweetened the invitation by adding I thought I had a couple of cold beers in the fridge. The men would be leaving in the morning for Nashville. Too soon this wonderful weekend would be history, and for some reason something inside of me would not let it end.

As Carl declined, saying he was too tired, Christopher agreed to come with me. Armed with the knowledge that Christopher also was not ready for this night to end, I felt a tweak of apprehension gradually creep into my brain. Maybe it was the thrill of anticipation.

As soon as Carl disappeared into their motel room, the once relaxed ambiance inside my car instantly switched to awkwardness, similar to the flipping of cool and warm water layers in a deep lake during spring. Maybe there was not enough of Christopher and me to fill the volume of the car's interior; or perhaps, with Carl no longer present to dilute the presence of Christopher, there was simply too much of Christopher inside my car for me. Whichever the reason, I found it crushingly difficult to breathe, and I could not comprehend why Carl's departure created such a difference. We drove the three miles separating their motel from my cabin without exchanging a single word, with everything about being alone with him seeming uncomfortably left-handed.

Peering through the windshield at the black new asphalt passing beneath the hood of my car, I was lost in thought as judgments rapidly trained through my mind: I have never known when enough is enough—I should have never mentioned the cabin—I should have said good-bye to them both at their door—I should have—

Oh, damn, we're here!

After I turned off the engine, we walked in silence to the door. While Christopher stood behind me on the narrow front porch, I fumbled with the keys in the lock, the hollow sounds of closing car doors still echoing in my ears. I sensed Christopher was not standing that near to me, yet somehow he seemed much too close for my comfort.

"I'm not really nervous," I announced, speaking aloud for the first time since Carl had left us at The Tanglewood Inn. "I've just not owned this place very long." Although lying about being nervous, I spoke the truth about my length of ownership. I needed to fill the empty, heavy silence with light conversation, if only for the slight comfort it afforded me.

Immediately, I regretted having keys to my house, to Mom's condo, to Margaret's place, to the restaurant, to my post office box, to the cabin and to my car all on one key ring. With the metallic jangling, I worried that Christopher would think I moonlighted as a janitor. After trying the different keys for what seemed to be hours, I found the correct one and heard the tumblers click. The front door swung in as a rush of stale air, pent up for too long, fled past us to join the freedom of the night.

My small cabin was homemade from leftovers and sat on a tiny lot sandwiched between the old road to Sunshine and the banks of Little River that merged later with the Tennessee River, somewhere between the cities of Alcoa and Knoxville. The cabin's rooms were damp and musty and furnished with secondhand items I was not even certain Goodwill would take as contributions.

For years, I had yearned for a place in this location where houses so rarely became available. I had learned the cabin had remained unoccupied for months after its last owner had passed away. About the time that my accountant had suggested I could spend some money, it came on the market. In fact, I had been driving by the very afternoon the realtor placed the For Sale sign. After stopping my car in the middle of the road, I had called out to her to take that sign down because I was buying that cabin right then and there.

Before the purchase from the estate was completed, his attorney had removed the old man's personal effects, but had left his furnishings. I would redecorate someday, maybe. Then, again, maybe not. Considering the all-invasive dampness, the periodic flooding and the possible break-ins, I did not worry at all about the items now in my cabin. I would have need to worry if its furnishings were upgraded.

"It's not much, but I love it," I explained to Christopher as I moved ahead of him down the short hall toward the main room, turning on the overhead hall light and the living room ceiling light when I reached the switches on the wall. "Whoever originally built the cabin must have stumbled upon a good buy," I explained the obvious, "because every room in the place, except the bath, is lined with dark walnut sheet panelin'. I can get away from the world here. Only Mom and a couple of friends have the phone number. No one else can find me when I'm in my hidey-hole."

I walked toward the table lamp on the near side of the couch. With the night's darkness, the cabin's paneled walls and dampness lent its interior an earthy, primeval feeling.

"Hidey-hole?" Christopher questioned.

I stopped to consider the type of childhood this man might have had.

"You don't know about Uncle Remus and Br'er Rabbit and hidey-holes?" I asked while I turned on the table lamp.

"No," he answered curtly, "I'm afraid not."

Bracing both hands against the doorframe, Christopher leaned into the first doorway on his right, the opening into my bedroom. The space was just big enough for a thin person to ease sideways around the iron double bed and the single chest-of-drawers. Because there was not enough floor space for night tables, lamps had been attached to the wall on either side of the bed.

Continuing his tour, he next walked past a closed door down a widening in the hall to the open bathroom door on his left. After flipping on the wall switch for that room, he grimaced immediately as the bright glare assaulted his eyes.

That abrupt contrast had also gotten my attention the first time I stood in the bathroom with the ceiling light on. Even the realtor had cringed when she had shown me about. A previous owner had put up plastic-covered panels in an unsettling hue of yellow, an uneasy alliance among the color of a free-range hen's egg yolk and a grammar school safety patrol's yellow rubberized rain slicker and the glow-in-the-dark decoder ring I played with as a child. That small room allowed for one person at a time to stand comfortably amongst the sink, commode and tub.

When I was alone in the cabin, I left the bathroom door open because I felt trapped inside the room with its door closed. Besides, I loathed the brightness of the walls under the glare of the naked bulb that served as the room's sole light.

Directing Christopher's tour of the cabin onward, I turned off the hall light when he entered the compact living room/dining room/kitchen combination. The space was much too small to be called a great room. An ancient, broken-down Naugahyde sleeper-sofa occupied the wall that faced the river. Crowded bookcases with sagging shelves lined the wall to its left. All had belonged to the previous owner. An over-sized, ornate, wooden console TV from the 1960s sat catty-cornered under the window next to the far end of the bookcase. I had been pleased to find the set displayed a decent enough picture, as long as the neighborhood cable service lines remained intact.

I used the former owner's folding wooden card table as a dining table whenever I had Mom or Liz or Margaret over for meals. This evening it was covered with stacks of old magazines I had been sorting through, after discovering them just last weekend when I decided to clean out what the old man had stashed away under his bed. I really should have just thrown them out, but I had uncovered a treasure trove of girlie magazines from the 1940s and '50s amongst his sedate collection of *Life*, *Newsweek* and *National Geographic*.

Standing across from the taller bookcases, a third bookcase served as a waist-high dry bar and room divider between that space and the kitchen area. I had scooted over the old man's 1950s-era, dome-top refrigerator to bring my Grandmother Taite's marble-topped kitchen table for added work space and hung my great-grandmother Jubelle Lee's cupboard for needed storage above it. These additions faced the white porcelain double sink embedded in a long counter set under windows that looked out over the narrow river flowing behind my snug retreat.

When I acquired the cabin, I also became heir to a hodgepodge of lamps left on the card table as well as the unmatched end tables by the sofa. I turned on the remaining lamps as Christopher wandered about, feeling they would show our surroundings to better advantage than the room's ceiling fixture, which I quickly turned off.

A 1950s vintage, blond-wood coffee table with splayed legs squatted on a braided rag-rug in front of the sofa. The rug had most likely been colorful when purchased, but had dulled over time. Brown linoleum in a generic, wood plank design covered all the floors. Repeated footsteps over untold years had worn the pattern down to the backing, leaving an inviting black trail that started at the front door, fading off toward the bedrooms and bath, continuing on into the large room to the bookcases on the right and back door in the middle and on over to the kitchen sink on the left. The narrow footpath widened into black stepping stones where the refrigerator had stood and in front of the three bookcases.

I remembered what Mom had said when she first saw the cabin's interior. She had kindly pronounced that the place looked 'lovingly lived in.' Her Southern lady comment actually translated into 'Damn, child, what have you spent good money for!' I was glad that she had not spoken the condemnation of 'There's no accountin' for taste.' As I waited patiently to hear Christopher's judgment, I wondered what this stranger from California thought about my folly and instantly found myself curious as to why his opinion would matter.

When he completed his walk-through inspection of the three rooms, he pointed to a closed door to the left of the bathroom.

I cautioned quickly in mock panic, "Sweet Jesus! Don't open the door! That's the junk room, and I haven't worked up enough nerve to tackle that mess yet. It'll give me something to do this winter."

"It is . . . rustic." Christopher gave voice to his measured first comment. Some moments later, he asked, "How long have you owned this place?"

"About three months. It came up for sale early last fall but bein' a female and a small business owner to boot, it took time for the bank to approve my loan." I could tell by his tone that the man saw only the clutter, not the eccentric charm. "Just you wait. Get a beer out of the fridge and come outside on the porch."

I clicked on the small radio tucked away among the liquor bottles on the low bookcase dividing the main room. Music from the oldies station broadcasting from Sevierville filled the cabin. "You'll soon understand why I love it here." After I adjusted the radio's volume, I moved over to the sink to get a glass.

"I think all this place needs is a lava lamp," Christopher judiciously suggested, going to the ancient, scarred refrigerator to open the door. Leaning inside to look for his beer, he asked, "Do you want one?"

"No, I don't drink beer. I'll have water. Get out the jug for me." Almost as an after-thought, I added, "Please."

"You don't like beer?" He handed me the water jug before pulling the tab on his beer.

"Nope, it's just that I heard the Japanese use beer to fatten their beef cattle. I'd rather get my calories elsewhere. Want a cold mug for your beer? There's one up in the freezer compartment." I placed my eyeglasses atop the windowsill above the sink.

"No, I'll drink from the can." Christopher watched as I filled my glass and handed the jug back to him to return it to the fridge. He asked, "Do you believe everything you hear, Rachael?"

I assumed that his amused tone applied to my comment concerning the process for fattening Japanese beef cattle. "No, I first must have two pieces of substantiatin' evidence," I quipped as I walked past him to the back door.

That was an odd question. My twin had found his question puzzling.

I think so, too, I told her.

After unlocking the rear door, I stepped onto the porch that ran across the back of the cabin. Not wanting to turn on the overhead outside light, I eased cautiously through the darkness to the wooden swing hanging in front of the kitchen windows. Beer in hand, Christopher followed. Wordlessly, he surveyed the property beyond the low porch railing before joining me on the swing.

Every quality belonging to the night surrounding my cabin seemed excessively rich and, if I could have found the appropriate dials, I would have lowered their intensities. Frogs croaked too loudly in the grasses flanking the river. Too many fireflies blinked high in the overhanging too dark trees. The sprightly water sparkled in the too bright moonlight. In the distance, a truck downshifted as the vehicle passed above us on the new road on the other side of the river, its gears grinding too noisily in protest. We sat in the shadows swinging with the rusty chains connecting the swing to the rafters making hoarse chain music overhead.

I felt clumsy and wooden sharing the swing with Christopher. We sat as close as possible to the opposite armrests, leaving sufficient space between us on those hard slats for a third rotund individual. Like waiting for that legendary second boot to fall, we shared a painfully pregnant silence. I remembered feeling that same way one afternoon long ago while I waited, in vain, for Mackey to reveal who had been sharing our marriage bed.

I noticed Christopher shivering, despite wearing my thick sweatshirt. The breeze coming off the river did not seem that cold to me, but after all he was not from around here and maybe Californians had thinner blood.

"Do you want a blanket?" I asked, most grateful to have something to say.

He abruptly stood and curtly announced, "No. Let's go inside."

The man was through the doorway even before I could uncross my legs and make my way off the bucking swing.

Being inside the cabin felt just as awkward to me as being outside on the porch.

From the radio, Otis Redding crooned that his arms longed to hold someone. Acting upon the lyrical suggestion, Christopher put his beer down by the liquor bottles and extended his hand. "Shall we dance?"

Since his face wore the unfathomable mask of a stoic manikin, I reasoned his offer had to be better than standing about, staring at each other. Placing my water glass on the coffee table, I nodded as I walked closer to him. Within his arms, I could feel the man's body actually shivering against mine.

Oh, my sweet Jesus, this is even worse, I told myself.

"I've never done this before," he said haltingly.

As we moved about the living room to the music, his last sentence pounded in my head. Each word echoed separately like hard-soled boots tramping across wood floors in an empty room.

Now that's an original statement, my twin barked out. *Like we've not ever heard that before!*

Part of me wanted to believe him. But he hadn't lied last night about the matches, I pointed out to the other. Reminding her of her observation earlier this evening before supper, I added, You were the one who suggested he couldn't be completely bad since we even wear the same style of Sebagos and sunglasses. Remember?

And that's lame, too. What do matches and shoes and sunglasses have to do with what he said?

Ignoring her last remark, I wondered how two people, after chatting away for hours on various subjects, could become so tongue-tied. I asked myself, What is happening here? What did I miss out on? Where was the transition?

Back in the car, Baby Girl. Back during the drive from the motel. Weren't you there?

Redding's plaintive song ended, another slow one began. We danced on, moving to the music of Neil Diamond, the Righteous Brothers and Diana Ross, with and without the Supremes. Gladys Knight and The Pips, followed by Miss Aretha, worked their magic until he stopped shivering and until, once more, I began to feel comfortable having his right arm about my waist, my left arm resting on his shoulder and my forehead tucked beneath his chin.

Throughout the late night as the oldies station played without commercial interruptions, we shuffled smoothly through countless songs. Johnny Rivers' "Poor Side of Town" and Brook Benton's "Rainy Night in Georgia" added fuel to the fire. Forgetting that we were strangers and overlooking his estranged wife in California, we gave ourselves over to the music. I draped my arms about his shoulders while Christopher held me close against his body, both his arms clasped behind my back at my waist. We became as partners who have danced together for ages while those old songs wove their spell tightly, binding us with tender chains.

Unable to remember when he started his trek, I became aware that Christopher was leaving soft, whispered kisses on my forehead, slowly moving his lips to my closed eyelids, then down to my cheeks and onto the tip of my nose. His wandering trail of downy kisses seemed endless. The music on the radio continued, but we ceased swaying to its rhythms. I felt the pulse pounding at my wrists and at the base of my throat. I heard my blood rushing past my eardrums.

Sweet Jesus, this is pure torture. Isn't this man ever going to kiss my mouth?

Upon opening my eyes to find him studying my face, I momentarily played with the idea that the man had been memorizing my features. He moved his hands up to cradle my head between them. Without his arms to support me, I nearly lost my balance and swayed backwards, but he steadied me against his body.

Christopher had stopped shivering soon after we started dancing. I, however, was shuddering now that we had stopped.

"I've never done this before," he repeated softly, searching my eyes for answers to unspoken questions before he leaned down to kiss my lips.

The chasteness of that first, true kiss expressed everything his words had not, and this time I thought I could believe him. His touch was gentle. He tasted slightly of beer. I stood close in front of that man while his sweet and tender kisses softly rained upon my face, washing away any doubts as to the truth underlying his words. Such gentleness, such earnestness, such innocence Christopher's kisses had. I placed my hands on either side of his face to begin kissing him in return. Searching, caressing, shy kisses we exchanged. Soon I became aware of nothing except his mouth.

Sometime later, when standing required too much effort, we moved from the center of the room to the couch. He sat in the middle of a cushion. I chose not to sit beside him. Instead, I straddled his lap, sitting face to face, my knees bent back at his hips with only a few layers of clothing separating what made us different. As our bodies settled comfortably into that almost intimate position, I was amazed that everything we had done since his first kisses had felt so uncommonly natural.

We continued flirting with our kisses. Tongue tentatively touched tongue. Hands clasped as fingers laced and unlaced together. Teasing kisses, laughing kisses. As if we had done this before, all happened smoothly. Not even our noses got in our way. Whereas our conversation at supper, hours before, had been with words, we now communicated with kisses and touches. The feel of this man. The taste of this man. The warmth of his breath against my face. All this was home. Strangely, all of this was familiar to me.

Without warning, the spirit of our kisses changed. Tongues plunged deeper. As quickly as a match thrown into a barn filled with last summer's hay creates an inferno, the heat between our bodies rose. Sweat trickled down between my breasts. My forehead became damp. My body felt hotter than two hells. Somewhere along the way, our innocent, childish parlor game of necking had changed into an adult war game, demanding we take no prisoners.

While speculating which of us would call out "Halt!" first, I considered the curious way simple, sweet kisses could become dangerous assault weapons. Later, when I experienced an immediate urge to rip off his shirt and scratch my nails deep into his back, I quickly realized I had to cool down before I did something really stupid. Those nearly uncontrollable emotions were more than I wanted to deal with. It would be me. I was chicken.

Uncle!

I pulled my hungry mouth away from his. I heard us both breathing hard before noticing Christopher's forehead glowed with perspiration. I found myself staring at his mouth, amazed that his lips looked as swollen as mine felt. I looked closer at his face and saw reflecting back through his eyes the same passion I had burning inside me.

Sweet Jesus, what have we started?

"So, Christopher," I asked between ragged breaths, "what is your last name?"

Instantly, the man lost that ravenous look in his eyes and laughed deep and heartily, filling the entire cabin with his voice. I had successfully defused the explosive atmosphere, along with his hot, hard penis on which I had been perched.

"You know what it is!" he exclaimed. "I told you Friday night."

I explained in a pitiful voice, "But I forgot. You see, I'm terrible with names."

"Saracini."

I don't remember that name.

Better to see him, I drew back farther. For several moments, I studied his face intently for features that could be considered Roman in origin. Christopher's light brown hair was lightly flecked with gray. His eyes were pale gray-blue.

"Funny, but you don't look Eye-talian," I teased.

"My family comes from northern Italy, near Germany and Switzerland." He went on to explain why he did not have the dark hair, eyes and coloring of the Italians I knew. "My ancestors intermarried many times with those blond barbarians from the North. But check this nose." He turned proudly to show his profile. "Just like Caesar's."

I managed a small 'hah' before a wave of such unforgiving sleepiness came over me that I whimpered, "I'm tired."

I knew, without looking at any clock, it was almost morning. I had spent two long days filled with plenty of physical activity and not enough rest. Although I hoped I knew in advance what his response would be, I asked in all polite Southern-ness, "Do you want to sleep here or do you want to go back to your motel?"

"I'll stay here." His voice sounded exhausted, as well.

My eyes felt scratchy, and my eyelids were too heavy to be held open much longer. I was pleased that it would not be necessary for me to drive right then. In any case, I could not have been a safe driver as drunk as I was from lack of sleep.

Preparing for bed, I lent Christopher a fresh toothbrush. We crowded about the sink to clean our teeth, taking care not to bump heads when we spat out used toothpaste. He flicked off the bathroom light before following me into the tiny bedroom where the bed beckoned my tired body. I made my way to the far side of the mattress because somewhere in The Manual it is written that the man must sleep nearest the door in order to protect the woman. Modestly, I turned away to undress down to my skimpy lacy panties. Joining Christopher under the covers, I discovered he still wore his boxer shorts. Bless him, the man had not assumed that we would do anything more than share the bed. I knew those boxer shorts were my second piece of substantiating information. After we braided our arms and legs together, I felt comfortable and safe and at peace.

Before drifting asleep in the darkness, I thought, in spite of myself, Oh, God, I hope he doesn't snore.

Closer to day break, I was awakened by Christopher kissing me, wanting me. His demanding hands were everywhere, kneading my breasts. Cupped under my butt, they pulled to position my torso against him.

Praying that the gentleman of the night before had not been replaced by his evil twin, I responded calmly in a measured voice, "Christopher, I'm not ready to share my body with you."

His hands immediately stopped. "OK," he sighed as he moved slightly away. He held me in his arms tenderly. Not dejected. Not pouting. No bruised male ego here. No begging. No snatching. His response was an unqualified acceptance of my request.

Again, this man amazed me because his actions were directly opposite to what I had experienced from other men. I placed my head against his chest where I felt, as much as heard, his heart pounding against my ear.

While staring at his graying chest hair in the murky light of the coming dawn, the thought occurred to me that Christopher Saracini was, indeed, a man, not a spoiled little boy's imitation of a man to which I had been exposed in my past. Here was a true man who knew he would diminish himself if he, in any way, diminished me. Here was that unicorn I had spent years searching for. He had wandered across my path two evenings earlier while I was on top of the mountain. I would never see him again, and yet I would never forget him. For those reasons and many, many more, I wanted to give Christopher a memento by which he would remember me. Not merely a souvenir that would sit upon a shelf gathering dust or some trinket too soon tossed in a drawer simply becoming lost under a mess of stuff, but a sensually laden memory to carry with him that could be replayed whenever he wished.

"Lie back and enjoy," I whispered. After gently pushing Christopher onto his back, I eased onto my hands and knees to straddle his body. Bending down, I kissed first his right temple, tenderly moving across to his eyelids. I took my own sweet time covering his face with soft, wet kisses before nibbling at the right side of his neck near his pulsating artery. His arms came up across my back to bring me down onto him, but I stiffened my elbows to resist.

"No, this is for you to enjoy. Put your arms down," I softly insisted.

He did not release his strong grip.

"I won't go on if you don't let me go."

Although my words were not intended as a threat, I had no desire to share any part of what would occur next. Selfishly, I only wanted to indulge his body. As seconds passed, I knew he was silently considering my last words. I waited, without moving, for his arms to drop away.

When, at last, he released his grasp and allowed his arms to fall onto the bed against his sides, I continued paying homage to his body with my mouth and hands until he shouted out, "Rachael Taite!" as he came to climax.

Five

What the hell was I thinking when I stayed up most of Saturday night nuts-ing around with that man, after hiking up and down that mountain? Mondays at the restaurant were always busy. At some point, I would have to dissect what had occurred these past two days before filing him away with those dangerous memories that would not get trotted out too often. Right now, all I wanted was some shut-eye.

Falling across my bed back home in Knoxville and wrapping a corner of the bedspread over my exhausted body, I promised myself that the next time I woke up, the first thing I would do would be remove my clothes. Secondly, I would wash the make-up off my face before finally going to sleep between sheets, for real. With my mind on overload and my body hungry for sleep, I justifiably felt rode hard and put up wet.

Sometime later, I heard a phone faintly ringing in the distance. As its insistent noise became louder, I questioned why some fool did not pick up that annoying contraption. More rings jarred my reverie until it dawned on me that damn phone was beside my bed and I was that fool. Forcing myself to concentrate on which body parts needed to function in order to get the receiver off its cradle and over to my ear, I fought my way back to the land of the living. I knew someone must really want to talk to me if they let the phone ring for that length of time.

Managing to position the phone near my face, I mumbled, "Hey."

"Rachael, I've got this wonderful idea!" Christopher's voice sounded disgustingly energetic as if he had enjoyed eight full hours of sleep the night before. A child describing its first ever circus parade could not have been bubbling over with more excitement. "Come over Tuesday night for supper," he invited. "There are two different dinner parties we could go to. You choose which one."

I croaked, "Where are you?" Not fully awake, my voice sounded rusty and little used.

"Nashville." Ignoring the curtness in my response, he pushed through the shroud of sleep surrounding my awareness. "I've got the brochures right here in my hand. I'll read them, and you can decide which one you like best."

I heard him rustling about. Adding dramatic interpretative flourishes, he proceeded to read verbatim from two brochures. How anyone could sound so awake on such little sleep was, at that moment, beyond my comprehension.

Am I awake? I must still be dreaming, I thought, because this couldn't be happening. The man wants me to come to Nashville. That city is a bit more than a hop, skip and jump away. On a Tuesday night, too. The middle of the week isn't an easy time for me to get away from the restaurant. And he wants me to choose between a dinner cruise on a riverboat or a dinner at a private club overlooking the city. Either will suit me just fine.

Damn, I hated making decisions. Especially those where I knew the proper one was clearly not the choice that held the possibility of being more fun.

He stopped reading and waited. Silence stretched from Nashville to Knoxville indicating it was my turn to speak.

"I'll have to see whether or not I can get away." I knew that was a lame excuse the minute I said it.

"Come," he coaxed. "Please."

I stalled for time. "Let me do some figurin'. I'll get back to you tomorrow night."

I wrote down his phone number in Nashville, knowing that the honorable thing would have been to lie when asked if I had pencil and paper handy. I knew the truly correct, respectable answer was a non-negotiable no to dinner. Given the opportunity for a few more hours in his company, however, I would gladly take my chances on an eternity in hell.

Upon placing the receiver back on its cradle, I was just too astonished for words, to think that man would have called from Nashville, Sunday afternoon, after we had said what I considered were our final good-byes before seven that same morning in Townsend. I had fully expected never to hear from him again. California was too far away from Tennessee to start any kind of relationship. Besides, what kind of a relationship, other than tawdry, could we have?

I leaned over the edge of the mattress to rummage through the wastepaper basket beside my bed. Considering that I might have need of it after all, I retrieved his business card I had discarded a few hours earlier.

◦✼◦

The rest of Sunday and all of Monday, I periodically mulled over his invitation. Actually, my twin and I silently argued the dilemma between ourselves.

If you're smart, you won't go.

But it could be fun. Besides, I want to be with him again.

What for? He is married and lives in California, of all places.

I thought I'd never see him again.

It's at least a three-hour drive to Nashville. You've got to work Wednesday. You've got a dental appointment Tuesday afternoon. If you care to recall, she snipped, *the man has a family.*

He's excitin' to be with. Anyway, he did say he and his wife were separated.

It's foolish to drive that distance for one dinner.

I've done stupider things before.

Tell me something I don't know. You two don't even live in the same time zone.

I'll probably be through with the dentist by five and could be there by seven-thirty, Nashville time. I've never met anyone like him.

I've heard you say that before, too.

If we don't go on that river cruise, I can leave right after dessert and get back here no later than two in the mornin', my time.

Why go through all this effort for someone who isn't from around here?

Dinner's at eight, I can be there by then.

There are just too many problems with this relationship. It cannot be allowed to go any further.

If I flew, I could get there in about the same amount of time and wouldn't be so tired.

Flying costs too much, and you would have to wait until Wednesday to fly back.

I'll just drive my car.

Our seesaw continued all my waking hours. We were so preoccupied advocating both sides of the quandary that I was all but worthless at the restaurant. Liz politely pretended not to notice. Margaret bluntly asked what was wrong with me. Since I had no answer prepared for Christopher, I certainly was not ready to dissect my distraction with my two friends.

Monday night as I dialed the number he had given me to request his room, I still had no decision until I heard Christopher's bright greeting, simply asking, "Hello. Are you coming?"

"Yes," I answered before adding in a lower voice, "This is not a wise thing to do."

"I know," he acknowledged in a tone more subdued than he had used for his question.

From its opening, I had made it a point to create a homelike atmosphere at work. I wanted customers to feel as if they were family when they walked through my restaurant's doors. Unfortunately, I had accomplished that goal almost too well. My best customers knew about my parents and me, Liz and her history and they were getting to know Margaret. When they came to feel like kin, our public grew proprietary about the restaurant and us. They knew a little too much, and they took on a little too much. They were forever introducing Liz and me to every bachelor they considered eligible on their list. Soon, I knew they would be doing the same for Margaret because those customers, like our mothers, did not want us to go through life without somebody to share it with. And like all mothers, they knew when something was up.

Tuesday fast became the slowest day of my life. I managed to negotiate the morning and lunch without too many mistakes, except I sported a band-aid on my left forefinger from a self-inflicted wound incurred dicing celery while doing preps that morning, and I had called the mayor by the sheriff's name in the afternoon. Both of those boo-boos would heal with time. I was not too sure about the one involving the Ob/Gyn's wife and his girlfriend whom I had seated at adjacent tables. I knew that would probably take more smoothing over than a single phone call to Doc Thornton's office and duplicate bouquets of identical spring flowers sent to his separate residences.

During serving hours, I overheard Liz fielding numerous inquiries as to my distracted behavior by saying she thought I had been kidnapped by space aliens and replaced by some poorly programmed clone. She had hoped by teasing me in public I would spill the beans. I ignored the bait.

Margaret had been picking at me all morning to gather details about my weekend, and normally laid-back Liz had begun nibbling for facts by that afternoon. Having known me too many years not to know that when I do not say much I have too much to tell, they were over waiting for an account of my weekend. Perversely, I chose the close of the business day, after the restaurant's doors were locked, to put my prying friends out of their misery.

Waiting until Liz and I stood in the center of the empty kitchen putting plastic wrap over the last of the cooled lemon squares and I could hear Margaret moving chairs just on the other side of the door in the dining area, I casually mentioned, "I'm thinkin' about leavin' for Nashville today after I'm through with the dentist."

"You're doing what!" Liz screwed her expression into a scowl.

Before I could answer, Margaret pushed through the swinging door. She had no intention of being left out of this particular conversation. "She's doing what?"

"Driving to Nashville to have dinner with a man," Liz answered before I had the chance to utter the first word.

"I knew it! I just knew it!" Margaret leaned against the prep counter, a Cheshire cat grin on her face. "She was acting too quiet yesterday and today. It had to involve a man. So, tell us all about him." Her tone implied a command, not a request.

I rolled my eyes. "It's just some man I met on the mountain Friday night." Since I had waited this late in the day to make certain I would lack time for a drawn out narrative, I hoped to brush aside their inquiries with only a sketchy outline. I began slowly, "He's—"

"A mountain man?" Margaret interrupted, impatient for me to complete my sentence.

"A California mountain man," Liz put in.

How could she know that? I squinted at Liz, at the same time pushing my glasses back against my face. And how did she know about our dinner date?

Liz shrugged her shoulders at my confusion before she nonchalantly explained, "I asked your mother what happened on your all's hike when she came by for lunch today."

Pragmatic Margaret pondered for a moment. "That's just too far away," she proclaimed, shaking her head at my impracticality. "Does he have a beard?"

"Yes, that's too far away. No, he doesn't have a beard. And," I said as I picked up my purse before heading for the back parking lot where my packed car awaited, "I'll see you in the mornin'. I don't plan on bein' late."

As the door closed behind me, I overheard Margaret tell Liz, "I bet you he's married. She shouldn't be goin'."

I was almost seated in my car when both friends stuck their heads around the restaurant's back door. Together they yelled, "Drive safe! Have a good time! Be careful! Break his heart!"

❦

Waiting in the reception area for my name to be called, I worried that I should have cancelled my dental appointment. I imagined the scenario that would take place later that evening. Christopher and I would be seated alone at a round table set for eight. The entire complement of conventioneers would be huddled en masse a few feet away, whispering among themselves. Occasionally, one would turn to look in our direction and nod knowingly before turning back to the huddle for further conferring. Above the murmurings, two voices would finally be loud enough for me to hear.

The first one would ask, "Who is that strange woman Christopher Saracini is with?"

The second would add, "I don't know, but isn't it too bad about the paralysis on the right side of her face."

Luckily, I discovered, when I was led into the hygienist's room, I was only getting my teeth cleaned that afternoon. I would have hated going to dinner with a half-numb face in the company of such an extraordinary man.

❦

I left her office at five. It was on the west side of town. That saved some time. Mom had agreed to walk over to my house and feed the girls. That saved some time. I drove at my usual five miles over the posted speed limit. That saved some time. I experienced no traffic tie-ups and no highway construction to maneuver my car through. That saved some time. I did not get lost finding his hotel in downtown Nashville. That saved some time.

And yet, until the very moment when I picked up the lobby phone to be connected to Christopher's room, part of my mind was saying, *Go back. This is foolish. He has a life that cannot include you.*

While another part of my mind was saying, *This is a special man. He will be the standard by which we will measure every man we meet in the future. Only a few hours more*, this part begged.

During the entire drive to Nashville, my body had simply allowed the debate to go on above it, unconcerned with those mental gymnastics, because my mind was not in charge here. My body knew that we were, all of us, going to be where that man was.

When he answered the phone, I heard myself say, "Hey, I'm downstairs." The wall clock above my right shoulder showed six-thirty, Nashville time.

⚘

At my first knock, his hotel room's door moved inward. Before it was fully opened, a hand holding a single red rose extended from inside the room.

"Welcome," he said as I crossed over the threshold, "I didn't expect you this soon. It took us over three hours to get here Sunday."

Taking the flower from his right hand and with my voice sounding more calm than my insides felt, I joked, "We drive differently in East Tennessee. Didn't you ever see the movie *Thunder Road*? Bearden Hill where Mitchum's wreck occurred is right near my house. Where I come from, moonshine runnin' is considered an Olympic sport." More realistically, I added, "I thought we could make happy hour if I got here early enough."

Stepping into the hallway, Christopher picked up the blue makeup case that I had placed on the floor prior to knocking. Venturing farther into the room, I lifted the fragrant rose bud to my face and took a deep breath, hoping to slow down my beating heart.

'Come into my parlor,' my twin ominously quoted that old nursery rhyme.

When we stood facing each other inside the room, I noticed how striking he looked in dress clothes. He wore a three-piece, navy, pin-striped suit over a fashionable, light blue shirt finished with a crisp white collar and cuffs. A geometric print, red silk tie was unknotted at his neck and matched the braces buttoned to his trousers and the silk handkerchief softly tucked in his jacket's breast pocket. Attired as he was, barefooted Christopher appeared ready for the quintessential *GQ* photo shoot.

In the canvas carry-bag draped over my shoulder, I had a navy dress. A bitchy observer might have cattily remarked that we had discussed what to wear during our phone call the previous night.

"We're goin' to make a handsome couple at the party. You clean up right nice," I complimented him while I hung my carry-bag on the clothes rack just inside the room. "I'll take a shower and freshen up my face. Give me about ten minutes."

I carried my makeup case into the bathroom and closed the door. Starting the water, I adjusted the temperature before shedding my travel clothes. After tossing aside my gray scrub pants and oversized T-shirt on the wide vanity counter, I stepped under a shower of hot water. I hoped it would be steamy enough to make my hair curl about my face, softening the severity of my customary, plain bun.

While I stood with the water beating down across my chest still wondering what business I had in Nashville, Christopher pulled back the opaque plastic curtain and stepped into the tub behind me. He had undressed. And, technically speaking, since we had kept our skivvies on Saturday night, this became the first time we had been naked together.

Reaching around to soap my breasts, he explained his presence in the shower by saying, "I thought I could help."

We laughed and touched and played. He was not much help.

"We're never goin' to get out of here if you keep this up," I chided, stepping out of the shower to hurry us along.

From behind me, I heard him say, "Here's a towel."

Turning to take the towel, I found nothing in his hands as Christopher had draped the item over his erect penis.

"What a novel idea! A phallic towel hook." I shook my head, explaining as I removed the offered towel, "I'm afraid it will have limited acceptance here in the Bible Belt."

We shared the bathroom's dual sinks as if we had for years. As I stole glances in the mirror at this man, the ease with which we meshed surprised me. His being naked in front of me, being naked in front of him, was one of the most natural things I have ever done. I had never been this relaxed with either of my two former husbands.

Looking closer at our bodies reflected above the vanity, I saw his scar for the first time. A long, pinkish-silvery gash indicated where his kidney had been removed years ago in Vietnam. I had a few scars of my own: remains from an old appendectomy and, more recently, one from gallbladder surgery. We resembled Frankenstein's monster and his bride. The figures in the hotel's mirrored wall were not young, untested bodies with taut muscles and sleek lines. They had been lived in for many years. Like an old, favorite pair of shoes, they were run-down in some places, scuffed in others. We had comfortable, user-friendly bodies.

Christopher leaned over to place a light kiss atop my ear. "Let's hurry. We can still make happy hour."

Before we left his room, he presented me with a second long stemmed red rose to carry to dinner. We briskly walked the few blocks from his hotel to the nearby skyscraper housing the private club where we would dine. When I first caught our reflections in storefront windows as we hurried past, I verified I had been right in my prediction. Despite dressing quickly, we did make a handsome couple. I decided we almost could have been mistaken for a successful corporate duo in our power navy blues. Alone in the elevator during the long ride to the top floor, we sneaked hugs and light caresses before the door opened and we drifted over to join the party in progress.

Shortly after Christopher returned from the bar with two glasses of white wine, a business associate of his walked over to discuss the conference. While I listened politely to them, I fixed a practiced, pleasant smile on my face. Since nothing in their conversation applied to me, I found myself wondering how I would be introduced.

How curious, I thought, that I had never stopped to consider what he would say when confronted with that moment of truth.

The men continued commenting about a session they had both attended earlier in the day before his friend said, "Chris, excuse me, but your pants are unzipped."

Oh, fuck!

Christopher and I blushed in unison.

That was one vignette my fertile imagination would never have conjured up. I had worried only about the possible drooling effects from dental anesthesia, not the assumed reasons for a zipper faux pas. I wanted to explain in excruciating detail to this stranger that we had not had intercourse, and that even by the most literal interpretation we could only be considered intimate friends, but it was not my place to do so. He was Christopher's acquaintance, not mine. More importantly, however, I could not quite put my finger on the reference for the proper response for this predicament in the abridged Manual my mother had engraved in my brain.

Christopher handed me his wineglass, leaving me to stare at the man I did not know and to whom I still had not been formally introduced while he turned to face the elevator doors and took care of his omission.

Attempting to mime innocence, I felt a sudden kinship to a cat I once owned. I remembered seeing my sweet kitty returning from an afternoon in the yard with a downy breast feather caught between the base of her whiskers and her feigned innocent smile. That cat had acted guilt-free, as had, too, my three-year-old cousin coming to Aunt Maurie's dinner table with Oreo cookie crumbs haloing her cherubic mouth.

Although I still wanted to blurt out that Christopher and I had not done anything yet, I did not think the man would believe me. I sensed he would go to his grave knowing we were guilty as sin. All I could muster was a frozen smile and the hope that my mouth turned up sweetly, like those smiles worn by my old cat and Aunt Maurie's youngest daughter.

What a horrific start to dinner.

Mutely, I waited for Christopher to turn around, longing to beg that we leave now because I had just endured all the fun I could stand for one evening. Before my silent date could utter the first word in our defense, dinner was announced, and my red-faced escort steered me into the room set aside for our last supper together.

We entered a dining room where the outer three walls were windowed. Beyond the glass, the Nashville skyline sparkled as brilliantly as one of Porter Waggoner's spangled shirts under banks of studio lights. The sun had not completely set for the evening, and the sky was nearly robin's breast red at the far horizon, fading into deep plum back toward the east. Christopher led me over to the side of the table where we would face the sunset as we ate. Thankfully, he guided us clear of the man who had delicately pointed out Christopher's indelicate omission.

Easing my chair up to the table, Christopher leaned over to whisper in my right ear. "Sunsets will always remind me of you and Lee Contie," he said, hoping to put me in a lighter mood for our coming meal.

I chuckled. "That's Mount LeConte," I gently corrected him, simultaneously putting the zipper incident completely out of my mind.

Other conventioneers were soon gathered on either side of a long table centered in the middle of the room, facing expansive, formal place settings arrayed with more than enough flatware for three normal meals. I know we ate, but I do not remember what we ate. Christopher and I were not congenial dinner companions to the other attendees. We talked only to each other, skillfully blocking interference from extraneous conversations floating around us. We talked as old friends do who after having not seen each other for years had much to catch up on. We did not hold hands or whisper in each other's ears. We succeeded in looking reasonably reserved above the tablecloth. Under the table, however, I had removed my right high heel, Christopher, his left shoe, and we intimately touched toes throughout dinner.

As the evening progressed, I told him some of the not-so-wonderful things I had done or were done to me in my life: about watching kittens being born and then later learning Daddy had thrown them all into the lake to drown; about Mom always making me select my own switches; about all those close calls while driving and dating and drinking too much alcohol; about dalliances that kept me from being bored back when I was employed; about that so-called business associate I surprised Mackey with; and about a number, but far from all, of the poor choices I had made earlier in life. Just minor little things that I had kept to myself for fear that no one would still like me if they knew. Those individual events, when twirled together with all the rest, made up threads that my mind had woven into dark fabrics that my active imagination later had fashioned into shadowy shapes for appliquéd tableaus used to illustrate *The Book of Rachael, According to Rachael* that I presented to the world.

As a rule, I permitted a person no more than three short forays into my dark files. In this one aspect of my life, I had always felt there was safety residing in low numbers. But I found myself sharing surprisingly much more than three with this man whom I hardly knew. That Tuesday night in Nashville, I felt compelled to point out some of the damaged trees to ensure that this man would eventually come to see the living forest of my life. I needed Christopher to know some of my scars in order to understand me, for without shadows a picture lacks depth. Closely watching his eyes to gauge his reactions as I confessed each sin, I noticed nothing I said altered the tenderness there. Amazingly, the man heard me out and did not judge.

In turn, he shared the reason behind his parents leaving Italy and about growing up with seven brothers and sisters in America. He spoke briefly of his time spent in Vietnam. I listened to him talk about the woman he had married and the love he had for their two children. He mentioned his company and described some of his employees.

As Christopher related his history, I realized his memories were as dear as sweet cream, whereas mine recalled blinky milk. I found the comparison a sadly amusing commentary on the differences of our upbringings.

A favorite childhood memory of my mother's baby sister sprang to mind. Aunt Maurie had told me she was about eight years old at the time she and a cousin, who lived on a brood farm outside Lexington, made up a game while jumping rope. With every flip of the rope, each girl had to curse. She reported Maggie Elaine had cussed a blue streak so deep it turned purple and never repeated the same word combination twice. Maurie said the only word she thought sounded the least bit dirty was 'peacock,' so my aunt had said that word every time she jumped.

Christopher finished the last swallow in his coffee cup, and with that the dinner was over. He was quiet for a short time before he added softly, "I cannot possibly explain why I called you Sunday night and invited you to dinner."

Hell, I can't even tell you why I drove to Nashville for this dinner. I did not give voice to that instantaneous thought. Instead, I sat silently staring at my cup half-filled with Earl Grey tea, listening to the muffled conversations as the other guests emptied the room.

He sighed before saying simply, "I just had to see you one more time."

Too soon, the reason for our stolen Tuesday night was over. Christopher left me alone at the table to find his host and thank him for the invitation. I accepted his explanation that there would be fewer words to speak if I did not accompany him. As I looked around the room, waiting for his return, I knew I had done my Southern mother proud because we had eliminated all forks and spoons and knives laid out for our use. Not all of the other diners had been as successful as we.

Above the elevator doors, I saw a wall clock showing the time to be almost eleven, Nashville time, much later than I had originally planned to drive back. This present-day Cinder Ella needed to get on the road before midnight. Holding hands, we walked quickly back to Christopher's hotel, neither of us talking or joking now. The evening was finished. I must leave him soon and drive east to my home, and he must leave tomorrow and fly west to his family.

⚜

"I've something for you," Christopher said after closing the door.

Those were his first words since entering the elevator after dinner, and their sound echoed against the walls in the quiet hotel room. Going over to the dresser, he picked up a brown paper bag to hand me. Opening it, I pulled out first a fortune cookie sealed in plastic. Smiling a puzzled smile, I lifted my gaze to his face.

He explained, "Carl and I walked all over downtown Nashville to find a Chinese restaurant to get that."

The second object I retrieved was a third red rose.

He said, "I want you to have a fresh rose on your drive home."

The third item I removed was a diet cola. Again, I waited for his explanation.

"Some caffeine. This late at night, I didn't want you to stop to get coffee in case you became sleepy."

Finally, I withdrew the T-shirt Christopher had worn down the mountain on Saturday.

"I wanted you to have something of mine to remember me by. I washed it out in the sink to get it clean, but I don't think I did such a great job." His voice trailed off boyishly as he completed his last remark.

I felt tears stinging my eyes, and I so did not want to cry. What could I possibly say that would accurately convey my feelings? I managed to stammer, "I don't think I can forget you. I've never met anyone quite like you before. I know all the reasons I should not be here tonight, but I'm here anyway." Despite all my efforts to the contrary, tears welled up in my eyes and inched down my cheeks. I hated the finality of this parting.

Christopher moved closer to me and gathered me in his arms. "I want you to understand," he said, stopping before completing his thought. "All I know is," he continued, allowing for lengthy pauses between phases, "I had to see you . . . one more time . . . before I left Tennessee."

I looked into his eyes to search for the lie usually associated with that frayed and tarnished sentiment. I could not find it. Intuitively accepting, without having definitive proof as to the reason I could not find it, I understood the lie simply was not there in this man. I leaned my head against his shoulder. Within his arms, I knew no harm would ever come to me. This was my rightful place. I was supposed to be here, despite the reality that was outside this room.

Sweet Jesus, why did we ever meet, and why did I ever drive here?

Christopher and I clung tightly to each other. While using the following precious few minutes in a foolish attempt to memorize the rhythm of his beating heart, I wished the hours we had shared could be stretched into days that could turn into a lifetime, but that was not going to happen. When I acknowledged that unhappy thought, I knew it was time to leave. I relaxed my arms.

"I must go," I whispered.

When I tried to pull away from his embrace, he tightened his arms about me.

"Not yet," he whispered, leaning down to gently kiss the tip of my nose before moving lower to nibble on my lips.

After those first gentle, inquiring kisses, I knew I would not be going anywhere any time soon. His hands found the buttons at the back of my dress. I reached up to loosen his tie, but before I had untangled that knot, I stopped.

"The windows," I said, "people can see in."

We stood in a rented room on the fifteenth floor, about to do the unlawful, and my only concern was that the curtains were not drawn. As if drawn draperies would make the act more acceptable because no one else would see, just like reasoning a bag of potato chips eaten alone in my bedroom would not show up directly on my thighs.

Instead of walking to the window, Christopher returned to the door and bolted it. With a flip of the wall switch, he turned off the lamp hanging above the low dresser. The room became dark except for lights from neighboring skyscrapers.

I walked toward the window, but he suggested softly, "Leave them open."

Upon hearing that request, I turned in his direction and stopped, waiting for my eyes to accommodate the room's dimness. When I was able to see him in the city's soft neon glow, I was reminded of our lying together at the cabin in my bedroom, his body lit by that Sunday morning's easy dawn. I remembered how his skin felt under my hands. And how he tasted. After that last memory, I shuddered. I took my glasses off and placed them on the dresser. With our eyes locked together, we stood separated by the foot of the king-sized bed, slowly undressing. Like layers of civilization and laws of conduct being stripped away, our garments dropped to the floor. As I stepped toward him, I took away the pins securing my prim bun. My long hair cascaded over my shoulders to curl about my breasts. When I reached him, Christopher nuzzled his face into my hair and then nipped a kiss on my neck.

"God, how I love how you smell," he groaned, the pleasure in his voice becoming pain.

※

Retreating to a safe plane somewhere above the bed the better to observe our actions, I separated from my body. From this familiar distance, I would remain aloof from the events occurring below me. As during all those other times before, I planned to maintain control of my body while my mind wandered at will. Wanting to ignore what was making the physical act of loving this man, this night, so special, I told myself he has the same number of body parts, arranged in the same locations, as any other man I had screwed. I pondered the positions I saw my body assume. Intellectually, I knew there are only so many ways two people can engage in sexual exploration without the presence of props, and I came to suspect Christopher wanted to try most of them. I next considered the emotion called 'love' and its relationship to the sexual act called 'love,' concluding that not just one single element was capable of changing pure fornication into a shared union of two bodies. Consideration, gentleness, acceptance, respect and a thousand other minute little things also contribute to that transformation.

I found myself consciously struggling to keep my separation intact. In the past, I had always been successful in remaining a disinterested third-party observing my body engaged in sex. That customary trick was not working well for me this time.

Sweet Jesus, the man was proving to be everything I had always thought, back when I was young and hopeful, a lover could be. I had never before found that lover. So, why tonight?

With that realization floating through my brain, I asked aloud, "Who are you? Where have you been all my life?"

No answer was given. None had been really expected.

Where Christopher's body ended and where mine began soon lost definition. Being wrapped around him was both sacred and profane. Initially, passages from Tchaikovsky's "Violin Concerto in D Major" played in my head as we entwined bodies on that big bed. Why music from the concert I had attended the week before would drift into my consciousness was beyond me, but it complemented what I saw occurring on that bed below me. Shared bodies. Shared sensations. We became first-chair musicians, playing each other's bodies as if they were finely tuned instruments. We caressed with fingertips soft and tender. We moved hands roughly and passionately over each other. As our performance progressed, pagan drums savagely overran that controlled, civilized musical score, and we transitioned smoothly into a primitive mating ritual, keeping pace with rhythms that drowned out any awareness of our surroundings. We then began ancient, intricately complex dance sequences which had been carefully choreographed centuries before, orchestrated down to the minutest movement.

Slowly, I became amazed that during this, our first time together, I never geed when I should have hawed. Just as our noses had never gotten in the way that night we first kissed, we fitted together perfectly and moved easily together as if our bodies had been customized for the other.

Several times, feeling Christopher growing larger and harder inside me, I recognized he was close to climaxing. But whenever the man moved too near to the edge, he whispered, almost in agony, "No, not yet."

Each time, he gave it as an order for us both to stop. Each time, I paused until he had himself under control and was glad to wait for I, too, needed to catch my breath. In the past, I had taken pride in that I had never lost myself in the sexual act. Of course, I would get tired and out of breath, but I had never lost control.

So, the other demanded, *what in the hell is this man waiting for?*

Beats me, I answered my twin, I would have thought it would be over by now.

Next, the oddest thing happened. I could swear I heard Christopher say "I'm waiting for you."

At the very sound of his voice inside my head, I felt a jolt of electrical conductivity pass through my body. I had read somewhere about the transference of thoughts, yet this was the first time I had ever encountered such an experience. From that moment onward, Christopher's touch anywhere on my body caused me to tremble. When I opened my eyes to see his face above mine, I found it to be tortured in pleasure. His expressions, however, were too raw for me to view for long, and when such incredibly delicious sensations began to occur inside and outside my body, I lost all strength to hold my eyes open. Blinded by passion, I welcomed his assault of hot, wet kisses in the tenderest of places: the insides of my elbows, the crooks of my knees and the small of my back.

When he entered me for the last time, I surrounded him for the first time. Now that my mind had ceased its wanderings, I concentrated on the feel of his wiry chest hair soft against my breasts and the wetness of his shoulders under my hands. I became aware that our bodies were slippery with sweat and that my stomach muscles ached with each contraction of my torso. Finally relinquishing my role as play-by-play analyst, I consented to being steered and guided. Shortly after which, all sensations blurred as a sensory overload burst through my body and camouflaged our exact movements. Somewhere amidst all those guilty pleasures, I lost the last rein I had used to maintain control over myself and needed to hold onto Christopher to keep from falling into oblivion. Muscle groups I did not even know existed responded to that man's exquisite touch. Wherever he wanted to go, I followed. And somewhere, in the depths of me, he found a hidden me and released her. By means of his delays, he had unerringly sought her out so we all might climax together.

When the end finally came, Christopher called out, "Rachael Taite!"

Sweet Jesus, that's what he was waiting for.

Lying in the comforting warmth of his encircling arms, I sobbed hot, nearly endless tears. My body was bathed in sweat. Pools of that liquid puddled at the base of my throat, in my belly button and on the back of my knees. My heart pounded against my chest walls, as if wanting to escape the prison of my body. I was forty-two years old, I had been married twice, I could not even remember the names of all the men I had screwed and yet, until tonight, I had never before climaxed.

A numbing sense of loss settled over me. Had I known Christopher was in my future, I would have waited for him. Until this very moment, I had never regretted that part of my life. Forty-two years of living and now I will never see him again. I felt very, very sad and so very, very much alone.

"Promise me," I heard a voice pleading, "if anything ever happens to you, you will have Carl call me."

Even I knew that to be an unfathomable request coming from someone he had met only the Friday before, but she had to know that I would be contacted as if we were next of kin. I would have liked to explain the reasoning behind her words, but I did not completely understand myself that urgent need.

I stammered, "I've . . . I've never had anyone affect me like this before." As if it justified my plea, I added lamely, "We are a part of each other now."

What I did know was that he had uncaged a person inside me whom I had never been aware. But how to explain this woman, whom I never before knew existed, to Christopher when I had never told another living soul about the voices of the others who resided inside my head? With this new voice demanding assurances that I would be contacted, I was inexorably compelled to extract his promise for her. Even though Christopher and I would never be together again after tonight. Even though after that phone call, there would be nothing I could do.

After I implored many times, Christopher reluctantly agreed. "All right, I'll tell him to call, but, Rachael, nothing bad will ever happen," he reassured me, softly stroking my face, gently wiping away my tears.

As soon as he addressed that primal fear, a new one loomed to take its place, ringing itself in with the clarity of a chiming clock announcing the midnight hour. How would I ever make it through the rest of my life knowing that he was in the world, but not in my world?

Six

With the haste of a bat rushing home to her cave, I scurried across and down the Cumberland Plateau in a face-to-face race with the coming dawn. The glare from the rising sun proved to be more troublesome than the slower cars in my path. Reaching the outskirts of town, I wove through the early rush hour traffic on I-40 as skillfully as any NASCAR driver taking back the lead after his last pit stop.

Had they been riding with me, I felt my moonshine running uncles would have beamed their approval.

The clock at my bank on the Pike indicated the hour was minutes before seven when I sped by. I was unlocking the back entry to the restaurant when Liz and Margaret drove up in their cars. True to my word, I had not arrived late for work, but I was none too certain that I would be able to manage my share of the morning's chores.

Liz walked toward me, carrying a plastic grocery bag with celery stalks peeking over the top. I recalled yesterday that I had been unable to purchase enough celery for two days when I left the wholesalers on Forest Avenue, but I had gotten the best of the lot. Reliable Liz had made certain we would have enough of the green crunchies to get through one more lunch until I went back to market Thursday.

Stopping, Liz stared into my roadmap eyes. Shaking her head in disapproval, she ordered, using a stern tone that allowed for no negotiation, "Get back in your car. Go home. Margaret and I can handle the prep. Come back at eleven, . . . " slowly adding, ". . . if you wake up."

Truly grateful that she had sent me packing, I nodded my thanks and stumbled, exhausted, to my car. Since she very seldom ordered anyone to do anything, I knew I must look rough. After the exhilarating events of the past twelve hours, I also knew I had no business around sharp objects and hot stoves.

I heard Margaret comment before they disappeared into the kitchen, "Looks like our team didn't do good."

I managed the short drive to my house. Once inside, I listened to my cats fuss about my being gone all night and the emptiness of their food bowls and how I had best take care of them before I did anything else. My Daddy had always said there was nothing like two hungry Siamese cats to put a person's problems into proper perspective.

After I fed the girls, I pulled my tired self up the stairs. Using the phone by my bed, I made the call Christopher had requested. I reported arriving home without incident and wished him a safe flight to California. Since I could not bear to think of his final destination, I did not bid him a safe flight home. Too spent to shed any more tears, I placed the receiver down before crawling between the sheets.

After three hours of much needed sleep, I returned to the restaurant. As I entered the lobby from the back, Liz pushed open the front doors for our usual eleven o'clock launch. I noticed she and Margaret had all employees in place and the kitchen ready for the first hungry customers who were already waiting outside our doors. Although I sported frog-eyes from crying and lack of sleep, I greeted all that day, smiling as if nothing was wrong and defiantly, silently daring any inquiry into the cause of my swollen eyelids.

※

Perhaps Mom had spoken the truth when she instructed that ladies do not sweat, they glow. Failing that qualification for Lady-hood, my body fairly dripped with moisture. Being much too hot from the heat in the kitchen and from the humidity reached that day, I questioned how the teams would manage the muggy weather at kick off for the season's first football game this coming Saturday, the last in August.

Thankfully, my workday was over, and all employees were gone. Taking the opportunity to cool down, I sat alone inside the front window watching Kingston Pike's Friday rush hour traffic wandering in and out of the strip mall's parking lot in front of my restaurant. My body ached from the effort needed to have twenty additional sheet cakes baked and frosted for tomorrow's pre-game, tailgating festivities.

Sipping a glass of water, I impatiently waited for a painting contractor to arrive to give me an estimate. As the refreshing liquid played over my tongue, I considered that it tasted the way all water should taste, subtly flavored as if it carried life-giving strength from trace minerals naturally absorbed as its molecules perked through the earth. As a child, I had drunk well water drawn from Mammy's backyard that tasted this way. City water had never smelled right to me. Once while visiting on Little River, I was given water from a spring that flowed out of the mountains near Sunshine. After that first glassful, I vowed never to drink treated water again and, thereafter, maintained a private supply of spring water at the restaurant and at my house.

Recalling my good fortune last November when I had been driving up to replenish my cache of water, I smiled. That was the day I saw the For Sale sign being hammered into the ground in front of the cabin that soon became mine.

Hunching my shoulders over my glass, I played with the ice. That same activity had seemed more productive, however, when I was in my twenties and the glass held scotch on the rocks. I sighed, wishing for a cigarette. If I still smoked, I would have had something to do with my hands to help pass the time while I waited.

My thoughts next drifted to Christopher Saracini. Living had been without light since I returned from Nashville. That Wednesday morning seemed like another lifetime ago. I knew I had wandered through the last few weeks feeling like a third thumb, for Liz and Margaret had told me so. Many times, in fact. I had managed the restaurant with few glitches and without zest. By the first of June, several of my steady customers had pulled me aside to ask discreetly if I were ill and to give me the name of their internist should I have need of a good doctor.

I knew I had not been my old charming self. I kept hoping one morning I would wake up and the darkness surrounding me would lift with the morning's fog, but that had not happened as yet.

I had taken to sleeping in Christopher's old T-shirt every night because it, comfortingly, smelled like him, and I was grateful he was not better at washing out clothes in hotel sinks. After he sent me a postcard while he was on vacation, I mailed one when I attended Aunt Maurie's youngest daughter's wedding in New Orleans. Those cards had been our only contact.

My body was in Tennessee, but pieces parts of me were in California. Not even the proposed new color scheme for Rachael's raised me up from the land of the living dead.

Those grand plans to enlarge my restaurant, mapped out on the hike up LeConte last May, had fallen apart when I learned I would need to borrow too much money. Later, when the adjacent office space did not become available, I regrouped and rethought, settling on paint changes for the present.

I continued to wait for the painting contractor. I had set the appointment for six. He was late. So what else was new about me waiting on a man? It seemed I had been doing that all my life. Old habits die hard, as my dear sainted Daddy would have said. I took a deep drink, swishing the cold liquid about my mouth to warm it up before swallowing. I decided, as the tepid water slid down my throat, that a mouthful of Dewar's, neat would have better suited my mood.

Life's a bitch, and then you die.

As I pushed my chair back from the table, I told my twin, "Thanks for sharin'."

I left the restaurant before the tardy man could show up.

⚜

Two weeks later in mid-September and still no painter had graced my doors. Another Thursday had arrived, however, bringing the dreaded payroll chores.

I stared at the calendar in the cluttered cubbyhole, which served as my office at work. My high school class reunion was being held the second weekend in October. As usual, I had no date.

Our first class reunion was held while Richard, husband *numero uno*, and I were waiting on our divorce to be final. I was working on my engineering degree when the second one rolled around and was not seeing anyone anywhere close enough to my age to want to drag to that celebration. I chose not to show up with the grad student who was my sweet darling during my second stint in college because I knew too well those high school classmates of mine, who had married just in time to beat the stork, would have commented that they had children near his age. Mackey and I had broken up housekeeping before the third.

Here it was, two weeks before my twenty-fifth high school class reunion, and I still had no suitable male available to escort me. Good thing this was 1989, or else I would have been considered a failure, despite having two college degrees, two residences and my own successful business.

Putting my palms piously together as I had been taught at vacation bible school, I leaned my head forward and shut my eyes. I did not expect an answer, but had decided prayer could not hurt this late in the game.

I whispered, "Please, please, couldn't I just this once have a date?"

That futile plea voiced, I started working up payroll. Before I had signed the first check, Margaret opened my closed door to slink inside. She never slinked unless there was an eligible male about, and I knew by the twinkle in her blue eyes that he must be a handsome hunk.

Assuming the artful pose of a Roaring '20s vamp, she leaned backwards against the edge of my disorderly desk, turned her head sharply in my direction and archly announced, "There's a man out there askin' for you. If you don't want him, may I have him?"

Memories of Christopher almost had me say 'He's yours,' but hating to give away something I had not even seen yet, I answered, "Better let me check him out first."

After following her to the lobby, I saw Joe Bill Everhart standing there, glancing over a menu. Damn, what a difference since I last saw him. Instead of the tall, bony kid I remembered hiking with, he had filled out with more muscles than The Creator should allow one man to have. Even with the manly changes in his physique, I would have known that face anywhere.

Leaning over to Margaret, I said just loud enough for her to hear, "I think I'll keep this one, old girl. Time for you to disappear."

Joe Bill looked up from his reading as I approached. I walked toward him taking in the handsome specimen he had become, while something in the back of my mind made me think that I had heard he had married. He smiled. I smiled back. I had forgotten his eyes smiled whenever his mouth smiled.

"Joe Bill! It's been too long! How have you been? What are

you doin' now?"

We stiffly hugged in greeting, as old friends do when too many years separate the current hug from the last. I noticed immediately that his body felt strange against mine. He was much taller than Christopher, his chest thicker and harder with more muscles, his stomach flatter and narrowed down to more of a vee. My head did not fit as perfectly under his chin. My hands crossed closer in back about his waist. Standing in front of him, I had to tilt my head back to look into his eyes. That much of a tilt had not been necessary with Christopher, and I had also forgotten that Joe Bill's eyes were green.

It was a short hug as hugs go. When we stepped away from each other, I felt hungrier for Christopher's arms more than ever.

"I'm still down in the mouth," Joe Bill joked in reply, "but I've recently moved my office to Deer Springs."

"You're about too late for lunch, but I can make you something simple if you're hungry, or how's about some tea, if you're not?"

I said what I said not because we stood in a restaurant. I paid honor to the old Southern tradition of offering refreshments to callers. Like my mother had taught me, and her mother had taught her.

He looked down upon my face from his height advantage and smiled. "No, I don't need anything. Just wanted to see you. How are things?"

"I'm fine. The place here is fine. Mom's fine. You got that copy of Daddy's eulogy I sent?"

Although we had dated some after he left Knoxville for dental school, Joe Bill and I had not seen each other in over fifteen years. Despite that fact, we had always exchanged Christmas cards with a few sentences jotted down to keep the other updated.

"Yeah."

"Good." I looked about my now empty restaurant. "I'm goin' to change the colors here if I can ever get hold of a painter. I've contacted two so far, and neither one has bothered to show up."

Clearing his throat, Joe Bill hesitated before revealing the reason behind his visit. "I'm in town for a dental meeting. What say we get together for dinner while I'm here?"

"OK." I paused before asking, but a second married man was two more than I wanted to be involved with. "Will your wife be joinin' us?" I inquired politely.

"No."

I waited for his excuse explaining her absence.

"I'm not married anymore." His voice hinted of a sadness that he was unwilling to share.

"I'm sorry, Joe Bill." As soon as I caught the flash of pain in his eyes, I became truly sorry for him. His expression grabbed at my heart, and I did not have to know the details to understand the ache I saw there.

Liz butted through the swinging door from the kitchen. Her hands were busy with a dishtowel. She called to me, "Rachael, there's a man back here who claims to have an appointment with you. Says he's a painter."

Puzzled, I looked at Liz. "I thought this one was supposed to be here tomorrow."

"Well," she said, "he's here now, waitin' at the back door."

Joe Bill seemed grateful for the rescue. He quickly concluded, "How's about Saturday night at seven?"

I nodded. "Works for me."

When I attended high school, no self-respecting girl accepted a date for the weekend this late in the week. The Dating Rules, specifically spelled out in The Manual, dictated that she must sit at home on the weekend if she had not been asked by Wednesday before nine in the evening. Of course, if she and the young man who was doing the asking were going steady, that rule might be superseded, but only at the girl's discretion.

"Until then, 'bye." He turned and walked out the front door.

I called after him, "See you at seven. Have a good meetin'."

"Mm-mmh! That's one fine lookin' man!" Coming to stand by me, Liz watched him go to his car. "Isn't that What's-his-name who went to dental school?"

"Yep."

Our eyes remained on his dwindling backside while Joe Bill sauntered as if he were accustomed to being watched as he walked away. He waved before he got behind the steering wheel.

"Nice butt." Because Liz was raised under the same Manual, she added, "A dentist. Your momma will be so pleased."

"Yep."

❦

Although I found him to be less talkative than Christopher,

Saturday night's dinner progressed well enough. I did not ask about the no-longer-present wife, nor did Joe Bill volunteer any information. We discussed neutrally charged subjects, starting with the changeable Knoxville weather, our parents, UT's chances for another SEC title in football come December and our businesses. I considered the possibility of asking him to escort me to my looming high school class reunion, but hesitated for some unknown reason. Over dessert, I invited him to the cabin.

Thinking I could smoke out Christopher's memories with some new ones, I considered handsome Joe Bill might do the trick. Well, that was certainly a huge error in judgment on my part.

Joe Bill refused my offer of a beer when we arrived at the cabin. Although I snuggled close when we sat on the porch and he did put his arm across the back of the swing, the man did nothing to pull me under his wing into an embrace. My body did not fit against his massive body as easily as it had fitted against Christopher's. Our silence was not awkward. It just was not companionable. As we swung on the porch, my little radio played the old familiar songs that we had necked through in college, but the music did nothing to build a fire under either of us now. After an interminable hour of hearing chains squawk, Joe Bill announced he needed to get back to town as he was leaving early Sunday morning.

I was relieved the evening was finally coming to an end and that I had not issued an invitation to my approaching class reunion. What a waste of perfectly good moonlight, sparkling water, singing frogs, crisp mountain air and a hunky man that evening had been.

Margaret and I were frosting the last two caramel cakes needed for tomorrow's catered luncheon when Liz came into the kitchen with breaking news of a major earthquake in San Francisco. Feeling the blood rush out of my face, I dropped my icing-covered spatula and ran to the telephone back in my office. I had my hand on the receiver before I heard the utensil splat against the floor.

Wondering if Christopher was alive or if he was hurt made my knees wobbly weak. I was way past frantic. Not knowing if he was safe was as vexing as having a contact lens off-center in my eye. With my hunger to know so great, I could not wait for a delayed call from Carl bearing bad news. Without considering the consequences of my actions,

I uncovered his hidden business card and dialed his office.

The other worried, *But what if all the lines are down, and we can't reach him?*

My call went through without a second's delay. While the rings vibrated against my ear, I prayed it was a good omen that telephone lines to his office were still intact. In the middle of the fourth buzz, a woman answered by saying the name of a company so fast I failed to understand her words.

Damn, not who we want to talk with! Well, you're certainly not about to hang up before we find out something.

I tried to sound regionally non-specific when I asked, "May I speak to Christopher Saracini?"

"He's not in the office," she answered in a bored voice.

After taking a deep breath, I blurted, "I've just heard about the earthquake and wanted to know if he's been hurt."

"He's all right." Irritated by what she considered to be the frivolity of the call, she would volunteer nothing else.

Beginning to wonder if Liz's source of information had been accurate and whether there had really been an earthquake, I still needed to learn more. "And his family?"

"They're all right, too." The woman's disinterested tone implied I had no business taking her away from an important task.

"Thank you," I said before hanging up. And thank God, too, because I could now relax, knowing that piece of my heart was not in harm's way.

※

The following weekend I waited at the cabin for UT's football game to be televised. To burn the time before the telecast, I listened to John Ward's pre-game radio show while I pored through the old man's collection of blue magazines. The black rotary phone by the couch rang. I reached over to pick it up, expecting to hear Mom's voice but hearing Christopher's instead.

So, how did he get this number?

He told me of his adventures during the recent quake. After he finished, I hesitated to tell him about my call to California, not knowing what his reaction would be.

"How did you get this number?" I asked, stalling for time.

There was a short silence before he explained, "I copied it down before you took me back to the motel that morning."

"Oh?" With the cabin's phone being unlisted, I had not expected that response. "Copied it from where?"

"Rachael," he curtly answered, "your number is on your phone."

I looked on the phone to find the number written in Mom's precise style on a strip of paper taped across the center circle. Never having noticed the number there before, I waited for him to start a new subject.

When he did not, I took a deep breath before confessing, "I called your office as soon as I heard about the earthquake. I spoke with some woman there." I squinched my eyes and waited for a sharp reproach.

"I know. I heard," he replied.

With my next breath, I quickly added, "I didn't give my name." I wanted to assure him I had been discreet.

"After Rita said a woman with a southern accent had called, I knew it had to be you." Next, Christopher laughed. "Don't worry about that call, but if you call in the future, use my private number."

I smiled and felt the world smiled with me.

Future calls. He thinks we have a future!

"That'll be nice," I answered calmly. Sliding down the wall to sit on the floor with my back against the front of the bookcase, I went on to tell him what all had been happening in my world since we parted in May. I made no mention of Joe Bill.

By mid-November, I had given up my good fight. I needed to throw myself a grand pity party because the man I wanted was a man I could not have.

Unable to muster the will for the drive to the cabin that dreary weekend, I stayed in my little house in Knoxville. With a cold rain steadily falling outside in gray sheets, I assured myself that the water would benefit the flowers come spring, but thoughts of that distant reward did nothing to raise my spirits now. Most of this year's crop of oak leaves was on the ground, lying about in clumps like crumpled wet blankets. For days, I had been unable to summon the energy to complete raking them. The fire I lit Sunday afternoon did nothing except smoke and sputter up the chimney. In a further attempt to withdraw from the world, I walked about the house closing all the wooden blinds on both floors.

After I curled up in the wing chair near my sad excuse for a fire, my companion cats nosed themselves a place on either side of me. Opening a book based on a fictionalized account of Sally Hemmings' life, I stared at the blurred pages on my lap, then over to the smoldering fire, back to the book again, unable to drum up interest in either.

The phone beside my chair rang. Glaring at it for crashing my private pity party, I debated about letting my recently purchased answer machine get it before reluctantly reaching for the receiver. When I moved, the sleepy sisters mewed their protests.

"Can you get away for a few days?"

I sat up straight when I recognized the voice. "Yes! When? Where?"

Grunting disgust with my sudden change of position, the girls jumped down from the chair, landing stiff-legged and loudly on the oak floor. As I frantically grabbed a pencil and searched for paper, he told me the dates in December and the specific flight numbers I should request.

After having no luck finding paper, I flipped to the title page of my book. Preparing to copy down the numbers, I requested, "Tell me again. I've something to write on now."

Christopher patiently repeated the needed information. "Call me back when you get it all arranged." He added, "Use my private number."

When our conversation ended, I put the phone down and suddenly noticed what a beautifully fine November day it had become. The fire blazed away in the fireplace, popping and crackling a happy tune. On the other side of the French doors that opened to the deck, wonderful silvery rain nourished glorious spring flowers now stored away in bulbs underground. Posing by the hearth, even my cats had little cat smiles on their faces. As fiery, liquid joy throbbed through my blood vessels, I knew I had more than enough energy needed for two lifetimes.

❦

Delayed by strong winds in the upper jet stream, my flight landed in San Francisco a full forty-five minutes late, docking at the far end of one terminal with only ten minutes before my connecting flight's scheduled departure from the last gate of another terminal four concourses away. That distance was according to the helpful airport layout given me by my Delta flight attendant as our pilot drawled apologies for the lateness of our landing. While waiting to rise from my aisle seat, my stomach tied itself in knots as my fertile mind conjured up worse-case scenarios to entertain itself.

We're too old for this.

In a desperate attempt to make my connecting flight, I rushed through the long passageways. My damaged knees ached from the pounding as I jogged on the exposed concrete floors past numerous Pardon-Our-Renovations-In-Progress posters.

We're way too old for this!

Panting and sweating, I arrived at the gate. According to my wristwatch, I had missed the scheduled departure time by a mere five minutes. No passengers were lined up for boarding and the gate area was deserted, except for one uniformed attendant shuffling boarding cards. Regretting my lack of daily exercise, I gulped for air and considered the possibility of changing my poor habits when I got back home.

When able to speak, I asked, "Has the flight for Arcata left yet?"

Although I had stood there for some time while catching my breath, the unconcerned, tanned gate attendant did not bother looking up from her paperwork until after I had spoken. She pushed locks of her sun-streaked hair behind her ears before she intoned, "We're having some problems. Don't know when we'll be taking off. I'll call the flight when it's ready." Her bored voice implied she had given this speech many times, not just this afternoon. When she bent back over her papers, her hair fell back to cover her rather large ears. As far as she was concerned, our conversation was over.

Welcome to the real world. Bitchily, my twin added, *Damn, but she has big ears, bless her heart.*

That woman might have looked up when she spoke, but I was not certain she had seen me. After her blasé regard, I concluded I no longer rested in the comfortable cocoon of genteel Southern-ness in which Delta had enveloped me on my flight to the West Coast.

What the hell was I thinking? After all, this was California, and how foolish of me to consider that a commuter airline would be run with any attention paid to time.

With my achy knees reminding me why I gave up jogging on pavement ten years ago, I limped to the passenger waiting area. Sitting down in the nearest row of linked seating, I opened my book on Sally and waited for my flight to be called.

When the plane at last leaped off the runway in San Francisco, I glanced at my watch. The hands showed the exact time I had been scheduled to arrive in Arcata.

This place is just too laid-back for me.

I nodded in agreement with my twin before settling back in my seat, reading about Sally and Thomas Jefferson at his home in the hills overlooking what would become the University of Virginia.

***

As I deplaned in northern California, I was reminded how much airports had changed since the late 1960s when I was in my teens and saw Rob off to Korea. In present-day Arcata, as it had been some twenty years ago back home, there was no metal, intestinal-like tubing to walk inside and no gauntlet of a terminal to fight through. I simply stepped out into sunshine, moved down steep, metal steps at the plane's door and walked across the tarmac to an opened sliding gate in a chain-link fence. Outside the lacy boundary, people clustered to greet arriving passengers. Back in that kinder and gentler world, back before hijackers, that was how I pictured airports still should be.

Walking toward the small, boxy terminal, my thoughts raced as rapidly as my beating heart. Would Christopher be here with the crowd? Or would he be inside the building? Or would he not be here at all because my plane was so late in arriving? Would I even remember what he looked like? Would he recognize me? Would we have changed so much in these past months that we would have lost the magic between us?

Oh, Rachael, what are we doing here?

While my eyes searched the tight knot of people for a familiar face, a man moved free. He stood apart from the others, with the biggest smile on his face and crooked in his right arm a huge bouquet of long-stemmed red roses mingled with baby's breath. I hoped that man, waiting just outside the gate for someone to come to him, would be Christopher. As I walked closer, I happily discovered he was.

When he gathered me into his embrace, I had all my pieces parts back together. At last, I was home.

While going to reclaim my luggage, I learned he had flown in on the same commuter airline that morning and had already checked into a motel. He casually mentioned, in passing, his travel bag had not arrived with him, but had been told it would be on my flight. We picked up his suitcase at the baggage claim area, but my three pieces of luggage were not there. The uniformed employees behind the counter were not ruffled in the least bit that my clothes did not arrive with me.

Dutifully, I stood back to watch Christopher manage my crisis. I also stood awkwardly aside in an unaccustomed role as bystander. Since I usually had to step on my own spiders, having a man tend to me and mine was a luxury I did not often enjoy. I intently listened while one worker assured Christopher that my items would arrive, with any luck, on their next flight scheduled in at eight in the evening and would be delivered to our motel.

No one employed by the airline expressed concern about my missing possessions. I, on the other hand, worried that this was Saturday afternoon and that I was leaving Monday morning and that I had no idea where my next change of underwear was coming from. Christopher seemed unperturbed, as well, by their absence.

"Oh, yeah, sure," I laughed, when we later strolled through the parking lot to his car, "you know where your underwear is."

After exiting the airport, Christopher drove us about Arcata where I found a landscape much different from what I had expected. The Wednesday before leaving home, I had dropped by the library to research Northern California where I had found pictures and detailed written descriptions depicting rugged mountains, tall trees, quaint townships and narrow, two-lane blacktop roads. Those pastoral scenes were not what I was now being shown. The area I saw was too urban, too crowded, too paved over by concrete.

As he pointed out sights of possible interest, we sat far apart in his compact rental car, separated by more than the space between the bucket seats. Since Christopher said countless times he wanted to give me a feel for the area, I began to suspect the man was as uneasy as I had been about this visit.

After the exciting rush of first greetings and after the handling of my missing luggage had been worked out, I withdrew within myself. I needed time to get into the rhythm of this man. With his speech patterns sounding foreign to my ears, I kept asking him to repeat himself. I listened hard to each sound he uttered to understand the gist of what he was saying. I found myself having to repeat my words for him, too. It seemed as if, during the months of separation, we both had become hearing impaired, and each set of hearing aids had been forgotten on bathroom sinks at our respective homes. I thought I recalled his being much easier to understand when we had been on top of LeConte.

Rachael, I heard her say during one of many long lulls in our conversation, *it's been over six months since that hike. What did you expect? You both have changed.*

"How's your mother?" Christopher suddenly asked.

Startled, I jumped in my seat. "She's fine." Politely, I asked in return, "How's your family?"

"They're fine."

With that short exchange, we established the status of everyone on both sides of the continental United States. Small talk. Nothing talk. Mere sounds to fill up the empty spaces surrounding us. More miles turned over on the odometer.

"How's your work goin'?" I inquired.

"Well."

Well? That one-word answer isn't going to help fill this vast awkwardness.

Minutes later, he asked, "How's your restaurant?"

"Growin'," I answered, allowing that two could play this game.

During the drawn out drive that painfully slow afternoon, we tentatively crossed over into each other's physical space by briefly touching fingers to arms while we stalked about in hobbled attempts to flush up a conversation. Each time, the contact lasted longer until, boldly, we threw all caution aside and held hands. The matching smiles we shared as we clasped hands confirmed I had been correct in assuming he also had been apprehensive about this first meeting.

After meandering through town, our so-called joy ride turned westward toward the ocean, terminating at long last on an isolated lane paralleling the backside of an industrial complex, its gravel roadbed resting upon a slip of land separating the beach from a wide marshy pool. Sometime during our wanderings, gray clouds had pushed inland, filtering out the winter sun and muting its brightness. The brackish water on our left was surrounded by clumps of grayish-green grasses. In the far distance, geometric blocks of gray buildings stood like those factories pictured in my grammar school geography books. From several tall stacks, white smoke billowed against a bleached-out sky. Nearby, tall grasses swayed in the strong wind coming in from the flattened greenish-gray Pacific resting well beyond the low dunes on our right.

The surrounding view was an austere study in shades of gray. As seen framed through the car's windshield, the monochromatic landscape dredged up memories for the opening sequences of a 1950s television program shown early Saturday mornings. While my parents slept in, I would sit cross-legged, spellbound, on the floor in front of my family's black-and-white Capehart TV, waiting for the Indian test pattern to fade into the opening credits for *Industry on Parade*. I had always found those promotional industrial shorts more fascinating than *Winky Dink and You* which aired next.

The bleak environment outside our vehicle was not an inspiring example of nature's wonders or even of man's handiwork, but this was where our drive had ended. Staring at the barren scenery, waiting for his tour to continue, I realized I had always been comforted by shades of gray. Besides, in its utilitarian starkness, being here on this sliver of land with this man felt safe and familiar in an *Industry on Parade* sort of way.

Minutes went by before Christopher turned to me saying, "I'm so glad you're here. I had to see you again."

Hearing happiness in his voice, I turned to observe the emotion shining in his eyes. I felt gentleness in the way he cradled my hand. After lifting my hand to his lips for a kiss, he squeezed my hand once before letting me go. He reached up to drop the transmission into reverse.

"I know this isn't much time to spend together," he apologized, "but it's the best I could arrange."

Before I could do more than smile in agreement, he steered the car in the direction from which we came. After reaching the main highway, he went on to tell me what he had mapped out for our next few hours together. While listening to all the man had planned, I decided he was going to keep us busy sightseeing. I began to wonder when would there be time for us.

We walked the quiet, dim second floor hallway leading to his motel room. He carried his one suitcase, packed with clothes to last the week he would be in town. I carried his floral gift.

When he had checked in that morning, Christopher said the front desk clerk indicated this back wing would be unoccupied except for us. The hall felt abandoned and unloved. Our muffled steps on the padded carpet broke the heavy silence in that long corridor as we became strangers again with each step.

Soon after closing the door to the room, he pointed to a bottle on ice in the plastic ice holder, provided by the motel, and two crystal wine flutes. "This is one of my favorite wines," he proudly explained, "and I bought these flutes especially for us."

After depositing his bag on the floor, Christopher uncorked the bottle and poured the wine while I ran water in the short trash can for my roses.

As we clinked rims to our glasses, he said, "Welcome to Northern California."

Upon touching, the rolled lips of the thin flutes made a rich, melodic sound that contrasted with the surrounding generic accommodations. The bottle had been chilling all afternoon. Its cold bubbles tickled my mouth, twinkling chills down my throat.

Before we drank our glasses half down, he put his flute on the dresser and took mine to place beside his. He tentatively kissed my lips. Without further delay, we removed each other's clothing. Moving to the bed, Christopher eased me back on the bedspread before kissing me hard and deep. His hands traveled expertly over my body. Quickly he entered me and was finished before I was ready to start.

Although he called out my name when he climaxed just the same as he had done in Nashville, it was not the same. Shortly after his explosive use of my name, he pulled out of my body and rolled over beside me. The uneventful act was over too soon. Afterwards, the man did not even offer to reach over to hold my hand.

My, oh, my. Now, that was short, but not sweet.

I was glad our first time together since Nashville was over for its existence had been hanging over my head like that sword of Damocles, but I had not expected the much-anticipated event to be a rabbit special. I lay beside Christopher disappointed, knowing this trip was a total mistake and that these coming next few hours had fast turned into one long, long weekend. I was now happy he had a lot of sightseeing planned. At least, I could look forward to that.

What if that night in Nashville had just been a fluke and sex together would never be that good again? I pondered.

Damn, Rachael, what a horrible thought!

Without a word, Christopher left the bed to stroll purposefully into the bathroom, his footsteps making no sound against the carpeted floor. I heard faucet knobs turn, instantly followed by the hollow sound of water loudly striking the tub's acrylic surface.

Wonder if he would notice if we got a flight out of here tomorrow?

He returned to stand at the edge of the bed where I remained, stunned as a deer caught in headlights. Backlit by the bathroom's light coming around the corner, his darkened body presented an ominous shadow of a man I did not know. Silently, he stood at that distance for a moment before issuing the invitation, "Come shower with me."

Obeying his implied command, I pushed myself off the bed and allowed Christopher to lead me into the bath and place me under the brisk shower. I did not need to put my hair up to protect it from the hot water because, before taking my body earlier, he had not given me time to remove any pins that kept my bun twisted in place. Stepping behind me into the tub, he took soap in his hands and lathered my body. Too numbed by the events in the other room, I remained silent, unable to think of anything to say, while his soapy hands gently touched and glided over my back and arms and legs.

"I couldn't wait for you this time," Christopher began explaining, his tone soft and apologetic. "I wanted to be inside you too much. I had waited far too long for you this whole day to wait any longer." His soapy-slick hands washed away my travel tiredness and smoothed away the uncertainties of the last few minutes.

Before we had completely toweled off, he took my hand, leading me back to that rumpled bed and welcomed me, in slow earnestness this time, to Northern California. He became the lover my body remembered. Being here, I knew afterwards, was definitely not a mistake.

Christopher circled the outside lanes of a small shopping mall, looking for street numbers, but was unsuccessful locating any. For thirty minutes, we had driven the streets of Arcata, searching for a specific Italian restaurant that he had read about last summer. Aware my voice was growing testy, I knew that small can of tomato juice and package of pretzels served on the flight up from San Francisco were not going to keep the hounds of hunger at bay much longer. I thought it odd that the establishment had no brightly lit signs to direct first-time customers to its whereabouts and had said so many times before noticing that my companion's voice had acquired an unkind edge, too.

During our fourth lap, he decided to seek assistance. "Rachael, help me look for someone to ask directions before we miss our reservation altogether."

We craned our necks about the closed and all but empty shopping center. The only soul we spotted was a vagrant, hunkering in front of a closed florist. His worldly possessions rested in a tattered, bulky, tall backpack beside him. Christopher pulled the car near the curb.

In an imperious tone one reserves for subordinates, he said firmly, "Roll down your window and ask him."

I recognized that tone because sometimes I had to use it in order to get the best quality produce from my suppliers. I knew it for what it was, and I did not appreciate his using it with me.

I intentionally mumbled, almost under my breath, but loud enough to be heard, "How's a scruffy derelict goin' to know?" I reluctantly rolled down my window. To make certain he heard me this time, I said louder, "He's not goin' to know where."

"Go on," he insisted, again in that hated supervisory tone, "ask!"

Although I felt strongly that poor man was too drugged-out to know his right hand from his left foot, I asked for directions just to humor Christopher. It was the correct Southern woman thing to do.

The young man looked at me before slowly stroking his stubbled chin. Settling onto his haunches, he replied, "Across the parking lot. Two buildings up. Its entrance is on the lower side." His no-accented, highly educated voice would have served well in a self-assured, measured defense of a thesis.

"Thank you!" Christopher called out, stepping on the accelerator to speed us on our way.

Knowing that I had just been exposed as definitely not being from around here, I muttered, "Well, y'all certainly have a better educated class of street people out here."

We were only a little bit too late for our reservations, but did not have to wait long for another table to become available. Even crowded with other diners, the candle-lit restaurant was invitingly intimate with dark, heavy wooden beams intersecting against roughly textured, cream-colored plaster walls and ceiling. We were shown to a table nestled into a far corner where a welcoming candle dripped down the sides of an empty Chianti bottle.

Finding the candle's flame barely provided sufficient illumination to read the menu, I placed mine aside before asking, "Honey, what do you suggest?"

As soon as my question was posed, Christopher transmuted in front of my eyes. I quickly discovered that the man ordering a meal in a restaurant on his turf was far different from the man who ordered fried chicken in Tennessee. He had been normal when we ate in Townsend, but here, he was clearly on a mission. First, he carefully studied the wine list to decide which wines we would have, which he next cross-referenced, many times, with the dinner menu to determine which foods would compliment his chosen wines.

His choice sequence was the reverse to what I was accustomed. Then again, I had never dined with a man who required a separate wine to accompany the main course or who considered the supper meal as an evening's entertainment. With our entire pre-dinner conversation revolving around wine selections and food possibilities, I could not decide if it was just Christopher being Christopher, or if I had been dating a less gastronomically evolved class of men. Back in Tennessee, back when I used to have dates, the only question would have been did I need another scotch with my dinner.

I relaxed comfortably into my chair to watch this amazing flurry of decision-making. An image of Christopher Saracini at the Smoky Mountain Market and Service Station on Chapman Highway popped into my head. I could see him leaning against the counter, consulting with the short-order cook as to which hot dog selection would complement his previously chosen soft drink. I imagined myself nearby standing next to a metal rack that held individually packaged servings of beef jerky, salted peanuts and fried pork rinds. I could hear hidden bells ringing sporadically whenever cars drove across the black cords stretched across the pavement by the gas pumps outside. My conjured-up vision of him ordering at the Market put a smile on my face.

Does Pepsi-Cola go with chili? Does a Mountain Dew call for onions and relish? Will we be having a Little Debbie or a moon pie for dessert should he choose a Yahoo?

"Are you very hungry?"

His question, the first to be sent in my direction for some time, jolted me back to the reality of our table in Arcata. When I failed to respond promptly to his query, Christopher looked up from his dinner menu.

"What has you smiling?" he asked.

"Oh, nothin' really," I answered. I would not tell him about my recent visions. They would take too many words to describe. Besides, it had been much too long since that in-flight snack for me to be willing to waste further time setting up that scenario for him. "I'm just happy to be here, but I'm so hungry that my stomach thinks my throat's been cut. You decide. Anything you order will be perfect. Just feed me," I urged, "please."

"OK." He put down the smaller menu. "I've decided on the wines, and I think we'll go with a shared appetizer and meal."

As he named wine selections of which I had no knowledge, I nodded my agreement to each of his choices. When our waitress returned, Christopher began our order. With the white wine, he ordered antipasto. After that, he ordered one salad with blue cheese dressing.

Oops, had I spoken too soon? Should I tell a man I'm just getting to know that I think that blue cheese dressing tastes like stale armpits?

"Honey," I tentatively interrupted him, "I can't eat that dressin'. Could we have something else?"

Stunned by my first refusal of the day, his look implied I had uttered a dietary *faux pas*. "You don't eat blue cheese? Harrumph."

Turning to our waitress, he asked, "What other dressings do you serve?"

She listed their choices, and I quickly opted for raspberry vinaigrette.

Christopher said, "Make that two salads. One with blue cheese and one with the raspberry." He next ordered one baked ziti dinner for us to share, requesting she check with him before starting each course.

The evening progressed slow and easy. He taught me to dip bread in olive oil and pepper, instead of spreading it with butter. While discussing the aborted renovations for Rachael's, we sipped white wine and picked our way through a heaping plate of Italian appetizers. We grazed through separate salads, relating our flying experiences of earlier in the day.

"You know, Honey," I told him, "until this afternoon, comin' up from San Francisco, I've never flown any carrier but Delta. As usual, I had the customary layover in Atlanta this mornin'. My Aunt Maurie and I used to joke that when people died in the South they would have to transfer in Atlanta before goin' on to their reward. And when she died and her body was flown back home, our plane did stop in Atlanta." Recalling that ironic layover, I smiled a small, sad smile and finished the last of my white wine. "Maurie would have laughed had she been sittin' beside me when her flight stopped there."

Our waitress appeared to remove our plates and empty glasses. I waited until she walked away before continuing.

"Christopher, I'm so glad we met on the mountain."

He nodded his agreement.

She returned with round goblets for our red wine. For the second time that evening, they went through the bottle-opening ritual. He pronounced it fit for consumption before she poured my glass. A second waiter appeared with one large plate mounded with baked ziti.

"And damn, I'm glad we're splittin' this!" I added, "This plate is huge."

"Rachael," he started to speak, then stopped. He picked up his fork before placing it back down on the table. Looking directly into my eyes, he haltingly began again, "My sweet Rachael, you have added something to my life that was missing. Whenever I see a sunset, I think of you."

I took my first sip of red wine and shuddered as it fell down my throat, hitting the appetizers and salad already in my stomach. With its taste much bolder than the white, the red almost took my breath away. Recovering from that surprise gave me time to consider how to respond to his astonishing declaration.

How to explain to this dear man what meeting him had done for me when I still did not understand what all that meeting meant myself? I felt as if I had been around him for years, instead of hours snatched from a few days. How would I tell him that I had never climaxed before that night in Nashville, when he probably thought me more experienced in love than I am? I knew about sex, not love. How could I describe feelings to him that I was barely aware of?

Sitting across the continent from my home and across the table from a man to whose side I would gladly heel whenever he whistled, I knew wherever he was, that was where I wanted to be. Having no concise response at hand, I replied generically, "My life has been altered since our meetin', and I've been happier because of you."

Our conversation during the main course was much slower than our eating. I attempted to put my feelings into words, but found that a daunting task. Taking longer to select the appropriate words than to speak them, I translated from the language of my heart to the language of my mind and feared choosing the wrong word to represent my true meanings.

Although Christopher spoke in a matching measured way, I discovered that I learned more about his feelings when I watched his eyes and his hands than when listening to his words. I saw tenderness and longing in his eyes that closely mirrored emotions deep within me. I understood his need for connectedness whenever he put down his fork and reached across the table to hold my hand, or when he brushed his fingers against the back of my hand holding my wine glass.

As soon as the last ziti tube was eaten, I realized that all the words uttered since we began the pasta had been superfluous. By the Blood of All we held Holy and on some deep level, we understood each other, we knew each other, we trusted each other and spoken language could never fully explain the bands that connected us. I also accepted that in no way could I satisfactorily explain how I knew those profound concepts to be true.

While Christopher drank coffee, I lingered over the last of the red wine in my glass. Realizing that sitting across a table of disappearing food from him had been seductively intoxicating, I hoped we had displayed better table manners than those shown in the scene from *Tom Jones*. Mentally reviewing our behavior since ordering, I prayed that we had not appeared that obvious to the patrons in our restaurant as had Albert Finney and that actress, licentiously devouring the meal placed before them.

Returning my thoughts to the wine, I announced, "It's taken all of my half of the pasta to become accustomed to this red's sharp taste, but I like it. You've certainly expanded my wine horizons." Having said that, I again became pensive. The anticipation that having Christopher in my life would expand other horizons as well was one thought I chose not to share.

Resting against the back of his chair, he said, "You know, Rachael, my expectations for the future changed in May. I can't begin to think of my life without you." As he had for much of our dinner conversation, he spoke slowly, giving weight to his voiced sentiments.

I took a deep breath before emptying my glass. Just as my body felt warm and tingly from the alcohol, my heart felt warm and tingly from his last remarks.

Christopher quickly leaned forward, taking both my hands in his. His voice became more playful as he jumped to a lighter subject. "How's about some tiramisu? We must keep up our strength to have sufficient energy to make love."

❦

Since we made love again before we fell asleep and again after waking this morning, it was a good thing we both ate that dessert! scampered through my mind after I stepped away from the tub.

Wrapping a towel about my clean body, I walked out of the bath to ask what had he planned for our breakfast, but found the room empty. I stared at the heap of clothing I had worn since leaving home early the day before. They were as tired looking as I was tired of looking at them. I wished I had taken the time to hang them up or, at the very least, had washed out my undies before I had fallen asleep.

Perhaps I could wear my panties inside out today, I thought.

Sweet Jesus, what a skanky thought!

"Would you rather we went without?" I responded aloud since the other and I were alone in the room. "I'd be too embarrassed if some emergency room tech cut off my clothes and found me naked underneath. Inside-out, used panties would be better than no panties at all."

As I finished my last word, the door to the room opened. Whooping loudly, I jumped to grab the bedspread the better to cover myself before recognizing the intruder to be Christopher with my luggage in hand.

"Sorry, Rachael. I thought I could get back before you got out of the shower."

The door closed behind him as he put down the suitcase containing my folded clothes in order to hang up my carry-bag of hanging garments.

"You scared the very life out of me!" I scolded.

As he placed my make-up case on the counter in the bath, he further explained, "I wanted to surprise you by having your things here before you finished your shower. I didn't intend to scare you."

He returned from the bath and lifted my suitcase to the low dresser's surface where last night's empty wine bottle still sat. After the case landed with a weighty thud, he asked, "Rachael, why did you pack so much if you were flying out for just two nights?"

"Honey, I did pack light." I went on to justify my three pieces of luggage, "I just didn't know what to bring. Besides, Margaret would have brought more." I dropped the clutched bedspread to walk over to give him a peck on the cheek. "Thank you for my luggage. It's a comfort to know where my next change of underwear will be comin' from."

The downtown area of Eureka was much more picturesque than

what I had been shown of Arcata the afternoon before. Here the residents had reclaimed many of the old structures that had been built around the turn of the century. Some wooden Victorian 'ladies' had been restored to their old genteelness, now providing homes to yuppie families. Others had been gussied up with gaudy color combinations, returning to life as bed and breakfast inns.

Coming to the end of our early Sunday morning walking tour, we strolled nearly empty streets, peering into closed shop windows in the town's small historic commercial district. I had enjoyed our walk through this old section where the cancer of urban renewal funds had never been well-seeded. Old storefronts faced the coming century as front men for pastry shops and antique stores and clothing establishments. Stopping to admire a huge decorated Christmas tree behind the glass windows of a hardware store, one ornament, a green, realistically warty pickle about the size of my forefinger, leaped out to catch my attention from among the hundreds of festive others hanging there.

That represents you and Christopher, my twin informed me, *in this pickle of a relationship.*

He tugged at my hand. "How's about this for breakfast?" He pointed to a small coffee shop across the street before adding, "Gotta keep up our strength."

The more time we spent together, the more I sensed he never stayed in one place very long. Eager to learn much more about Christopher Saracini, I quickly followed him.

After sharing a freshly baked bear claw, we hopped into his rental car, heading to redwood country. Past Arcata, the countryside opened up and settled down into how I had imagined Northern California would look. The highway soon became almost free of other motorists. The wild Pacific Ocean relentlessly pounded the flat shore to my left while dark emerald green trees stood tall on the mountains to my right. Up the highway a bit, the roadbed veered away from the water, and dense vegetation soon blocked any views of the ocean.

Above Trinidad, Christopher pulled off the road briefly to show me Patrick's Point. We strolled to the parking lot's edge. Towering cliffs and rocky shoreline had replaced the sandy beaches we had driven beside earlier in the morning. The deep water's sapphire surface was rough with heavy swells, and its waves crashed with bleach-white foam against massive crags. I watched miniaturized people walk along paths on the distant rocks and was amazed how the cliffs dwarfed those adults.

Apologizing that there were too many other favorite sights he wanted to share to allow time to go hike up the actual Point, he sped to Crescent City where Roosevelt elk, instead of domesticated dairy cows, grazed beside the highway. We wound into the hills past Lady Bird Johnson's personal grove of redwood trees.

Driving back to the coast, Christopher pulled the car into a ranger station for the Redwood National Park. Thinking it odd that a ranger station for a redwood forest would be situated near sand dunes and the ocean, without a single redwood tree close by, I wandered about the exhibits while he conferred with a female ranger. Unexpectedly, he grabbed my elbow, rushing us back to the car.

As we returned to the hills and surrounding redwoods, Christopher commented, "This weather is unusual for Northern California this time of year."

"Really?"

First looking out my side window and next through the windshield, I found not the first cloud in the sky. After the dense, rain-threatening clouds of yesterday evening, Sunday had dawned a surprising pleasantly bright, cool December day and had remained so.

"Yes. Fog should be covering the views," he continued, "and it should be raining. During World War II, the Army Air Corps used that airstrip down at Arcata to train U.S. flyers how to deal with the English fogs."

After turning to beam my companion a toothy, smug grin, I boasted, "The good weather today is here only because we're together. You'll have your rain back after I leave."

As Christopher pushed the gas pedal down, he drove up the steep road faster than we had an hour earlier. Later he announced cryptically, "I got the code."

"What code?"

"For the lock on the gate across the road leading to the grove that contains some of the largest known redwoods. The ranger said we needed to get in there and out before dark. In the summer months, only tour buses are allowed into the valley. During the off-season, rangers give the code to motorists who know to request it. That was why I was talking to the ranger. She said we were the first to ask for the code today."

"Does that mean we'll have the trees to ourselves?"

"We should," he answered. "The code is changed every few days to keep down the traffic. She didn't know if anyone was in yesterday to ask for it."

Within minutes, we stopped in front of a gate barring access to a nameless side road. As Christopher fumbled about the lock a couple of times before it opened, I thought it was interesting he had trouble with locks the same as I.

After I drove our car past the barrier, he carefully closed the gate and replaced the stubborn lock before taking back the driver's seat. He slowly steered the steep, narrow, winding dirt road to reach the secluded valley guarding the tallest tree. We passed areas where timbering continued. Here the sides of the ridges looked like the flanks of dogs with mange, and red clay slides bloodied the mountainsides. As we descended, I hated what I saw even as Christopher explained that timber must be managed. I saw no honor in this type of management. The land looked raped. I felt uncomfortable as I gazed around at downed, ravaged trees lying about like broken, used bodies.

Eventually, the roadbed widened into a deserted parking area. Having arrived late in the day, we discovered we had the valley with its special redwoods to ourselves. While I read aloud the printed information at the small shelter, he conversed with the trees behind me. According to the sign, we had a half-mile walk to view the world's tallest redwood.

The valley was an ancient quiet place. Whenever we talked, I found myself whispering to give honor to the living cathedral through which we walked. The trek down the ridge through the redwood grove assumed the sacredness of a religious experience. Akin, I imagined, to walking the Stations of the Cross for the Faithful. In this primeval forest, trees that had stood long before America became significant surrounded us, generations of trees withstanding and surviving the forces of nature. Trees that would stand here long after civilization was gone, providing some fool lumber company did not manage their species out of existence.

Rough-textured, reddish trunks of the big trees stretched tall to hold the towering green canopy above our heads. Scattered colonies of darker green ferns clustered about the ruddy brown, needle-littered ground at the massive trees' spreading bases. Hidden overhead, scattered birds called occasionally to each other, their subdued songs muffled by the vast openness under the distant greenery.

Strolling among these giants, I was ambushed by a frightening experience I had considered to be successfully forgotten and buried. I had hoped never to feel that lost ever again, but now that memory had returned toting awful anxieties with it. As my grown-up body responded accordingly and panicked, my mind became further unnerved by old visions.

In mid-September in the early 1950s when Mom and Daddy and I were walking about the grounds during the TVA&I Fair, I had become entranced by some sideshow and let go of my Daddy's hand. When I turned to take his hand again, I found I had been abandoned in a crush of tall adults with only unfamiliar knees at my eye level. Neither Daddy nor Mom were anywhere in sight.

My adult mind now vividly recalled the prickling, hot-cold terror of that sultry fall afternoon when I searched for my parents. With my grown-up heart pounding from the sudden assault of that horrifying childhood episode, I reached for Christopher's arm, clutching it tightly against my trembling body as we walked farther along the steep path through the redwood grove.

Smiling, he looked down and kissed me lightly on my forehead. After untangling himself from my grasp, he draped an arm around my shoulders, snuggled me close. Putting my arm about his waist, I pulled myself closer to him as my mind revisited terrifying events.

I gradually noticed that the longer Christopher held me, the less my mind was able to rehash that almost paralyzing fear and the slower my heartbeat became. I watched that dreadful scare from over thirty-five years ago fade, its power over me neutralized by his nearness. I had laid on hands, but amazingly Christopher had been the healer. And I was the one who was ultimately healed.

How did that come about? She wanted answers, but I had none.

By the time the sloping path had flattened out, the frightful incident within me had been replaced with an unfamiliar, pleasant feeling that merely required the comfort of Christopher's hand lightly clasped about mine. I considered telling him what I had recently re-experienced and how I now felt, but was not certain exactly how that scary memory had at last been put to rest.

If I shared what had just happened inside my head during our walk through the redwoods, I was afraid he might think I was too unstable emotionally and my poorly inadequate description too far fetched to be credible. After examining that chilling possibility, I reconsidered sharing. Maybe I would tell Christopher later when I felt my place more secure in his heart.

Upon reaching the marker at the foot of the world's tallest redwood, we stood in quiet awe of this wondrous creation. Living up to its billing, the tree was huge and just too tall. I could not lean back far enough to see its crown.

"It would take too many people claspin' hands to reach around this sucker," I announced as I continued to stare upward.

Christopher read aloud the measurements for this prized tree. Afterwards he said firmly, "I think we should christen this tree."

I quickly dropped my gaze from the tree's top to look directly at his face. To more fully express my puzzlement, I wrinkled my forehead before I asked, "You want us to pee here? I don't think I can. I powdered my nose back at the ranger's station."

"No," he explained patiently, "I want us to make love here."

"OK," I amiably agreed. "I can do that." I looked around for a soft place at the base of the world's tallest redwood tree. I would do anything for this man but, being in my early forties, I wanted to be somewhat comfortable when I did this anything.

Having carried nothing with us to spread on the ground, our choices were limited. We spent several minutes searching for a location on the deep carpet of needles strewn about the tree. After a couple of tentative starts, we opted for Christopher sitting on a fallen tree trunk with me facing him on his lap. That position was not as comfortable on old bones as the worn couch back in my cabin, but the downed trunk was tolerable. After a few kisses and caresses, we soon ignored the primitiveness of our surroundings and lost ourselves while making love in that isolated wilderness.

When we climaxed together, he shouted, "Rachael Taite!"

His voice pierced the almost palpable silence, staking claim to me in our private world populated by just us two. Afterwards, naked in the quiet solitude of the redwoods, we sat motionless and joined together. While waiting for our ragged breathing to return to normal, I soon felt the sun's heat leaving the valley and heard the wind overhead picking up. As soon as a quick, brief breeze off the nearby water came through the trees, chilling the sweat on our exposed bodies, we separated to scurry about the forest floor in search of clothing.

With panties here, boxer shorts there, tossed about in our haste, the base of the world's tallest tree was as littered with scattered garments as any co-ed's dorm room following preparations for a big prom. Unlike Adam and Eve in their garden, however, we were not ashamed of seeing each other's nakedness. We were just too frazzling cold to dress leisurely.

Before continuing along the Stations for the third- and fifth-tallest trees, we went off trail to stand on the rocky banks of the wide Redwood Creek. As Christopher stood behind me with his arms draped around my shoulders, the combined heat from our bodies warmed us. The blue reflected in the shallow water matched the blue found in the late afternoon winter sky. Mesmerized, I turned my head around once to verify that the colors were the same as those in my sweet darling's eyes before relaxing against his body to enjoy the wild beauty before us.

"This has been a wonderful day, and it's not over yet," he said softly in my ear.

When I turned around to kiss him, I caught movement out of the corner of my right eye.

"Oh, Sweet Jesus, Christopher!" I tore away from his embrace. "We're not alone! There's a man and a woman standin' at the foot of our tree!"

I grabbed his hand, pulling him onto the trail. We walked briskly out of their sight.

"Oh, damn, oh, damn, oh, double damn!" My rapid low curses almost kept pace with my feet. "Oh, Christopher, they know what we just did! Oh, how embarrassing!" I was so distraught that I explicitly pronounced the ending g-sound in 'embarrassing'.

"They don't know." He attempted to restore my lost composure.

"Honey, they heard you call out my name." I stopped my wild flight in order to look him squarely in the face. His tone had done little to inspire my confidence. I felt the heat of a caught-in-the-act blush warming my neck and creeping upwards.

He grimaced. I watched that expression slowly ooze into a sly smile.

"I did do that pretty loud, didn't I?" He sounded almost pleased with his earlier vocal efforts.

I barked back, "The entire national park knows who I am and what we were doing!" Finally, I chuckled. There was nothing else to do but laugh at our predicament. Calmer, I added, "At least, we weren't caught with our pants down. Literally!"

He squeezed my hand. "Come on, Rachael, we have some more trees to see. I don't think we'll try to christen them."

"Good idea."

We continued at a slower pace, enjoying the majesty of the trees and the sounds of the river and the magic of our closeness. Occasionally, we caught a glimpse of the other couple. Not much later, a second couple with a teenager in tow appeared not far behind them.

"Damn, Honey, there's more people. They probably heard you, too." I was beyond mortified.

Christopher thought for a moment before commenting, "That family won't know which one of us two couples it was, will they?"

His statement did not make me feel any less embarrassed. Unaware that I spoke aloud, I issued a torrent of sentences, filling the serene forest's quietness as rapidly as the thoughts came to me. "That first couple knows it was us. I know it was us. I'm thankful that I'm not from around here and there is no possibility of my ever seein' those five people again. And, thank God, we're in your rental car and not in my Caddy with its vanity tags. Damn, what an afternoon's walk in the park."

❦

Farther along our drive returning to our motel, we stumbled upon a restaurant situated on a bluff overlooking the Pacific and the setting sun. At the same time we drove onto the unpaved parking area, an employee opened the entrance. As their first guests that early Sunday evening, she offered us our choice of seating. Upon entering, Christopher requested near the fire where we could look out on the sunset.

The old bungalow had been gutted and reconfigured into one huge room below, with a loft above for additional seating. Two Christmas trees, both heavily draped with strings upon strings of tiny white lights, decorated its festive interior. One was in the far corner of the main room and the other at the top of the steps in the loft. The long, west side of the house held a bank of windows capturing the ocean's view. White votives flickered atop white linens in the center of each table in the lower seating area. A cheery fire blazed in the oversized, rock fireplace on the short wall opposite the steps leading to the loft.

I pored over the menu as Christopher cruised the wine list until our waitress returned to announce that they did have Dungeness crabs. For this meal, he allowed the food to dictate his choice of wines.

We split an appetizer of goat cheese and fruit, sharing one bottle of white. After my first bite of goat cheese, I silently wondered if blue cheese could taste as stout and proceeded to eat mostly fruit. For our main course, Christopher picked out meat from a large Dungeness crab while we shared a dryer white. As he handed choice pieces of crab to me, I ate chunks of that rich meat, feeling as pampered as any Roman noble being hand-fed by a devoted slave.

"What a wonderful weekend! I'm so glad I'm here."

In addition to enjoying his tender ministrations, we had the entire restaurant to ourselves, leaving me to feel absolutely decadent and spoiled, far beyond being spoiled. The converted house seemed exceptionally romantic with its primary illumination coming from softly glowing candles and twinkling holiday trees, with low seasonal music easing through the expansive dining space and with the burning of the setting sun outside matching the glow in the fireplace within. I was content and would love becoming accustomed to this kind of treatment.

He smiled his agreement, going on to say, "You've added something to my life that was missing. I'm just a simple Italian boy who does nothing out of the ordinary. I always follow the rules." He popped a lump of crab into his mouth.

I reached to take his right hand in my left. "Honey, I think we're breakin' a few rules here," I corrected him. To come clean with his Catholic God, I knew he would need to confess his sins and renounce the error of his ways. I reminded him, "You'll have to go to confession some—"

He interrupted. "I told my priest about you when I was on retreat this past summer."

Damn, how's that for a reality check! Has he also explained to his children why daddy never takes communion with them?

My heart went cold, my body stiffened as I tightly gripped his hand. "And what did he say? How many Hail Marys do you have to recite to atone for me?" I stared down at our joined hands to await his answer.

Responding in the quiet tones of a condemned man who freely accepted his sentence, Christopher explained, "No, I've not made confession. We merely talked during the retreat. He told me I was old enough to know the difference between right and wrong."

Continuing my tight hold on his hand, I kept my eyes focused there because I could not bear to look up. I feared hurting more if I read the emotions on his dear face.

Priests in California, I thought, must be more relaxed about the sin of adultery than the Baptist preachers I know back home. But we are just too perfect together. I am forty-three years old, and I am having dinner with the man I want to spend the rest of my life with. And yet, because he has previous claims on his life, I will get on a plane in less than twelve hours to leave him.

I knew I had no business dining with Christopher beside the Pacific Ocean. At the same time, my heart wanted to know how soon would I see him again.

Finally I said aloud, "Life isn't supposed to be this difficult."

A solitary tear burned down my cheek. We both ignored it.

Seven

Before leaving Arcata, I had carefully rolled the crystal flutes inside separate sweaters for the return to Knoxville but found, upon unpacking, only one made the journey home intact. I did not know whether it was his or mine that had shattered. I did know those jagged pieces reminded me of how I felt now that we were apart. Realizing days later I only felt whole when Christopher and I were together, I decided mine must have broken.

Rachael's became too small, too quick before the 1989 holiday season ended. During most days, customers had to wait nearly an hour for a table to free up. In their attempts to appease our hungry masses, my harried servers ran into one another. Our lone busboy, Joey, was hardly able to keep Lightnin', the newest dishwasher, supplied with sufficient dirty flatware in order to have enough clean utensils for the busy servers to wrap for the next table set-up.

The catering and carry-out portions of the business needed more space, too. Back in the compact kitchen, tempers occasionally boiled over as we tried to satisfy every order without stepping on each other. Yet no matter how busy I became, thoughts of Christopher Saracini were only a heartbeat away.

Christmas, New Year's and Valentine's Day all came and went without the sound of his voice. Although we exchanged clever greetings cards, words printed on paper were not as satisfying as having his arms around me. Strangely enough, I did not miss our sexual couplings as much as I missed his body asleep beside mine. Sybyl and Beatrice bundling under the covers alongside my body were not nearly as comforting. Too many mornings blurred together before I stopped reaching for Christopher, needing to feel his chest rise and fall as he rested next to me. Around the Ides of March, I finally mustered a stretch of days without wondering did he miss me, did he think of me when we were not together?

◦✥◦

After securely locking the restaurant's front doors, Margaret, Liz and I sprawled on chairs in the lobby, our heavy arms much too tired to brush back the strands of hair falling onto our faces and our aching legs too spent to stand even long enough to remove our stained aprons. Studying the furrows between their eyebrows and the tightness about their lips, I saw they were as stressed as I by the crowded conditions.

"Ladies," I begged, "tell me when we start havin' fun."

Both groaned.

"If I had something in my hand," Liz half-heartedly threatened, "I'd chuck it at you." She closed her eyes while Margaret glanced about for a toss-able object.

"The lease will be up shortly." I went on, explaining my nearing dilemma, "We can't enlarge here. The watch repairman next door doesn't want to move, and the knit shop owners on the other side have just remodeled so they won't be leavin' any time soon. We need to go scoutin' for new digs."

"Got any ideas?" Margaret asked.

"Just that we need to stay somewhere close. Not more than, say, two miles away." That was the only firm condition I had for the change.

"Not even that much," Liz suggested. "Our customers are accustomed to the Old Brickyard area. I think we'd be too far west if we went beyond Bearden Hill." Because Liz had been reared in the area, she knew its business potential and understood the mind-set of the people who lived and worked nearby.

I looked about my recently redecorated surroundings. I liked the soft teal tint to the walls and shiny enameled, white wood trim. I liked the lush, lifelike, plastic greenery entwined across white latticework at the large front window. I liked the splashes of teal and mauve flower bouquets depicted on the plastic-coated tablecloths and the crisp white, molded plastic chairs that tucked under the tables. I liked the compactness of the tidy space and truly hated the thoughts of moving, but we could not stay here much longer and keep our customers happy and our employees sane.

"OK, let's start lookin' about. My lease is up late this summer," I said, resigning myself to the inevitable.

Hugh Ed's lean body took up most of the available height in the doorframe. He wore the whites of his painting profession and freshly polished, alligator hide cowboy boots. The graceful, artistic fingers of his big hands cradled a carry-out order, making the white paper bag holding his lunch appear smaller than it was. I always imagined Michelangelo had hands like that.

To announce his presence, he cleared his throat. "Miz Rachael, Ah think Ah might have found you a place."

Hugh Ed Dalton became my painter last fall, by default, when he was the only one to show up. From coastal Alabama, he talked in a rich, deep-brown voice and in a Slow-School-Zone speed that would calm a hurricane-force gale back to a summer's cooling breeze. In five months, I had yet to see his clothes spattered with paint. He always wore white pants and a white long-sleeved shirt when he worked because that was how he was taught. He was very neat when he painted because that was how he was taught. He kept his billfold in his left hip pocket tethered by a chrome chain to his black leather belt because that was how he was taught. Since I was better than ten years older than Hugh Ed, he always respectfully addressed me as Miz Rachael because that was how he was taught. His pants, whether they were his on-duty painter's whites or his off-duty narrow-leg jeans, always had a deep crease down the front. I had no idea who or what had inspired that trait.

I peered over the rim of my glasses at the man towering above me. His gaunt, sinewy appearance masked the kind, caring soul beneath. His baby-fine brown hair was held securely in a neat, thin ponytail at the nape of his neck. No stray hairs dared to float about Hugh Ed's head, and I envied how he managed that. This afternoon, he had his sleeves rolled back, exposing vein-blue tattoos of a swirling dragon on his right forearm and a skull on his left.

When I had first seen Hugh Ed, this lanky giant of a man had frightened me but that was before I heard his voice. After I got to know him better, I trusted the man with his personal set of keys to my house and to my cabin and to my restaurant because of the ways he had been taught.

I put aside the mock-up of the proposed spring menu and swung my office chair around in order to face him. "Oh? And what have you found?"

"Well-a, Ah was workin' over here to th' frame place when Ah heard about this space just off th' Pike. It's over in th' corner near those foreign rug people. Thought you might be interested, seein' how y'all's so crowded here now."

I pictured the shopping area he described and thought I knew the location to which he referred. "Thank you, Hugh Ed. I'll check it out this evenin'. By the way, who told you I was lookin'?"

"Well-a, Ah overheard Miz Liz and Miz Margaret one day last week. Ah reckon you'll be needin' me to get th' place ready."

I laughed. "You know I wouldn't have anybody else."

He smiled his molasses-slow smile and at the same time bobbed his head once to indicate he was leaving.

I had been most fortunate last fall when no other painter showed up to give me an estimate because I got this capable, quiet man. He eased his way into my life as easily as he rolled out paint onto sheet rock. He hardly spoke except when spoken to. He never left dollops of paint on floors or painted over light switch covers. The afternoon he drove by my house to check on painting the exterior, Hugh Ed met me at the front door and drawled, "Well-a, Lady, you do need me."

And I did. Besides painting, he could fix plumbing, he could remove leaves from gutters, he could replace wiring and he could repair appliances. He knew skilled tradesmen who would come when the work I needed done was more than he could do by himself. Also, he had three high-school-aged sons who raked leaves and who knew not to step on flowers and other plantings when doing so. Hugh Ed Dalton was invaluable to have around because I was a single woman who owned a fifty-seven-year-old Cape-Cod-style residence in town and a pieced-together cabin in the mountains and a restaurant stocked with used equipment.

During the morning of the first Wednesday in April, revised plans for the new restaurant's design were delivered to me. When I had first pictured the changes in my mind, I imagined that the new Rachael's would be wonderful. However, after my initial look at these latest drawings, the lines appeared generic and lifeless, and I could see nothing. Overwhelmed by all the fine lines that gaumed together, I put the plans aside until the lunch rush was over and all the other hectic activities at the restaurant had ceased.

More spiders for me to step on. Sweet Jesus, how I hate dealing with details.

Carrying a glass of spring water to my compact office, I planned to spend the remainder of the afternoon poring over the drawings. With the only competing sounds coming as employees straightened up chairs and tables, I thought I could make sense of those architectural scratchings if I got quiet and concentrated. As I opened the door, my phone rang.

"How's about Boston and New England in May?" a familiar male voice asked.

Teasingly, I countered, "I think the time to go there is really September when we could catch the fall colors."

Christopher brushed my suggestion aside. "I'll be in Boston for business. Come up for the weekend. What do you want to see while we're there?"

"I've always wanted to see L.L. Bean. When are we goin'?" Not giving him time to answer that question, I pleaded, "Christopher, you must promise that no matter how hard I beg, you won't stop at any antique stores. The loan officer won't allow it, and my credit cards couldn't stand the strain."

"OK, L.L. Bean it is, but nix the antiques." His voice became all business when he began, "Here's what you need to do . . ."

As I hastily jotted down the times and flight numbers, doubts concerning whether he thought of me when we were apart washed away. Hanging up the phone after his call ended, I told myself aloud, "He thinks about me or he wouldn't be making these arrangements for us to be together."

You are far too old to be that naïve. You're just a good fuck. That's all we are to him.

Not wanting to believe my twin, I ignored her. "No, it's like havin' a personal travel agent!" I defiantly announced to the empty office before settling at my desk to study the drawings for the new restaurant space.

Margaret, Liz and I sat around the table on sun-warmed, black metallic-mesh chairs on the deck outside my living room. Good weather had arrived promptly on schedule for opening week of the Dogwood Arts Festival. Jonquils and phlox and azaleas were in glorious bloom. The air was heavy with fragrances from dozens of flowering trees and shrubs in my garden and from those throughout the neighborhood. As the warm spring wind teased at its edges, the tablecloth tickled our knees while we sipped Bloody Marys and enjoyed Sunday brunch on the first morning, since last fall, that the weather allowed for such sweet decadence.

Although I had invited my friends over to announce my coming trip to Boston, I dreaded telling them. Since my flight to California last December, each woman had been subtle but pointedly vocal in her comments about my budding relationship with Christopher. Considering the topic too personal for the rest of the ears in the restaurant, I thought it best to make my plans known when there were just the three of us. I would break the news to Mom later tonight.

Having finished the last of the strata I had prepared, Margaret and I watched Liz, the only person I knew who ate slower than Mom, complete her serving. During the lull before dessert, I casually inserted my announcement.

"I'm thinkin' about meetin' Christopher in Boston."

In obvious disgust, Margaret exploded loudly, "Why the hell for! He doesn't belong to you!"

Before she spoke, Liz touched her napkin to her lips. "I agree with Margaret," she said quietly in a much more lady-like tone.

"I know," I countered, "it's not a great idea, but I really want to spend more time with him."

"You don't need to throw away your time on that man, Rachael!" Margaret tossed her napkin between our empty plates. In more control of her voice, she added, "I see no benefit to this relationship. His wife won't allow it."

"But Christopher told me they're separated," I said, playing my only trump card. Mine was a weak defense, at best.

Nearly interrupting me, Margaret stated emphatically, "His eyes are brown!"

I frowned. "No, his eyes are blue," I corrected.

"No, Rachael," Margaret spoke slowly as if she were explaining the obvious to a simpleton, "they are not separated. The man is married. He is so full of shit that his eyes are brown. You'll never be mentioned in the will."

"Margaret, that's cold!" I protested.

She did not miss a beat. "Can't you find some man who's not married? Whatever happened to that Joe Bill?"

"I don't know," I waffled. "I never heard back from him after he left last fall except for his annual card at Christmas."

"Rachael," Liz added, "you know your bein' with Christopher isn't right. This relationship will come to no good end."

At the very least I had expected some emotional support from my two friends. Instead, I got a dour Greek chorus intoning cold, hard logic for the next two hours. By the time we cleared away the dishes, I had been thoroughly briefed as to their sentiments: they wanted me to be happy in a relationship with neither of them feeling that relationship would ever involve Christopher.

Every rebuttal I gave in response sounded, even to my ears, as substantial as a piece of overcooked macaroni. I did not go into detail how Joe Bill had not felt right when he held me. I could not explain to them why my naked body felt such contentment whenever my skin touched Christopher's skin. I dared not tell them about the hidden Rachael he had revealed to me in Nashville and that she only came around when I was with Christopher Saracini.

Later that evening, when I asked Mom to baby-sit the girls while I was out of town, she answered, "Of course, I will." She paused before adding, "But, Darlin', you know your goin' isn't right."

Bless Mom, she might not agree with what I chose to do, but she supported me in the doing. I figured, in this case, she was being accepting of the sinner but not the sin.

Much later that same Sunday night, long after the eleven o'clock news ended, I lay in bed listening to the clock on the living room mantle chime the quarter hours. Despite what my friends might think, this was not the first sleepless night I had wrestled pillows because that man was on my mind. I knew he had a life and a family that did not include me. I also knew I could not go on dreaming about the man because that interfered with my daily living.

I was not a mean-spirited person, but for weeks, I had been wishing bad for a woman I had never met. I had fleeting visions of receiving a call one day when Christopher would tell me she had died crossing the street and would ask me to come to California to live with him. Sometimes that imagined call became one where he announced he was leaving California and his children because he could not live any longer without me. Despite wanting us together, I knew I could never make my happiness out of another's sorrow. I would have to give him up and soon.

As Monday morning crept closer, I finally reached what I considered to be the most righteous conclusion that this, our third adventure, would be our last. I decided it would be far more honorable of me to tell him in person, and we Southerners must always allow for the concept of honor in any morally trying situation. I could not bear to end our relationship during an impersonal telephone call. The man meant more to me than to be blown off as easily as that. Besides, never having been to Boston, I rationalized that it would be a shame to miss out on such an opportunity.

In the approaching daylight, I perfected my speech. I pictured the scene playing out our last night together in New England, when I would simply tell Christopher that he should be traveling with his family. I would virtuously finish by adding that I could no longer continue taking away from their time with him.

As the alarm clock across the room sounded, anticipation for our final trip together took on a bitter sweetness that appealed to the part of me that understood why Scarlett always craved the man she could never have and why Rhett joined the Confederacy when the Conflict was nearing its end. Being a child of the South, I had been steeped in the seductive mystique surrounding lost causes.

Armed with the private knowledge that I would be giving up something I so desperately wanted, I knew being in New England would be just too romantically poignant, taking on the epic proportions of a last supper for the condemned because I would be with the one whom I was happiest one last time. Then alone for the rest of my life. As difficult as it was to look forward to my pending execution, I grew impatient waiting to be held again in Christopher's arms.

Upon landing in Boston, I walked from the plane with my parting lines securely entrenched in my brain and all my clothes for the weekend crammed in one rather large suitcase. I also had a huge herpetic lesion squatting on my lip and ten extra pounds padding my butt and thighs. The emotional turmoil surrounding my decision to give up Christopher had inexorably extracted its physical toll during these last few weeks.

I had no trouble picking my man out of the crowd waiting beyond the restraining gate. He was the only one holding a pink carnation.

A single carnation. I'd wondered how he would top those roses in Arcata.

I walked into his welcoming embrace. As he leant down to kiss me, I cautioned, "You can't. Look what I acquired this week."

Halting his kiss in mid-flight, Christopher tightened his arms about me instead. "That's OK, Rachael. I'll forego kissing this weekend. At least, you're here. Where's your luggage?"

"I checked it back in Knoxville. You'll be so proud of me," I teased, "because I only packed one bag."

As if bestowing an honor for a feat well done, he handed me the carnation.

"How did you know that this was my sorority's flower?" I asked before I put the blossom near my nose to inhale its familiar fragrance.

"I didn't know you were in a sorority." Taking my hand, he led the way to the baggage claim where we waited until the last piece of luggage appeared, but my blue suitcase never did slide down that conveyer belt. After the machinery stopped, we found the lost luggage claim department to learn my bag was still in Charlotte and should arrive in the morning.

"No toothbrush. No make-up. No fresh underwear for sixteen hours," I wailed. "I'll never check my luggage ever again." I pouted and pitifully moaned, "I can't even kiss you."

Laughing, he kissed my forehead before commenting, "Don't worry, Rachael, you do have other talents." He gave me a huge bear hug and twirled me about.

⚜

Walking hand in hand into Copley Plaza's grand lobby, I was so elated being with Christopher that my feet barely touched the plush carpeting. Still, being luggage-less, I felt a bit like a hooker because somewhere in The Manual, it is written: Upon first entering into a hotel, a lady must be accompanied by her suitcases.

After locking the door behind us, Christopher led me on a tour of his charming suite. I was enchanted by the inside wooden shutters and tall ceilings in each of the three rooms. The spacious bath was equipped with two snowy-white, thick terrycloth robes and a deep tub big enough to hold a small party.

"That tub has room for six people," I announced as I followed him to the sitting area, "and they needn't be too friendly."

Nodding agreement, Christopher pointed to the waiting bottle of chilled wine. "Ready for a drink?"

When I saw the wine, I replied, "Such a shame that one flute broke."

"Yes," he agreed, "I had meant for you to bring the flutes each time we met. If I had saved the box they came in, they would have traveled better. Let's not worry about it."

As I enjoyed a sip of wine, he retrieved a brown paper bag hidden under the small divan where we now sat. "I have something for you," he said, handing the package to me.

From the bag, I pulled a coffee-table-sized book of Boston's famous public gardens. Leaning against each other, we thumbed through the colorful pages.

We were not halfway into the pictures when Christopher huskily announced, "You can do this later."

Closing the book, we put down our glasses. Placing his arm around my waist, he escorted me into the bedroom. Cradling my face with his hands, he stood in front of me, branding soft kisses on my forehead and marking other facial landmarks as his as well. Because he did not want to own it, he did a satisfactory job of dodging that mother of all fever blisters on my mouth. After he pulled away the pins holding my bun securely in place, he buried his face into my hair, breathing in deeply. Finally, he slowly undressed me, kissing body parts as he exposed them.

Bless that man's heart, he said not one word about my added poundage.

I have never been known for my patience. Grandmother Taite always told me that when I was going through the assembly room in Heaven when God was making me, I got tired of waiting in line at the station where the angels handed out patience and left before getting any. After exercising as much self-control as I could muster for as long as I could, I allowed my hands to play over Christopher's body, removing his garments. There were such delightfully erotic things I wanted to do to him in return, but could not because of the herpetic sore on my mouth.

Despite that god-awful-looking impediment, we managed, as we made love, to erase the claims that our other lives had on us. After he called my name, there was no one else in our world, and the incompleteness I had endured for the last five months was completely gone.

❦

We explored Boston on foot, following the painted lines of the Freedom Trail from tiny, cobblestoned Acorn Street to Paul Revere's petite, two-storied house. Although we found the neighborhood bar where everyone knows your name, no one knew ours. We clinked our drink glasses there and did not resist toasting each other with 'Cheers.' Dinner was a boiled New England lobster at a nearby seafood restaurant. Following our meal, we entered a liquor store after Christopher decided to replace that empty bottle of wine back in our room.

Becoming quickly lost amid towering canyons of boxes filled with alcoholic libations, I had no doubt that this cavernous Bostonian store held enough alcohol to stock every liquor retailer in Knoxville. We wandered by hard liquor in assorted bottle sizes and discovered wines in gallon jugs, but there were no small bottles of wine to be seen.

Following his meandering footsteps, I decided Christopher had no plans to ask for directions any time soon. When I located a clerk, I approached the man.

"Where do y'all keep your small bottles of California wines?" I asked.

"Lady," the employee chuckled, "you're in an Italian neighborhood. We sell no small bottles of wine."

I looked in Christopher's direction. He shrugged his shoulders before commenting, "Guess we're not from around here."

"Hey, that's my line," I teased.

❦

I sat alongside Christopher on hard plastic, molded seats, watching the cityscape whiz by. We rode the subway back to the airport where I hoped to retrieve my luggage and he planned on picking up a rental car. During yesterday's trip into Boston, which had been my first experience on a subway, the railed system had proven too fast for me. During that ride, I decided to rely upon Christopher to determine which side of the tracks to be on to wait for the trains and which stops to get off. Knowing that was one skill I would never need at home, I saw no good reason to acquire it.

Later, as we maneuvered through a paved maze of interstates, leaving town reminded me of steering amid electric bumper cars at the fair, except the stakes were higher. No one here would merely laugh should we snag chrome or rear end them. I was, however, prepared for the worst in my handwashed undies. Outside the city proper, we left the efficient interstate system for the narrower blue highways. Skirting the coastline, it was my assignment to select whichever state route was closest to the ocean.

I soon discovered how quickly minor personality quirks could be revealed when two people are confined in a small, unfamiliar car. Before leaving California, he had done extensive research and was well provisioned for explorations. As a result, I had two unfolded road maps and three opened tour books spread across my lap. Early on in the day, I learned that he liked to know where we were on the highway in relation to the little lines on the maps. He also wanted me to read aloud about the area we were currently passing through so we could confer whether to stop for closer inspection. Unfortunately, since he did not always remember from which book he wanted me to read, I had to do some fancy juggling to find the correct tour book, while simultaneously pointing to our exact location on a map at that precise moment.

When we reached Marblehead around mid-day, Christopher interrupted our motoring. Since his pre-trip investigation had determined this to be The Town to explore on foot and to sample indigenous food, we left our parked car. Heavy with the fresh aroma of fishy saltiness from the adjacent clear water, a gentle breeze carried strong hints of the town's seafaring origins. Having been designed for carts and carriages and pedestrian use, the secondary streets in this old village splintered off its narrow main drag at interestingly odd angles. The prim, sensible homes we walked beside were well tended.

From inside a darkly weathered, plank building by the harbor came the tempting call of cooking seafood that lured us to lunch. Once inside, Christopher chose to sit at a makeshift counter added under windows overlooking bobbing boats. We ate mussels and drank white wine while tethered sailboats lolled about the small harbor under a cloudless, robin's egg blue, bright spring sky.

Before we resumed our peaceful, turtle-slow journey northward,

Christopher marched us into the town hall where a famous Revolutionary War painting hung. Having seen that picture in schoolbooks many times, I had never imagined the inspiring colonial figures would be impressively life-sized.

Farther away from cosmopolitan Boston, intersections became poorly marked. Only with both of us reckoning hard, did we keep the car headed in the right direction.

As the day progressed, I grew annoyed that I was unable both to sightsee and find information that he requested as quickly as he wanted it. Soon after our lunch stop, I decided I would prefer to drive and enjoy the sights, thus affording him the pleasure of poring through the extensive arsenal of maps and books with which I had been armed.

After the latest demand for coordinates, I slammed *Fodor's* shut while I curtly suggested, "Honey, suppose I drive for a while!"

Christopher was silent a moment before responding in a contrite tone, "Am I asking for too much too quick?"

"Oh, no, not at all," I purposely lied, allowing nothing to mask the exasperation in my reply.

He attempted to make amends. "Rachael," he courteously began, "I appreciate the great job you're doing with the books and maps. I enjoy seeing where I am on the map when I drive and hearing about the places I'm driving through." Christopher further explained, "When I take the kids on trips, they get carsick and can't read the books or maps for me."

I bet they wised up to you years ago and now just pretend to get carsick.

I took a deep breath. "Honey, I'd still like to do some of the drivin'. I am a good driver, you know."

"No, you can't. I'm the only driver listed on the rental form."

Although I was fast losing any hopes of getting out of the shotgun seat, I defended my proposal by suggesting, "They'll never know."

He countered. "What if there's a wreck?"

Mentally chalking up a point for his side, I recorded my loss.

Despite our mastery of the maps, a poorly marked intersection did us in. After managing to get off the main road, we found ourselves circling the beach side of an island. We made the same mistake twice more. On our fourth arrival at the intersection from hell and since, on this lap, a man stood near the passenger side of the car, I was granted permission to ask for directions.

"When all else fails," I grumbled as I rolled down my window before calling out politely, "Do y'all know the way to York?"

"Eh?" the man responded.

I asked louder. "Do y'all know the way to York?"

"Eh?" he answered loudly.

Thinking the bystander must be really hard of hearing, I asked again louder still. "Do y'all know the way to York?"

"Eh?"

Turning my head, I glared at Christopher. I understood that I talked differently from New Englanders, but this current exchange was past bordering on the ridiculous and, after three tours of that boring island, I had lost my pleasing personality. Through clenched teeth, I demanded, "Christopher, you ask him."

Leaning over my body, he called through the window, "Which road to York?"

That damn Yankee then pointed out the correct road and off we drove in the appropriate direction.

"Not only do people up here talk funny," I huffed, "they hear funny, too."

He patted my knee through two maps and three tour books. "Rachael," he pointed out, "you have the accent here." A moment later, he added, "At least you didn't use 'you-ens.'"

We spent most of the day traveling to York Beach where Christopher had planned to stay the night. Each township we encountered was a picture postcard for coastal New England. Keeping true to his word, he had sailed by each one of the numerous antique shops we passed. We had taken the time, however, to walk New England-quaint fishing villages dating from colonial times, to rub the bronze statue of the Gloucester fisherman for good luck and to wander alone through an abandoned oceanfront rock quarry first mined prior to the Revolutionary years.

Having no reservations for the coming night's lodging, Christopher wanted to select a motel before finding a restaurant for supper. His amassed guidebooks were of no help since their recommended inns were still closed for the season. The resort appeared more deserted than Cherokee had been that May night when I drove Carl and Christopher into North Carolina.

Remaining in the car while Christopher checked into the only motel with a lit vacancy sign, I glanced at my surroundings, noting this flat Maine beach lacked sand dunes and was much different from the Carolina beaches I knew. Here the main highway separated the sand from a single long row of motels. The generic building looming before me would be considered second-row accommodation at North Myrtle Beach, seeing as how it stood across the road from the beach proper. In Carolina, the desirable first-row designation was given only to those establishments situated on the ocean side of the pavement.

While following Christopher to the second tier of rooms on the building's backside, I considered asking if he had noticed whether the manager on duty was named Norman Bates. Upon entering our assigned room, we were greeted with a stench as stale and moldy as any high school gym's locker room.

I walked into the bath. The facilities there were less than perfect and, since the towels were rather thin, I knew my Daddy would have never considered staying. These accommodations were a disappointment and a huge letdown after the Copley, but I would remain here if he wanted.

When I returned from the bath, I found Christopher facing the drawn curtains with his back toward me. Unsure how to comment, I waited for him to break the silence.

He turned to face me. "This is awful," he finally said.

I nodded my agreement. "I've stayed in places at the beach that smelled this bad when I was in college." I wrinkled my nose before adding, "That was a long time ago, and I'm not in school anymore."

With that said, we left the room, both relieved neither wanted to remain the night.

Wondering if we would find another motel open before darkness arrived, we drove the next miles in silence as night crept in from the east. After the narrow roadbed for U.S. 1 rose up to negotiate a mound of scattered, lichen-covered boulders and eased around a curve, we came upon Perkins Cove at Ogunquit. After agreeing, without hesitation, that this was our kind of place, Christopher stopped the car to inquire about lodging.

The area looked just too wonderful to me. The orderly setting had been tastefully designed to entice tourists. A white pedestrian drawbridge linked the manicured grounds surrounding a low motel, painted white, to a colorful, tight cluster of quaintly crafted, new shops and indigenous restaurants across the water. Bobbing, pristine white sailboats were moored to precisely aligned slips. To the left of the motel, a creek emptied with the flourish of a stout waterfall into the calm waters of the serene cove. Beyond the small knot of buildings in the near background, a black paved walkway followed the rocky Atlantic coastline, linking the designer village to some destination we had yet to discover.

The drive from Boston had been under sun-drenched skies and approaching spring's early fragrances carried by the constant breeze had teased through our hair whenever we explored outside the car. I had left dogwoods blooming in Knoxville, but here in Maine leaf buds remained only tightly held promises at twig tips. When we crossed the drawbridge on our way to supper, the strong wind coming across the Atlantic nipped at our heels, hinting of an imminent change.

While waiting inside the restaurant's entry, we stood beside huge holding tanks containing our coming meal. Feeling numerous pairs of little, beady eyes staring at me, I almost lost my appetite. Although I had seldom turned down an opportunity to enjoy a good lobster, seeing my soon-to-be supper this fresh was chillingly uncomfortable. When the hostess directed us over to the tanks to select the individuals we wanted to eat, I almost asked if I could just have an order of fries and slaw instead. Unable to condemn a living creature to be boiled alive, I stared horrified at my soon-to-be-supper while she explained that our selections would be prepared and the plates properly dressed before our waitress carried them out to us. Graciously leaving my escort the honor of choosing two victims, I opted to select a vacant table in a distant corner of the crowded dining area.

Having wrung my fair share of chicken's necks in the past, I was not against the slaughter of animals for food, yet I never made the life-or-death decision. My grandmothers had always judged which past-laying hen was to be the main course for the family's next meal. And the remembered, quick snap had always seemed much kinder than watching the agonizingly slow, futile struggle of a desperate lobster in a pot of boiling liquid. Of course, now, after the prepared crustacean was lying motionless on a plate with drawn butter and a serving of slaw, I never experienced any such qualms eating the poor, tasty, little dear.

With the surrounding din making lengthy conversation difficult, I concentrated on getting the succulent meat out of the shell and into my belly. I was quiet, not simply due to the noise inside the restaurant, but because I knew this was our penultimate supper. Tomorrow night was the appointed time to tell my lover good-bye and farewell forever.

After we had cleaned our plates, Christopher studied guidebooks for the coming day while I observed people. Older couples with graying hair occupied several tables nearby. I watched their ease of being together that I quickly assumed had been forged over many years. As they wordlessly dined, I saw one woman touch the corner of her mouth, indicating to her companion to wipe a swatch of cocktail sauce off his. With their meal completed, another couple read separate sections of the newspaper while sipping coffee. Christopher and I would never have that future.

Other tables within the busy restaurant contained young couples coping with small children. I watched mothers and fathers cut meat, enabling children to feed themselves with spoons awkwardly grasped by immature hands. Some mothers held glasses of milk to mouths of chubby-cheeked toddlers. One good daddy ate while cradling a sleeping infant against his strong chest. And we would never share that past.

With the anticipation of what I planned to tell him tomorrow saddening me and with the remembrance of the special day we had just shared piercing my heart, I envied every soul in that restaurant for their seemingly normal lives. Most importantly, I had drunk too much wine.

I stared at the table directly across from me as a young mother gave her baby a bottle and her husband fed their toddler. Without forewarning, I turned to Christopher, bluntly confiding, "I've always been too scared to have a baby. Never did trust either of my two husbands enough to want to have their children. I was afraid they would leave me. So, I left them instead."

Putting his book aside, he waited for me to continue.

Silently, I recalled how my first husband, King Richard the First as my Daddy had christened him after we divorced, had treated me. During those horrid few months of marital un-bliss, I had always puzzled how I had been able to get through college if I were the Dumb Dora Richard often told me I was. Of course, I had been stupid enough to marry him.

Next there had been Mackey with his coal-black hair and cold, green eyes. I had simply been too foolish about that second husband of mine. Later, before we divorced, I had learned several men and most women Mackey had met throughout our marriage had found him irresistible, too.

As if my dinner companion had been privy to my actual thoughts, I suddenly remarked, "I could have trusted you." Tears blurred my vision and trickled down my cheeks. "Just look at that older couple over there. That will never be us."

He quickly interrupted, "Let's just enjoy the time we have together."

Not wanting to open that door any farther, we began plotting the next day's journey.

⁕

We awoke to discover that winter had reclaimed Maine. The morning was cold and gray, all fogged in and drizzly. We bundled up in extra sweatshirts under our jackets and hoped those additional layers would be sufficiently warm. After deciding over breakfast that we could not find a more delightful place to stay, Christopher arranged that we would spend our final night at the Cove, after which we drove off for L.L. Bean.

The farther north we wound, the rockier the coast became. We tarried at the Cape Elizabeth lighthouse long enough to walk in the engulfing damp, hardly seeing the ocean for the thick fog. As morning progressed, the sun gradually burned through the low clouds, unveiling still more picturesque New England villages and rugged farmlands. When we reached the mother store for L.L., we separated to purchase souvenirs to carry home to our families. While lunching later on authentic New England clam chowder, we laughed upon exchanging the same colorful T-shirts we each had selected for the other as a remembrance of our trip.

⁕

Late that afternoon, we followed the Marginal Way toward Ogunquit. The wind blowing across the angry, gray Atlantic was bitingly cold as it whipped spray off the barren rocks and into the air above. We sensed a storm brewing. Not long into our walk, I placed a torn piece of tissue in my right ear because that side of my face had already begun to ache from the bombardment of the icy flecks of foam, and I feared an unwanted earache might soon follow.

The pavement shadowed the shoreline, weaving in and out of clumps of twisted greenery and broken boulders. We slowed in the shelter of wind-sculpted bushes. When we were hidden from sight, Christopher pulled me into his arms. He kissed my forehead. Stepping back to unbutton my jacket, he put his cold right hand under my shirts, reaching for my breast.

With only the wind and us present, I decided this would be the appropriate time and place for my well-rehearsed speech, giving up my forbidden love. Fearing that if I waited until after dinner, I would have had too much wine and not enough courage to give it.

After lifting my head to be able to read his eyes, I began tentatively, "Christopher, I can't . . . I won't see you after this weekend."

Upon speaking the first line, I started hyperventilating and hiccuping. In addition, I shuddered hard from head to toe, sporadically shaking like a wet dog drying its coat. Two rivers of tears immediately began flowing down my face. Those clustered fever blisters, which had already turned my lip almost inside out, burned when my salty tears found them. I felt the spray-dampened Kleenex sticking out of my right ear flutter in the wind. Ocean spray spotted my glasses, blurring my vision.

Pitifully, I struggled to pull up the rest of my well-practiced words. Stuttering, I was finally able to continue, "I . . . I . . . I want to be able to say to you, 'Come . . . come grow old with me, the best is yet to be.' I . . . I want you to say you will, but you can't. You . . . you won't. Bein' with you, knowin' you, has been the best thing that has ever happened to me. You will always be a part of my life. I will never, never forget you, but our bein' together can't go on. I'm . . . I'm stealin' time away from your children."

When my nose began to drip, I sadly wondered what other body part would be the next to betray me.

Listening intently, Christopher observed my face while I spoke. When I stopped talking, he pulled my head to his chest. Silently, he held me closely until my tremors and hiccups ceased.

When I could again breathe normally, I said into his jacket, my voice muffled by the fabric, "I haven't had a single fever blister since 1977, when I was workin' for the state with that horrible man." When I pulled my head back from his shoulder so my next words would be clearly heard, I stuttered once again, "I . . . I've . . . I've been wantin' to tell you how I felt, b-but didn't want to do it over the phone." I blurted out in anguish, "I . . . I ca-can't ever see you again!"

"Oh, Rachael," he crooned softly, reassuringly, "my Rachael."

He held me tightly against his warmth. While drawing comfort from the steady beating of his heart, I heard the wickedly cold wind sneaking through the branches overhead.

"Did it ever occur to you, my dear, that your body is trying to tell you, that despite everything, we're supposed to be together?" He leaned down to kiss the safe corner of my mouth. "You've become very important to me." He waited a moment before continuing. "I love my children, and I'm responsible for them. I pledged my word to care for my wife when I married her, and I will not abandon her. However," he paused, kissing my forehead before completing his sentence, "Rachael, I cannot imagine my world without you." Again, he waited before continuing, "My life in California is like cake. It's good and fulfilling, but you, my sweet Rachael, you're the icing on my cake."

I interrupted. "If we keep meetin' . . . how do you explain? . . . you can't go to confession because of me."

He shushed me. While dense boughs swayed above us in the intensifying bitter wind, we clung tightly to each other. I felt without him there to anchor me to the earth, the next strong blast of air would surely blow me away.

"If I don't leave you when I fly out tomorrow," I pleaded, my resolve weakening, "I'll get so deep into you, I won't be able to leave."

My throat tightened to such an extent that I was afraid I would not be able to draw in air past its knotted muscles. At that very moment, I realized for the first time the crux of my fear—being that vulnerable and that dependent on another person terrified me.

Cupping his hands on either side of my tear-streaked face, Christopher spoke slowly with deep conviction, "Believe me, I'll never keep you against your will. You're free to go whenever you need. I'll always be there for you. You've already given me such joy. I'm just a simple Italian man from a small town. I've never been with a woman, other than my wife, until I met you. I want us to be together as long as you want us to be together."

"I want forever," I begged.

"But, Rachael, I may not live forever," he answered solemnly.

Before I could respond, he nodded in the Cove's direction. I turned to see another couple heading toward us. We four spoke in passing before they strolled on.

The moment was lost. In silence, we resumed walking toward Ogunquit while the coming storm strengthened in its approach from far out over the Atlantic. The unresolved conflict that could not be solved without causing someone pain followed in our wake. The door, which should never have been opened back in Townsend, remained open.

We left Perkins Cove early Sunday morning to return to Boston. The same distance, which had taken the entire day Friday to cover while following the regional map's blue roads, took less than two hours to retrace by interstate. After returning the rental car and checking his luggage with the airline, we stowed my bag in a rental locker at the airport before catching the subway to downtown Boston where we planned to kill the hours before his 1:50 flight.

We strolled through the Commons and explored a nearby graveyard containing pre-Revolutionary markers before walking toward Christopher Columbus Square to view the wooden ships moored there. For lunch, we decided upon a restaurant that was celebrating twenty-five years in business. Waiting for the establishment to open, we located the nearest subway entrance and, while there, Christopher purchased tokens for our return to the airport, allotting our remaining money for food and drink.

Throughout the succulent meal of mussels and lobster and wine, we lovingly called up vignettes of our times together, each special scene flowing into the next as if we gazed into a crystal ball. Beginning at the beginning, our memories melted together:

"When I first saw you and Carl sitting close together at LeConte, I thought you both were nancy boys."

"Have you found a lava lamp for the cabin?"

"Can you believe that I've flown to meet you twice, and each time my luggage didn't get off the plane with me?"

"Remember christening the world's tallest tree?"

"How's about that liquor store not having any small bottles of wine?"

"Wasn't Perkins Cove perfect?" Christopher asked before taking a sip from his wine glass.

"Everything is perfect when we're together," I gently chided him. "Remember how great the weather was in California?"

He reached for my hand across the table. "I want you to know that as soon as your plane took off that Monday morning, clouds rolled in. It rained the rest of the time I was there."

Paraphrasing a 1970s song, I informed him, "Ain't no sunshine when I'm gone."

Continuing our litany of special memories, we shared a desperately lovely lunch as if neither of us wanted to notice the minutes slipping away. Reluctantly, Christopher checked his watch.

"Damn, Rachael, it's already one-twenty! I've thirty minutes to get to my plane," he pulled out his roll of money and started counting bills, "and we haven't even settled our bill."

Raising my hand, I got our waiter's attention. Thankfully, he came immediately. When I explained our need for urgency, the young man hurried away to total the tab, trotting back when he had finished.

As Christopher stood up from his chair, he glanced at the ticket before leaving another five on the table. We walked quickly through the restaurant, before galloping to the subway entrance as soon as we exited the doors. Tossing tokens into the slots, we flew down the steps to the tracks.

No trains were in sight, and we were in the middle of Boston.

"Maybe we should take a taxi," he muttered under his breath, but not talking to me. "Damn it!" he cursed. Dragging me after him as he took off running, he explained over his shoulder, "We're on the inbound side. We have to wait on the outbound side to get to the airport."

When we reached the opposite side of the tracks, there was still no hint of a train.

Impatiently, he calculated, "If I miss this connection to New York, I'll have to wait until Monday to fly out. There isn't another plane this afternoon."

Since my flight out of Boston was much later than his, I felt no pressure associated with my departure to Charlotte. When a train at last approached, we rushed to board. Even after we reached the airport stop, we still needed to catch a bus to get from the subway station to the terminal. I watched his anxiety increase by the minute.

We jumped off the train as soon as the doors opened. Before reaching the staircase, I glanced at my left wrist to see that my watch showed 1:40. Racing up the stairs to the street, my knees ached as I pushed my body to keep pace with Christopher. My lack of exercise and those additional pounds were exacting their price.

Upon reaching the outside to find a bus waiting, I knew God was good. After I caught up to Christopher, I heard him explaining to the bus driver, who sat alone in the vehicle reading the Sunday comics, about his 1:50 flight before asking the man to start the bus immediately.

"No," the portly driver answered calmly, "I've got a schedule to follow. My bus won't move before its time." The serene driver returned his attention to the funnies.

Realizing it was pointless to argue, Christopher literally gnashed his teeth. While thinking I must not care for my companion as much as I had previously thought, I was secretly glad it was his 1:50 flight and not mine. Unable to offer anything more than moral support, I sympathetically watched his jaws clench and unclench.

"Just take a seat. You'll make your plane," the unflappable driver confidently assured us.

Waiting for the bus to move, Christopher formulated an alternative plan to reach his gate. "Rachael, we'll hop off at the first transit stop, run across the parking lot and get to that last concourse quicker than if we wait for the driver to make all his stops."

As the vehicle lurched forward to follow its appointed route, the man behind the wheel cautioned, "No, sir, it'll be quicker to stay on my bus."

I looked at Christopher. "Honey, I bet he knows what he's talkin' about." I had done about all the running I could do today. I silently vowed to start exercising tomorrow.

"OK." Exasperated, Christopher reluctantly accepted the driver's and my suggestions, but sat the entire lumbering ride with his left leg furiously moving in time with some out-of-control metronome that only he could hear.

We arrived at the final stop at 1:48. Christopher leaped through the opening doorway as soon as space was available, his feet hitting the pavement at top speed. Due to my bad knees, I entered the terminal at a much slower pace.

I watched him speeding up the moving escalator, taking two of the moving steps with each stride. From across the gate area for his flight, I saw him stop at the attendant who appeared to be checking boarding passes against the passenger list. I was still far behind when he turned back to wave before exiting the terminal. I arrived at the windows in time to observe him walking up the rear service steps to board the waiting plane.

Suddenly he was gone.

God, I hate good-byes!

After the New York-bound plane taxied away, I returned to the main hallway to retrieve my suitcase and check in with my airline. I still had two hours to while away before my flight.

That was no good-bye, my twin snapped, *that was an escape!*

Ignoring her tart observation, I settled into a waiting seat in the spacious Boston terminal, reaching into my over-sized purse for the counted cross-stitch of Charleston's Rainbow Row with which I had been torturing my idle hours for months.

Not finished with the subject, she prodded, *Your I'm-Leaving-You speech did little to convince him or me of your noble intentions.*

Well, at least I spoke my piece, I informed her. He knows where I stand, and I know where he stands. Maybe he is more Continental than American, and maybe he can justify a mistress while remaining a family man. I think, as a good Catholic, he won't be able to go to confession as long as our relationship continues. I can accept that he feels that a good Catholic does not divorce. I can understand his children's need for him during their teenage years. Damn, I know how I would have felt if Daddy had left Mom when I was in junior high, but I need him, too. Perhaps his family and I could share. Christopher could live in California for six months and, then, in Tennessee for the next six months. Maybe we could activate a hetaeristic chapter in the United States.

That would make you his concubine. Margaret would argue that, legally, you would be better off if you three converted to Mormonism. Rachael, you are simply being ridiculous! This daydreaming won't get you what you want. You need to end this relationship and get on with your life. Nothing was resolved at Perkins Cove, you ninny! You were reared in the hellfire and damnation of the Southern Baptist Church of the 1950s so I know you were taught right from wrong.

But if we weren't supposed to be together, why did we meet? Why are we so damn perfect together? This is the first normal male-female relationship I've ever had.

No matter what you think, Rachael, this is not normal. You are correct, however, on one point, she added sarcastically, *it is damned.*

Ignoring her taunts, I concentrated on visually untangling the charting, hunting the location for my next stitches, effectively pushing the other out of my consciousness. Upon hearing the initial boarding call for my flight to Charlotte blare across the concourse waiting area, I stabbed the needle into the fabric before stuffing the work back into my satchel-sized purse. I hated arguing with myself because no one ever won and no one ever lost, it was simply an exercise in futility.

Eight

The Friday following my Boston trip was the date for my spring reservation at LeConte. Up the trail Friday, I explained to Mom how I felt I could trust Christopher because I had never caught him in a lie. I told her I liked myself better when I was with him although I was not able to unscramble why. Most importantly, I wanted my mother to know that I had tried to give the man up.

Down the trail Saturday, after listening to a comedic rendition of my failed, farewell address, Mom tactfully suggested I drive to my cabin the following weekend after the restaurant was closed. She advised me to get where I would not be disturbed and make a list. She said she trusted me to make the right decision.

The longer I considered what she said, the more I thought her advice sounded similar to that the priest gave on Christopher's retreat.

※

Listing was her approach to most quandaries. Mom's method consisted of two columns side-by-side on one sheet of paper, detailing the pros and cons of any problem that resisted solving.

I had been making lists all afternoon. Crushing each one after I glanced over it, I had thrown the balled-up papers onto the floor. I did not like any of them.

Rolling onto my back, I contemplated the ceiling's excruciatingly white panels above my utilitarian, iron bedframe. Last week, Hugh Ed had painted the discolored tiles with Kilz. He had said yesterday at lunch there was a surprise waiting for me at the cabin. Well, he had certainly succeeded in his attempt to shake me up. With the unaccustomed brightness making the rooms lighter and out of sorts with the rest of my retreat's lived-in, shabby interior, I knew I would need time adjusting to the change.

The playful, four-legged girls enthusiastically batted my discarded papers across the floor in the other rooms. I heard one cat slam into a wall in the hall. Soon afterwards, Sybyl jumped onto the bed and flopped her body near mine. Her heavy panting and heaving sides betrayed her recent physical activity.

Carrying a crushed ball of blue-lined notebook paper in her mouth, Beatrice shortly joined us on the bed. She dropped her toy by my hand before collapsing with a grunt beside her sister.

After uncrumpling the paper and ironing the sheet smooth with my hands, I stared at the two columns. The pro side held line after line of nebulous reasons to stay in the relationship such as: Makes me laugh, Makes me feel safe, Great sex. The con side held just two: Only separated and Never will leave family.

If I followed Mom's method, I was to base my final decision on the side with the longer list. I looked in the direction of Beatrice's masked face before asking, "In this situation, shouldn't the cons outnumber the pros?"

Meowing enigmatically, Beatrice left her sister's side. After butting her head against mine, she purred an inscrutable response. Patting her squared head, I told my furry companion, "Precious, you're no help, but I love you anyway."

❦

I called California the following afternoon. Despite quitting caffeine and cigarettes cold turkey years ago, I needed to taper off gradually from being with that man.

"Wait," he said upon learning I was on the line, "until I close the door."

When he returned to the phone, I justified my call by saying, "I needed to hear your sweet voice just one more time. Did you make the flight back safely?" Any excuse for talking with him. Besides, I considered my greater number of pros far outweighed those two cons.

"Yes, it was fine." Christopher became distracted. "Damn it," he cursed before muttering into the phone, "there's someone at my door." Louder he said, "Come in."

I overheard a female voice asking questions in the background.

"I must hang up," he said abruptly.

"Bye," I responded as a click, signaling the connection had been broken, was followed by a deafening silence. Our conversation had ended before my need to hear his voice had been sated.

Now, that was as comforting as a hard slap in the face.

⁂

The next months, we exchanged unsigned cards with only postal marks betraying their cities of origin. I decided against phoning again because I could not face the possibility of another curt dismissal like the one occurring during our last, abruptly terminated conversation. Resisting written correspondence, I did not want traceable evidence of my sentiments to come back to haunt him or me. In any case, I was not certain that writing could express my gut feelings for that man. If I had never easily found the words to speak that adequately described my emotions, how would I ever find enough paper to hold my tangled ramblings?

The reality was I hoped if I did not initiate the contact, he might not call in regards to another meeting. I knew if he never asked again, I would never be tempted to say yes.

Monumental decisions, such as this one, were always easier when someone, other than me, made them. Even so, I found myself in March changing the days the restaurant was open to Monday through Friday. Five working days netted nearly the same amount of money as six. Saturdays, with the area's businesses closed, were no longer worth the added effort and overhead.

In some hidden cranny of my mind, I wanted to have two-day weekends set in place because with that scheduling, it would be simpler to get away to meet Christopher, just in case he should ever invite me to travel with him again. What was that old saying about Hope springs eternal?

Later that April, after almost twelve months since seeing him board the plane in Boston, I accepted that my flawed speech recited along the Marginal Way had actually worked and that I would really never see him again. I was ambivalent, somewhat happy that decision had been made for me and somewhat saddened that our relationship was finished.

⁂

Upon reaching the narrow black top to Sunshine, I ran all the windows down for the remainder of the drive. The low, hovering, gray clouds hinted of coming rain and hid the crests of the approaching mountains. The warm air and spring aromas were intoxicating this Friday afternoon, and my car's interior was peaceful without my raucous Siamese backseat drivers.

When I last checked on their whereabouts, the girls were asleep on their favorite chair by the fireplace with plenty of spring water and dry food in their matching pink porcelain bowls to keep them satisfied until my return Saturday evening. Their inquisitive damp noses and insistent black paws had been too much help during my previous forays into the junk room. To make any real progress, I really needed to tackle that mess without their questionable assistance.

After arriving at the cabin and before doing anything else, I splashed a little vodka into a tall glass of cranberry juice. As I plaited my hair into two braids, I smiled, remembering how Grandmother Taite had done my hair when I stayed with her as a child. Attempting to tame my flighty tresses, she would pull the strands tightly as her gnarled hands fashioned my unruly locks into trim, neat ropes, never paying any attention to my complaints that she would permanently slant my eyes with her precise braiding. Finally, Grandmother would pin my taut plaits into a narrow, figure-eight bun that matched the one above the nape of her neck.

Her coif would be as neat at night when she took down her braids as it had been in the morning when she had twisted in that last hairpin. My hair, on the other hand, would have broken free before lunch. So, since my hair refused to be confined in a symmetrical bun like hers, I never tried mastering that technique.

Now that I was grown, the bun I managed was a single knot twisted over that flat spot at the top back of my skull. My hairdo always started out neat enough in the mornings, but short curls would soon softly halo my face and kiss curls would grace the nape of my neck. When I was not going to be seen in public, I often allowed long braids to dangle free, squaw-like behind my ears and over my breasts. That style would do for this evening's chores.

I retrieved my favorite T-shirt from the top drawer of the dresser. As my thoughts returned to that night in Nashville, I buried my face into the softness of its faded green fabric and breathed deeply, hoping to inhale his smell, but any trace of the man was long gone. I carefully folded and replaced the shirt, regretting not safekeeping his scent in an airtight container instead of wearing the T-shirt whenever I wanted to feel close to him. I quickly downed the tart cranberry drink before mixing a second, using a heavier splash of liquor.

Upon opening the cabin's backdoor, I saw a soft, misty rain in which the water dripping off the roof and nearby trees made more sound than the barely-there drizzle itself. Ignoring the call of the porch swing, I turned to face my challenge.

Staring at the small inroads made during my previous attempts at sorting through the untidy second bedroom, I took a deep drink from my tumbler. I found myself wondering if the old man had thought he would live long enough to catalog his treasures or had he, perversely, planned on dying ahead of his heirs, leaving them this mess to sort through.

The phone rang.

"Saved by the bell," I muttered, reaching for the receiver. "Hey," I said into the phone, relieved to have been given a concrete excuse to put off the inevitable.

"I have to fly to Atlanta. Can you come?"

I exclaimed, "That's wonderful!" Wasting no time weighing pros and cons, I offered without hesitation, "I'll drive my car down."

"I've heard the South has good barbeque. Thought we might try some while I'm there."

"Oh, Christopher, there are so many regional recipes. Each area thinks its method is the best." Beginning a culinary excursion, I listed, "There's North Carolina style which is much different to South Carolina's Low Country version. In East Tennessee, some of us do ours with molasses and hard liquor. Memphis does their ribs dry-rubbed with sauce on the side for dipping. There's vinegar-based or there's ketchup-based. Pick a style. Any style. How many days do you have? How much drivin' do you want to do?"

He answered cryptically, "Not that many. Not that much."

❦

With T-DOT's never ending improvements to the interstate between Knoxville and Chattanooga preventing an unimpeded flow of vehicles, I followed U.S. 411, thinking I could make better time using that old route. Outside Maryville, the countryside soon became rolling farmland, and the traffic quickly thinned out. Since this highway was as familiar as a dear friend, my mind felt free to wander as I aimed my car southward, my right foot firmly pressed against the gas pedal and my bent left leg propped against the dash.

I recalled one wild trip Margaret and I had made when returning from a midweek party in Atlanta. We were living in the dorm and had to make curfew or face being grounded for Homecoming the following weekend. We burned up the old blacktop that night, making the journey from downtown Atlanta to inside the dorm's front door in less than three hours. And in a four-cylinder Ford Falcon at that.

I chuckled aloud. That had to be a land speed record of some type.

Almost four full days with Christopher, I thought. Be still my beating heart. That will be about as long as our last two trips combined.

I next ran over in my mind the coverage I had left back in Knoxville: Mom, bless her, will help Liz and Margaret with the customers during the lunch rush these next two days. Liz and Margaret can manage the preps just fine without me. And Liz will drop by to feed the girls while I'm gone. They always eat well for her. Oh, hey, that's where I get my bacon. Damn good stuff! Almost as good as Granddaddy's.

I had driven past the building that housed a small butcher shop outside Madisonville. The thoughts of that wonderful bacon reminded me of the additional ten pounds I had gained since Boston.

I will diet for certain, I vowed, come Monday. I'll start exercising, too. Wonder what type of flowers Christopher will have for me this evening? At least, I know this time my luggage will arrive with me. Oh, fuck.

Oh, fuck.

Blue lights flashed by me in the oncoming lane. I glanced at the gauges behind the steering wheel.

Double damn! Those lights are for me.

I slowed down and eased my car off the pavement. While waiting for the trooper to come back around for me, I hunted my license and auto registration. I hated being this old. Twenty years ago I never got fines. Just warnings. Liz always complained it was because I had big boobs that I never got ticketed.

After a girl gets past forty-five, the dating pool dries up, and it starts raining speeding tickets. There's just no justice in this old world.

I touched the button lowering the driver's window when the officer appeared beside my car.

"M'am, do you know how fast you were drivin'?" he asked politely. "I'll need to see—"

"No, officer, not really." Equally polite in return, I handed my documents through the downed glass before he completed his scripted request.

"I'll be back," he said.

In my side-view mirror, I watched his diminishing figure stroll to his vehicle.

So much for your idea about making better time on the old road. Traffic jams around Chattanooga wouldn't have cost this much in wasted minutes.

Watching cars and tractor-trailers I had passed miles ago now passing me by, I took a deep breath and drummed my fingers against the steering wheel, knowing I would have to get around them all over again. Double, double damn!

The officer returned. "Knoxville, eh? I was up there a few weeks ago visitin' my mother. Nice town."

"Yes, it is."

"So pretty with all the dogwoods bloomin'. I took her out on a couple of trails."

"That was nice of you." *Sweet Jesus, where is this line of conversation going?*

The trooper continued filling out paperwork. "Say, M'am, you wouldn't happen to be the same woman who has that restaurant in Knoxville, would you?"

"Yes, I am."

"I thought I saw this car when I was eatin' there last week with Momma."

I nodded. That was the thing I most dislike about driving a car with vanity tags because in one glance, people know who you are and where you are.

"Most women don't spell their name the way you do." The officer continued, "That hummin'bird cake of yours is mighty fine."

I smiled. "Glad you liked that cake. It's one of my favorites, too."

Noise crackled across his car's radio, and he glanced briefly in its direction. "My momma's awfully partial to your caramel cake. Says it tastes like her granny's." He removed the paper from his clipboard. "Where you off to this evenin'?"

"Atlanta," I answered.

"Well, try and stay a little closer to the speed limit," the officer suggested as he handed the paperwork to me. "Troopers down in Georgia might not have tasted your hummin'bird cake." He added, "I'm givin' you a warnin' this time."

Because no sane traveler driving through Georgia wants to be caught on Atlanta's puzzle of an interstate system during peak traffic hours, I arrived in that fair city at early dusk. An out-of-state driver might inch through those motorized parking lots once, but never on purpose a second time. It was just as well that Tennessee State patrolman stopped me when he did. Although I had meant to leave home late enough to miss Atlanta's rush hour, I had been making too good of a time before being pulled over north of Tennga.

The hotel I sought was located off Peachtree, near the heart of the city. Following Christopher's suggestion, I left my car in a paved lot across the street. Strolling through its doors with my roll-along luggage rumbling behind, I felt less like a woman of questionable virtue than I had upon entering the Copley. After I located the lobby's house phone, I asked to be connected to his room.

"Come to the twelfth floor," he instructed. "I'll meet you at the elevator."

On the ride up, I anticipated the variety of flowers he would offer when I stepped off the elevator. After three single roses in Nashville, a bouquet of roses and baby's breath in Arcata and one carnation in Boston, I decided a woman could get right spoiled, real easily, by that man.

When the elevator doors glided open, Christopher immediately greeted me with a huge hug and a quick kiss, but no flowers. As we walked the hall, I considered one possible reason behind his floral oversight: We had met over two years ago and, by now, the honeymoon was over. Nevertheless, I was more than slightly disappointed, having become conditioned to receiving flowers from him.

With his arm about my waist, he ushered me toward his room. "Rachael, it's so good to see you! How was your trip? Let me have your luggage. Here's my room. Close your eyes until I tell you to open them."

His rapid deluge of sentences never gave me the chance to respond except for a single "OK" when we reached his room's door.

"Are your eyes shut?" He waited with his hand on the doorknob.

"Now they are."

I heard the door open and allowed him to lead me into the room. We walked about ten strides before he stopped.

"Rachael, you can open them now."

I opened my eyes to discover the ceiling covered with helium-filled balloons. A multitude of colorful balloons, each with brightly-hued, curled ribbons dangling from their knotted ends, bobbed in the air currents which had been created by the recent opening and closing of the door. On a far circular table, I noticed a small bottle of champagne breathing in a true, metallic wine bucket, not in the usual generic, plastic, hotel ice holder. A compact, clear plastic box sat nearby.

"And I have a special treat for later," he informed me.

Christopher poured champagne into stemmed, plastic beverage cups. After he handed one to me, we touched their rims. "To us," he said.

"To us," I toasted back.

Although the plastic glasses made no proper toasting sound, fanciful balloons and chilled champagne substituted nicely for fresh flowers.

Not sporting fever blisters made loving less problematic than it had been in New England. Although I felt a raw hunger for him, I relished the familiarity and the ease of being together that had not been present during our previous couplings. Despite a year's separation, our first coming together was more time consuming than it had been in Arcata. Executing movements that were excitingly similar, yet tantalizingly different, our bodies lingered in erotic positions, remembering what went where and when and for how long.

His body felt right under my hands. His skin smelled the way a man's skin was supposed to smell. His hands knew the proper pressures to apply. His mouth tasted sweet, and I simply could not get enough of his sweetness. Whenever my body was ready for a different position, his was ready, too. For the longest time, we kept our eyes open while we shared bodies, not wanting to miss seeing the feelings and emotions that played across each other's faces. Later, when the time came that all I wanted was the sensation of his touch, I shut my eyes, the better to concentrate freely on the reception of the stimuli coming from inside and outside my body.

Whoever said a person could not go home again had never made love with Christopher Saracini.

Afterwards, as I lay sprawled across the bed, my body felt like one of my faded linen calendar towels from Williamsburg looked after I had dried the dishes. Cast aside, limp and damp.

"Why do you always call out my name when you climax?" I asked when I at last had regained the ability to speak.

Christopher turned so I would be certain to glimpse his smile. "Because you're mine," he answered smugly. Groaning with the effort necessary to sit up on the edge of the bed, he rose to walk toward the table.

"I'm yours?" I questioned with my voice rising, pretending to get on my high horse. Teasingly, I added, "And just when did I become yours?"

He returned to my side of the bed before opening the small box. "Here's your surprise."

With effort, I raised myself on one elbow to peer inside. I found one decadently fanciful dessert.

Describing the confection as I looked at it, he began, "A little cup made from hard, just like I used to be, chocolate filled with chocolate mousse, topped with real whipped cream and one cherry." He generously offered, "You can have the cherry." He picked up a brown spoon that was also inside the box. "We eat the whole thing with this little spoon fashioned from hard, just like I used to be, chocolate."

"That'll do," I said. Returning to my last question, I asked, "And when, pray tell, did I become yours?"

Christopher scooped up some of the mousse and whipped cream before feeding me the first bite. He replied, "You've always been mine." His regal tone was bathed in disbelief that I was not aware of his ownership.

The rich, smooth chocolate eased down my throat, replacing his salty, male taste that lingered there. Before popping the cherry into my mouth, I responded matter-of-factly, "Well, at least, you could have said it was because you love me."

Instead of offering a breezy comeback, he retrieved the bottle of champagne to pour the last of the liquid into our plastic glasses. "Finish your drink. Let's go to the Top of the Mart before it closes. It's beautiful up there at night. Have you ever seen Atlanta from there?"

"Not yet."

◦❈◦

Ignoring the stares from the two employees manning the front desk, we strolled outside, toting two balloons. Mine was pink. His was blue.

Standing beside my parked car, we watched the just-released balloons float up into the hot Georgia night. We stayed with our heads thrown back and our arms linked and our eyes following their erratic progress as the pinpoints of color became smaller and smaller.

"There go Christopher and Rachael's hearts floating away together," he said solemnly.

Oh, he loves us even if he won't say it.

The balloons vanished into the darkness.

"We better hurry," I suggested, "if we're goin' to catch those bird's-eye views before that restaurant closes."

Christopher looked around the street to get his bearings before turning to face what he considered to be the proper direction for us to walk. He took my hand, saying, "We go this way."

Introducing a new subject, I volunteered, "I got stopped by a cop on the way down here."

"How much will that fine cost?" he asked.

I chuckled. "Nothin'. Seems that the man likes my hummin'bird cake. I got a warnin'."

"You bribed him with a cake?"

"No, Honey," I explained slowly, "the trooper ate at Rachael's a few days back when he was up to see his mother. He recognized my vanity car tags."

He laughed. "Your fame is spreading. Soon we'll have to meet using assumed names."

❦

Although we reached the lofty revolving restaurant only minutes before closing time, the manager agreed to serve us while he and his two bartenders totaled the day's take. With the lights of Atlanta passing slowly beneath our chairs, Christopher and I sipped white wine accompanied by the sounds of dueling cash registers ringing in the background.

I leaned over my chair to idly ponder the sparkling city below us. "Wonder if this is how astronauts feel when they look down at the earth?"

Christopher pushed a stray wisp of hair behind my right ear. "How's your restaurant?"

I sighed deeply. "Oh, Honey, on the days when we're not busy, I worry that I've bitten off more than I can chew. Then, on those days when we could use ten extra tables, I wish I'd held out for a bigger location. I like the new place OK, but the whole thing seems just too big. I really liked it better when we were smaller. Oh, well." My voice trailed off. In a little bit, I inquired, "What about you? How's your company doin'?"

"Doing great except for that new woman I wished I'd never hired. She's good but a real pain in the ass. Business is booming. The need for our type of consulting work is really out there. We're looking into putting on training seminars in Europe."

"Did I ever tell you that my passport is current?" I slipped in.

He smiled. "I'll keep that in mind."

"How are the kids?" I wanted to get that inquiry out of the way.

"Victoria has become an honor student. Straight A's, that girl but my son." Christopher ran his hand over his face while he considered that child's progress. "My son, Vincent, is not like my daughter. He's smarter, but just damn immature. Vinnie makes the stupidest choices." He stopped at that, saying no more about his younger offspring.

"And your wife?" I really hated asking that particular question, but felt it impolite if I did not inquire about her, since I had brought up the subject of his family.

"Well. How's your mother?"

"She's doin' OK. Mom will work the front so that Liz and Margaret can be free to run the kitchen."

He tentatively approached his next question. "Is your restaurant doing well enough to support all of you ladies?"

Before I could answer, I spotted the manager walking toward us. I silently admired the fashionable cut of his suit. Businessmen in Knoxville were not quite up to speed with that style. Next, I noticed his big city attitude. He was a young, handsome man feeling his own importance, wearing a custom-fitted suit on his climb up the corporate ladder. I was old enough to be his mother and grateful I lived in a much smaller town.

"It's time," the young man said firmly yet politely.

During our return to the hotel, I explained my friends to Christopher. "Daddy provided handsomely for Mom. Liz and Margaret work at the restaurant to get their quarters in for the Medicare coverage they'll need later on. Liz's parents owned one of the first motor courts on Kingston Pike. When they got too old to keep the place up, Liz took over the family business. That was some years after the interstate came through town and changed the traffic patterns. The first thing Liz did was to tear the old cabins down and put up an office complex. She kept the land and leases out office space. And, I think, she's got some rental houses scattered about town."

"And Margaret?"

"How to explain Margaret? Now that's tougher." I thought for a few seconds before saying simply, "She gets mentioned in wills."

"Mentioned in wills?"

"Yeah, you see, Margaret likes older men. Much older men. And older men like her. They like doin' little things for her, like givin' her a car to drive, providin' her with credit cards. Just little things to make her life easier." I knew that abbreviated explanation did not do my dear friend any favors.

"Sounds like a kept woman to me."

I shook my head. "No, it's not like that at all." Going into greater detail, I described Margaret's imaginative master plan, "Those men ask her to marry them, and Margaret accepts. While they wait for the weddin', her fiancés want her to be comfortable. They're always rich, and their families or lawyers always insist on a pre-nupt. Legal stuff gets taken care of. She's in the will, so to speak, but the men die before she can become Mrs. Whoever."

"Looks like if they never marry, she wouldn't be entitled to anything." Christopher had not quite grasped the creative concept my beautiful friend had perfected in her youth.

I stopped walking. He stopped, too. To complete my sketchy explanation as to the source of my friend's financial independence, I added, "All I know is she gets honorably mentioned in the wills. The woman has amassed a tidy sum on two or three occasions that I know about. Margaret invests the money and does quite well for herself. So, you see, my friends work with me for their 'Social.' I'm the only poor soul who must work to earn a livin', not them."

He shook his head. "Has anyone ever told you, Rachael, that you have unusual friends?"

✣

"Doesn't it amaze you that we ever met at all?" I asked as we recovered from our third round of lovemaking that first evening in Atlanta.

"Yes." He slowly drew in a breath before exhaling deeply. "What really amazes me, however, is that I can't get enough of you. I'll soon be fifty, and you make me feel and act like I'm eighteen again." He rolled over on his side to face me. Taking my nearer nipple in his fingers, he squeezed it playfully as he said, "Rachael, my sweet Rachael, you do such exciting things to me."

"'It's a poor rule that don't work both ways' as my Granddaddy Taite would say," I replied. Idly, I ran my fingers through the hairs on his chest. "But to meet by chance in the middle of a wilderness . . . "

I had decided during the long drive to Atlanta that being with Christopher was similar to a progressive dinner. We met in different states, made love two or more times a day, visited interesting sites, ate fabulous meals and drank good wines. I had found it to be a wonderful arrangement, but it was not real life. We were never together long enough to get on each other's nerves. I did not have to iron his shirts and pick up his dirty socks. He did not have to remember to put down the toilet seat and carry out the trash.

"Christopher," I asked rhetorically, "can we go on meetin' like this forever?" I did not expect or even want a reality-based reply.

His tone became serious. "Rachael, I don't want you to sit around waiting for me to call. I want you to date. Have a good time with some other man."

Well, maybe, he doesn't love us after all.

His calloused suggestion was definitely not what I wanted to hear. My throat tightened while tears filled my eyes. "Yeah, sure. Like, I can find someone like you. Honey, don't you know that it took me forty-two years to find you? At that rate, I'll be eighty-four before I can find someone like you again."

In contrast with the harsh realities associated with his words, he gently nuzzled my ear and kissed my neck. "No, don't replace me," he explained selflessly between sweet kisses. "I want you to find someone who will make you happy when you're not with me. Someone you can leave whenever I can get away to meet you. I don't want you to be lonely when you're not with me."

"You're unbelievable." I laughed at his audacious suggestion. "Like that man could exist."

<hr />

We waited until well after morning rush hour traffic dwindled to a steady roar before leaving for Orangeburg, South Carolina, where I planned his initiation into the Southern barbeque experience at a family-owned establishment there. I remembered the place was open only Thursdays through Saturdays and had some of the best Low Country, chipped pork I had ever tasted. Unfortunately more than ten years had passed since I had been to that town and with coming from a direction other than Columbia, I worried I would be unable to find the building. Unable to phone ahead for directions due to my inability to recall its name, I really could not be certain the establishment was still in operation.

I did not voice my doubts because he thought I was perfect. Despite entering the city from the west, I directed him to the restaurant's location without the first false turn.

Maybe we are perfect, the other mused.

With the exterior of the restaurant as utilitarian and minimalistic as I remembered it being, I made no comment as Christopher took in our surroundings. The parking lot was sparsely graveled. The white, squat building was constructed from no nonsense, plain cinder blocks. Once inside, we walked across bare concrete floors to the rear where the fare was held in stainless steel, buffet-style servers. On our way to the food, we passed between two rows of long picnic tables that filled the big room. The wooden tables were placed perpendicularly to the unadorned white walls. Their red-and-white checked tablecloths were the owner's only attempts at decoration.

Inching down the crowded cafeteria line, I instructed rather than invited, "Have some hash over your rice."

Christopher was quiet, before slowly asking, "What's hash?"

"You don't really want to know," I answered truthfully, "but do have some so you can say you've tried it." I repeated the same explanation Margaret had given me when I had first inquired about hash some twenty-four years earlier.

I knew my companion entertained doubts about this restaurant and its lack of ambiance as soon as we separated thin paper plates on which to ladle our food selections, but I made no apology for that economy. His eyes widened in disbelief after he sat down in front of a loaf of white bread, still in its plastic wrapper. Astounded, he turned, without a word, to check every table to find each had a loaf awaiting the restaurant's patrons, and neither did I address that presentation. The sweet iced tea, however, just about put him over the edge and sent him out the door. I could not keep from laughing when I saw the man's puckered face after his first swallow.

"Not from around here, are you, son?" I commented sagely before going back to the ladies behind the counter to request unsweetened tea. Learning they had none, I returned with plain water.

"You'll have to make do with water. I'd forgotten we're so far south that it is sacrilegious to offer unsweetened iced tea." As I stepped over the bench to sit beside him, I explained Southern sweet tea. "When I was comin' up, all we drank was sweet tea. My grandmother, Big Momma, taught mother how to make it. My Mom taught me. You add two cups of sugar to one quart of hot, freshly brewed tea."

"Oh, God," he swore low in disbelief. It was his only comment.

Recovering from the exposure to sweet tea, he ate seconds of the Low Country barbeque with its tangy, mustard-based sauce. The local men at our table were friendly and shared conversation with us. All in all, I considered it a good experience, for Christopher said even the hash was tasty.

"Honey, do you want any dessert?" I asked after we tossed our used paper plates into the gray trash cans positioned near the front of the restaurant.

"No, thank you." He quickly explained, "I've had tea."

✻

Leaving Orangeburg, we took the interstate toward the Atlantic Ocean. Upon reaching Charleston, we caught the ferry to Fort Sumter.

Despite all my visits to the area, I had never made that pilgrimage. Since early childhood, all Southern battlefields had made me wary, because I have always been able to feel the mangled lives and tattered dreams left strewn about them. I have never been able to find honor in such wastefulness. Even though history records no battle-related deaths occurring on that tiny bit of Carolina soil, I had no desire to travel there, but my companion wanted to see the fortifications. So, in my Southern-bred attempt to be a good hostess, I bit my tongue, steeled myself against what I would sense and went along for the ride.

Being a first-generation American and being reared in California, Christopher knew little of Civil War lore. His information was gleaned mainly from school textbooks, which are written, as are all accounts, from the winners' bias. Because of how and where I was raised, I knew there was almost a state called East Tennessee, just as there is currently a state named West Virginia. He had not been taught that. Also, seeing as how I had been born in a state that had been the last to secede and the first to rejoin the Union, I knew the South was not a part of the whole, even today.

    I had read the schoolbooks, but I had also been exposed to oral histories. I came up around families who had fought through and then stayed after the War. All my Daddy's people wore blue; whereas all my Mom's kin wore gray. None of them owned slaves, and all had survived the hell of Reconstruction. The only skirmishes Christopher had heard discussed over dinner centered around Italy and her past wars.

    This was not my first attempt to share the mystique of the South with a foreigner. My first husband, who was born and reared in England, had a hard time understanding the monuments to the Confederacy as he traveled in the South. In Europe, Richard had patiently explained to me, you only find statues to the victors. Pointing out that the Daughters of the Confederacy had placed most of the statuary down here, I had to spell out a fact I thought blatantly obvious—the men of the Army of the South may have surrendered to Grant at Appomattox, but the women of the South had signed no such agreement.

    Under the hot, late afternoon sun, I walked uneasily over the island where the War Between the States began. As I followed Christopher, I passed solemnly through an unseen, but tangible to me, thin mist of heated emotions that those long-ago soldiers had left behind. Each breath I pulled in brought me air tainted by the stench of that pending war's costly doom. I watched my companion's growing fascination with the siege as he studied the exhibits and read the posted signs.

    Even Daddy had been like that. It had to be a man thing.

    We stayed Friday night on Folly Beach. Returning to the city the next morning, we followed a pamphlet's walking tour around the Battery. Under countless blue plastic tarps, work to repair the damage from Hurricane Hugo was in evidence, but Charleston was a well-schooled, Southern lady who had been knocked down before and knew how to pick herself up. In the Old Market, we passed vendors selling wreaths fashioned from popcorn plants and baskets woven from sweet grass. We peered through iron bars on ornamental side gates guarding private gardens. The faded colors of Rainbow Row were kind to our eyes. Briefly, we studied the indigenous architecture of the old houses crowding narrow Bay Street. We lunched on she-crab soup at my favorite restaurant on Queen Street.

Since I did not want my shoe fetish to interfere with my time with Christopher, I ignored that fabulous store on King Street where I went yearly to purchase footwear. Besides, my hands were already full with amending his perceptions of the South without diluting the validity of my arguments by exposing him to my strong weakness for shoes.

All morning, Christopher had walked with his customary quickness. Learning from our previous meetings, I made it a point to keep up because he seldom slowed down. Still, I was amazed how much territory we covered, which I attributed to his being well organized. And yet I was aware that time was passing by much too fast. I found myself wishing the cosmic clock's hands had to move through chilled molasses while we were together. Maybe then, perhaps, I could have enough time with him.

By mid-afternoon, we had checked off each line of his entire Charleston to-see list. During our drive toward Savannah, I suggested a side trip to Beaufort where I could show him my most favorite Carolina site. I had been a little surprised that section of the Low Country had failed to make his original list of required sights to view in the Palmetto State.

When we arrived at the ancient church grounds, I parked my car under the shade of centuries-old trees. While we gazed into the sunlit clearing where vestiges of the old structure remained, I retold some of the romantic history I loved about the place.

"I drove here for the first time back in 1977, when the wisteria was in bloom. That's when Margaret showed it to me. That day, those blossoms hung in purple swags on the trees surroundin' the church's ruins. As you can see, only the outer shell of brick stands. The plaster that once covered the four brick columns of the front portico fell away long ago. The congregation built the original church when South Carolina was just a young colony, only to have the British torch it durin' the Revolutionary War. The faithful rebuilt the church on the same foundations, only to have the Yankees burn it down durin' the War of Northern Aggression. The elders of the church probably decided that God was tryin' to tell them somethin', and so they built a third time on a site closer to town. That buildin', I believe, has yet to be touched by fire. But this is the South and old habits are hard to break, so the second Sunday followin' Easter each year the congregation returns to hold services here."

When I finished speaking, we exited the car. Waiting until after

Christopher read the historical marker that confirmed my verifiable statements, I added a piece of additional lore. "Someone told Margaret that the very first church was wooden. It was burned durin' an Indian uprisin'. Which makes me think, perhaps, Native Americans could have held tribal observances here and wanted to take back their ceremonial grounds."

"That's not on this marker," Christopher responded.

"I know. That's why I didn't say anything about it earlier. I don't know whether it's true or not." I explained further, "I didn't want you to think I would lie to you. It's very important to me that you know that." On a level deep inside me, I understood only truths could be spoken while one stood on the soil surrounding this crumbling edifice. By relating that belief, I hoped he would come to accept that I would never lie to him.

After studying the shell of the small church for a while longer, he commented in a pensive tone, "OK."

We moved toward the ruins. Minutes later, I shared a secret hope. "When I marry again, it will be in this place."

Standing together outside those thick brick walls, I came to sense he and I were old souls who had crossed over onto ancient, consecrated grounds. Studying the symmetry of the old church, we slowly walked around the ruined sides, imagining stained glass in the now empty, gracefully arched window openings.

At first, I was surprised by the amount of time he spent exploring the grounds before gradually coming to appreciate that Christopher felt its special draw as well. He was usually easily bored and ready to be off to new sights. I was pleased that he chose to linger here.

Later, wandering alone inside the old walls, I bowed my head and found myself silently petitioning the Eternal God of this Sacred Place. I prayed first for Christopher's health and safety and for that of his family; later, for that of my mother and friends. Within these broken walls, I felt an easy acceptance of our clandestine relationship.

Unexpectedly, I heard a solemn benediction acknowledging that I belonged to Christopher as surely as he belonged to me. In amazement, I searched the heavens through the church's nonexistent roof for the source of those words, knowing full well that strong, feminine voice did not originate inside my head. I never had heard her before this afternoon. A second blessing, coming immediately after that first, intoned that as we had come to this place together, we would leave this place together.

Finally, a third pronouncement assured me that we had always been together and that we would always be together.

Double, double damn, I instantly thought, that's just too, too strange!

Out of nowhere, Christopher appeared beside me. Holding out his hand, he asked, "Rachael, it's time. Are you ready?"

I nodded before placing mine in his. At the very moment our hands touched, I became more united with him than I had ever felt joined to either of the men with whom I had purchased licenses and had legally wed. Hand in hand, we strolled to my car.

Savannah proved impossible to negotiate by automobile the next morning. Due to a scheduled parade to honor its Desert Storm returnees, city crews had placed wooden sawhorses to block many of her streets. Fortunately, we quickly stumbled upon the tourist information bureau because Christopher required city maps and directions to a barbeque establishment he had read about in one of his many tour guides.

A pleasant-faced, young black woman was helpful with all his requests except for the restaurant. "Sir, I was born and raised right here in Savannah," she apologized in her coastal drawl, "but I've never heard of that place." Turning, she called to an older white woman for assistance.

I whispered an aside to Christopher. "I think that's a bad sign if a native Savannah-ite hasn't even heard of that barbeque. Are you sure you have the name right?"

He thumbed through his guidebook to verify the name. "Yes, that's the correct name."

As the older woman came toward us, she volunteered, "Oh, yes, Aneece, I've eaten there. It's wonderful. Y'all are in for a treat." She flipped over the city map that was in front of us in order to read it better. "Let me show y'all its location."

That's a good sign, I thought.

For some minutes, the second woman pored over the line drawing, using her perfectly manicured index finger to guide her eyes. "Well, I'll be. I can't find that street on this map. Now, where are y'all from?"

That's a bad sign, I thought.

"California," Christopher replied quickly, knowing a one-state answer simplified things.

She smiled. "I'm amazed that visitors from California would know about such a little ol' obscure restaurant!"

"Oh, yes," I added my two cents' worth proudly, "this man does his homework before travelin' to a new place."

Tactfully ignoring the obvious differences between our speech patterns, the older woman checked the map once more before replying, "I can get y'all in the general vicinity. Maybe y'all can get directions once you're in the neighborhood."

After we left the tourist bureau, Christopher insisted we watch the festivities before touring the town by foot. Like most Vietnam vets, he had never gotten a homecoming parade. I have always thought that my generation's soldiers, who fought in that unpopular war and who were not recognized by their country, wanted to make damn sure that no American soldier was ever treated that way again. Probably for those two reasons alone, we stood along a parade route, in an unfamiliar city, to cheer men home that we did not even know.

While watching men and women dressed in desert fatigues march by, I remembered my friends who went to war back in the 1960s and '70s. I found myself softly crying for them and for the cheers they never heard.

After brushing a heavy teardrop off my jawline, I told Christopher, "Everyone I knew came back from 'Nam with no visible wounds, but their wives say sometimes they still have bad nightmares."

"Have I ever told you how I lost my kidney?" he asked abruptly.

I shook my head. On previous trips, he had discussed some of his experiences at OCS, but 'Nam was one subject he had never said much about. If I were this moved by Savannah's military parade, I knew the man must be mired armpit deep in his memories.

He was quiet for a long time before he finally spoke. "The most dangerous time for a soldier in 'Nam was the first two months when he's green and the last two months of his tour of duty. That was when he's thinking about getting back stateside. I made it one day past that first two months and thought I could relax. That night, our camp was overrun, and I got hit. I got hit real bad."

As soon as his last remark ended, I felt a fearful dread settling down to blanket my heart. Knowing I had to protect myself, I quickly threw up firewalls against the events through which he had lived. Refusing to allow my mind to conjure up scenarios for that night, I shielded myself from his pain of those many years ago. I willed myself to hear his words dispassionately because I knew, without one doubt, I would be unable to remain standing if I went there.

"My kidney was removed in a field hospital," he continued in a voice devoid of emotion. "After I stabilized, I was sent stateside to heal. Later, I was discharged."

When he stopped talking, I waited wordlessly, dreading any elaborations. When none came, I relaxed my guard and gave thanks his life had been spared and also gave thanks I had been spared all the gory details he had endured.

Finally adding, he announced, "I've done well with one kidney. It hasn't hampered my life at all. I was lucky."

As we continued watching the parade in silence, he seemed caught up in memories for a good long while. After he finished his thoughts, Christopher said aloud, his voice trailing off, "Most of the other boys that night weren't."

I waited for him to continue. Uncertain of what he would relate, I again prepared to hear the worst.

His voice was stronger, more natural, a short time later when he said, "I acquired two good buddies in OCS but I lost track of them when we got to 'Nam."

After the final tank in the parade had passed by, we drifted the sidewalks of the town, using the maps Christopher had obtained at the tourist bureau. After strolling beside beautiful brick homes, we later sat on park benches under dense, leaf-laden ancient trees. We were grateful that the city fathers had pled their case well to Sherman to prevent their town from being torched. In our continuing quest for Southern barbeque, we left Savannah's historic district.

Entering a once elegant neighborhood where venerable houses carried their advancing years with worn gentility, I was reminded of a velvet smoking jacket I had once seen hanging in a back corner of Big Daddy's Elegant Junque and Thrift Store on Central Avenue Pike. Hinting of a storied past, the well-lived-in burgundy garment sported a frayed, black satin shawl collar and matching cuffs, and its once plush elbows had been rubbed down to the dull sheen of the fabric's woven backing.

The farther we walked into the area, the more black faces we saw than white. During the morning's parade, I had noticed that several street vendors offered beer. As a result, some of the passersby on the sidewalks, as well as some of the porch sitters, had consumed more than their fair share. I became uneasy because I knew we could quickly become an unpleasant racial incident written up on page two of the local Sunday paper.

One charming aspect of an old town, Christopher was learning, was how some of the streets do not appear on the newer maps. Whereas, I knew that was also a troubling aspect of an old town. We eventually found the street, but not the restaurant.

As a pair of beer-can-toting black men wobbled by us, one said loudly, "Git back to th' waterfront! You don't belong here!"

I grabbed Christopher's hand. "Sweet Jesus, Christopher!" I whispered. "Let's do as he says. This could get nasty."

"No, we'll be all right," he calmly assured me.

I was not reassured in the least bit. My companion definitely was not from around here, but I was and I definitely knew enough to be frightened.

Sweet Jesus!

A WASP-y appearing mailman, dressed in postal blue Bermuda shorts and matching short-sleeved shirt, turned a corner, coming toward us. Immediately, Christopher questioned him as to directions to the elusive restaurant.

"Oh, sure, I know the place," the man answered. "I carry their mail. Never eaten there, though. You say it's good? Y'all did right good gettin' here. You're less than a block away. In Savannah's old sections," he explained, "the alleys parallelin' the streets have the same name as the streets, but don't have any street signs."

"No wonder we couldn't find the place on this street," I said aloud as the realization dawned on me, "it's on the alley."

The carrier nodded. He looked at me before turning to Christopher. He also had heard the veiled threat that drunken pedestrian had sent our way. "It would be better if y'all walked the rest of the way with me."

I was relieved at his offer. Since the man distributed the neighborhood's mail and the residents knew him, I hoped anyone walking with him would be granted safe passage. I figured, also, by the time we were finished eating, the drunks would be off the streets and be passed out, we would be safe. Christopher seemed naïvely pleased with the man's helpfulness.

We were escorted a half block onward to an alley behind the street on which we had first met the mail carrier. Our postal guide pointed to a nameless structure that had started life as a single-car, cinder block garage. The unpainted structure's exterior made Orangeburg's barbeque building look positively baronial.

We stepped inside to find a massive, young black woman singing a hymn as she chopped meat behind a chest-high, homemade counter, her tune sounded like "Rock of Ages" to me. Since that robust figure wielded a meat cleaver as if it were an extension of her hand, I knew we surely would not want to make her mad.

Five rescued diner booths lined two walls. Even dulled by the passage of time, their mismatched yellow and red plastic-covered seats were garish splashes of color in the otherwise gray room. Behind her and against a short wall stood a well-used refrigerator, a twin to the one that I had inherited back at the cabin at Sunshine.

"Hello," Christopher sang out in his best California accent.

"Hey," she drawled in return as she laid down the huge knife. Turning away from the large, square worktable, the young woman royally eased her bulk over to where we stood. Resting her elbows atop the high counter, she leaned forward to wait for our order.

"I've read that you have the best barbeque in all Savannah," he continued, enunciating his words carefully as if in a foreign land speaking to a native in her own tongue, "and I have come all the way from San Francisco to taste if that's true."

She smiled at him, flashing deep dimples and beautifully white teeth. "That be right," she modestly answered.

They proceeded to discuss what would be the best for us to order. When I asked about preparation, the woman knew her stuff. She talked about the variety of wood the restaurant chose to burn, how the pig was smoked, the basis of their sauce and the secret precook rub especially blended for their ribs. All the important aspects that people who barbeque know about. Having competed three times in the whole hog division for Memphis-In-May, I appreciated her explanations. She understood it was attention to such details that make the difference between dry, tough, stringy meat and juicy, tasty, melt-in-your-mouth-sweetness meat that is almost as good as hot sex.

"We gots sweet tea or Cokes to drink," she added after they had settled on our lunch selections.

"Do you have water?" Christopher asked quickly.

The young woman thought for a moment before gliding to the old refrigerator. She pulled out a Gatorade bottle, its original labeling still attached, filled with clear liquid. "This be OK?"

Assuming it contained water and grateful that he would not have to drink anything sweet with his barbeque, he answered, "That'll be wonderful."

We watched her make up our orders. The woman wasted little motion as she moved around her prep area.

Before we carried our heaping plates to a booth, she offered, "Here's a crab apiece. They on th' house. We be known for them, too."

The barbeque was as good as her description of their technique had led me to believe it would be. The crabs were a spicy delicacy, too. For dessert, we shared a fried sweet potato pie, which Christopher told her was his first, adding there were not too many opportunities for such good food in California.

⚜

It was early afternoon before we drove west toward Macon. This trip, with Christopher in charge of maps and tour books and me driving, had been a pleasant change for us both. I was able to enjoy the drive and the scenery, leaving him free to sightsee or peruse his books or pinpoint our precise progress on whichever map he chose.

I had mixed emotions about our next city. The sections describing sites that Christopher read aloud sounded like places I would like to see, but I had been near the town as a child when Daddy was stationed at Warner-Robbins Air Force Base for the start of the Korean Conflict. I remembered the days being so hot that sweat dripped off my earlobes and the nights so muggy that I hated my skin touching my body. I remembered one summer having a succession of ailments: German measles, red measles, chicken pox and an ugly eye infection, caused by ever-present swarming gnats, that required the twice daily application of refrigerated penicillin salve behind each lower eyelid. I remembered when the ceiling lights were put out at night, I could hear the clicking of countless roach feet as those insect battalions participated in maneuvers throughout the married enlisted men's quarters. Since I was not tall enough to reach the pull cord for my bedroom's bare light bulb that would send those creatures scurrying for dark nooks and crannies, I had been too scared to go to the bathroom during the night. I so dreaded the crispy crunch and gooshy feel of unseen, monstrously huge roach bodies under my bare feet that I would rather, come morning, endure my parents' wrath directed at me and my sodden bedclothes. I also remembered spending long, dark, frightening hours standing on tippy toes atop my mattress until my calf muscles cramped from looking out my bedroom's solitary high window, pleading the next headlights I saw would be Daddy Pop's car coming to a stop at our front door, crying each night for deliverance from my hell.

Later when I was an adult, I learned my parents had suffered through their own nightmares there. Although their experiences involved reasons different from mine, that base had been a place of torment for us three.

I did not care to recount my horrific childhood existence at Warner-Robbins and felt Christopher did not need to learn about my family's dirty laundry. I simply saw no good reason to go there.

"I don't remember much about the place except it was hot and buggy and I hated livin' there," I finally told Christopher, thereby condensing my military-induced incarceration to one terse sentence.

He answered, "Well, it's either Macon or Atlanta tonight because Savannah is too far a drive tomorrow."

I took my gaze off the oncoming pavement to glance in his direction for a moment. "I don't want to have to think about your leavin' just yet." Suddenly sad, I returned my concentration to the road.

Christopher gently placed his hand on my shoulder. "I know. Me neither." He added tenderly, "Rachael, Macon will be better this time because we're together."

With my voice sounding strangely childlike to my ears, I pleaded, "Just promise me, we won't stay at any place that looks like it has roach bugs."

※

At its location inside the converted Macon railroad station, the town's tourist bureau was inconveniently closed. A thoughtful employee had placed a plethora of pamphlets, however, on racks in its lobby, enabling Christopher to happily plot our visit.

The atmosphere outside the imposing building's cool interior was as hot and breezeless and muggy that late afternoon as I remembered. Most of the places of interest were not open, but he decided we would meander around the town while waiting for a reasonable hour to eat.

We found the streets deserted as the town's sensible residents took refuge from the high temperature and brilliant sunlight. We located the famed house that had a Civil War cannon ball stuck in its exterior. The antebellum frame residence with its war relic strangely brought to mind the image of an elderly lady with a blackhead marring her complexion.

Soon after I shared that unsightly thought, we came across a Catholic church. Christopher disappeared inside to check out the architecture of its interior. While I hesitated outside, my vision followed the rows of chiseled rock upwards to the towering, forbidding steeples. Realizing the God of this church was unsympathetic to our plight, this stern structure seemed much less welcoming to me than the lovely, decaying ruins near Beaufort.

Despite fearing a bolt of lightning arising from His Mighty Wrath, I entered to find the dim sanctuary's coolness providing instant relief from the sun's breath-robbing heat. While he explored the nave, I perched uneasily on a pew in the back, hoping to make myself small. I knew I was not wanted here. And my feelings for the man, whose movements I followed with my heart, did not belong inside this place of worship. I soon walked outside, where I was spiritually more comfortable, to wait in the heat.

Upon leaving the church, we came upon an inviting city park situated on a sloping hillside that faced the soon-to-be-setting sun. After making ourselves comfortable on the grass, Christopher seemed in a mood to discuss subjects he did not ordinarily bring up.

"Did I tell you how pretty Victoria was in her white dress when she graduated junior high? She looked like an angel." He added, "So much like the pictures of my dead mother as a girl."

"How's that?" Using a leading question, I took the opportunity to learn more about his children.

"Thick, curly brown hair. Soft brown eyes." He smiled. "She has the sweetest smile. Like Momma's. And so, so smart. Makes all A's, just like her old man wished he could have done." He laughed. "I wasn't a good student. I studied just enough to get by. My son is like me in that regard. He likes to build things. Vinnie's good with his hands. I know he's smarter than his sister, but he won't apply himself." He changed the direction of his elaborations. "I've started letting Victoria drive when we go on trips. She's fearless behind the wheel. That scares me."

More descriptive than usual, Christopher continued with anecdotes involving his children. I could tell by his voice that he was proud of them and their accomplishments. Even those of his headstrong son. I heard the words less than I saw the love as he talked. His face and hands became animated while the emotions he felt toward his children glowed warmly in his eyes.

"I took my children to visit my grandparents in Italy a few years back. What an experience it was for them. My family's village is in the mountains to the north. It's small, difficult to reach. Both kids said they were glad they didn't have to grow up there. You know, my grandparents don't have indoor bathrooms. You should have seen her nose wrinkle when I showed Victoria the toilet facilities." Remembering the incident, he chuckled softly. "I was so proud of them and their manners and the respect they gave the old ones."

I waited, allowing time for Christopher to add to his remembrance. When he did not, I shared some of my family's background with him. "Mom's grandparents in Kentucky had an outhouse, too. I visited them a lot when I was in grammar school. That was where I learned to light an oil lamp. Mammy and Pappy were so old by then that all they kept on the farm were chickens. Big Momma would fix a huge Sunday dinner on Mammy's old wood stove. After church services ended, all her people would drop by. The men would eat first, then the women and children. I'd help Big Momma kill and dress a couple of old hens. Have you ever done that?"

He shook his head in the negative before asking, "Your grandparents were rich enough to have a cook?"

I laughed heartily at his question. "Oh, Christopher, you're thinkin' about Mammy in *Gone With the Wind*." I patiently explained, "We all called my great-grandmother Mammy, and Big Momma is what everybody called my grandmother. I thought I'd told you that."

We were quiet for several minutes until it seemed time to ask about the other member of his family. I requested, "Tell me how you met your wife."

Slow to answer this query, some time passed before he said, "My father worked with her father. She's from a nice Italian family, like me." Christopher stopped there. I could almost hear the wheels turning inside his head as he sifted through their history for information he felt free to share, but there was none forthcoming.

"And you love her?" I finally asked.

"And I loved her," he responded. He waited a long while before explaining, "I respect her for her kindness, for how she is raising my children, for how good she was to my parents when they became old and sick. She's a good person."

"Of course she is or you would have never chosen to marry her." I spoke my true feelings for I had never expected his wife to be otherwise. I did not inquire further into the reason or reasons that undermined his love for her. That line of questioning was too invasive. Besides, as much as I might wonder, I really did not want to know.

After my first divorce, I had adopted the policy that whatever happens between a man and a woman to sever their bonding should stay just between them. A simple public declaration of 'It's broke, and we don't want it fixed' by the couple should be all that the law required instead of an assignment of blame to justify the societal cost of divorce. Later after my divorce from Mackey, I had decided that, based upon what originally was his and hers first, stayed his and hers, then what assets acquired together could be divided down the middle. I had further reasoned that children should be nurtured by both parents equally, so that no child would feel the need to side with either parent.

Divorce codes based on guiltlessness made perfectly good sense to me. It was just not the legal system under which I lived.

Hearing Christopher describe his family did not seem odd because I had never felt we were rivals battling for his affections. After all, he had said I was the icing on his cake. I had opted to accept that his world in California was a segment of his life that did not include me, just as my life at the restaurant did not revolve around him. By considering that when we were together our other lives did not exist, I had chosen to believe only our time together was real, everything else was simply flickering images as shown in a nickelodeon.

The ability to ignore easily what one did not care to see was merely another aspect of the Southern experience in which I was well versed.

I changed the subject. "My hunger alarm is about to go off." I looked at my watch. "Good gracious, it's almost eight o'clock. No wonder I'm starved."

"What are you hungry for?"

I smiled a lascivious smile. "For you always, of course." I inhaled deeply. "You know, Honey, I do think I smell seafood."

After helping me to my feet, Christopher lifted his head and took a deep breath. "I believe the lady is right."

Returning to our well-appointed motel room following a seafood buffet served by a restaurant behind Mercer College, I turned on the television. After I tossed the remote near where Christopher was stretched across the bed, he picked up the black plastic as soon as it landed. With the remote in hand, he mindlessly changed channels every few seconds. Amazed, I sat on the foot of the bed to observe this stranger with his battery-powered slave.

We had never watched television during our previous meetings. Although Christopher and I might have had the set on in the mornings while we dressed in order to catch the weather forecast, we had never taken time to watch TV together. I had no reason to turn the damn thing on this evening but I did. After his umpteenth rotation through all the available channels, the man continued clicking. I had not realized Christopher had this affliction. He was not perfect after all.

If he doesn't quit, I thought, I just might have to kill him.

It would be justifiable homicide. No female jury would convict you.

"Christopher, Honey, if you don't find a channel and light soon," I said sweetly, "I will have to break your fingers."

"Oh," he commented absentmindedly, "does this bother you?" With one final click, he cut the set off and rose from the bed. I watched him repacked his suitcase for tomorrow's flight.

When would I see him again? I hated this part of our time together when we both became quiet and self-absorbed. Similar to alien space creatures preparing for take-off, we seemed to concentrate all our energies in morphing into our alternate life forms, with the reverting as awkward as changing horses in midstream.

Not ready to lose him to California so early our last evening together, I walked to where he leaned over his opened suitcase. Pulling the shirttail out of his pants, I kissed his exposed back. After Christopher straightened up, I raised his shirt up to his shoulders, baring the rest of his back. With my fingernails almost not touching his skin, I lightly traced where muscles tied into his spine.

He turned slowly to face me. He leaned down to kiss me gently, encircling my mouth with gentle, nibbling kisses before he began unbuttoning my blouse.

"No," I whispered, "this one's for you."

Understanding my intentions, he allowed his arms to rest against his sides. I undressed him slowly, caressing each segment of his skin I revealed. Leaving trails of soft, wet kisses on his skin, I became a tigress marking her territory. I knew an untold number of months would pass before we were together again. I wanted to memorize his body, to drink in all that I could of him. I planned things to do to him so that he would never ever be able to forget my touch or me.

Slowly, deliberately we made love. His sweat mingled with my sweat. As sensual sensations became so intense as to be painful, I realized I had never seen Christopher's expression so contorted. Salty moisture dripped heavily from his face onto mine. Putting off the inevitable conclusion, we moved through a varied sequence of positions. Our breathing became ragged, our bodies so slippery with perspiration that our torsos coming together and pulling apart made sloppy sounds. Every muscle, every thought, every feeling I owned became focused where Christopher and I were joined. Nothing else existed for me.

All our efforts were finally rewarded. As he called out my name in a thunderous sound ripped from his lungs, I placed my hands over his mouth to mute the noise.

I managed to gasp, "They'll hear you in Atlanta."

Christopher sprawled beside me in bed. Our bodies were too hot to be touching but, like moths drawn to flames, neither of us could pull away, so we remained joined. I turned my head in order to see his face. Although his skin was flushed, glistening with sweat, his precious features were now relaxed. I watched his blood pulsing under the skin at the base of his throat while I felt the throbbing of my blood marking time with his.

"I love you," I heard myself say.

Where did that come from? Sweet Jesus, you've just said the unspeakable!

He briefly smiled before weaving his fingers into my tangled hair. Exhausted, we both fell asleep.

Limiting our conversation only to what pertained to our current travel, we completed the remaining distance to Atlanta in silence. What I had confessed prior to falling asleep the night before played on my mind. Perhaps it was on Christopher's, too, but we elected to keep it shelved.

Upon reaching the turn-off to the airport on the outskirts of Atlanta, we reviewed the highlights of our current trip. Drawing upon earlier meetings, we included the beauty of Perkins Cove, of almost being caught with our pants down along Redwood Creek, the zipper incident in Nashville and the moon glow atop LeConte. Our sporadic memory replays lasted until we reached the airport. When Christopher gave me final instructions, I nodded in agreement that I would simply drop him off and drive away, knowing all the while I could not possibly leave him that cavalierly.

While he carried his luggage to the curbside check-in, I pulled out of traffic to park my car. He would have to walk away because there was no way I could drive away while watching his image shrink in my rearview mirror. In any case, I could not see through my curtain of tears to steer safely.

After pulling the keys away from the ignition, I ran to where he stood, driven on by the strong desire to be with him as long as possible. Crying but trying not to cry, I smiled and held his hand tightly as his luggage was tagged and checked in by the skycap. Christopher talked to me, yet I comprehended nothing he said. We hugged one last time before he entered the terminal, then I slowly walked back to my car. Hating that he would remember me with tears streaming down my face, I steered my car away from the Atlanta airport.

I knew I had changed everything with those three words I had said prior to falling asleep the previous night. What did I really want from this relationship? Could I still share? My life was certainly less complicated before that May when the man hiked into my life.

Unaware of my surroundings, I returned home on the interstate, praying for angels to watch over me and the other drivers because I could see nothing clearly through my tears.

Nine

The verdant trees of late summer embracing the deck behind my house had been turned to autumn's gold by some itinerant alchemist passing through on last night's vapor express. With sunlight filtering through them, the shimmering leaves acquired a molten quality that brought to mind that bead of melted gold Joe Bill had once shown me as he prepared to sling metal into the burned-out mold for a molar crown. By just looking at nature's bounty in my yard from my elevated deck, I became a queen whose coffers had suddenly been enriched by a king's ransom.

Saturday afternoon I sat centered on the black metal glider with the head of a sleeping Siamese cat on each thigh. The girls and I lazily waited for the Vols to play South Carolina. Since the game would not be televised, I had carried a radio outside, planning to listen to John Ward's play-by-play and to enjoy the patchwork of colors and heady aromas of fall in East Tennessee at the same time. I liked the sense of efficiency that doing two tasks together gave me. Years back that same efficiency, however, had gotten me to an emergency room when I sharpened steak knives while watching a *Star Trek* rerun.

The warmth from the midday sun was kind against my body, but it made the girls' fur almost too hot to touch. From my gently gliding black throne, I surveyed the small city lot on which my house sat. The land was just big enough for me to maintain without hiring a lawn service. The actual acreage might have been small, yet the sense of belonging it gave me was enormous. Sleeping that first night on my then-empty bedroom's bare floor, I felt grounded. Literally grounded. I knew I finally belonged somewhere because I resided on land I owned. That feeling of connectedness had been missing from my life before I purchased my house.

There had been another vacuum in my life before Christopher Saracini hiked into it. I just had not been quite able to put a name on what need he fulfilled. Whatever deep emotional void that was satisfied by our relationship felt much too complex for a one-word definition, such as belonging or connectedness.

Just what did I get from that man? I got no demands on my time. I got no one to take care of. I got great, steamy sex without being concerned about contracting social diseases.

How brazen those reasons sounded. How heartless I sounded when putting them into words.

Whenever we were together, I felt free of chains. I became the woman I would like to be, living the life I would like to live. Whenever we were together, I could be playful and sensual and cared for. When we were apart, I had wonderful memories. By tending to all the details I found so annoying, he assumed the man's proper role of stepping on spiders. All I had to do was show up in far-away cities whenever I was issued an invitation.

There had been no one else like Christopher Saracini in my life. He was the perfect lover. Never underfoot when I had things to do, only around when I could give him my undivided attention. He was intelligent, interested in just too many subjects. He had a wonderful sense of humor, a great spirit of adventure. He told me I was special, and because he had said that, I truly believed I was. I felt like a heroine in a bodice-ripping novel. Being with him seemed so opposite from my actual, mundane existence. He brought to me a quality that had been missing from my days. Because of that man, I had Romance with a capital R.

If I were the icing on his cake, he had become my meat and potatoes. I could not imagine my life without him in it, some way, somehow. Because he cared so deeply for his children, I feared that he would return some day to live under the same roof with them and their mother. The pressures applied by his son and daughter and his church pushed him toward reconciliation with his estranged wife. No one in California was my champion. Not one soul there spoke out on my behalf. All I had was a precarious toehold in his life.

Hell, my twin chortled, *you don't even have a ticket to watch the fight.*

I knew only that Christopher had my heart. What would I have to look forward to if he stopped planning our times together? Where would be my Romance?

An enthusiastic radio voice broke into my thoughts with the announcement: "It's football time in Tennessee!"

I looked around the deck for my girls. They had eased out of the direct sun while I mulled over my rat's nest. I located Beatrice under the glider in the shade created by my body, while Sybyl posed like a single bookend on the railing near the back wall of the house.

"Well now, ladies," I called to them, "you wouldn't happen to have a knife to cut through this tangled knot of mine, would you?"

Unlike my two-legged friends, my furry companions offered no opinion.

After tucking away all completed bank slips and facing the money into the zippered bag for today's deposit, the impact created by the restaurant's move to its larger space fully sank in. For the first few months after the reopening, I had been afraid that the newness would wear off for our patrons and the volume of business would drop, leaving me holding an empty money bag with no way to meet the increased overhead. Too many nights, I had experienced a recurring nightmare in which I was kicked out onto Kingston Pike with my arms loaded with cooking pots and pages of family recipes tucked under my chin. Despite my fears, the daily take had grown steadily. Weekly payrolls and monthly payments were met on time. The ladies loved us, and businessmen had taken to returning in ever increasing numbers.

Today's totals were the best to date, and it was not even a football Friday. The restaurant gods had been good.

The only drawback was my lost freedom. The amount of time the restaurant consumed was in direct proportion to its growing success. Stolen weekends at the cabin were the only islands of quiet in my busy days. Because Mom, Christopher, Liz and Margaret were the few who had that number, the phone seldom rang there. For the most part, Liz and Margaret left me alone on weekends. The rest of our crowd did not know I owned a place on Little River, or they would have thoughtlessly felt free to drop by without first calling ahead. Months ago, I stopped scheduling any time off because I wanted the ability to drop everything to meet Christopher whenever he could get away. I imposed enough on Mom, Liz and Margaret to tend to the business and my four-legged girls for those special trips, especially since none of the two-legged trio thought much of my reasons for maintaining that long-distance relationship. I felt too greedy in planning more vacations away from my responsibilities. That was the penance I paid for my Romance.

Mine was a pleasant enough existence. An outsider, I guessed, would envy me.

"Well-a, Miz Rachael," Hugh Ed said, coming to lean against the doorway to my office, "come see what you think about your new doors."

"You through already?" I was shocked at the speed the man worked.

"Yes'm." The tall man smiled. "Ah think you'll be right pleased with how th' entrance looks now."

He turned, and I rose from my chair to follow him. Last week, Hugh Ed had haltingly suggested I needed a smarter entry than the plain brown doors the restaurant presently had, offering to paint them with the colors I had chosen for its interior. Although he already knew exactly how he wanted them to look, Hugh Ed would not tell me precisely what he had in mind, wanting to surprise me. Silently, I prayed those doors would not be the shock the stark-white ceiling tiles at the cabin had been.

"Well-a, what do you think?" He stepped back allowing me full view of the entry's new appearance.

"Damn!" I exclaimed soon as I had an unobstructed view. The once generic, six-paneled double doors now made a dramatic statement. "Hugh Ed, you definitely changed them up. They're beautiful." The man had painted the rails, styles, face and butt edges of the doors the dark teal I liked. The inner panels were my favorite shade of mauve, and the molding framing those panels was dull gold. The fresh paint glistened richly in the light. "How could you tape and paint them so fast?"

He smiled his shy, little boy smile. Holding a freshly cleaned paintbrush close to the closed door, Hugh Ed demonstrated his technique in the air with a quick flip of his wrist. "Well-a, no tape. I cut in to th' wet edge."

"Damn, you're good!" I exclaimed. "That must take a steady hand."

His smile widened. "Yes'm, it does, and I am good," he modestly concurred.

After Liz and Margaret joined us, I noticed the big man's face reddened and his eyes lowered. With both ladies being lavish with their praises, he became more tongue-tied than I had ever seen him.

Wanting to more fully inspect the doors, I reached for the inside pull. "Can I see the other side now?"

The now mute man barely managed a nod. We all went outside to admire the colorful change as Hugh Ed stood near, soaking up compliments as fast as a damp sponge soaks up spilt water.

Having delayed my escape from work long enough, I grandly announced to my friends, "Ladies, Hugh Ed, if y'all will excuse me, I have a date with the bank and then some Christmas shopping to complete. See y'all Monday."

※

"Go! Go! Go!"

Half the people gathered in the living room moaned in mock pain when the stretched out receiver dropped the forty-yard-long, desperation pass thrown as the last seconds ticked away. The rest cheered their relief as their team's defender slid face-guard forward on the artificial turf. With that mote of excitement over, the long first half came to a close.

A station break preceded the start of this year's Super Bowl half-time show. As with most years, the games leading up to this season's grande finale had been more exciting than the first half I had just witnessed.

With the game's progress halted, I surveyed Liz's crowded living room. Since graduating college in 1968, I had run the streets too many nights with most of the people present. I really could not name the year Liz started her bowl tradition, but it seemed like we had been showing up since the games started. And, yes, the usual suspects had congregated again.

Over the years, a few in our crowd had married and now brought their spouses to the gathering. While we old-timers welcomed the new additions warmly, should divorce proceedings crop up the departing spouse never retained custody of the Super Bowl invitation. Occasionally, someone would drag along a serious date, but mostly we came alone to touch base with long-time friends. Just like those California swallows that return every spring to the old mission.

I noticed Hugh Ed lurking in the far corner behind a table crammed with food. He stood stiffly, as if it was his job to brace up those two walls. Since this was his first year to be invited, he appeared almost comical in his obvious discomfort at being surrounded by an unfamiliar horde.

Although most of the crowd stopped by my place for lunches in or for carry-outs, some I never saw except at Liz's annual party. A couple of us had been hanging out together beginning with Knoxville's initial attempt to create an opportunity for singles. Back in the late 1960s, the local movers and shakers deemed it proper that the clubs be segregated by sex, an approach that I had considered to be truly backward, but segregation was an established Southern habit back then. Sometime during my first marriage, Liz helped organize the area's first mixed-singles club. Rejoining the dating scene after my divorce from King Richard, I met Liz at the first Friday night social I attended. All the women at the bowl parties, except for Margaret, I had come to know through Liz and that club.

Over near the steps leading downstairs, Carson Peoples was talking with a man I knew to be in the ski club and whose name I had never bothered to learn, seeing as how I did not ski. Carson and I had chaperoned a sorority formal when we were in our early twenties. I thought I recalled we had more fun at the dance than the girls, but I drank so much

Wild Turkey back then that I would be hard pressed to say what actually had happened. I did remember, however, that had been the night Carson lit my nose when he went to light my cigarette. I had failed to notice his poor marksmanship until the next afternoon when the sensations from my seared nose beat out those from my throbbing head.

I heard Lynnette's trilling laughter ring out and followed its sound until I found her talking with Margaret. With her too beautiful green eyes and café-au-lait skin tones, she could be a poster child promoting racially mixed marriages.

A tall, feminine back disappeared into the kitchen. That figure had to belong to Saralyn, the only human I knew who could go eyeball-to-eyeball with Hugh Ed. She had played center on the Lady Vols' basketball team and now taught PE at Oak Ridge.

Squeezing by her as he left the kitchen was Old What's-his-name, who fucked as fast as he shagged. Having always considered speed inappropriate when it came to either of those activities, I smiled at my choice of words because my English-born first husband would have been quick to point out I was redundant by using those two verbs. I never, ever went out with Old What's-his-name again after our first encounter, or perhaps he never asked me out again. Failing to recall which, I noticed that it looked like he had bellied up to the feeding trough one time too many since last year's party. Nancy, who sat in the recliner across the coffee table from me, and I had locked horns over him shortly after Old What's-his-name joined the crowd.

What the hell had we been thinking when we did that?

Coming down the hall from the bathroom, Dunkin' Doug, who had more notches on his gun than John Wayne, entered the living room. I had dated him back in my hazy, liquor-drinking days. Liz had told me last week that his wife had left him, taking their four daughters with her. Must have been the case of one indiscretion too many for the woman. I found it dripping with poetic justice that Doug sired only daughters because, when his girls reached dating age, that man would have to worry that randy boys, like he had been, would be asking them out. Since he had not attended a Super Bowl with the crowd after marrying, I wondered what he was doing at Liz's party, because all the women here knew to steer well clear of him. Maybe Doug felt he had nothing left to prove among those who knew him well.

During my misspent youth in the 1970s, I had followed the philosophy celebrated in one of that decade's hit songs: *'If you can't be with the one you love.'* Just about everyone crowded into this house had done the same, but so much had changed in twenty years. Back then, clap was subdued with penicillin, and crabs were killed with an over-the-counter, blue ointment. Now that AIDS stalked the sexually active, my cohorts and I had grown either older and wiser or flabbier and less interested. I considered tallying up the number of men present I knew biblically, but decided against it.

Perhaps Dunkin' Doug and I had more in common than I cared to think.

Old What's-his-name wandered over to where I sat on the end of the couch near the television. His plate was piled high with taco chips and Liz's famous bean dip, barely leaving room for two slices of my almond skillet cake. I briefly wondered why I had never been able to recall his name.

"Hey, Rachie," he called out, "why don't you ever have this almond thing at your place?"

I smiled sweetly, despite despising his irritating shortening of my name. "I'm no dessert whore," I joked. "I don't sell all my goodies. I do keep back some treats for my special friends."

He nodded vigorously and chortled, "I'm glad I'm your friend!" Next he suggested, "Looks like you've been enjoyin' some of your own desserts a bit too much. Put on some love handles, haven't we?"

I stared pointedly at his receding hairline. "Losin' a little tactfulness along with our hair, aren't we?" I replied. We fired forced grins at each other before he carefully wove his rotund body through the people sitting on the floor and disappeared into the kitchen.

Our terse exchange brought to mind why I never tried to remember his name. Maybe, I silently considered, I had best redefine some of those present as acquaintances, not friends.

Margaret worked her way through the crowd. After she sat beside me, she nodded in Hugh Ed's direction before she whispered, "Watch him when Liz comes back into the room."

"OK," I agreed, but returned my attention to the set when the game resumed for the third quarter. Before too many formations played out, Margaret jabbed her elbow into my side. I looked for Hugh Ed and noticed his eyes riveted on Liz's every movement.

Margaret whispered, "He's sweet on her. Haven't you paid any attention to how often he's been comin' by for lunch?"

Losing count of the numerous times I had seen Hugh Ed at the restaurant since Christmas, I frowned. "You mean," I asked in mock incredulity, "it's not because of Big Momma's pimento cheese receipt?"

With my reply and its archaic word for 'recipe' catching her in mid-sip, Margaret snorted, almost spilling her drink. She shook her head. "Liz and I have a bet on how long it will take the man to screw up his courage to ask her out. Want a piece of the action?"

"Hell, Margaret," I blurted in mock anger, "I'm a small business owner. Because I gamble every day I open my doors, I don't mess with small stakes." I looked around Liz's house crammed with nearly forty people, some of whom I had known for better than twenty-five years. "Too bad this game isn't any better. I'd leave now, but I wouldn't want to be the first to go. Y'all might talk trash about me."

Liz waved across the crowded room, mouthing the words, "Thanks for the cake."

I nodded my acknowledgment. I always carried that particular cake to her parties. After the year I failed to make the game due to my coming down with the flu, I was told by more than one attendee that the least I could have done was to send the cake on in my place. It had been a small comfort to learn that my absence had been noticed.

"You seem in a good mood. What's up?" Margaret asked.

I smiled. "Christopher called this mornin'. We're meetin' in Orlando next month."

As disapproval slowly scrolled across her face, a picture of the pulsating sign at Times Square entered my mind. After her judgment vanished, she looked deep into my eyes, searching for answers. She finally asked, "He makes you happy, doesn't he?"

"Yep," I replied, my answer followed by a too quick smile. After my smile faded, in all seriousness, I shared the one truth I knew about Christopher's and my relationship, "Margaret, he's the only man I can trust. I've never been able to trust a man before."

Slightly nodding her head, she weighed my words. When she sighed, I knew she had accepted his place in my life. Later during another lull in the game, she lightened our conversation by asking, "How many states does this make where y'all have visited?"

"Six or seven, I think," I answered. "I do believe the man is tryin' to screw our way through all fifty states."

Margaret rolled her eyes before warning, "You won't be mentioned in the will, you know, so he better be givin' you some great memories to keep you warm come time to go to the nursin' home."

Watching the bright, big-city lights of Orlando flash by, I sat in the airport shuttle with strangers, allowing my body to slump in exhaustion. The unaccustomed heat of the Floridian night and the faint scent of tropical blooms combined to reek of decadence, especially after the puritan chill of winter I left behind in Tennessee earlier in the morning. The two flight legs had been pleasant enough, but the hour the plane remained on the ground in Atlanta, allegedly due to mechanical problems, had been a bitch. Since the airline refused to allow us to deplane, we passengers had sat, penned up like a truck full of hogs en route to slaughter, breathing in stale air. God only knew what communicable diseases I had sucked down all those minutes. Not being allowed back into the terminal, I had been unable to get to a payphone to tell Christopher I had no idea when he could expect me. This trip, at least, I knew the exact location of my single piece of luggage, having rolled it on board myself and placed it in the overhead luggage compartment.

Neither had I wasted precious minutes phoning ahead when I finally stepped into the terminal in Florida. I knew the man well enough to know he would have already checked with the airline and had probably learned my ETA quicker by phone than we did from the pilot while the plane was still in the air. If a shuttle had not been ready to pull away from the building as I walked out the terminal's main doors, I might have considered calling. Of course, I would still have had no clue as to when I would actually reach his hotel.

As my luck for that day would have it, I was the last of nine passengers to be taken to their final destination. Once inside, I wandered the lobby in search of a house phone and was ready to ask for its location when I spotted the corner in which the little dear was cleverly hidden. I propped myself against the wall while waiting for Christopher to answer the ring.

"Hello! Where are you?" His greeting sounded as bright as sunshine.

"I'm downstairs. Finally. What a god-awful day." My voice was a passionless monotone.

"Come on up." His voice changed to welcoming and warm, sounding as comforting to me as flannel sheets felt on a cold night. "I've pushed our dinner reservations back an hour."

With more effort, I found the elevators. After stepping inside, I leaned against the far wall.

Instantly recognizing the ambient music when I heard the notes that went with the familiar line, '*Got mad and closed the door*,' I thought, God, we're getting old. Since when did Blood, Sweat and Tears become elevator music?

You've lost at love before. My twin erroneously sang the opening line before adding, *That's your theme song all right.*

As the elevator climbed the distance toward his room, my spirits rose along with it. Yes, it had been a long day and I was tired, but that tiredness could be easily dealt with when I got home Monday night. Ruling out flowers and balloons, I did not speculate further upon what special welcoming might await me. This trip I carried along a surprise for Christopher, consisting of two bottles of Crossville wine as well as Tennessee-produced cheese and crackers.

Arriving at the room, I found its door slightly opened. That sight was unsettling, as I knew Christopher would not normally leave his room vulnerable. He was far too experienced a traveler for that small carelessness.

Something's wrong, maybe.

No, I reasoned, that couldn't be because I just talked with him minutes ago. He was fine then.

What if someone broke in and killed him as we were coming up in the elevator?

I hesitated outside in the hallway. Not wanting to push the door open any farther than safely necessary, I called his name softly. With no answer coming from within and with my heart rate ratcheting up, I realized that I could easily allow myself to become frightened.

"Christopher?" I called louder.

"Come in," he answered in a normal speaking voice.

By his calm response I knew all was well and I would be safe after I entered. Taking in a deep, relaxing breath, I opened the door wider. With his special greeting immediately in sight, I hurriedly shut the door behind me. Christopher stood in the middle of the room, posed like that famous line drawing Michelangelo once sketched to study proportional relationships in the male figure, only this male figure held a plastic hotel drinking cup containing white wine in each outstretched hand and had a beauteous smile on his face. Obviously, he was happy to see me and packed no banana in his pockets because the man wore nothing but a wonderful smile.

"Welcome to Florida!" he grandly proclaimed, walking toward me. When he reached where I stood, Christopher closed his arms about me and kissed my forehead. After relaxing his hug, he presented me with a frosty cup of chilled wine. "I'm so glad you finally arrived. I've missed you."

I noticed his eyes twinkling with happiness.

"Me, too," I answered. In his eyes, I saw reflected back the twinkling in mine and a smile that was a twin to his.

Tired? Who said anything about being tired?

Since the restaurant was located on the top floor of our hotel and we would not have far to travel, even after my flight's delayed arrival, we could have hurried and made his original dinner reservations, but Christopher had other ideas and had pushed the time back. He wanted us to touch and to kiss and to reclaim each other's bodies before stepping outside his room to join the world. We put our wine down and began to remove my clothing. After a few kisses, I had to agree with the wisdom of his thinking. Had we left immediately for the restaurant, our need to be together would have been too strong for us to play pretty at the dinner table.

Lying on the bed as his tongue circled my left nipple, I said, "You know, if you did this upstairs, an irate maitre d' would ask us to leave before our appetizers were served."

Later when he entered me, I shared the image that flashed through my mind. "And if we did this, an insensitive waiter would toss a pitcher of cold water on us when he returned with our entrée."

Those two visions brought to mind Daddy's clever mother. Back when my aunts and uncles and Daddy were little people and the family was to attend her girlhood church's yearly homecoming in Union County, Grandmother Taite always prepared fried chicken, potato salad, deviled eggs and two huge bowls of banana pudding the day before. At her house that Saturday, she made sure her children ate their favorite foods to their hearts' content with sly Grandmother insisting on third and fourth helpings for each child. Come Sunday at the covered dish picnic across the road from the church's graveyard, hers were the only children who did not act like starving piglets, piling their plates high with food which had been arrayed across bountiful tables set under the trees. Grandmother Taite would sit back, smiling sweetly, and accept, with the dignity of a benevolent queen, the compliments paid on her children's wonderful manners as her brood sparingly helped their plates, like little ladies and gentlemen.

I decided against imparting that particular memory. As brief as the footnote was in my brain, that poignant bit of family history would have required far too many words to describe, and I certainly had no intention of distracting the man with unnecessary words while we got down to the serious business of making love. Besides, for all I knew he might consider grandmothers and sexual intercourse to be diametrically opposed concepts that should never be entertained together at any juncture in time.

"Rachael Taite!"

My name poured out of his mouth with the same abrupt force that his seminal fluids entered me. I found it amazing that after all these months and all those climaxes, he continued to call my name with each ejaculation. It was the only true consistency he maintained when we made love.

As soon as my breathing returned to normal, I kissed his shoulder before requesting an explanation. "How come, each time we do this, you manage to make it all new? Tell me how you do it."

"It's not me," he answered. "It's you. I'm just . . . "

". . . a simple Italian man," we said together, laughing, "from a small town."

"Yeah, sure." I did not believe him tonight nor had I believed him the first time that sentence left his mouth years back. "You're a magician."

"You missed a fabulous sunset this evening," our waiter informed us as he handed over bound, oversized menus. "Is there anything I can get you from the bar?" His question was directed toward Christopher, not me.

Christopher shook his head. "No, thank you. Let me see your wine listings."

"Certainly, sir." From behind his back, the waiter produced a third bound book I had noticed tucked between his white shirt and maroon cummerbund. It was much narrower than the ones containing the food offerings. "I'll return with water."

After flipping open both books, Christopher appeared engrossed in comparing wines against this evening's food selections. Waiting until the waiter had completely disappeared from view, he said, "I requested a table facing west. Had your flight been on time, we could have shared another sunset together. Rachael, I still can't see one without thinking of you."

"A covert symbol for our little ol' secret club." Although I joked about his comment, I felt the same about sunsets. My stomach rumbled. "What looks good to you?" I asked as I closed my menu, waiting to be told what I would be served.

Why should I bother with selections when I had Christopher to order for me? When seated in an elegant restaurant, this simple Italian man, who could no doubt transform a shared, square Krystal hamburger into a romantic interlude, became a culinary maestro orchestrating a sumptuous repast.

He named a white wine he thought would be well complimented by oysters Rockefeller. "I thought we would have a red with the veal, or the lamb might be interesting. That strawberry dessert would be nice with a . . . "

As I listened to Christopher discussing our options, I looked at our surroundings. The section of the restaurant where we were seated was arranged so that each table was visually isolated. Each richly tufted banquette, which had been designed to be both generous and yet spacious enough only to seat two comfortably, faced a floor-to-ceiling window with its own private view. Looking over the twinkling city lights floating in an ocean of night, I snuggled against the rounded booth and nodded my agreement as Christopher charted the courses for our meal.

Meandering through each shared dish from appetizer to dessert, as we previously had lingered over each kiss and caress, dinner became an extension of our earlier slow, sensuous lovemaking. We sat joined at the hip, running fingertips lightly over nearby forearms and resting hands on adjacent thighs, remaining as discreetly well-behaved, like the well-bred couple we were, as Grandmother Taite's children had been during homecomings on the church grounds. He fed me my half of the oysters. I fed him his. As we nibbled on a single salad, I discovered that blue cheese dressing was not as yucky as I had once thought. We ate fork-tender veal medallions artistically strewn over an array of steamed, julienne vegetables presented on a white porcelain platter. To end our meal, Christopher requested only fresh strawberries and champagne.

The next morning we arrived as the gates opened at Epcot. Having been informed of our itinerary over breakfast, I drew in a deep breath upon entering the resort property in preparation for the oncoming day. Christopher planned to show me the world in ten hours or less. We would lunch in Italy, have a late supper in Paris and, in order to miss the long lines of fellow tourists, he would begin our tour in the middle of the park, thereby increasing our chances of making all the sights in one day.

Mid-afternoon, Christopher stopped in front of a Disney-sanitized English pub. "Rachael," he began haltingly, "I need to phone the office. Why don't you wait over there?" He pointed to shaded benches by the man-made lake. "I'll come back as soon as I'm finished."

"OK," I said agreeably. After he kissed my cheek in parting, I headed toward a bench facing the water while he went in search of public phones.

Calls to California were not unusual when we were together. Sometimes, he would contact his office; sometimes, the call would be to his children. Although he never hid the calls, thankfully he never talked where I would overhear his side of the conversation. That was fine as far I was concerned. This was my time with Christopher. Being an only child, I did not share well, but I tolerated those intrusions into our special hours because I felt his family and his office held tenure in his life, whereas I did not.

According to The Manual, a well-schooled Southern woman knows her place. Therefore, I always smiled and practiced waiting patiently until he completed his calls.

From the very first, I had decided that I would prefer to know about the calls rather than have him hide them from me, otherwise I simply did not care to be a party to them. After he returned from those necessary check-ins, I always politely asked if everything was fine in his other world. After each of my foiled attempts for a sophisticated, dispassionate rationalization, I always felt a certain kinship to a young girl child peering into a pet shop window, yearning for that puppy dog she knew she would never be given.

With my world on pause, I sat in the cool shade of the overhead branches as warm, soft Florida breezes brushed by my body. Waiting for Christopher to return and for my life to begin once again, I stared at the lake, aware of the bustling humanity around me. All morning I had been amazed by the presence of so many teenagers and children flitting about. This was a school day, so why were these kids not in class? My parents would never have taken me out of school just to go on vacation. Back when I was coming up, families only took trips during the summer when schools were out of session.

And you walked uphill to school both ways in hip-deep snow. Rachael, you're sounding too old with that line of thinking.

Before many more minutes ticked away, I realized Christopher had been gone an uncharacteristically long time. When the sunlight bouncing off the water became uncomfortable to view, I changed benches to spend the rest of my waiting more closely observing people.

I watched Goofy granting pictures to excited, tongue-tied children knotted about his knees. I studied the many family groups, speculating which ones were working on second or third marriages and which children had been sired during some previous pair bonding. I divided all young, childless couples into two subgroups. I decided those walking joined as closely as contestants in a potato sack race were newlyweds and at Epcot because they were too embarrassed to stay in their rooms all day screwing. Those couples who walked gingerly were those newlyweds who had failed to properly pace themselves and had rubbed raw certain sensitive areas. As they had obviously planned no other activity for their honeymoons, those unfortunate couples were left with uncomfortably strolling around the resort, surrounded by strangers, as their only form of entertainment.

I almost envied those men and women who appeared close to our ages and who had teenagers or grandchildren in tow. Seeing older couples, without offspring tagging behind, made me curious as to which ones were actually married, which ones were dating, which ones would be filing for divorce as soon as they returned home and which ones were enjoying an illicit tryst like me. I categorized childless, middle-aged and older couples using the following criteria: those not talking to each other were married, those holding hands were dating, those walking five or more feet apart would be shortly contacting attorneys. After close scrutiny, I decided that we must be the only adulterers meeting at such a family-oriented site.

After checking with my internal clock again, I knew Christopher had been gone far too long for a routine phone call. I had no room key and did not know how I could prove to hotel management I needed to get back into our room should that become necessary. Before my imaginative mind could compose dialogues for such an emergency, I turned to see Christopher striding toward me. Relieved, I smiled and rose from the bench. Waiting for him, I noticed he failed to return my initial smile as he continued striding vigorously in my direction.

Maybe there has been unsettling news.

He walked like a man with a purpose. He did not stop or smile or speak until he stood in front of me. Without expression, Christopher wrapped his arms around me, giving me a long, deep, passionate kiss in front of Goofy, the carefree children and God knows how many other people.

"Damn, how I've missed you!" he said when our kiss finally ended. He hugged me tightly before releasing me from his embrace.

As we continued hand-in-hand with our walk through Disney's version of England, I decided today was definitely not the day to inquire into the state of affairs back in California.

❈

I lay on my stomach diagonally across the mattress, my lower torso covered by a sheet. Too relaxed following my personalized, morning wake-up, I had fallen back asleep while he showered. I had good intentions of joining that shower, but had not been able to activate any muscles to get me there. Turning my head, I discovered Christopher on his hands and knees, checking under the bed for any overlooked possessions while he sang softly to himself, in Italian, a nameless happy tune. Out of the corner of my eye, I noticed his closed suitcase against the wall near the door.

What would it be like if we lived together? Would I still be the icing on his cake? I wondered if I would continue being a source of joy in his life. Would the physical side of our relationship become too familiar, too routine, too taken for granted that we would not crave each other as much as we did now?

Oh, Rachael, just shut up. Quit agonizing about this tangled mess and enjoy it.

After getting to his feet, he came to sit on the side of the bed near my head. "I'm leaving to rent a car now," he said as he brushed my hair over to one shoulder.

I murmured to acknowledge his statement. I felt his hand gently stroke my head.

"Rachael, you bring me such happiness. My life has been so enriched because of you." He leaned over to plant a light kiss on my exposed ear. "Our time together is so special to me." Leaning further to kiss my shoulder, he whispered, "I'm so lucky we met."

I became aware of his weight shifting farther on the bed. Next, I felt a wet kiss centered between the two dimples near the base of my spine.

"I'll be back as soon as I can." Speaking in his normal volume, Christopher added, "Be ready."

His last kiss had created an electric tingle that quickly spread heat throughout my body. I wanted him now as much as his body had needed mine earlier when he awoke.

"I'm ready right now," I volunteered truthfully, feeling his body lift away from the mattress. I quickly snared his knee with my right arm.

He chuckled. "I should have said, 'Be packed.' I'll be back in about an hour."

Purposely staying away from the interstate systems, Christopher steered our rental car through central Florida, heading toward St. Augustine. The slower tempo of the almost-deserted pavement and the tranquil rural areas that we drove along helped dampen the hectic pace we had maintained the day before at Epcot. Azaleas brightly dotted the yards of the small towns the highway bisected. Each community appeared color coded by those flowering shrubs, some pink, some red, while other townships exhibited only purple blooms.

"Did I tell you I stayed with Grandmother Taite after Mom went to work?" Distracted by our passing a huge clump of especially brilliant fuchsia blossoms, I interrupted my initial train of thought. "Honey, have you noticed all these azaleas?"

Christopher shook his head, keeping his eyes on the road ahead. "Not really," he replied.

"I've decided each town council must have bought just one bush and had all the residents take cuttings. That's why, in each of these towns we drive through, all the azaleas match."

"You were saying about your grandmother." He was far more interested in my history than flowering shrubbery.

"She kept me when Mom went off to work. She had a cow and chickens and put out a garden each year. She taught me how to wring a chicken's neck and clean it. Did you say you've done that?"

"No. Never."

"And she spoiled me somethin' fierce. She'd buy a day-old birthday cake at the White Store each Saturday so I could skin off all the icin' I wanted to. I never had to eat any of that icky cake part."

Of all her grandchildren, Grandmother Taite favored me because I was my Daddy's only child. Daddy had been her pet because only my father had her black hair and black eyes. The rest of her children took after Granddaddy's people. At her house, she allowed me the freedom to be the child I could never be at my house, and what a sanctuary her home had been.

"She had cherry trees and could bake the best pies." Recalling one chore I had inherited from my dad, I chuckled. "In the spring when tent caterpillars would weave their nests, Grandmother would send me to burn out the sinners. Daddy had done that for her when he was a boy. Daddy would preach the worms a sermon before he torched and sent them all to hell. So would I. That's why we called them 'sinners.'"

And, sinner, who's coming to torch you?

I ignored my twin, but she turned my thoughts to Christopher and me. Deciding that sleeping dog was about to get woke up, I inquired, "Honey, what would it be like to be together all the time?"

He was quiet for a few miles. Without taking his eyes off the asphalt ahead, he explained solemnly, "It would change everything. Since no relationship stays the same, we would lose what we have now."

Although I wanted to plead that it could get better, I said nothing.

"I know you won't stay with me forever," he continued, "and I won't leave my family, so let's enjoy our wonderful times together for as long as they last. Remember, Rachael, we're making memories for our old age. Thinking of you in my golden years will . . . "

I turned my head to view the passing scenery. While he ambled through his well-thought-out list of reasons why he stays in California and I remain in Tennessee, I merely tuned him out. Those statements might sound perfectly justifiable to him, however, my mind, like a badly scratched vinyl record, kept repeating, *We could be different. It could get better.*

Over the years, despite coming up schooled in the Southern edition of The Manual, I had successfully broken free from many of those old chains that tied down various aspects of my life. But I had not yet been able to shed that one cardinal law that had been engraved on me. Men know best. Although I tested out in the top two percent of the population in intelligence, I knew I was on the low end of the bell curve when it came to romantic expertise. After two failed marriages and countless dead-end relationships, I simply had accepted that I was not gifted when it came to male-female interactions. I labeled my sad condition as being romantically challenged.

If I knew what class to attend, I thought, I could sign up—

Hell, she butted in, *you couldn't even qualify for the prerequisite course.*

I desperately wished I had logical reasons I could eloquently present, detailing why we could be different, but I dared not voice my thoughts, even if they should come to me. I would not challenge Christopher because men knew best, and I had been trained to defer to them.

Was that a fallacy like the rest of the misinformation fed me?

※

Upon reaching St. Augustine, Christopher indicated we would find a bed-and-breakfast for our two nights in that city. With all his travels in Europe, he was experienced with this form of accommodation. Since I had only stayed in American hotels and motels, I deferred to his judgment as I had been so trained.

Just south of the historic district, we found an inn with a marker indicating the building had been originally constructed as a boarding house back in the 1800s. Its darkly painted exterior seemed foreboding, but inside we discovered it charmingly furnished with period antiques. The suite we were shown had in its attached bath a freestanding, claw-footed porcelain tub encircled by a suspended oval curtain. That great tub sold me immediately because I envisioned a romantically shared shower. On the other hand, Christopher took a fancy to the room's curtained four-poster bed.

Before we had taken the time to unpack, we showered together in that once inviting tub. However, the plastic curtain constantly surprised us with its coldness as its stiff surface kept sticking to our wet, soapy bodies. It became a third entity in the scheme of things, about as welcome as two wailing babies at a wedding.

So much for that dream. Some fantasies are better left not acted out.

※

While waiting on the weathered deck for a table to become available, we sipped wine, commenting on our great fortune in finding such interesting places to dine on each of our trips. Near our feet, bouncing tabby kittens playfully scampered around posts supporting the deck's aged wooden railing. The idyllic locale, where earlier our innkeeper had directed us, was a Hollywood-perfect backdrop for lovers.

"Remember that little place in Marblehead?" I asked.

He countered, "Don't forget the hash at Orangeburg."

Distracted by the pristine beauty of the surrounding tidal marsh as the daylight came to an end, I interrupted our listing of past restaurants. "Damn, Christopher, this is our best sunset to date."

Although the late winter sun had just dropped below the mainland, its last rays released a fan of glorious colors across the adjacent estuary. Above its intersection with the marshlands, the sky shimmered with blending shades of oranges, reds and tangerines. Molten clouds spilled across the deepening blues higher up. The open water carried a mirror image of the sky's colors on its still surface. Marsh birds flew low in silhouette near the horizon. A warm breeze, carrying aromas from the saltwater and from the restaurant's kitchen, played against our bodies and piqued our appetites.

Christopher pulled me against him and gently pushed back strands of my hair that were being blown into my face. He stared into my eyes. "I want only the best for you, my sweet Rachael," he said in a serious tone.

He leaned forward until his forehead rested against mine. I knew he wished only good for me as certainly as I knew the sun rose in the east and set in the west. While standing within his encircling arms with our heads touching, wave upon wave of tranquility washed over me. Intuitively, I knew their hidden source was centered somewhere within Christopher. Accepting his invisible almost intangible gift, I exhaled slowly before breathing in that comforting peace with each following intake of air. As gentle waves of his offering cascaded over me, I experienced a strangely glorious sensation passively accompanying the oxygen molecules carried by my blood as they crossed cell membranes throughout my body.

"Saranson, party of two," blared the outside speaker from near the restaurant's front door.

Christopher suddenly released his embrace. "That must be us," he said, moving toward the door. "No one ever gets my name right."

With its peaceful inflow of energy cut off from the source, my body jerked from the abrupt loss. Like an addict, having repeatedly used drugs recreationally and who becomes hooked after his last cavalier hit, longingly fixates on his recently emptied needle and requires more, I stared dumbfounded at his back as he walked away, desperately craving what my body had just enjoyed. Now, I truly understood what was that nameless something he supplied that had been missing in my life. And I, too, wanted more.

Every voice in my head screamed, *Come back! Hold us like that just a little longer!*

⁂

The following morning, we shared breakfast with a couple who appeared to be near our ages. While the woman and I sat together at the table sipping orange juice, Christopher and her companion walked around the reception area, munching sweet rolls. As he collected brochures, I overheard Christopher question the other man about what he considered to be the city's choicest historical sites.

My table partner remarked smugly, "My husband and I always stay here on our drives between our winter home in the Keys and our house in Connecticut. We've been doing that for years."

Admiring the room's comfortable antiques, I agreeably commented, "This place is just too neat. I can understand why y'all keep comin' back. This is our first time to stay here."

"Where's home for you two?" she asked.

Without thinking, I answered truthfully, "I'm from Knoxville, Tennessee. He's from San Francisco, California."

She shook her head in the negative, thinking she had not been given the correct response to her question. "Where do you live now?"

Not considering the consequences of my words, I repeated, "I'm from Knoxville, Tennessee. He's from San Francisco, California."

Looking inquisitively into my face, she waited some time before

replying, "*Same Time, Next Year?*"
Sweet Jesus, she knows!
"Not exactly," I replied casually, hoping my face did not look as if the woman had caught me red handed in the cookie jar. Oh, damn, oh double damn! "So, how long will it take y'all to get home from here?" I asked, hoping to steer the conversation to a safer subject.

Coming to my rescue, Christopher quickly called from the far side of the room, "We've got a lot to see today, Rachael. Have you finished your juice?"

<hr />

Escaping our lodgings without running into that inquisitive Yankee woman again, we walked the colonial district of St. Augustine, ending at the historic fort, the old city's main attraction. Christopher happily held a map of the fort in his hands. I knew that man possessed a contented soul whenever he had access to a map. His boyish pride in knowing his exact location in the world sweetly endeared him to me.

Following Christopher as he extensively explored the interior of the pre-colonial fort, I worried over the lives lost there through the centuries. Afterwards, on the grounds outside the thick walls, he stopped to study his map and looked toward the fort. He turned slightly, looked again at the fort, referred once more to his map, then repeated the process. He was uncharacteristically quiet, his face puzzled.

"Honey, what's the matter?" I had never seen the man look so confused.

He pointed to his map. "There's supposed to be two forts here."
What in hell is he talking about?
I scanned the map I held that pictured one fort with its two stories shown slightly askew, one above the other. I walked to where he stood to determine if he had picked up a different map. His was the same as mine. I studied his face, finding his expression one of continuing concern for the missing fort.

As soon as I realized the reason for his quandary, gales of uncontrollable laughter burst from my throat. I could no more contain the sounds welling inside me than I could have squelched the multitude of sneezes caused by my allergy to Paperwhite narcissus.

While hysterically convulsing at the expense of the man I loved, my control weakened over certain necessary body functions. As tears spilled out of my eyes, I could barely breathe between whoops of laughter, let alone speak. First, I feared I would faint from lack of oxygen to my brain, next I became scared I would wet my pants, and then I worried both would occur at the same time. My muscles barely maintained my skeleton in an upright position. When I could no longer trust myself to stand without assistance, I clutched Christopher's arm for support with both hands.

Startled by my unladylike outbursts, he focused concern on me, forgetting his missing fort. When at last able to muster connected words, I put an end to his dilemma.

"Just . . . one fort." Moving my hands in the air, I placed one atop the another. "Two stories."

"Oh," he said, comprehending the map at last.

Wiping tears from my chin, I added, "Honey, maybe you are just another pretty face."

By his changed demeanor, I knew immediately that I had seriously bruised my darling's pride and that my recent behavior had shattered a major tenet of behavior for polite Southern ladies. Despite my aching sides, I succumbed to a second, milder fit of laughter.

Touching his arm, I quickly apologized, "I'm sorry that I laughed at you like that."

With my guffaws diminishing to periodic giggles, I was relieved that I had not fallen out and, mercifully, had not peed in my panties.

"I'm so sorry," I repeated, hoping to make amends.

Wordlessly, Christopher studied the fort. Scanning his map a final time, he briskly folded the paper before shoving it into his pants pocket.

"You're right," he bit off his words concluding, "that was funny."

He turned on his heels, quickly marching away. I followed a respectful ten paces behind, thanking my lucky stars I had not committed the unpardonable, an undignified snort, while in the throes of unbridled hysteria.

Sharing the foodstuffs I had carried from home, we held a private picnic that afternoon in the garden behind our inn. While reliving memories from our past trips during those three hours, time almost stood still for me.

Later we walked the mile, a pleasant little jaunt to whet the appetite as Christopher had described it when he first proposed the idea, from our bed-and-breakfast to a restaurant housed in a converted Victorian cottage situated beside the town's main drag. Striding that distance was sobering, dissipating the effects of the two bottles of Crossville wine.

Still regretting my rude laughter earlier, I began beating about that bush to disguise my approaching apology. "Honey, did I tell you that I did a report on St. Augustine's fort when I was in the seventh grade?"

"No."

Taking his hand while we walked, I opened with, "I saw the fort first when I was eight. That was when I rode down with Daddy Pop to Daytona. Big Momma and Aunt Maurie were already there for vacation. They had ridden down with my great-uncle and his wife. We went right by the fort, but he wouldn't stop for me to go in it. Daddy Pop never stopped when he was on a trip unless the car needed gas."

Christopher interrupted my symbolic thrashing. "Didn't he take bathroom breaks?"

"Oh, no," I explained, "but Daddy Pop always kept a mason jar handy. I'd have to squat over it on the floorboard in the backseat. It was kinda hard for me to hit the mark when he drove around curves, especially when we were on the old roads goin' through Kentucky."

He snickered.

I chided, "Don't laugh. Be pretty." Returning to my task, I continued, "Anyway, I've always wanted to explore that fort ever since I was eight. Thank you for takin' me." I finally had reached the reason for sharing that memory. "Really, I have no idea why I laughed so hard when you were havin' trouble decipherin' that brochure. I guess it was because that wasn't like you. The Army trained you to read maps, and you've always been able to pinpoint our location on road maps right down to the exact millimeter. It was just so unexpected that you thought there was a second fort that I was caught off guard. That's why I laughed." I walked on eggshells while awaiting his response.

We covered some distance before he spoke again. His tone was serious, but contained no trace of hurt feelings. "You know, Rachael, I've been thinking about that this afternoon, too. I must have gotten so engrossed inside the fort that I'd forgotten about the stairs we had taken." He was quiet for some time before adding, "When you started laughing and couldn't stop, I looked around and couldn't see anything that would make you laugh like that. I wanted to share the joke, but didn't know what had caused your laughter."

Interrupting, I said softly, "And then, I told you it was you."

"Yes, then, you told me I was the joke." We walked in silence a while longer. "Rachael, my mistake was amusing, perhaps," he said firmly, "but hardly that funny."

I answered contritely, "I agree. I can't explain my rudeness. Please accept my heartfelt apology. I will never do that again."

He opened the door to the restaurant and allowed me to enter ahead of him. "Apology accepted. Incident closed."

<hr />

"This restaurant and dinner will go directly into our archives," I declared after swallowing my last forkful of key lime pie.

The meal had been a too perfect dining experience. Our waiter had been personable, and the atmosphere as cozy as sitting at card tables surrounded by family while eating at Big Momma's on Sundays after church. Individuals at adjacent tables on the enclosed front porch quickly became new best friends we would never see again. Christopher selected white wine to accompany our stone crab claws and a red for our entrée. Upon seeing my grimace after my first sip of the red, he ordered a second bottle of white for me. The chef's presentation of shark had been too good and went well with both wines. He requested another glass of wine each with our single serving of dessert.

Placing my fork across my plate, tines down, I looked up to find a man and woman standing at Christopher's side. They smiled. Wondering why these strangers stood by our table, I smiled a questioning smile back.

"Excuse us," the woman said, "But we were eating in the next room over and wanted you to know that we wished we had been seated in here because the porch sounded like it was having more fun than where we sat."

Christopher grandly waved his right arm in the direction of the opposite side of our table. "Come, join us for coffee."

The man laughed heartily, but refused. I caught a look of disappointment flittering across the woman's face. "I guess we'd better not," she made their excuses. "We have a long drive ahead of us."

After they left the room, Christopher tossed back the last in his wine glass. "Walk back or call a taxi?" he offered.

Although we had shared nearly five bottles of wine since three in the afternoon, I really did not feel all that drunk. The mile back would not faze me; after all, I hiked LeConte on a regular basis.

"After I go to the bathroom, let's hoof it," I replied.

After ten in the evening, the streets in the old town of St. Augustine were almost empty of traffic, and we were the only pedestrians strolling through the historic district. Despite all businesses being closed, the deserted area was well lit, and I felt little apprehension because I had Christopher at my side.

In front of the oldest schoolhouse in the United States, he abruptly announced, "I need to find a bathroom. Quick!"

We located the public restrooms we had visited earlier that day, but their doors now were locked.

Jokingly, I said the first thing that popped into my head, "Where's Daddy Pop's mason jar when you need it?"

"Rachael, please!"

By his tone, I knew he was not amused by my remark. As we had another half mile before reaching our room with its awaiting toilet, there was nothing left to do but forge on.

"This is terrible." Discomfort was evident in his voice as he picked up his pace. "Hurry. I'm desperate. Try to keep up."

Upon hearing his last remarks, I noticed a small public park ahead on our left. No lights illuminated its darkened greenery. As Christopher hotfooted past its surrounding ornamental iron fence, the idea occurred to me that since the man converses with trees while hiking, this park might suit his needs right now.

"How about the park?" I suggested. Watching Christopher make a sharp turn without breaking stride and race-walk through an open gate into the deep shadows, I called after him, "I'll wait here on the sidewalk."

Without a word of acknowledgment, he disappeared into the night. From within the darkness of the park I soon heard water running.

Suddenly, I heard an unfamiliar, outraged male voice demanding, "What are you doing!"

Sweet Jesus, it's a cop!

Expecting to find a blue uniform, I quickly spun around, knowing full well that Christopher was about to be arrested for urinating in public and probably would have an additional charge for indecent exposure tacked on. Yet, I saw no policeman in sight.

Not a cop, I thought. Could be a street person.

Next, I overheard Christopher defensively explaining about all the wine he had drunk and the unavailability of the public restroom. All the while hearing water flowing, I thought he must have been in dire need of relieving himself. Who would have thought one kidney could filter so much liquid?

After a moment, I heard the disembodied voice say in a hurt whine, "If I came into your home, I wouldn't pee in your living room."

Still zipping up his pants, Christopher burst out of the park. I grabbed his free hand as we raced, staggering drunk with ill-controlled laughter, all the way back to the inn.

We left St. Augustine early the next morning, driving down the coast as close to the ocean as the highways allowed. I wanted to show him the beach where I had spent childhood vacations with Big Momma and Daddy Pop before I met Margaret and she had introduced me to Cherry Grove in South Carolina.

With motorcycles crowded into parking areas for most of the motels lining the town's main drag, I realized too late that this weekend started Bikers' Week at Daytona. Spring Gathering's early arrivals must have partied hearty the night before because there were few bikers puttering on the streets when we pulled into town. Hoping to miss out on any rowdy participants, we stopped for an early lunch at a crab shack near the water.

Our crab cake meal began peacefully enough with only Christopher and me seated in the small eating establishment, but soon the room became populated with fringed, black leather vests and pants; densely tattooed arms and chests; heavy gold chains; massive watches attached to black, tooled leather wristbands and diamond stud earrings. With each opening of the front door, welcoming greetings among the bikers increased in volume. Some of the males were accompanied by biker chicks attired in skimpy, black leather bras and with discreet tattoos on exposed stomachs that just eased out of low-riding, skin-tight leather pants; delicate gold chains; diamond ring-encrusted fingers; jeweled watches affixed to gold wrist bands and perfectly coiffed hair.

These were no ordinary, single-wide dwellers. They were corporate and professional denizens belonging to a high-rent district's Wild

Bunch. Attired in khaki slacks and pastel knit shirts with our sockless feet shoved into Sebagos, we were definitely the most underdressed of those assembling for lunch.

Leaving the noisy establishment without considering dessert, we walked through a herd of customized hogs to our rented car. Each machine we passed priced out many times over what my recently purchased, used Olds Ninety-eight had cost new. Still absorbing what we had seen of a life-style so foreign to us, we returned to the town's Broadwalk and famous beach in silence.

Since Christopher had never before been where cars were permitted on a beach, he was intrigued with leaving Daytona via the deserted sand. Grinning like a young boy piloting a four-wheeler, he speeded up and spun the car around when he braked. He performed that stunt several times before we exited the packed sand. Appropriately squealing each spin, I enjoyed the brief glimpse into what he must have been as a child.

One biker back at the crab shack had looked familiar, but for the life of me I could not place where I knew her. I worried with that puzzlement for hours. Wandering through the Kennedy Center, the mystery was solved when I saw our reflections superimposed over a display of space suits.

"Honey," I announced, "I do believe I saw my dentist at lunch. She certainly looked different without scrubs, mask, and latex gloves."

We spent our final night together lingering over dinner at a Cocoa Beach restaurant specializing in fresh seafood. Enjoying too much wine while waiting for an open table and later when sharing scallops and shrimp, I was feeling no pain by the end of our meal.

"I don't think I can drive back to the motel." Having imbibed more than I, Christopher laboriously pondered the charges on our tab to verify the accuracy of their total before suggesting, "Let's have our waiter call for a taxi."

With some difficulty, I focused my eyes in his direction. "No," I insisted, "I can drive the fuckin' car."

Sweet Jesus, how much did I drink?

Every hair rooted in my scalp ached, blood pounded inside my skull, dried spit caked the left outside corner of my lips, my tongue stuck to the roof of my mouth and I was naked under the sheets. I remembered driving from the restaurant to our motel, I remembered parking the car without hitting the curb guard, I remembered walking through the door Christopher held open for me and that was all I remembered.

Why did I have to blank out when I get too drunk? Why couldn't I just pass out like your normal, run-of-the-mill drunk? I thought I had grown too old, too wise, to put myself through this again.

Maybe this is all a bad dream, I thought, hoping against hope that it could be true. However, when I turned my head, the room spun and my stomach churned. I knew I would have to sober up, not wake up, to feel better. Damn, this was one aspect of my life I never wanted to share with Christopher.

If all my blood cells had not been occupied with beating against my brain like calloused palms pounding against a council drum, I could have blushed with embarrassment from having no recollection of the events that I had been party to after I blanked out. Unfortunately, that had shamefully happened too many times in my past.

While steeling myself for the dreaded, coming confrontation, I dredged up the first time when I had called Margaret after a big party at Cooksey's frat house, and she had sounded uncharacteristically cool to me. When asked what was wrong, Margaret told me things I had said to her the night before that I did not remember saying. I was stunned. She said I had better call Cooksey and apologize to him, too. So, I made the call, and he accepted my apologies, but I still had no idea what I had said or done. Margaret forgave me and, later, became my roommate. Cooksey never again asked me out, and I never tried rum and coke after that night.

There had been too many times after college when I woke up to find some hairy arm draped possessively across my belly. Those embarrassing mornings stopped when I finally switched from hard liquor to the more genteel wine.

What if I had been ugly with Christopher? What if I had been one crude, sloppy drunk? Sweet Jesus, what happened?

My twin was silent. Since she made no accusations, I decided she must have been too embarrassed to rag me about my behavior and had slipped away, leaving me alone to face the music. I slowly turned my head to check if Christopher was awake. I found him beside me in bed, propped against pillows, reading the local Sunday paper. I had never seen him read a newspaper when we were together. Wearing reading glasses, he looked stern.

After making enough fresh spit to unglue my mouth, I spoke. "Honey, I want to apologize for last night."

I had no idea what had transpired last evening, but I wanted to be certain I first asked his forgiveness, even before I greeted him with 'Good morning' and long before I was told I needed to apologize.

He looked over the top of the page at the facing wall. With his patrician profile seemingly set in stone, my heart sank. Since my companion did not look over in my direction, I decided I must have been dreadful. Now I would have to add last evening to my long list of lost nights.

"What for?" he asked, matter-of-factly. Never once looking at me, he went back to glancing over the paper.

Oh, damn! Oh, double damn!

I sucked out more saliva in order to give my answer. "I was drunk when I drove us back last night. I don't remember much about what happened after we got in the car."

Dropping the newspaper to his lap, Christopher looked at me over the top of his reading glasses' frame. "At the restaurant, you said you were OK."

I took a deep breath before explaining the one flaw I had never wanted him to know. "I blank out sometimes when I drink too much, and then I do things I can't recollect the next day. I don't . . . I don't remember anything I did or said after we walked into this room. I barely recall drivin' here." As I waited for my statements to register, I prayed he would not ask about past examples of such behavior. I slowly resumed my apology, "If I did anything . . . or if I said anything terrible to you, I am truly sorry."

"You said you were OK," he repeated thoughtfully, carefully weighing what I had just said.

As if repetition was needed for its acceptance, I restated my contriteness. "It was our last night together. I was too drunk to remember anything after we got back here. I am so very, very sorry."

I sensed he was replaying the previous evening. As I anticipated him rejecting my confession, eerily familiar thoughts and feelings washed over me. I found myself praying there could be a reprieving order from the presiding cleric, yet knew no mercy would be forthcoming from such a stern-faced man. Awaiting his verdict to be carried out,

I had nothing to add in my defense. Lest I condemn the one I loved by gazing upon his dear face, I kept my eyes fixed on the twisted branches stacked about my knees. With my throat constricted with fear as tightly as the encircling rope bound my bruised neck and tortured body to the rude cross at my back, I stood amid a bed of faggots, awaiting the fiery kiss of a nearby torch. Soon a glowing vapor rose between me and the assembled horde, silencing the jeers and freezing the movements of those crowded about me.

I waited, for what seemed to be an eternity, before I heard Christopher say from a great distance, "You don't have to apologize for anything."

Immediately the frightfully real vignette faded in retreat, and I was back in a Floridian motel, feeling only the weight of a smooth sheet against my skin and wondering from where in the world had that vision arose.

I closely watched Christopher. He seemed to be carefully considering his next question before finally asking, "How do you know? How am I supposed to know when you're that drunk?"

Putting my personal confusion aside, I glanced down at the sheets covering my nakedness before saying sadly in a low voice, "When my favorite adjective is 'fuckin'.'"

Leaning over to place a chaste kiss on my shoulder, he replied sweetly, "I thought that was your favorite verb."

Perhaps you weren't too awful. My twin had returned from her hidey-hole.

Maybe I wasn't, but what did I do? What happened last night, and just where did that strange memory come from?

<hr />

Still too hung over to contribute much to any conversation, I said little during the drive back to Orlando's airport. I knew I was growing too dependent upon Christopher as I had found it increasingly difficult to leave him after each visit. I had gone to Nashville knowing that our relationship would not exist past dinner that Tuesday night. Now, nearly four years later and living a continent apart, we were still meeting. Those few years totaled longer than my two marriages combined. Victoria had graduated high school and started college, and Vinnie had made it out of junior high.

Our sporadic weekends were no longer enough for me. Like his children, I, too, had grown. Except where he was concerned. Although my needing him had never been part of the original deal, I had constructed my business schedule around our visits because I had fallen hard for a man who was never around to stomp spiders on a daily basis.

My heart wanted Christopher and me in the same time zone, in the same community, in the same house. I so wanted to enjoy again those wonderful feelings I had experienced at sunset in St. Augustine, and I wanted to have them all day, every day.

I had questions that wanted answers. Like, where do I fit into your future? Do you retire from me when you retire from your firm? If I move to California, would we be together more often, for longer periods of time?

There was so much I wanted to discuss, but remained quiet, memorizing his profile until I could see the man, line for line, feature for feature, with my eyes closed. I rested my left hand on his right thigh, feeling his muscles tense and relax under my fingers as he powered the car along the interstate. Speaking only when spoken to, I voiced not one question to the most important person in my life because I sensed he did not wish to answer any of them. In any case, I was not prepared to cope with a negative response.

Standing alone in the crowded Orlando terminal, I watched his departing plane, my body aching as if undergoing an amputation with no anesthesia administered to ease the pain. In the emotional wake created by his absence, a startling realization dawned on me. I was related to those downed hemlocks that I had seen wrenched from the soil on my hikes to LeConte for I, too, lacked an anchoring taproot.

Ten

After our weekend in Florida, re-entry into my usual routine proved easy because the next few weeks were jam-packed with catered orders for the opening of the Dogwood Arts Festival, Mother's Day celebrations, bridal luncheons, Derby parties, graduations, divorces and 'just-because' gatherings, on top of what we prepared daily for the regular onslaught of hungry mouths at the restaurant. I hardly had time to put plastic wrap over the last catered dish leaving the kitchen before making up a grocery list for the next day's orders. Liz, Margaret and I worked like demons possessed just keeping most customers happy. More and more often, Mom got called in to help greet and seat the lunch crowds. We were just too successful, and I almost wished for a late spring snowstorm simply to give us some down time.

Between the crunch for Derby Day and the flurry of high school and college graduations, I looked forward to a break in the action provided by another trek to LeConte. Even without Christopher present to celebrate our anniversary, I jealously maintained that special May weekend in order to sit on Cliff Top, watching the sun fall toward the west, hoping that he would be watching the sun go down with me, only three hours later.

Reasoning it was the same sun, the same sunset, what did it matter that we were in different time zones? Had not Einstein boiled down time to a brief mathematical exercise in relativity?

After icing the last five caramel cakes baked after lunch, I found the booth in the far back where Mom was finishing her chicken salad on whole wheat. I did not have to examine her plate to know she would have her sandwich on the heels of the loaf. Like her, I found those end slices to have better flavor. I slid opposite her and, moving her straw aside, took a deep sip of spring water from her glass.

"What do you want me to fix for our hike up Friday?" I asked. "Scott's strawberries are just comin' in. I could do a little something extra with them."

"Darlin'." Mom stopped before she started.

I knew what that hesitation signified. Even though I had no idea which tangent our conversation was about to take, I also knew I would not like what followed.

"Could I don't and say I did?"

Stunned, I peered at my mother over the top of my glasses' frame. Never before had she passed on a hike.

"Perhaps Liz and Margaret could join you. I just don't feel up to goin' this time."

I did not know what to say next. I knew she had not been feeling well. I knew Mom's feet had always been a problem when she hiked, however, the prospects of later lost toenails had never deterred her before. In the past, nothing had ever come between The Hammer and some goal she wanted. I recalled earlier this week when I had noticed that my mother now stood shorter than me. Mom was supposed to be two inches taller. Feeling a constant in my life growing dim for the first time, I became aware, at that very minute, the woman was slipping away from me, and that someday there would be a void I did not know how and would not want to fill. Although I wanted to ignore that possibility today, Mom backing out of this year's hike seemed like the first nail building her coffin that would not let me forget.

Intently, I studied her once ageless face. She was in her seventies. Hiking LeConte was a young woman's activity. I figured she must have thought out this request long and hard before voicing it. Realizing it was as difficult for her to utter those words as it was for me to hear them, I simply nodded my head in agreement. Having no unselfish argument available to change her mind, I reluctantly accepted that the time had come for her to stop hiking.

"I'll ask," I said softly, wondering how to handle coverage for my restaurant the morning of the hike.

***

Margaret walked in the lead, I stayed in the middle in order to be a party to both their conversations and Liz brought up the rear. As the hot sun beamed through breaks in the leafy canopy, I heard the sounds of the last creek we had crossed fading in the distance. Had Mom been my hiking buddy today, I would have been able to leave Knoxville two hours sooner and miss out on the heat this early into the trek. The stones in the trail clinked with our steps. My pack was heavier than usual, and it dug into my right shoulder. I decided to take two anti-inflammatories at our next water break.

Margaret's jaunty attire had been specifically purchased for this morning's adventure with each item carefully selected to enhance its wearer. A roguish straw hat, shading her tastefully painted face, sat saucily on her elegantly styled, bottle-streaked, natural blonde hair. The cotton bandana artfully knotted at her throat matched her red tank top and red rag socks. Her boots were unscuffed. Her gold jewelry added the proper sparkle to enliven the drab tan of her crisp, new cargo shorts. A navy fanny pack, holding her lunch and water and makeup, set off her small waist. She picked her way along the trail using a recently purchased walking stick tipped with a shiny brass spike. Liz and I carried the rest of her essentials in our larger backpacks.

I wore my favorites: worn gray scrub pants and faded navy T-shirt. The sturdy sapling I had picked up some twenty years ago along the way to Trillium Gap to use as a walking stick thumped against my hand as I strolled Alum Bluff's well-beaten trail. Liz sported distressed jeans and an orange Vols T-shirt. Our packs showed hard use, our hair was tucked under sun-faded blue Tennessee baseball caps, our boots were comfortably broken in and our makeup remained in jars on dressers back home. Margaret was a fashion-do, whereas Liz and I were primed for the ignoble, fashion-don't layout.

Since the last Super Bowl party, I had observed, with growing amusement, the sparring between Liz and Hugh Ed. With all the nonverbal positioning, their verbal engagements seemed more like unconventional warfare. I noticed that as his forces cautiously advanced, hers eased deeper into hiding.

Deciding now was a good time to get updated as to their status, I called back over my shoulder, "Say, Lizzie-Lou, when do you think you'll put Hugh Ed out of his misery and accept a date with the man?"

When Margaret stopped abruptly in order to hear Liz's answer, I bumped into her. With her path blocked, Liz took the opportunity to pull a tissue from her pocket to blow her pert nose. Only after placing her tissue into her waistband did she consent to respond.

"Well," Liz answered, "I don't know. I've been waitin' for the right man to come along for so many years now that I just don't think I want to date any more. He is a nice enough man, but I've been single far too long. You know, it's taken months, but I've finally gotten our customers to stop fixin' me up with dates."

Having heard Liz's non-committal answer, Margaret started up the trail again. She called back over her shoulder, "I think you ought to go out with him, Liz. If you married Hugh Ed," she pointed out, "you wouldn't have to pay money for a man to do maintenance on all your properties."

Margaret had always been practical when it came to choosing men to date. Her same practicality applied to packing because she never packed any more than someone else could carry for her, which was why Liz and I carried heavier packs than usual and why my right shoulder ached.

Liz called over my head, "That's no reason to marry a man for!"

"Then it's because he didn't go to college!" Margaret yelled back to Liz.

Before I could add my two cents' worth, Liz barked in a tone of voice that disallowed further discussion, "No! That's not it! Subject closed!" We walked a few yards more before Liz stormed ahead to Margaret, "Next time, buy a bigger pack!"

I was not certain, but I could almost swear that the implied 'bitch' was actually spoken. Attributing Liz's uncharacteristic irritability to the fact the three of us had put in double time over the last forty-eight hours to cover today's estimated volume at Rachael's while we hiked, I diplomatically placed all further inquiries into their relationship on hold.

When we reached the log steps imbedded into the steep rise at the foot of Alum Bluff, Margaret stopped to adjust the red laces on her new boots. When she raised up, she said, "You won't believe who Mrs. Marshall wants to introduce me to."

Liz and I waited for her to continue.

"Jackson Hodges."

After we failed to respond with what Margaret considered to be the proper enthusiasm, she went on to give the man's pedigree. "He's the one who owns all that land around Sevierville covered with all those malls. He's divorcin' his wife right now. And when that little ol' mess gets cleaned up, Mrs. Marshall, who's his mother's sister, is goin' to have a big party and introduce me to him."

"Will he have enough money left after the divorce for you?" I asked.

"Oh, Rachael." Indicating she saw no hope for me, Margaret sighed before starting the steps at the steepest incline along this trail to the Lodge. All conversation was put on hold until we reached the top. Stopping to rest, Margaret breathlessly explained, "Jackson hired a detective who . . . caught her . . . in the arms . . . of another man, so to speak. I don't think she'll be entitled to too much, . . . seein' as how she got caught with his pants down."

❧

Not until an unsigned postcard arrived from Hawaii wishing me a happy birthday in September did it dawn on me that was Christopher's first contact since March after his call reporting he returned west without incident. I had been just too busy with the restaurant to notice. I could have called him, I guess, but I decided that would be too forward on my part.

Somewhere, The Manual points out that a female must not appear forward, which is Southern speak for 'aggressive.'

He failed to call at Christmas. Neither did he send a card. This was the first year he had forgotten me. I was mowed down as if some juvenile prankster had sneaked up and sharply tapped into the bend at the back of my knees with his bent knees, the way I had done classmates on the playground during recess in grammar school.

I fumed that I was being taken for granted. I was hurt. I was mad. I was really much more disgusted with myself than hurt because I had let my guard down. My sheer stupidity had created this hateful dependence on another person. When we had stood with our foreheads touching at sunset in St. Augustine, I must have allowed the man inside my fortifications. He had come too close and studied my weaknesses far too well, for now the enemy owned the power to hurt me.

The honeymoon is definitely over this time, I thought. But, by damn, I can do without Christopher Saracini. What the hell was I thinking when I thought he could be trusted? I lived without that man for forty-two years. I can live very well without him for the rest of my life, thank you!

How careless of you, girl, allowing one man to control your happiness. That's it! No more! My twin was indignant for me. *Any man, even a separated man, can overlook special days for his family, but he best not ignore his Southern-born mistress.* She admonished, *Rachael, there are rules of propriety to be maintained here.*

Damn him, and damn the horse he rode in on!

Unwittingly, I had left my heart too vulnerable. Worse than parading bare-ass naked in front of him, I had stripped down emotionally. Regretting having been lulled into thinking I could trust any man and allowing Christopher to get close, I was maddest at myself for that lapse in psychic security

Rachael, my twin smugly pointed out, *he was on foot when we met. There were no horses there.*

And damn you, too, you literal bitch!

In January, I mailed a short note asking not to be contacted again. I wrote that I wanted more than he was willing to give. I suggested he take one of his children on his future travels and stop inviting me.

I felt my sentiments were noble and well intended. I carefully edited the message three days before I drafted the final version and posted my terse request. In reality, I wanted him to call, begging me to reconsider and pleading with me to sell everything I owned to come live with him by the Bay. What I got was a flowery card with a handwritten addition, saying sadly that he would miss me, but he understood my feelings.

Damn. Double, double damn. At the very least, I thought the man would call to explain his oversight so I could reluctantly allow him to persuade me to change my mind.

The Bible instructs: 'If your right eye offends you, pluck it out.' Some early translator must have left out the verses explaining how to adjust to that accompanying loss of depth perception.

All the literature I had ever read on the subject indicated that three weeks must pass before new habits become ingrained. Three months after receiving his unexpected response, I remained among the walking wounded. I thought I would be able to fill my time with activities that would help heal the hurt I had created. I spent time with friends. I took in movies with Mom. I walked the Boulevard in hopes of losing unwanted pounds. I researched new menus. I adapted old family recipes. I had quiet hours at the cabin with my four-legged girls. I explored unfamiliar trails in the mountains. I found the experts to be completely wrong or I had misjudged my feelings for Christopher Saracini.

As a ruse to prevent me from picking up the phone to dial his number, I began pretending he had died. That did not help matters much, however, because I was already haunted by the man. I felt his presence at the restaurant, in my car, beside me as I hiked. The worst times were at night. Sprawled out on my lonely bed, lying on my stomach, I could feel his arm across my shoulder, the weight of his leg over my leg, the length of his warm body against my side. Night, after night, after sleepless night.

True to my request, Christopher did not contact me after sending his last card. The ancient adage 'Be careful what you wish for, for you might get what you wish,' ran through my mind too many times.

After a mere four months into the new calendar, my resolve completely melted away. Having failed to realize how much I relied upon his viewpoint whenever I had a problem to confront, I played with the idea that we could become pen pals or, at the very least, phone pals. In the past, I could always get his take on a subject during a phone call or while driving through some countryside. I came to believe if I could only hear his voice or read his handwriting once in a while, I would be able to manage the rest of my life without actually seeing him. After all, I told myself, I have the memories of our times together that I could replay in my mind whenever I wished, as often as I wished. Surely, those remembered visions were enough to last a lifetime.

What a crock of shit.

Christopher away in California and me in Tennessee was like having a half-eaten bag of potato chips in the kitchen, calling my name. The need to hear his voice would drag me to the telephone, and I would start to dial before quickly slamming down the receiver.

I had taken seven days to get over caffeine. My body had required about five weeks to work through its craving for nicotine. After four months of no contact with Christopher, some part of me still coaxed, *Just call. Talk with him. One call won't start back anything. We can just be friends.*

I concluded it was a good thing I had never tried cocaine for I was having far too much trouble withdrawing from my addiction to that simple Italian man from a small village to try any substance stronger.

Maybe I was vulnerable because of the romantic movie I had seen the night before. Maybe my bio-rhythms were low. Maybe the Devil made me do it. Maybe I just needed contact of any type with that man to feel complete again. Maybe I was frustrated by the bad lettuce I found at the market that morning. For whatever reason, I found myself leaning against my kitchen sink at seven Thursday evening, dialing his private number and not able to hang up when he answered during the first ring.

"Hello." His beloved voice was business brusque.

My heart thumped so hard against my chest wall that I knew he could hear it over the phone line. I felt like a dog groveling before her master, hoping for one kind word.

"Hey." That simple greeting was the most I could muster.

As soon as he heard my voice, Christopher responded, not wasting one fraction of a millisecond, "When can I see you again?"

His question was music to my ears, a balm for my hurting soul. The one narcotic my body craved.

Two weeks later, I stood at the appointed gate in the Denver airport waiting for him to deplane. I might look to all the world like a solemn-faced, plump, graying-haired woman, rumpled from a cross-country flight, but inside I was jumping up and down, shaking with as much excitement as any little two-year-old girl awaiting her turn to tell a department store Santa her heart desires for Christmas.

With growing impatience, I searched for his dear face in the crowd of strangers streaming by on either side of me. Christopher was the final passenger to come through the door. My heart leaped into my throat. My cheeks hurt from the wideness of my smile. I wanted to throw my arms about him and cover his face with kisses. When he recognized me and a frown crossed his face, I quickly lost my smile and remained motionless. Scanning the concourse, he stopped a few feet in front of me. He appeared uneasy.

"Rachael," he said, speaking in a low monotone, "there was a couple on my flight who've known me and my family for years. We need to be discreet."

Damn!

Double damn! I nodded that I understood. "Does this mean I need to walk ten paces behind you?" I joked, wanting to put a smile on his face.

"No." He did not smile.

I half-heartedly teased, "I guess screamin' for joy and jumpin' into your arms is out of the question, too."

Still, no smile was forthcoming. "That's correct."

Adopting his serious demeanor, I said matter-of-factly, "OK, then, pretend that I just did."

Christopher allowed a brief smile to play across his expressionless face. Attempting to pass for two travelers who have struck up conversation during flight, we turned to stroll through the Denver airport, walking two feet apart, pulling our luggage behind us while discussing seemingly non-incriminating subjects.

"How was gettin' here otherwise?" I asked while I scanned the passageway, wondering if any of the couples I saw were the man and woman who knew him.

"Fine." We walked farther along the busy corridor before he asked, "And for you?"

"Fine."

After passing by the security checks leading into the concourse we were leaving, he asked, "How's the restaurant and your mother?"

"Fine." I found it bizarre that we could plan to meet in a city where no one we knew lived, yet Christopher could still run into friends on the plane. "How are the children and your wife?"

"Fine."

Running out of topics, I asked, "How is Carl?"

"Just talked with him last week. He asked to be remembered to you."

So, wonder how much Carl knows about us?

Beats me, I answered the other, but it is interesting that they discussed me last week.

Hearing an odd sound coming from Christopher's luggage when he rolled his case onto the escalator, I asked, "What's that clanking noise?"

"Two of my favorite wines from Napa," he said over his shoulder in my direction. I noticed his head turning as he scanned the area below us for those people he knew.

"That's nice," I answered. Like compromised, covert government agents on a secret mission, I sensed we were being watched while we walked through the airport. Having no idea who the opposition's agents were, I could not wait to be safely away from such a public place.

After checking the posted bus schedule to our hotel, he decided we would do better taking a cab. Could have been he was concerned that we would share the bus ride with that other couple, but it also could have been because I had started telling him in cold, scientific terms what I planned to do to his body when we got behind closed doors.

Far removed from the reserved traveler he had been in the airport, Christopher could not keep his hands off me after the taxi's door closed. He patted my thigh. Held my hand. Pulled me close under his arm. Nibbled on my neck. Caressed my breast. Brushed loose curls of hair away from my face. Repeatedly, he said how much he had missed me, how afraid he had been that he would never see me again.

Glancing forward into the rearview mirror, I noticed our cab driver raised his eyebrow more than a few times during the trip into the city, obviously taken aback by that staid, middle-aged pair who, once inside his cab, certainly did not act with the same decorum as when they had stood on the curb outside his cab.

Seconds could not pass fast enough for us until Christopher locked the door to our hotel room. Dropping our luggage in the middle of the floor and casting aside garments in all directions, not even taking time to reach the bed, we fell, giggling lasciviously, onto the floor.

❧

"Rachael Taite!" He called out when his time came.

Afterwards, still on the floor, we held each other close. Our fingertips slowly traced the other's facial features, as if to verify nothing had changed. Soft kisses trailed across bare skin. The five months since sending my naïve letter had seemed to me like five years in terms of separation. We had gone as long as eighteen months before between meetings, yet I had never felt apart from him, not anything like these last months.

"I thought I would never touch you again," he said softly, nibbling on my ear. "I'm not ready for you to go."

"I can't leave you. I tried, Honey, but you're in my blood." I knew it was not the excitement of the forbidden that drew me to this man. Whatever was the source of the attraction, I did not know. I just knew I had to be with him. However, certain realities were going to be faced during this weekend. Between hungry kisses, I warned, "We'll have to have some serious discussions this trip." I was not quite resigned to my limited options.

❧

Vibrant Denver was far different from historic St. Augustine where we had been the only pedestrians on the streets. Swarming with life, the downtown's seductive vigor lured us into joining its restless throngs. Sidewalk cafés were filled with patrons. The pavement was crowded with laughing people who hurried to get to wherever it was they were going. Walking amid these strangers, I easily absorbed their spilled over anticipations for the coming evening.

We strolled with arms around the other's waists, lovers lost in each other, lost in the crowds. After sharing an intimate afternoon with my heart's desire and dining in yet another fabulous restaurant, my body was just too sated by sex and food. Now, we headed back to our hotel where I would sleep peacefully alongside my sweet darling. My world was complete, if only for these two days. Without needing any verification, I knew my feet floated above the hard sidewalk on a cushioning carpet of happiness.

"Where do you find these wonderful restaurants?" I asked. "You've never picked a bad one. Our steak and all the accompanying courses were too good. "

Christopher snuggled me closer to kiss the top of my forehead. "Only the very best for my sweet Rachael."

"Chris Saracini!" a masculine voice called from our right.

Sweet Jesus!

Stopping dead in our tracks, we let our arms drop to our sides. Christopher cursed under his breath and turned. A burly man rose from a small table nearest the railing separating the open café from the sidewalk. They shook hands while the man's smugly grinning female companion remained seated. The pair appeared to be about Christopher's age. He introduced us.

Oh, double, double damn! I managed a friendly smile and shook each hand offered in greeting. By the ensuing conversation, I learned they were that couple who had been on the plane with Christopher. Sweet Jesus, now what?

"Isn't Denver a great city? I just love sitting here watching people pass by." The man, whose name I had promptly forgotten, reached back to pull up an additional chair to their table. "Won't you join us?"

I looked to Christopher for his reaction.

Before I could read his response, the man asked me, "Aren't you from Berkeley?" He loomed over me, too close for my comfort.

"Ah don't think so," I drawled, sounding more Southern than usual. Even to my ears.

Before this chance meeting could continue its downhill slide from awkward to incriminating, Christopher extracted us from the couple. "No, thank you. Rachael, here, has an early meeting," he improvised.

We walked away, without our arms around each other. We did not even hold hands. Those foreign invaders had soiled the fragile beauty of my lovely, play-pretend world.

Turning my head in Christopher's direction, I joked, "Do you think we should walk on opposite sides of the street all the way back to the hotel?"

I needed to make light of the encounter. With Christopher offering no response, I was left alone to wonder if he had been as shaken as I was by the brief contact with his friends from back home.

With the only illumination coming from the city lights beyond our window, we sat cross-legged on the floor in our shadowy hotel room solemnly discussing what the future might could hold for our forbidden relationship. The conversation was disjointed, with words slowly spoken only after responses had been carefully scripted. As we scouted out each other's expectations, heavy layers of silence insulated the long pauses between our statements.

"I want us to be together, either in California or Tennessee." I added truthfully, "The location doesn't matter much to me."

"There're my children to consider."

"You'll always be a good father, Honey, whether you are married to her or not."

"I can't divorce. I gave my word," he said.

I countered, "Other Catholics divorce."

"But that wasn't how I was raised," he replied.

Catholics aren't raised to commit adultery either. Rachael, if you're that gullible, I've got a bridge to sell you off Manhattan Island.

Thanks for sharing, I told my twin, but I want a dialogue here. I'll not put him on the defensive.

Thick, velvet curtains of unspoken desires woven from unparallel expectations hung about us, turning our surroundings into a large isolation booth while we separately worried with answers to difficult questions. Drumming sounds in my ears coming from the steady contractions of my beating heart supplied tense music to mark the passage of time.

Putting an end to the choking silence, he said, "Besides, if we were together, our relationship would change."

I heard that reason our last trip, I thought, and that dog isn't going to hunt this trip.

"We could be different," I said aloud, proud of myself for voicing that sentiment at long last. "Hasn't our relationship gotten better over the years?" I sat taller, visually empowered by the very utterance of my feelings. "Don't you agree?"

"Yes," Christopher answered, his voice falling into the room's darkness, "but . . ."

Rachael, you've just invalidated your own argument by agreeing with him!

"OK," I corrected myself aloud, "I'll grant you our relationship has changed."

I waited for his response. The ensuing silence was deafening, soon drowning out the beating of my heart in my ears.

At long last, he responded, "Yes, but even after all these years, I don't even know if you shit or fart in the mornings."

"Shit or fart? What does that have to do with anything?" I was astounded by Christopher's graphic remark. "That's the strangest comment I've ever heard!" Despite the gravity of our debate, I broke into gales of laughter.

Our discussion ended on that earthy note, as I had no defense prepared for that tack. Besides, never having handled confrontations well, I was relieved ours was over for now. I had faced all the seriousness I wanted for one night.

When I returned from the bathroom the following morning, he was lying on his side, facing where I had lain, his breathing soft and peaceful. After assuring myself that Christopher was still asleep, I leaped up into the air and, as if I fell back on a trampoline, flopped down beside him on the bed, very effectively bouncing him awake.

Sitting up in bed, he looked wide-eyed about the room, desperately searching to discover what had awakened him. Living in California, I guessed, must have made him first consider the possibility of an earthquake. Mystified, he finally focused his eyes upon me.

"What happened?" he asked, bewildered.

I answered calmly, "I only wanted you to know that I have just shitted and farted."

With the Rockies towering above us, we made a patented, Christopher-quick tour of Denver. Having reluctantly accepted that dress shoes were simply dead weight when traveling with this man, I had packed only sensible walking shoes this trip.

We toured Molly Brown's house and the Denver Mint. We climbed the stairs to the top of the Capitol's dome. I discovered that Denver proper had enough beautiful big trees to make this East Tennessee girl feel right at home. For lunch, we trekked to the historic restaurant by the railroad tracks to try their famous mountain oysters. I found their buffalo steaks to be tastier, less chewy. Later, I drank white wine while my companion taste-tested the products at a micro brewery. My body had trouble the entire day adjusting to Denver's mile-high altitude and, periodically, my nose bled. While sipping martinis at happy hour, we listened to the harpist at Molly's husband's hotel. After that, Christopher decided we should try Italian for dinner at a restaurant that was the better part of a mile away from our hotel.

He suggested we walk there. I thought I could manage one more march that day, so long as I did not forget and blow my nose.

After our waiter served dessert, I picked up my fork and requested, "Tell me again why we can't be together."

My tablemate was thoughtful and quiet while we ate and I awaited his answer. When we finished sharing our single serving of tiramisu, he finally looked in my direction.

Taking a deep breath, Christopher carefully began, "Rachael, you are the love of my life, but I have previous obligations. I want to educate my children. Having two children in school at the same time, even if they attend a community college, is expensive. The community property laws in California would make it impossible for me to give my children what I want them to have should I divorce now."

Finally, a reality-based argument I could understand. "So, don't get divorced," I suggested. "I'll move to California. We'll live together."

Out of nowhere, our waiter appeared to replenish Christopher's coffee and my glass of water. We remained silent until the young man left.

"I wouldn't know how to explain you." He continued, "My children think I'm their stodgy old dad. Your presence would make everything they believe about me to be a lie."

It must be all right to live a lie as long as the little dears don't get wind of it! my twin stormed out.

"Honey, you're anything but stodgy," I interrupted, finding it impossibly hard to believe this man, who had made steamy love to me in Nashville, could ever describe himself as boring.

He overlooked my comment. "Besides, Vincent is having some trouble with drugs. He got in with the wrong crowd this year in school. I need to be there for him until we get him through this rough spot."

That use of 'we' was not lost on me. That was a her-and-him 'we,' not a me-and-him 'we.' Unfortunately for my cause, one of the reasons I so admired this man I loved was for his strong sense of family. Reasoning they were minors and required his protection, I had decided long ago I never would put myself between him and his children and tell Christopher to choose. Now, as for his wife, their relationship was different because he had already chosen to move out long before we met on LeConte.

"Am I supposed to see you only when you can get away?" Tears of frustration filled my eyes. "You get to have your cake and icin' and eat it, too."

"Rachael, it's not that way at all." Although raw with emotion, his strained voice remained low and under control. A note of hopelessness that I had never before heard also was present.

"I want us to be together for the rest of our lives." I felt tears roll down my face. I hated each and every one because I felt they weakened my argument.

"My children . . . " His sentence remained unfinished. He was a man trapped.

"Christopher," I said firmly, "I need you just as much as your children."

Fine, I thought, I will own the premise that their education is a priority. I will not push the man any closer to the brink where he would feel compelled to choose between them and me. There are no winners in that tug-of-war. With tears dripping off my jaw, I desperately searched his face for possible solutions.

At long last, I sighed. "Honey, find us a country or a religion which allows for a second wife. That will solve this dilemma." That was the most equitable resolution I could devise. Where was wise King Solomon with his sword when he was most needed?

With tears in his eyes, Christopher looked at me sadly. With no reality-based answer forthcoming, we changed the subject, ignoring that door I had finally flung open.

Having only the responsibility of my mother, the restaurant and my employees, I was the less encumbered. My Mom only wanted for me what I wanted. She would come with me if I chose to move across country. If neither Liz or Margaret were interested in taking over, the restaurant could be sold, and the new owners could be persuaded to retain my employees. Christopher, on the other hand, was bound to his children by his love, to his wife by his sense of values. And his were very strong chains indeed.

Many thoughts raced through my mind during the quiet walk back to our hotel in the chilly Denver night. I used to say I would never settle for a lover who, if caught in a steel trap, would not chew off his foot to get to where I was. I found now that I loved whom I said I would never love. If I were strong, if I did not feel completed by him, if I felt there was another man in this world who could take his place, but I was weak and needed him much too much to leave. I would rather look forward to the occasional weekend with Christopher and the resulting memories than face the dreadful isolation of being entirely without him. Although I had been raised differently, tonight on a Denver sidewalk I reached the unenviable conclusions that life was compromise, not choice, and that brandishing a short stick was, at times, better than waving an empty hand.

Reaching for him, I instantaneously felt less alone when his fingers closed about mine. Holding hands, we walked several blocks, each lost in our separate thoughts.

"Christopher, I love you." I summed up my existence in those four words.

We continued another block more in silence.

"I love you, too, Rachael."

His admission halted me in my tracks.

My stopping to regard this man who had been my only lover for the past five years required him to stop as well. We stood beside a deserted side street near downtown Denver, our clasped hands bridging the gulf between our lives.

Since that first night in Townsend, I had hoped he cared for me, but this was the first time he had acknowledged his feelings with those specific words. A comforting warmth blanketed my heart. Through a veil of unfallen tears blurring my vision, I was able to see the unfallen tears glistening in Christopher's eyes, illuminating the truth found there.

Knowing that I would never again try to extricate my heart from the stickiness of our tangled web, I smiled in defeat. I stepped forward until our bodies touched. Rising to stand on tippy-toes, I kissed his cheek.

"I like hearing that," I told him.

Eleven

With the third Saturday in hot August came reunion time for my maternal grandfather's family. Dutifully, I drove Mom over for the day. This year the family was to convene at the former German prisoner of war camp outside Crossville, Tennessee. I found that odd location somewhat appropriate since Daddy Pop's clan had originally immigrated to America from southern Germany.

When I had attended church camp there as a teenager, the grounds retained the camp's original barbed wire fencing and guard towers. We had slept in the wooden barracks on narrow 1940s iron twin beds. On rainy days, we children had played games inside the gym where walls were covered in painted, romanticized friezes of the countryside the German officers remembered. When Mom and I arrived, the grounds looked different, yet felt the same. Sometime after my summer stints there, the camp had been updated in that the barracks and gym had been taken down; however, one rickety tower and the rusty, menacing, perimeter fencing had been left standing.

On a previous outing, I had decided that present-day family reunions must have evolved from a Stone Age tribal custom. For some reason, though, my family had never really been that close to his people when Daddy Pop was alive. I barely can remember meeting his mother, my Greatgranny Jubelle, and his sister, Martha Carol. I just have faded-picture memories of them and Daddy and Daddy Pop playing dominoes on a rickety, worn, cardboard-topped card table in the middle of the living room during their infrequent visits from California. Those old ladies never paid me much mind.

Why Mom insisted we attend every reunion, beginning with the first in 1981, was beyond me. I had spent my hours at those events staring at distant relatives while trying to figure out how I fitted into the equation. I did not favor them physically. My nose, my chin, my more-than-ample bosoms, my shortness all belonged to someone else's gene pool. These people looked like my grandfather. They were fair, tall and lanky, sporting pale blue eyes. None looked like me except for a scattered few immediate cousins with similar cheekbones and squared jaws.

I bet my great-grandmother and my great-aunt had also studied me during their visits to Daddy Pop's, trying to pick out features they could claim came from their branch of my family tree. Since the old ladies had poor eyesight, they must have come up empty-handed when they searched for recognizable signs in my childish, chubby-cheeked face.

Although Daddy Pop's surname was Germanic in origin, I had learned two years ago that it was rumored that the alpha male had come from the rocky lands along the cold Atlantic's northern coastline. His offspring resided in what is now Germany when it became necessary to tack on a last name to differentiate family groups. As his descendants came down the centuries and crossed over from Europe, the family's inherent skills were the additional threads that held the clan together, tying us back to that Norseman who first journeyed into the Black Forest region those many centuries ago. Daddy Pop's ancestors were bakers, weavers and farmers at first, then later followed trades requiring good hand-eye coordination. Today, the ones I had met were machinists, weavers, artists, airplane pilots, seamstresses, farmers and embroiderers.

My working with my hands and my single-minded stubbornness came from these men and women. Daddy Pop's family traits were there in me, I decided, even if they were not expressed by hair color or bust size.

Members from related yet distant family trees had occasionally attended our small, recently formed group's gatherings to collect our sapling's data and to share their more detailed information. This year a man from Indiana arrived for our weekend, bringing displays showing the villages where the two brothers emigrated some two hundred years ago.

I leaned over the picnic table better to study the pictures Keith had made during his last trip to Germany. He had affixed photographs, maps and brochures onto foam-backed poster boards. The land shown looked familiar to me. It was mountainous and forested like East Tennessee. I would feel at home there.

"Are you family or spouse?" Keith asked me.

"Family."

"And what do you do for a living?"

"Oh, I have a little restaurant," I replied. "I like to cook."

He smiled. "So many of the relatives have been bakers. Back in Germany, I discovered our family still bakes bread for the villages."

"Show me where . . . " With my Southern drawl, I decided against trying to pronounce the towns' names. "I have a lazy tongue," I brushed off an explanation, "and I can't say the names of those two places."

He turned the map so I could more easily decipher it. "Here's Italy." To orient me, he pointed to the color on the map that indicated that country. My eyes followed his hand. "Here's Switzerland." His forefinger moved to that country. "Remember the brothers came through Switzerland to get to America. Here's where . . . "

As Keith indicated the villages' exact locations in the Black Forest, the hairs on the back of my neck stood on end as the name of an Italian village fairly leaped off the map. The village of Saracini. A deepening chill quickly swept over my body. The only other time in my life I had felt body hairs stand erect was on the evening of July 4, 1980, when I jogged along the street near my former apartment. Some boys had driven up behind me and pitched out a firecracker before their car sped away. The explosion had gone off at my heels, scaring me half to death.

Sweet Jesus, I feel feet walking over my graves!

My knees went weak. I sank down onto the bench beside my Indiana kinsman.

"Are you all right?" I heard him ask, as if from a distance.

I heard myself answer, "I'm fine."

But, really, I was not fine. Not at all fine because I had become aware that Christopher and I had known each other for centuries because the area in Germany from where Daddy Pop's family emigrated was across the current Italian border from Christopher's family village. I felt lightheaded and tingly from the sudden rush of visions coming into my awareness. We had huddled in fear while frightful beasts roared outside our cave's opening. Side-by-side, we had cooked game our men had stoned. We had tended flocks in the mountains together. We had been siblings. We had been warriors, defending our village from outsiders. We had been foes, fighting each other to the death. We had been lovers. We had shared loveless marriages. We had taken turns being slave to master, servant to lord. We had been same sexed and, at other times, we had been differently sexed. We had been parent to the other's child. Braced against the roar of its citizens, we had stood together inside Rome's coliseum, waiting for the lions to be released. He had watched me be burned at the stake because I had kept to the Ancient Ways. When united by the Church to others, we had loved each other from afar and, sometimes, not from so afar. Our energies were inexplicably woven together. One complemented the other. Those fleeting vignettes presented me visual proof why we were drawn to one another from the very first evening on Mount LeConte. Sounds, smells, textures, tastes and emotions from all those instances washed over me, overwhelming the sensations coming from the present day.

I felt blood leaving my face and sweat breaking out on my forehead and upper lip. It had taken only nanoseconds for those eons of collective memories to flash at warp-speed through my brain. The knowledge was deeply unsettling because I had no logical, documentable, scientifically reproducible evidence to draw upon, only a visceral knowing of an immutable truth.

"Are you certain you're not ill?" my kinsman asked again.

"I'm fine," I again replied. "The heat just got to me for a minute. I've been dietin' too strictly, that's all." I pulled myself up from the bench. "I'll get some cold water, and I'll be all right."

He gently pushed me back to the bench. "You stay here. I'll get it."

Thankful for time alone to sort things out, I watched him rush away.

Rachael JubelleLee Taite, that is just too far-fetched! According to the Baptist church where we were raised, we die, our body is buried and our soul awaits the Second Coming to go to Heaven or Hell. There's none of this coming back to earth and having more life experiences.

I don't care what we were taught, I argued back. We are linked to that soul. You saw what I saw. This time around, we are female and the other is male. It has been many, many years since we have existed on the same continent, but we are together now. Our cycling was interrupted when the brothers left Switzerland. It resumed when Christopher's parents came to America after World War I. We belong together, and we will be together again. You heard what I heard at the ruins near Beaufort.

Just too, too weird! My twin did not comment again until seconds later when she asked, *Wonder which brother carried us?*

※

Labor Day weekend, three weeks later, found Mom and me up to our teary eyeballs preparing onions and hot peppers for relish. Through trial and error begun the year I had moved into my house, we had perfected the process. We learned to carry Big Momma's enamel topped, battered kitchen table out of the basement and set it on the graveled drive under the deck. While the juices from the onions and peppers fell harmlessly through stones to the soil, the deck kept the hot sun off our heads. Mom's job was to cut up the vegetables into manageable chunks. She would discard bad places and stems directly into the trash. I never recycled those scraps out of respect for the tender mouths of the hardworking earthworms in my composter. After donning dental exam gloves, I would grind the vegetable pieces, using Mammy's hand-cranked meat grinder. Finally, I would carry the heaping cauldron up the steps to the kitchen for cooking and canning. When he was alive, Daddy had carried the big pot to the kitchen, and he was the one who held his breath against the overpowering, caustic fumes when it came time to squeeze the water out of the chopped onions and peppers after they were scalded.

But before carrying anything outside, I first put a radio on top of the air conditioning unit so I could keep track of the Tennessee football game. Making pepper relish was a daylong exercise in a family tradition started by Daddy Pop long before football became the state's unofficial second religion. Keeping with his admonishment that if relish was not canned in the early fall, black-eyed peas traditionally eaten on New Year's Day could not possibly taste right or bring good luck for the coming year, I kept to Daddy Pop's handwritten receipt to maintain the proper ratio of white onions to red sweet peppers to green sweet peppers to red-hot, string peppers, adding only the radio broadcast of the play-by-play calls.

I was well into grinding peppers and onions, coughing from their choking fumes, when the extension in the basement rang.

"Damn," I muttered, removing my gloves. Discarding the glistening latex into the opened trash can near Mom, I hurried inside to catch the phone.

"Hey," I answered, impatient that I had been taken away from my grinding and a potential scoring drive.

"Rachael, will you come to Washington, D.C.? We'll celebrate your birthday there."

※

I leaned over in my seat to enjoy the crazy quilt of land crawling below the plane's wings. Before meeting Christopher in 1989, I had not traveled extensively. I had been to Daytona Beach a few times with Big Momma and Daddy Pop and had spent my summers during college away at Aunt Maurie's. Then there had been all those times Margaret and I had prowled Ocean Drive, but I had never really gone any place. Without a doubt, Christopher had added to my education and sightseeing experience. If nothing else, I had learned how little to pack for a weekend stay.

Becoming bored watching the passing landscape, I leaned against the plane's cushioned seat. As I fidgeted upon its rigid contours, I regretted my shortness because the curve for every headrest always hit me wrong. I tried the small pillow provided by the airline in several positions before finding one that took the strain off my neck.

With that physical need satisfied, my thoughts drifted to another need, the one I had for Christopher. One good had come out of our brief estrangement in that I could now empathize with his rushed lovemaking in Arcata. On my flight home from Colorado, I had reached the conclusion that it was impossible to act mannerly when bodies craved what they must have to survive and that we had been like animals marking our territories when we had intercourse on the hotel room's floor. Our actions that Friday afternoon could be compared to the desperate gulps of water a sailor takes after having been rescued following days at sea marooned on a raft. It was only after that critical deficiency was sated could he fully enjoy and appreciate the taste of fresh water, and it was only during our following, slower-paced couplings the remainder of the weekend that we had truly made love.

Sipping on bottled water the male flight attendant had handed me, my mouth broadened into a grin when my mind took off on a mental tangent. On commercial carriers flying in the 1960s, the hands passing out beverages were feminine and younger, and the job description was entitled 'stewardess.'

After that oblique observation, my mind re-examined Christopher's premise that our relationship would lose its special spark if we were around each other for any length of time. Finding fault in his logic, I felt alterations occurred with each meeting. Had he not felt those same changes? In some regards, we had become like those couples I had envied in that Ogunquit restaurant. As with partners of long-standing within my acquaintance, we had acquired catch phrases that had become entrenched in the comfortable, verbal shorthand we used, but unlike some couples I saw daily at my place of business, we had never sat through meals garnished with silence.

Feeling my anticipation building, my thoughts next wandered to our coming meeting. Since my first flight west, I had come to relish the romance and excitement associated with airports. Soaking up tensions that floated through the air from surrounding strangers and coupling them with the fact that Christopher and I had been or would be separated for months, I would free my fertile imagination, allowing my emotions to increase exponentially. Sharing good-byes with him always brought to mind Bogart and Bergman standing on a tarmac in North Africa. I believed our times together carried a movie script quality and knew they bore no relation to life-sustaining routines. Just as Susan Hayward and John Gavin never went grocery shopping while they played out their celluloid affair, we had yet to stroll the produce aisles at any Kroger's. Because he did not give our relationship or me space in which to expand and grow, icing, frou-frou, not substance was all it was allowed to be.

After learning my place in his scheme of things during last spring, my expectations for our future had narrowed greatly. I got to act out the part of Mistress, goddess of all things sensual and sexual. He left it for me to decide whether to accept or decline this imposed, restrictive, one-dimensional role.

What a pitiful choice selection. It was like having to decide whether to kill a living thing to have food to eat or take all nourishment from plant sources, all the while knowing plants were living organisms and could be harmed when harvested for food. My body's survival required amino acids whereas my heart's sustenance demanded Christopher Saracini. Perhaps changing to a synthetic, chemical, liquid diet would not harm any life forms while sustaining me. If my body could adjust to such austere nutrition, then maybe I would attempt to live without him.

Life was not supposed to be so damnably black-or-white. Where were all those lovely shades in between? I told myself I was not without morals. Despite everything, Christopher and I were meant to be together. He had told me so at Perkins Cove, and I had heard the benedictions at the ruins outside Beaufort. Besides, my visions at my family reunion were verifications from our past. While we were not above the law, we simply did not fall under this present paradigm of societal values.

Since I could not imagine my life without him to anticipate, I simply refused imagining life that way. I reasoned our relationship could not be judged immoral because we had existed before the Hebrews decided to limit worship to The One, True God and had been 'grandfathered-in,' so to speak.

As the plane began its descent, I toyed with sharing those shards from our past lives I had seen a month earlier at Daddy Pop's family reunion. Those startling visions had initiated my questioning the validity of current religious dogmas and had unearthed spiritual knots with which my mind fumbled, like numb fingers struggling with cold boot laces, as I daily diced freshly cooked chicken breasts for chicken salad at Rachael's. Since I had not told him about the voices in my head out of fear that Christopher would think me unstable, why should I now confuse him with those flashes of our shared past lives? He had already implied he thought familiarity bred discontent. Besides, he thought of me being special, not of me being strange and his was the illusion I chose to support. Having literally been burned at one stake for sharing my beliefs, I certainly did not want to chance, even figuratively, that experience again.

Since our flights were scheduled to land about the same time, Christopher had suggested meeting at a central location inside the terminal. After I deplaned, I searched the Washington airport for the local Travelers' Aid station. Since the crowded terminal was undergoing renovations and was as frantic with activity as a disrupted anthill, I found it a confusing hunt.

Although I waited only minutes at the temporary site for needy travelers, I still had sufficient time to worry if there was a second location for the agency where I should be standing. When he did appear, we did not hug in greeting, but tightly kept our hands on luggage handles. After his being on board with people he knew on that last trip to Denver, we no longer felt safely anonymous at distant airports.

"How's everyone back on the Coast?" I asked.

"Doing well." He pointed the way to the nearest exit. "We'll get a taxi to our hotel. It's near Georgetown. How is everything back home?"

"Fine," I answered. I saw he carried no flowers, I had not been handed a box containing a chocolate confection, I heard no bottles of wine clinking together in his roll-along suitcase, but we were in the same time zone, breathing the same air. That was gift enough for me.

⚜

With the sound of my name echoing in my ears, I teased, "They'll hear you all the way to Congress, Honey."

Our room was bright from the mid-afternoon sun coming through closed blinds. Before crawling out of bed, I waited until my knees lost their rubbery weakness so I could stand without fear of crumbling to the carpet. I went to our suitcases that had been left under the wall switch next to the door. I unzipped mine and hunted the vanilla-scented votives I had packed earlier that morning. Aware that the candles' low flickers would not change the ambiance of our suite, I hoped their aroma would clear away the staleness of the pent-up air.

Christopher lay on his back, partially covered by a tangled sheet. On the table by his side of the bed stood an opened bottle of champagne, two near-empty glasses and a half dozen red roses placed in a thick plastic water pitcher. I smiled, remembering how he had left me as soon as we located our suite, saying he wanted to purchase some wine and, when he returned, how delighted he was showing me the roses and the California vintage he had located.

After refilling both glasses, I handed his to him. Carrying my glass with me, I walked around the room, putting down and lighting votives.

I was standing near the small table inside the kitchenette when I asked, "Did you miss me?"

"What?" he called from the bed.

Thinking I must have spoken too low, I repeated louder "Did you miss me?"

He mumbled a one-word answer.

"What?" I entered the bath to leave a lit votive on the vanity.

"Always," he said slowly and clearly as he watched me move to the table near my side of the bed.

"It's nice to be missed," I replied as I sat on the bed, running my fingers over his chest.

"What?" Christopher asked before he drank from his glass.

I repeated slowly and loudly, "It's nice to be missed." After puzzling a moment, it dawned on me that despite all our years together, I still had to concentrate when we first met to attune my ears to the cadence of his speech. As slowly and as distinctly as a Southerner can, I announced, "You know, Honey, I sometimes still have trouble understandin' you when you talk."

He snorted, spilling his drink onto his chest. "You think you have trouble!" he exclaimed. "It takes me the first eight hours we're together to understand what you're saying, and that's not the worse part. It takes me two days after I get home to stop talking like you."

"Poor baby," I chuckled, offering no sympathy. After I leaned over and licked the spilt champagne puddled on his chest, I asked sweetly,

"Honey, did you understand that?"

Instead of a verbal response, he put his glass on the night table. Christopher took mine from my hand and placed it between his glass and the roses. Pushing me gently onto my back, he next dotted my face with soft kisses.

You understood me well enough that time, flitted across my mind.

Beginning a delicious sequence of sensuality, the tenderness shown by this man I so dearly loved almost made me forget to breathe while I concentrated intently on the sensations he directed my body to feel: the light brush of his hands over my breasts, his warm breath against my skin, his long legs draped over my thighs, holding me close to his body.

He might talk fast and clipped, but when we made love, Christopher could be real slow. I could live with that.

As part of the two-day celebration of my birthday at our nation's Capital, he came prepared with a shopping list of touristy activities to guide us. The first item to be checked off was Abe Lincoln. After viewing four sides of the Lincoln Monument and its ongoing refurbishing, we wove through the crowds, moving toward the Washington Monument. Not wanting to miss a single sight, my head swivelled from one side to the next as we walked along the famous reflecting pool.

Ever since leaving our hotel, I had been walking fast just to keep up with Christopher's long strides. Knoxville's summer had been too hot for me to maintain my after-work walking schedule, and my body, with its extra poundage that would not go away, had inched far beyond the state of out-of-condition.

Girl, you better take better care of us. Keeping up with that man is way too hard.

Hoping that if we talked, he would slow down a little, I cleared my throat. "I can't believe I'm here. I've always wanted to see Washington, D.C., but I never was in the safety patrol in grammar school or in the band in high school to be included in any of those school trips here." I quick-stepped a couple of times to gain back the ground I had lost while speaking.

"Just wait until you hear what I have in store for our next trip."

After I grabbed his hand pulling him to a stop, Christopher looked at me. I saw the gleam of the secret peeking from behind his blue eyes.

"Where?" I begged. "When?"

He shook his head. "Not before I know for sure will I tell you."

I pleaded and pretend-pouted, but nothing I said would change his decision to wait until all the details had been finalized. At least I had made him stop walking long enough that I had caught my breath.

"Let's go now," he said. "We've got a lot to see in a short period of time."

As we moved away from the reflecting pool, I stared above the scaffolding to the pointed apex of the Washington Monument. I repeated with awe, "I just can't believe I'm here." That said, I twisted my right ankle, falling unceremoniously to the ground.

Great, now we'll never be able to keep up with him.

The pain in my ankle was so intense that at first I could not even curse. Oh, my, this thing hurts! I'll have to stay back at the hotel while he sightsees alone. Damn, what if I broke a blasted bone! They'll have to shoot me.

He hovered over me, urgently asking, "Are you OK? Is your ankle twisted or broken? Can you get up?"

Exasperated with myself for falling, I refused his offered hand. After regaining my footing, I firmly told Christopher and myself, "I'm fine." Gingerly I placed weight on my right foot, feeling the sharp pain knife its way up from my ankle. Oh, Sweet Jesus, this hurts bad. "Just let me walk a bit," I ordered. "I'll be all right."

I had seen football players walking the sidelines after suffering a sprain. I could do that, too. To soften the rough edges surrounding my previous words, I added, "Some days, I'm just not as graceful as I am others."

I limped quite a bit during the first quarter mile while we chased after historical buildings and documents. Out of deference to my injury, Christopher slightly slowed his pace until hours later when we arrived at the base of the belltower for the Old Post Office. We double-timed up the remaining stairs to catch the last minutes of the sun.

He stood behind me, wrapping me in his arms just as he had done in the redwood forest, those few years back. Although there were only a handful of people at the top of the belltower, he spoke low into my ear, making certain no one overheard his words. "This isn't as crowded as the Washington Monument. I thought you would enjoy our sunset better from here."

Breathing in unison, we shared the most precious gift Christopher could give me: another sunset enjoyed with his arms about me. This evening the sun quickly became a fiery ball hanging in a cloudless sky above D.C.'s low skyline.

"I don't require much to make me happy," I whispered in return. "Just you and a decent sunset."

As the sun's measured descent gradually ignited the blue of the sky, I looked out across the darkening rooftops stretching before us like flattened hilltops. Although the orderly view from the post office's high belltower was not the wildness of the mountains back home to which I was accustomed, I was at home in Christopher's arms. Accepting, without a second thought, that he was the taproot through which I drew nourishment, I leaned into his body, contentedly soaking up all that I could from the bounty he had to give.

Before the sun left our sight, I asked, "Honey, aren't we lucky to have found each other?"

Christopher placed a kiss on the top of my head before tightening his arms about my shoulders. "I don't understand how we met," he answered. "I only know that I'm glad we did. I'm just a simple Italian man from a small town, and you're the romance of my life."

I had searched all my life for the peace I now found within the circle of his arms and wished it surrounded me always. I took in a deep breath before saying, "I love you."

"Me you, too." Quickly and quietly, he edited, rephrasing my three-word combination.

Later, making our way to supper, I found the Capital of the world's most capitalistic nation eerie at dusk. After business hours, Washington assumed another personality. As the suit-people vanished to their suburban houses, the homeless materialized, seemingly out of thin air, to putter around. The deserted streets were littered with scraps of paper that danced in the wind created by the occasional passing of a speeding taxi. The city had the feel of an after-hours amusement park. All the rides were closed for the night, and all the locals had gone home.

Christopher located an Italian restaurant in a restored turn-of-the-century townhouse only a short subway ride from our hotel. At dinner, we remained dressed like the out-of-town tourists we were as the rest of the patrons came attired in their date-night finery. That difference became even more pronounced while we lingered over dessert and more couples arrived for their fashionably late reservations.

As I admired the stylish clothing of the people around us, I felt out of place. I knew Christopher was never bothered by such minor details while traveling. Sometimes I had to agree with my Granddaddy about always having things handy, just in case they were ever needed. I knew Margaret would never permit herself to be without the proper garments no matter where she went. When I felt eyes boring in on me, I turned my head to find the lady sitting at the next table staring at my sneakers and white cotton socks. She wore pearls, a simple black sheath and a fabulous pair of black-strapped, high-heeled sandals that made my feet ache just to look at them.

I smiled at her and thought, Fuck you, Lady. Sneakers are not a capital offense. Besides, if you only knew, you would much rather be in my shoes this evening.

Ignoring her disdain-filled gaze, I turned back to Christopher to ask, "Tell me, how in the world do you keep findin' all these wonderful restaurants? Those homemade bread sticks were to die for."

"Nothing but the best for my Rachael." He smiled, counting out the money to cover our bill. Before he stood to help me back from our table, he added, "Actually, because you own a restaurant, I feel obligated to find you interesting places to dine."

"Oh, but if we keep eatin' like this, I won't lose any weight." I expressed an obvious fact, not a complaint.

As he offered his hand, he grinned. "I'll walk it off you."

After rising from my chair, I countered, "I'd rather you work it off another way."

❦

We started at the Capitol early the next morning, wandering through its cool passageways, squeaks from our rubber soled shoes echoing off all those hard, polished marble surfaces. We found the old Senate Chambers, the new House of Representatives and statues of former statesmen, lining hall after hall. We speed-read the base of each political icon we passed.

"Look, Honey." I stopped at the feet of a Southern Congressman who had served during the 1800s. "Here's a man who was also in the Confederate legislature."

While Christopher glanced over the inscription attesting the man's service to his constituents, both with the Confederacy and with the

Union, I told him, "I find that very admirable. I believe only a secure government would have a statue with this reference to a rebellious cause standin' within its Capitol's hallways. Bet there aren't too many countries that would allow it." I would never be able to explain why that statue and its single defiant line made my Southern heart right proud to be an American.

From the Capitol, we ventured down to stroll amid the jungle at the Arboretum. He next marched us double-time through the National Museum of Art. Striding through its great galleries, I saw paintings flash by as quickly as they had during art history slide shows when Dr. Ewing reviewed material for his exams. While he confidently lead me through all the building's twists and turns, I was as awed by the Old Masters on the walls as I was by the fact that Christopher never lost sight of me in the maze of the countless rooms. Next, using the provided underground passage, we surfaced at the Smithsonian's Air and Space Museum, completing that tour before lunch. After refueling our bodies, we wandered through a turn-of-the-century building that housed dusty machinery from an early Exposition. The machines were old and outdated but oddly brand new from never being used.

My twin commented, *Touring our nation's capital with this man is like flipping through Cliff's Notes for War and Peace. Too bad you had to go and buy new sneakers for this trip.*

We briskly took in the exhibits found inside the new Smithsonian before we crossed to the old Smithsonian building. Because I was too busy gawking at the approaching Castle to pay attention to my feet, I fell for the second time in two days.

"Damn it!" I cursed before my knees hit the curb.

"Rachael! Are you all right?" He quickly offered his hand to assist me to my feet.

Again, for the second time in two days, I refused his hand and rose up from the gutter, unassisted and none too ladylike, being more indignant than hurt.

Brushing myself off, I heard a solicitous Christopher say, "I know you must be embarrassed to fall like that in front of all these people."

Quickly, I glared at him and just as quickly thought, What the hell does he know how I feel? I abruptly answered his kindness by demanding, "Why? Did my skirt go over my head, exposin' my drawers?"

Surprised by my sharpness, he said, "No." He frowned, questions ready to pour from his lips.

"Then I'm all right." I forged ahead, not allowing him to voice even a second solicitous inquiry. "Some days, 'Grace' is not my middle name." My tone was brusque. I would not be made to feel that I should be embarrassed when I was simply furious about my lack of attention to the placement of my feet.

When I was a little girl, I had believed my family when they told me I was clumsy, judging me incapable of walking and simultaneously chewing gum. When I was in the eighth grade and grew, seemingly overnight, into a D-cup bra, I bumped into people and objects before I became accustomed to those new projections attached to my chest. Again I had been told I was clumsy. I had believed those people, too. Being clumsy was another lie I had been taught when I was coming up. At near fifty years of age, I refused to be made to feel embarrassment because I did something that was not graceful. Not even by the man I adored.

"I fell because I did not look to see where to put my feet." Still using my supervisory voice, I added curtly, "Did I embarrass you?"

Christopher responded quickly, "No." The puzzled look remained on his face.

"Good," I said firmly. "Let's go on." There were still too many items on his to-see list for me to explain my rudeness now. I might open that can of worms later when we had more time.

Later in the afternoon, we reached the Vietnam Memorial on Christopher's agenda. The scenes around the grounds appeared surrealistic. The linked, massive, polished stones curving against the green grass brought to my mind the vision of a great, muscular, pitch-black snake gleaming in the sun. War veterans in worn fatigues walked with the same dazed demeanor as time travelers set down in unfamiliar, yet strangely familiar, surroundings. Since all the boys I knew who went to 'Nam had come back, I had no names to search out.

Reluctant to look for the names of his two buddies from OCS, Christopher slowly approached the dog-eared master list of dead warriors. I watched his face carefully, not knowing what his search would find. Upon finding both names in the book, he learned that his friends had not been as lucky as mine. I noticed his mouth set into a tight line. I saw his eyes brimmed with tears. I watched his hands shake when he attempted to write down the location for the second name.

Wordlessly, I reached for the scrap of paper he had retrieved from the ground near his feet and removed the borrowed pen from his hand. My brain muted out the noise around us, leaving his halting words as the only sounds I heeded. His finger pointed out one location as he told me what to write. He thumbed over more pages until he found the first name a second time. I jotted down that location, too.

Silently, we went toward that glistening dark snake. The people walking alongside us and those who stood in front of the ebony stone wall were solemnly reverent. Occasionally, one would lean over and their lips would move, but I heard no words. We passed flowers, teddy bears, black lace panties, cards and letters nestled against the monument's elongated base. All were belated offerings to the dead.

MacAllister's name proved easy to find. As we stood before it, Christopher said haltingly, "He died about a year after I was shot."

When he was ready to continue the search, Christopher touched his right hand to the letters spelling out 'MacAllister' in farewell to his long-ago companion. We hunted for some time before he spotted Toby's surname.

Disbelief evident in his voice, he whispered, "Toby died our first month there." He stood with tears running down his cheeks, doing nothing to brush them aside. I watched the gathering tears bead at his jaw line before they dropped onto his shirt.

I found it uncomfortable to watch him cry while he stared at Toby's etched name. It was almost too intimate an occurrence to share.

I wondered to myself, Why is it so hard to see a man cry? Is it because our Society decrees real men don't cry? That is another lie. Real men cry because real men feel pain and love and regret and happiness. The difficulty must reside, I concluded, within that observer who cares for the man and who can only helplessly watch that dear heart weep. We watchers feel compelled to offer comfort, and what usually comes out of our mouths is: 'There, there, don't cry.' whereas we should say: 'There, there, do cry. I'll hold you and watch your back and let you go limp with grief until you are able to stand on your own again.'

I stood proudly with Christopher because he did me honor by sharing with me his tears for his fallen buddies. Shielding him from the other visitors, I remained slightly behind his body while he lingered at Toby's name. I had never known a man to cry openly. Even through all those hard times during my childhood, I had never seen my Daddy cry.

Had Mom? If he had wept, she had never mentioned it to me.

We stood together until Christopher had touched his friend's lettering and was ready to walk away. From the wall, we covered the short distance to the bronze memorial for the nurses who served in Vietnam.

The deeply evocative, female figures cradled the injured soldier in their arms while their sightless eyes searched the heavens for help. I found myself looking up, too, hoping for a glimpse of a helicopter that would carry the wounded to safety. Thinking of all the times that scene must have been played out, my eyes filled with tears. I looked away from the source of my pain to see three sobbing women about my age, huddled together, their arms thrown around each other.

One looked into my eyes and held out a camera to me. Without saying a word in reply to her gesture, I nodded and took the camera. Since this was an inappropriate time to call out 'Say cheese,' I counted aloud to three before capturing their images.

Still crying, each thanked me before the woman with the camera explained, "We were there. We did that."

From over my shoulder, I heard Christopher say in a choked, sad voice to the women, "Thank you for being there."

I took his hand and led him back to our hotel. In the privacy of our room, we held each other tight and loved away the hurt of his lost companions.

At the completion of supper at a Mexican restaurant, Christopher cautiously approached a new topic. "Rachael, I need to tell you something," he began.

I took in a deep breath.

Don't tell her. I think we already know.

Venturing into unfriendly territory, I looked into his eyes to gauge better the emotional shoals hidden beneath his words. "What is it, Honey?"

He looked away from my gaze. "Last February, I moved back."

I closed my eyes, allowing his words to seep into reality. I replied softly, "I thought so."

I had easily put aside that possibility when it first appeared, months ago, as a niggling irritation in my brain. Now that he had spoken the unspeakable, the once ignorable became a prickling thorn that must be dealt with. I opened my eyes to observe him closely. His expressions and body language would be factored into my final decision.

"Now what?" Trying to be casual, I sipped wine, intuitively awaiting further bad news.

"You're the romance of my life," he began, "but Vinnie was having bad problems, and I couldn't let her handle him alone. You see, he'd gotten in with the wrong crowd. We needed to present a united front. I had to be in the house for that."

United front, my ass!

My body went cold. "Are you sleepin' with her?"

Christopher slumped back against his chair before replying, "Yes."

"Sweet Jesus!" I felt icy hands encircle my heart and squeeze, restricting its beating. My almost empty wineglass slipped out of my hand, bouncing to its death on the tile floor.

Get us out of here!

I could not catch my breath inside the restaurant. "Get us out of here," I mindlessly repeated, obediently rising from the table to exit the room.

With the strength of my legs disappearing along with what remnants remained of my self-control, I leaned heavily on the wooden banister as I walked mechanically down the steep steps to the sidewalk outside. While the shockingly crisp fall air quickly expanded my lungs and the tightness around my heart eased, I stood alone on the sidewalk, not knowing which way to turn. Because I had failed to pay any attention, as usual, to the route we had taken on the metro to get to wherever we were in the Washington outskirts, I would now have to wait helplessly outside until Christopher appeared to escort me back to our hotel. With nothing else to do, my head rapidly filled with thoughts.

Rachael, what did you expect? You knew this would happen.

But I always thought he would choose me.

They have squatters' rights, not you.

But I'm the romance of his life.

That and some change will get you a cup of coffee.

But I don't do coffee. I want it to be different.

This is what you got.

It's not fair.

You're forty-nine years old. Sweet Jesus, woman, it's childish to think life has to be fair!

Almost immediately, Christopher joined me, and we walked the mile back to the subway along half-lit, suburban streets. We held hands and walked quickly, both aware that if we moved fast enough, neither would have sufficient breath available for conversation. In the artificial lighting on the metro, I noticed his drawn face looked as ancient as I felt.

Traveling away from the suburbs, I stopped thinking about our tangled situation and placed my body on automatic pilot. I would be like Scarlett and think about my problems when I reached Tara. The movement of the train rapidly rocked us to our station. Another brisk march through deserted Washington soon got us to our final destination.

Christopher fumbled with the cardkey at our room's door. Looking at the door, not me, he finally spoke. "Rachael, I never meant to hurt you."

"I know," I answered sadly.

As we prepared for bed, we walked from bedroom to bath and back again like ships that pass in the night, giving plenty of clearance for each other's emotional wake. When Christopher pulled the sheet over his body and reached over to cut out the light on his night table, we lay naked on our backs in bed. After mentally comparing our nude bodies covered by the sheet to corpses in a morgue, I regretted on several levels not donning a T-shirt before getting into bed.

I futilely stared at the ceiling in the dark for a long time before I asked, "Have you made your confession?"

"No, I can't do that," he answered.

While his unemotionally spoken words echoed in my head, I carefully considered the ramifications of that reply. The facts, as I knew them, were as follows: he won't confess because he has no plans to give me up and sin no more; he waited to tell me of his return to his family until our happy weekend was almost over, before revealing this reversal of his marital status when, together, we could confront it face-to-face; and he was leaving it up to me to decide, given these new circumstances, whether or not to continue our relationship.

Sweet Jesus, I hate making decisions!

I scooted next to his body. Christopher raised his left arm and pulled me against his side.

I sighed. "What are we goin' to do?"

"We'll keep doing like we've been doing. Seeing each other whenever I can get away." His voice sounded calm in the darkness, but his heart, thumping loudly inside his chest, betrayed his internal turmoil.

I might could live with that possibility. After all, it was familiar. In fact, I had already been living with it.

I finally said, "She knows."

His words came too quickly as he assured me, "No, she doesn't."

"Yes, she does," I disagreed. I knew whereof I spoke because I had known before Christopher told me that he had gone back to his wife. "A woman knows when her man is seein' another woman. She chooses not to acknowledge it. That's all."

Recalling that I had repeatedly put aside my gut feelings, I had known each and every instance Mackey had stepped out on me. Tears again filled my eyes and rolled down my cheeks. "I think I have cried more, since knowin' you, than I have at any other time in my life."

Having uttered that miserable fact, I left the bed and marched into the bath for tissues to blow my nose. When I returned to his arms, extra tissues in hand, I defiantly announced, "I'm not ready to give you up. These past seven years have been the best of my life because of you." I blew my nose a final time. "I'm here for the duration, I guess."

Covering my face with soft kisses, Christopher draped his leg possessively over mine. "You'll be leaving me," he informed me between kisses, "but I'll always be here for you."

When I started my reply to that remark, his tongue entered my mouth, halting further discussion, and I allowed that distraction to happen. We continued with touches and tongues and hands and bodies, showing each other how much we cared. It was simpler that way, because our sentiments never were waylaid by realities during the passages of time required to select the proper words.

※

We strolled into Georgetown for Sunday brunch at a sidewalk café. On our way to the Jefferson Memorial, the only attraction we had missed seeing the day before, the blister that came up Friday afternoon broke on my little toe. Silently, I vowed never to wear new shoes, ever again, during a weekend with Christopher. We returned to our hotel in time to grab our luggage, hail a taxi and arrive at the airport with enough minutes remaining for a quick drink together before his flight was called.

Sitting side by side at the bar near his gate, I sipped wine while Christopher enjoyed a beer. Realizing that I had missed inquiring about his kids' educational progress, I asked, "How are Victoria and Vinnie doin' with school?"

"She's about ready to start graduate school." He took a long swallow of beer before saying wryly, "My son barely has the grades to qualify for junior college."

Sarcastically, my twin commented, *With our luck, he'll want to be a neurosurgeon.*

I realized that somewhere inside me some foolish someone still hoped after the boy's schooling was completed, Christopher would come to be with me. Later when I was alone, I would correct her fallacy.

Christopher delayed boarding his flight until its final call was announced. Leaving my unfinished drink, I accompanied him as far as the check-in counter. Despite all our experiences with good-byes, I was taken aback with the raw pangs I felt while watching him walk away.

Alone, I returned to my wine. The bartender, who had earlier served us, strolled in my direction. Seeing I was near tears, he said kindly, "Good-byes are hard."

Although I nodded my agreement, I was thinking that I should be used to them by now.

The bartender brought a second glass of wine. When I opened my purse to get out some bills, he refused payment. "Your money's no good. Your husband took care of me and the tab."

Twelve

Sybyl and Beatrice continued joining my escapes to the cabin for needed peace and quiet. Bright and early this crisp October morning, however, that calm had been invaded by a squirrel that must have recently claimed the back porch as his own. Awakened from a deep sleep by an ungodly racket coming from the kitchen area, I stumbled into the main room to find the girls standing with their back feet in the sink and their front paws on the windowsill, nattering curses at a squirrel perched on the back of the porch swing, barking taunts at them. After yelling for the three to shut up, I returned to my bedroom, worrying that the solitude of Sunshine would never be the same ever again.

Later that afternoon, I sat motionless on the swing watching the sparkling surface of Little River undulate toward its rendezvous with the larger Tennessee River. As my concentration easily floated away along with that glittering, seductive water, my restaurant drifted into mind. It had far exceeded my expectations. Most patrons and most employees were delightful, but there were always those few who put my teeth on edge, making me wish they had never crossed my threshold. Because many of our patrons were employed by the locally based home and garden network, we were featured on national television when they put together a segment on regional places of interest. Business really picked up after that spot aired, even drawing out-of-state tourists driving through Knoxville. I found myself praying we would never be blessed with an article in any future *Southern Living* because my restaurant lacked the space for any additional customers, even the good kind.

Gathering my awareness back to the present, I checked my watch. My girl friends would soon be here for dinner. Having dieted all week, I looked forward to my favorite meal of grilled salmon and spinach Maria. After Liz offered to bring dessert, Margaret had volunteered to buy the wine. Depending on the amount of alcohol consumed, I had been forewarned they might or might not stay the night.

When tires crunching on the graveled pull-in next to the cabin signaled a car's arrival, I left the back porch. Once inside the cabin, I spied both my four-legged girls asleep on their backs, imitating dead bugs, in front of the short bookcase with their bent, dark paws poised in air. That trusting position left their tender bellies unprotected, exposing their breed's characteristic brown tummy patches. I smiled at the always comical sight.

"Ladies, are your backs painin' you?" I questioned as I passed over their relaxed bodies on my way to the front door. Since after eight years I had yet to step on them, the girls trusted me and did not move, not even a whisker.

I greeted my two-legged friends through the latched screen door. "Come in this house!"

"You owe me money!" Margaret exclaimed from beside her car. "They're goin' to the movies!"

"Who?" I asked as I opened the door.

"Me and Hugh Ed," Liz answered, brushing by me on her way to the kitchen. Her arms held two plastic bags filled with her mystery dessert.

"Watch out for the girls!" I alerted my guests. I looked at Margaret. "I never said I'd take that bet." I turned around to call to Liz, "I thought you weren't datin' anymore."

Margaret and I followed Liz into the kitchen to await further details.

When we stood facing her, Liz smiled a coy smile that hinted volumes but offered nothing concrete. "A lady can change her mind. Speakin' of change, let's change the subject. What's for supper?"

Before I could answer, Margaret said, "Salmon steaks and spinach casserole. Where's that cork thingie?"

"Damn, am I that predictable?" I pointed to the corkscrew by the radio before going to the card table to clear away the books I had begun reading earlier in the day.

In unison, they answered, "Sometimes."

I laughed. "Thanks for sharin'. I'll set the table. Then I'll do the fish. The Maria is coolin'."

"Those are awfully thick books. What in the world are you readin'?" Margaret came to look at the stacks covering the card table. She frowned. "Rachael, have you gone and gotten born again?" Paraphrasing one of the titles, she asked, "And just what did Jesus actually say?"

"Oh, you know how it is. You get to be a certain age, and you have questions that didn't get answered. So, the other day, I went to the bookstore and picked up some stuff. Did you know there was a Wicca book on the same shelf as all of these?" I hoped that sketchy explanation would be enough to satisfy her curiosity, because I was not ready to share with anyone the visions that had prompted my research.

After sundown that evening, with our stomachs full and our wine glasses half emptied, we retired onto the back porch to share in the dwindling riches left at the end of a long Indian summer. The surrounding night creatures were well into renditions of their species-specific late summer music. Tunes from our twenties and thirties filtered through the screens from the radio in the living room. The cabin was dark behind us.

Liz and I rested on the swing, taking turns keeping the cat going whenever the swing required a kick-start. Resting her heels on the railing, Margaret propped herself in a chair between the swing and the door.

"I feel like a frog," I announced during the latest lull in conversation.

After a while, Margaret offered the appropriate comment to move the conversation forward. "Why on earth for?"

"Well, I read somewhere if you toss a frog into hot water, he has enough sense to hop out. But, if you put that same frog in cool water and gradually raise the temperature, you can cook him because he won't jump out."

Liz was horrified. "What heartless scientist would do such a cruel thing to a poor little ol' creature!" She thought a moment before adding, "And what a waste of a perfectly good frog. You couldn't eat the meat because he hadn't been cleaned first."

Steering the conversation back onto the subject I had intended, I explained, "Lizzie-Lou, I feel like a frog because of work. Last week was a bitch. The food police dropped by. We had all those catered luncheons to do. Everybody who came to the restaurant must have not eaten for days because they ate up every dish we cooked each day. I'm almost sorry I opened the damn place."

Margaret sat up, causing the front legs of her chair to thump hard on the wood plank porch. "Yeah, I thought it would be easy work before I came."

After observing Liz nod her head in agreement, I suggested, "We need to change somehow, but how do we go about downsizin'?" I had no answers. Hell, how could I worry about the restaurant when I was wrestling with larger religious quandaries? "If it wasn't for Christopher," I began.

Liz interrupted. "Speakin' of him, how's that frog-cooker comin' along? You haven't said much about the ol' boy lately."

Thinking I ought to kick Liz, I kicked the floor instead, getting the swing to moving again. "Well, we've lasted longer than my two marriages combined. He's the only thing I look forward to these days, so I guess it's goin' OK."

Just then, I heard a cat's insistent bark in the window behind me.

Liz jumped. "What the hell was that?"

"It must be about eleven. Sybyl is tellin' us it's time for bed. Y'all are stayin' the night, aren't you?"

The cabin became a religious retreat the next three weekends as I pored over my recently purchased bibles and related books. The thought-provoking subjects I delved into made uncharacteristically slow reading for me. With so many points of interest referenced by scraps of paper, marking salient points to revisit, my books soon resembled porcupines sporting flat, short quills.

Mid-afternoon Sunday, I slammed a thick tome shut. I had read all I needed.

"That's it!" I loudly proclaimed to the cats, the only ones present. Sybyl raised her head from her nest against a lap-throw in the far corner of the couch. "I'm over this! Pompous men with huge egos thinkin' their narrow-minded way was the only pious way to worship. Probably had small dicks, too." I stood the better to argue my points. "No one knows what actually happened or what was really said. These books are really nothin' more than rehashed rhetoric taken from oral sagas. Not much different from Homer basin' his *Odyssey* on those old folk tales floatin' around Greece back in his day. And," I pointed to a yawning Sybyl, "you know about that old child's game of whisperin' a phrase and how words get changed with each retellin' as the phrase is passed around the circle."

I stepped over Beatrice who had been napping on the floor at my feet before my heated outburst flooded into the quiet cabin. "And those church henchmen, back in Germany, they wrote the first how-to books on torture. Women in entire villages were slain because those holy gooddoers decided those ladies, with their handed down potions that could cure the sick and ease the dyin', were in competition with the fledglin' Church. Damn them! And so those ego-maniacal, prayer chanters conjured up charges of witchcraft and made those learned healers into somethin' evil."

Leaning to pet Beatrice's head, I continued in a softer tone, "And little kitties, like you and Sister, were supposed to be in cahoots with those poor, accused women, and so your relatives were slaughtered. Then the rat population ran wild. I read somewhere, but don't ask me where, that decrease in your ancestors set the stage for the Plague." How any self-righteous fool could harm sweet pets, such as mine, sent indignant shivers through my body. "And if you were tried as a witch, you lost your property, whether you were found guilty or not." I muttered, "Damn church-goin' land grabbers."

I paced between the television and the sink. "Then Henry the Eighth came along and arbitrarily changed the Church's chain-of-command to justify his changin' wives. The balls of that man! He even had his buddy, Thomas More, killed because ol' Tommy refused to change his religious views to match Harry's. What a sanctimonious, randy, selfrighteous prick!"

"Whatever happened to 'Love thy neighbor as thyself'?" Agitated by the contradictory messages uncovered during my research, I was in a state that was near approaching hissy-fit classification. "So, who died and made those pompous asses God?"

Whoever wins the war, she said wisely, *writes the books. You know that.*

Still mentally sifting through all I had read, all I had been taught, all the documentaries I had sat through and everything I once believed, I walked over to the fridge, jerking the door open to get at the cold water.

"Hell, those Wicca incantations over there, they were compiled this century after the author did some delvin' into some old manuscripts. So, how much different is that compared to some bearded, Middle Eastern man in a cave somewhere writing down the Sermon on the Mount hundreds of years after it could have been spoken, followed by some religious scholar centuries later insistin' with his red ink that was exactly what Jesus said? There are only two differences, ladies. That Wicca stuff just hadn't been widely available in print for as long, and its followers prayed to an older god who happened to be female."

Damn, Rachael, what's got into you?

"Nothin's gotten into me," I yelled. "I'm just gettin' rid of some mental cobwebs!"

Well, she cautioned, *keep in mind we do live in the Bible Belt. Stick with your cakes and salads. And don't start lookin' now for frog eyes and bat toenails. It's bad enough that you talk to your cats.*

I carried the water jug to the sink, then stood motionless, staring blindly out the window. I wanted to discuss with Christopher the multiple light bulbs flashing on and off in my mind, but it was Sunday. He would be with his family today. My call would have to wait.

Although I had both his private number at work and his home phone number memorized, I had never considered calling his house, nor did I phone his office that often. Either one would be considered Bad Form. In addition to that, it would be unseemly of me to encroach into his other life. There were rules here that must be observed.

"Hell, there's always rules!" I fumed, feeling immobilized by cultural chains of every description.

I wondered if he would understand the journey my mind had been on, should I share it. Would those pieces, torn from so many sources, realign themselves as precisely when I related them to him? Had I merely been trying to justify my being with Christopher, and this was the only way we fitted?

And we did fit together so well. I could not remember when I stopped looking for a local man to date. Maybe it was the age I had attained. Maybe, because I had felt married to Christopher ever since we drove away from the church ruins near Beaufort, I shunned involvement. Maybe my body naturally released pheromones that repelled gentlemen callers. Whatever the reason, I was not bothered that no man hovered around because I knew, without one doubt, that whenever Christopher could get away, we would be together. Because the man I waited for was worth the price, I did not mind skirting around in the shadowy edges of love.

During the middle of last summer, I had come to realize that Christopher must have been serious when he said he had missed me because he had taken to phoning on a monthly basis since I returned from Denver. Thinking back over our last few conversations, I doubted an eavesdropper could deduce the exact nature of our alliance. I recalled we had discussed my work, his office, his children's educational progress, their sports activities and our most recent hikes. We had laughingly exchanged recently heard jokes, sounding more like high school friends playing catch-up than lovers. These latest calls were never long but were as welcomed as any bouquet he had ever handed me.

After learning of his change in residence, I stopped asking as to his wife's health. This inquiring mind had acquired more information than it wanted to know about her.

Sybyl jumped up on the counter and butted her head lovingly against my hand that gripped the jug of water.

"Hello, Sweetness," I calmly greeted her and gently stroked her soft fur. After reaching for a clean glass in the dish drain, I filled it with water. Yes, I was indeed over it.

My throat suddenly felt dry. I downed the entire contents of the glass in a series of long gulps. Replacing the water container in the fridge, I returned to the books scattered on tabletops and across the living room. With a serene mind, I made room for them on the dusty shelves behind the television.

The only book I left easily accessible was the one on the Ancient Ways. The words there had felt right when I read them because its invocations instructed: Above all, do no harm.

Fall finally came and quickly went in a glorious riot of leaf colors.

Christmas swept in and out, cloaked in carols. Winter-like weather was late in arriving, but hit with a vengeance in mid-January. On the morning of the sixteenth, I measured fifteen inches of snow on my deck. It melted all away in five days. Then more of the white stuff cascaded from the sky about four days later, accompanied by frigid temperatures that prevented Knoxville's usual quick melting.

I closed the restaurant during both snows. Although trees fell in yards all around my neighborhood, fortunately for the girls and me, at no time did my house lose electrical power. Margaret and Liz, however, kept me updated by phone with the now-you-see-it/now-you-don't comings and goings of their electricity. Mom sensibly stayed inside her condo at Cherokee Heights under a quilt, eating vanilla ice cream and watching TV, while all I wanted was just one spoonful of the snow ice cream that Daddy used to make.

During the second 'unprecedented' snow event, as the television's weatherman blandly referred to the snowy headlock gripping Knoxville, the girls ate all their favorite salmon cat food and staunchly refused any human food I offered. With heavy, wet, white clots falling off trees and landing noisily all around me, I gingerly crunched through the boot-deep snow to the grocery for canned salmon. Luckily for me, their cat litter supply held out, because I dreaded the thoughts of lugging a heavy bag of litter uphill through the snow from the ever-faithful, always-open Kroger's.

Since Christopher had called to check on me after he heard about our first snowfall, I decided to call him after the second storm when the skies had cleared and no more accumulation was expected.

"So, Honey, how are things in sunny California?" I asked brightly as I stood looking at the fairyland outside the French doors leading to my deck. Upon hearing an oak log pop loudly in the fireplace behind me, I turned to watch the explosion of sparks wafting up the chimney.

"It's raining right now, and visibility is near zero. It's like my office is inside a gray cloud." His voice sounded depressed and matched the weather I pictured outside his window.

"I'm sorry but ask me how deep the snow is this time on my deck."

"Five inches," he ventured.

"Not even close. Twelve," I announced cheerfully.

I enjoyed snow in Knoxville because of the festive atmosphere that always blanketed the area. In the North where deeper snows occur, residents there laugh at our inability to clear streets and get on with our lives, considering our few inches of accumulation and all. They fail to understand the mind-set we natives have toward snowy, wintry conditions. Perhaps if no black ice lurked beneath the snow, my city could be more aggressive in its approach to clearing the streets, but it is hard to do effective salting when maintenance trucks slide off into ditch lines. We native-born Knoxvillians regard a day with six inches of white stuff as an unscheduled federal holiday, an excellent excuse for business not as usual, an unexpected reprieve from drudgery. With ten or more inches we locals morph into black bears, hibernating until the streets melt clear once more. Those two back-to-back snows, both greater than ten inches and less than ten days apart, were a better gift than that puppy I never received for my sixth birthday.

"Jesus," Christopher swore before changing the subject. "Listen, Rachael, I think I've got everything lined up for the end of March. How does England sound to you?"

"England!" I rested my forehead against the chilly glass in front of me. "Be still my beatin' heart," I whispered in amazement.

The girls and I spent the remaining wintery holiday in front of crackling fires in the living room. I cross-stitched on a pillow front I had been working on for five years. When my fingers grew tired of that, I reread my favorite Francis Parkinson Keyes novels. The girls languished on their favored wing chair or hung off its companioning footstool in positions that defied the laws of gravity. Being idle those days did little to pay bills, but certainly renewed my body's batteries and gave me time to consider my upcoming transatlantic flight.

During that last phone call, Christopher had said he would meet me inside Gatwick's main terminal soon after I deplaned. I looked forward to flying halfway around the world, knowing without question that he would be where he said he would be, at the time he said he would arrive, because I, who in my past had trusted no man, knew I could trust him.

We would just have to find each other in a crowded foreign airport. No trouble. Just no trouble at all.

✳

"Ohmygod!" I screamed as our toy-sized transportation rolled to a stop at the first tangled intersection that the witty English euphemistically call a traffic circle. Christopher eased the front bumper of the rental car toward the oncoming traffic, coming on from entirely the wrong direction. "Thank goodness, you're doin' the drivin'. Sweet Jesus, you're too close to the shoulder!"

I shut my eyes, being just too unnerved sitting on the left side of a vehicle without a steering wheel in my hands and brakes under my feet. After I thought enough time had elapsed for him to negotiate the intersection and merge properly with the traffic, I peeked through one eye to determine if I could safely open both.

"Bein' a passenger in England will take some gettin' used to," I added in a much calmer tone now that our car was briskly flowing alongside the other vehicles. "Sorry I yelled at you."

"That's perfectly all right," Christopher responded sweetly. "I'll need all the help I can get."

I so wanted not to miss any view that my head twisted and bobbed atop my neck, seemingly without any meaningful purpose. The English countryside south of London rolled like the hills below Lexington, Kentucky, where Mammy's farm was located. For some reason I had imagined the land would look alien or, at the very least, English. But trees were trees, grasses were grasses and daffodils blooming on hillsides were daffodils blooming on hillsides, no matter where the political divisions might be.

"I just can't believe we are here!" I exclaimed.

He threaded through the next, much smaller traffic circle with ease.

"You did good," I complimented him on his skillful driving in a foreign country. "Honey, wonder how many American tourists never make it through that first traffic circle after Gatwick? I bet a lot of them just drop the transmission into reverse and back right back to the airport."

He laughed. "I bet a few stay on it, circling until they run out of gas."

"The English probably placed that intersection there as a tribute to Peter Sellers." I continued my musing, "They probably have a TV show, like our Candid Camera, devoted to nothin' but Americans tryin' to exit Gatwick while drivin' backwards on that traffic circle."

"Got the map?" he asked.

"That was a rhetorical question, wasn't it?" I answered as I turned to rummage around in luggage that had been strewn across the backseat. "Travis loaned me an Ordnance Survey map. It should have enough information to keep you happy."

"Who's Travis?"

"Hugh Ed's oldest boy. He and his girlfriend, Holly, took some time off from college to bum around England. Travis said he found this map to be right handy."

"Tell me the best way to get to Winchester. I thought we'd stop there first to see the cathedral. Then up to Stonehenge. Then, to Bath. I thought after that we'd drive to . . . "

Names of towns and churches and archaeological sites rolled easily off his tongue. Places I had never dreamed I would ever see, we would shortly visit. And we would have almost two weeks together. The sum of all our previous trips hardly added up to fourteen days. What if he was correct and our relationship soured by being cooped up in a compact car and in isolated bedrooms in a foreign country? No doubt we certainly would come to know each other's morning ablutions more intimately.

"Sweet Jesus!" I slammed both my feet onto non-existing brakes on the floorboard in front of me. While thinking our relationship might not survive the first three hours in England, I screamed, "Christopher!"

A traffic snarl on the streets leading toward the old section of Winchester soon became an Arthurian exercise in courtly behavior and vehicular restraint. The other drivers were polite, yet assertively determined to get where they intended to go. My Christopher was just as determined to drive like a native.

Surely, it had to be a man thing.

I felt crammed inside a too-small car in the middle of too many small cars, all driving on the wrong side of sharp-cornered streets originally designed for carriages going at a slow horse's walking gait. Not that we were moving much faster than a crawl, mind you, but I found that rate too fast for strangely worded road signs, for cars suddenly merging from unaccustomed angles and for stone buildings and walls towering over my head and lining the too narrow lanes that appeared, to my tired eyes, to be becoming even more constricted.

I felt my stomach knot. I heard my voice rise. I watched tempers flare inside the confines of our cramped car. After one heated exchange, we glared over our respective sunglasses' rims at each other.

Fourteen fuckin' days to go. We'll never make it.

After pushing his glasses up on the bridge of his nose, Christopher said in a more rational, controlled voice, "Let's get out of this traffic."

He found a car park behind a huge stone church. Outside in the fresh air, my unleashed spirits soared. Much relieved, I joined in his singing the chorus from "Winchester Cathedral" as we made our way from our petite car to the huge church's doors. I felt free to hold his hand or to drape my arm about his waist, knowing that our chances of being seen by someone he knew were slim to none. From the church, we explored the ancient city where I found it much safer to gawk at centuries old buildings on foot rather than by car.

After my initial encounter with British public toilets, I crossed the square to the bench where he waited, sitting awkwardly, with one arm behind his back.

"Sorry I took so long." I went on to explain, "It took me a while to figure out how to flush the john. I finally found a pull-chain danglin' from the ceilin', of all places. I guess you could say that I'm not from around here."

He shook his head and chuckled. "No, you're not." He abruptly changed the subject. "Shut your eyes. I have something for you."

I complied with his request.

"Now open."

In front of me was the largest, most beautiful bouquet of spring-yellow daffodils I had ever seen.

He began apologetically, "I wanted to have flowers for you at the airport this morning, but there were no vendors out that early. The woman I bought these from didn't have any roses. Hope these will do instead."

I had been so thrilled with the prospects of England and so exhausted by the flight over that I had failed to wonder what surprise Christopher would have for me this trip. He had not.

"You're wonderful." I leaned across the flowers to kiss him tenderly on the mouth. "They're wonderful. You are too good to me."

As I kissed him, the fresh scent from the cut blossoms reached my nose and almost tickled, causing me to nearly sneeze. Their aroma recalled spring's hope-filled promise of new beginnings. I had been a short fuse when we were embroiled within all that traffic and knew my actions earlier had not merited flowers of any type, but bless his dear heart for choosing to overlook my behavior and wanting to start over on a sweeter note.

He handed me the flowers before kissing my forehead. "It's my pleasure to give you flowers," he said in acceptance of my implied apology. "Are you hungry?"

As my rumbling stomach answered for me, signaling that airplane food had been just that and reminding me that I had not eaten well since

I left my house in Knoxville the previous morning, I nodded. We bypassed an American franchised restaurant, opting instead for a local pub.

While studying selections in smaller sized menus showing lunch-sized portions pricing, a woman sharply informed us those were for OAPs before speedily handing us much larger menus with much higher prices. We pored over the choices a second time, opting for steak and kidney pie so as to be done with that British experience our first day.

After lunch, we returned to the back roads with a slight hint of a plan to follow. We had no reservations, no set schedules and, surprisingly for us, no laundry list written-in-blood of sites we must see. Only the winds of whim would guide our passage into the Cotswolds where Christopher said we would confine our wanderings. Within a short span of time, we came upon Stonehenge, one of my two requested sites, and stopped to admire that ancient feat of engineering. I walked reverently around the outside of the stones, wondering if any of the chants I read last fall in my Wicca book had been used here.

Late afternoon we turned off the main road for a side trip to the city of Frome, thinking we might stay there our first night. At the interface between Today and Yesterday, the change from our jet-age century to the shanks' mare century of this original section of town was abrupt. Near the original center of town, the cobblestone streets were so narrow that I knew my Ninety-eight Olds could never negotiate their tight twists and sharp corners. I told Christopher the area felt as if we had stumbled onto a deserted movie set depicting a village created for Robin Hood and Maid Marian, for there in the middle of the charming community's oldest streets—which were not as wide as my driveway back home—were gutters filled with running water, still removing refuse same as in medieval days.

A deserted movie set or a town decimated by the plague, the other dryly commented.

While gawking at early buildings constructed from dark local rock, we drove by an appealing inn where Christopher suggested we might spend the night. After we were shown to our room, he left to inquire about dinner.

Alone, I explored the sunlit room, repeating what Dorothy had said about not being in Kansas anymore. The room had four walls and a ceiling and a floor. It contained all necessary furniture, and curtains hung at the windows, yet there was distinctly something about the space that was not American in feeling. It was not the jarring difference that driving today on the wrong side of the road in a pre-shrunk, mirror-imaged car had been. It was as subtle as the sweet aroma wafting through my backyard when the deadly angel's trumpet, a plant native to the tropics that I kept near the deck, opened its fragrant blossoms during late summer nights. The contrast teased my senses, daring me to find all the what-is-wrong-with-this-picture details.

Since the inn's walls were over two feet thick, I perched in the wide window well to look through diamond-shaped, leaded panes onto the cobblestone parking area below. With the age and thickness of the glass distorting my view of the outside, I sensed vague transparencies of horses and carriages, of men with swords at their sides and plumes in their broad brimmed hats and of women in billowing long skirts and swirling cloaks. These, however, were not visions from my past. These figures descended from Anglo-Saxon and French bloodlines. These events belonged to my daddy's people and I was just eavesdropping, so to speak. Since it was a blessing to realize that this was our first visit to English soil and that we would be making new memories here, I relaxed against the stone blocks at my back, watching the shadowed flurry of their activities. When Christopher returned, I turned my head and noticed he carried a vase.

"What do you see?" he asked.

Looking back through the glass into the parking area once more, I saw the shadows immediately vanish.

"Nothing, really," I replied truthfully.

He placed the container by the television. "You can arrange the flowers later. I've waited long enough." He started to pull his knit shirt over his head. "Come to bed, Rachael."

We hurriedly undressed and fell back onto the bed. As we made love this afternoon, I became aware that Christopher's body felt strangely older to my hands. He had turned fifty-six this past winter, and his skin had lost some of its elasticity since our last meeting. His precious face was more lined. His torso muscles were less defined. A slight paunch padded his belly. Most shockingly of all, I noticed that his chest hairs had aged. They had turned entirely gray and were longer and sparser.

My body felt older to me, as well. Getting into and out of that compact car all afternoon had been slow and required more effort as my knees failed to bend as smoothly as they had only months before when I was younger. My bosoms were closer to my navel, my skin was not as soft, and my love handles had grown into surplus rolls about my middle, whether I sat or stood. I hoped he would not find those gray pubic hairs I had discovered a few weeks back. Some of the positions I moved into while on the bed were not as easily reached or maintained as they had been on previous visits. I wondered if Christopher made note of our physical changes the same as I did.

Maybe love affairs were for the young after all. But then again, the physical sensations he aroused in me that afternoon and the emotions I had for this man were just as intense as they had been that first night in Nashville so many years ago. Perhaps, like youth, love affairs were wasted on the young. In any case, despite our advancing years and deteriorating bodies, he called out my name three times before supper. And neither one of us spoke to those inconsequential physical signs of aging as we shared our bodies hungrily with the one we loved, who had never aged.

Waiting for dinner to be announced hours later, we sat alone in the compact pub located at our inn. I glanced over tour books while Christopher investigated the Ordnance Survey maps.

"Oh, do you know what OAP stands for?" he casually asked.

I looked up from my reading to give that question careful consideration. "Only Anglican People?" I still smarted from the hostess' jerking the menu from my hand before lunch.

"No. Old Age Pensioners. Those smaller menus are for senior Brits on welfare." His voice sounded distracted as he continued to pore over the detailed drawings. He went on to explain the source of his knowledge, "I asked our innkeepers about that when I checked us in."

"Well, that bitch at the restaurant could have been nicer," I half-heartedly snapped.

Suddenly, he put the map book down, blurting out, "Do you realize how old I am?"

"Why, yes," I replied. I knew his date of birth as well as I knew mine. I looked down to finish the paragraphs about Frome.

He waited a minute before asking incredulously, "Do you know how many times we made love in that hour and a half?"

"Yes," I answered, closing my book, "I was there."

He went on, "Do you know that's supposed to be impossible for a man my age?"

"My Precious," I explained, putting aside the book, "don't you know our relationship defies all laws currently known to mankind?" My flip answer sounded matter-of-fact, but my heart caught in my throat when I looked at his happy expression. I felt such tenderness toward him and I felt so safe being with him. How I could feel both protective of and protected by the same man, at the same time, was beyond my understanding.

"But," Christopher continued, his mind still not accepting what his body had accomplished that afternoon, "I'm an old man!"

"Can't prove that by me." I placed my hand on the inside of his thigh. Feeling his body's reaction under my fingers and noticing the latest twinkle in his eyes, I asked archly, "And what will you be wantin' for dessert?"

An obscene chuckle was his only reply.

We traveled west toward the City of Wells, as our innkeeper's wife at dinner had insisted we needed to do, carrying my yellow daffodils in a plastic bag, their stems nesting in dampened newspaper on the backseat of our car. Wrong turns and wrongly given directions did not matter because we were together and had the riches of days, not a few penny-pinching hours, to share. The cathedral there was even more impressive than she had described and well worth the side trip attached to our wanderings through the British countryside.

When we pulled into Bath late Saturday afternoon, most of the inns were full or required two nights' stay for the remainder of the weekend, which refused to fit within the rigidity of our unplanned, semi-fluid itinerary. After hours of disappointing refusals, we found a bed-and-breakfast that was accommodating.

After he completed the paperwork to check into the uninspected room, Christopher manfully hauled every piece of our luggage up the three flights of stairs in one trip. He allowed me only to carry the key, tour books, maps and flowers. With each floor we mounted, the stairways became narrower and the landings more confining. Since I could see only legs under the burden of our possessions as he staggered and bounced off walls and railings on the trek to our accommodations, I had no difficulty mentally transporting myself to Tibet where I became a Western tourist following behind a heavily laden Sherpa guide ascending a steep mountain trail.

The fourth floor hall leading to our room was just too narrow. With

Christopher and our amassed luggage blocking my access to the door, I handed him the key. Recovering from our climb, I announced, "Honey, I think we were assigned a room that belonged to a servant or to a red-headed stepchild back when this house was a private residence."

I heard Christopher curse as he fumbled the key in the lock before the door consented to open. Toppled over by the weight of our combined possessions, he lunged into the room, collapsing face forward on the bed. I crossed the room to sit on the bed beside the fallen mound from which his breathing escaped in hard rasps.

"Poor baby. Next time let me help you with the bags." I leaned over to kiss chastely the tip of Christopher's ear, before explaining sweetly, "Honey, I don't want you to injure yourself." I quickly blocked out visions in which a massive heart attack preceded my married lover's death in a foreign country.

He forced a short laugh. "Don't worry," he said, still gasping for air, "I'll never disappoint you. Just give me a chance . . . to catch . . . my breath then . . . I'll make you lose yours."

After sharing our first British sunset, we strolled the almost deserted streets and avenues of Bath, discovering theaters and storefronts right out of a BBC production of Jane Austen's *Persuasion*. We even stumbled upon the top of medieval walls that once had guarded the ancient city. Again, we bypassed familiar American fast food restaurants in search for a local pub for dinner.

After the bartender called that our food order was ready, Christopher carried two heaping plates to our table. The food smelled wonderful to me. I examined the generous serving on my plate before confiding, "My first mother-in-law once told me that English food wasn't all that tasty and English restaurants only served small portions."

"Maybe she didn't find the right places to eat when she visited," he offered.

"No, Honey, she really was from around here," I told him, "but maybe there's another England she ate at," I laughed, "or maybe we're not in England after all."

Christopher had already started his meal. "This food is wonderful. Good flavor," he pronounced. "Much better than that steak and kidney pie we had back in Winchester."

I allowed, "Hell, plain grits is better than that!"

I looked around the crowded pub where we sat. The noisy room was filled with gregarious people from Bath, and its atmosphere felt warm and welcoming. No one appeared to care that I wore sneakers this late on a Saturday night.

"Christopher, this is more fabulous than Washington. You know, this past fall I was watchin' a *National Geographic* segment on the Roman baths here, and I promised myself that someday I would get to Bath. And less than six months later, here we are."

He took a long drink of the local beer he had ordered. "Be careful, Rachael, you might get what you wish for."

I ate a few bites before I said quietly, "I wish for you."

Christopher looked a long time into my eyes before finally replying, "You'll have me for almost two weeks."

That's not nearly long enough, I thought. I smiled anyway, my lips forming the passive, sweet smile of resignation that I had been taught long ago.

We found crocuses blooming in a riot of spring colors on the grassy mound in the center of the Circus. The graffiti on the walls down from the Crescent's elegant townhouses revealed British humour, which I found to be a pleasant change from Knoxville's gang rhetoric and gutter language. We stood in queues with other tourists to inch our way through the baths while I wondered to myself if English tourists millimetered alongside us.

After we exited Bath Abbey, our third cathedral in as many days, Christopher announced, "That's all the cathedrals I want to tour this trip."

"Yep, me, too," I agreed as we stood back to admire the imposing building one last time. "That one at Wells was the best, I think, and the little church at Frome was sweet, but I felt the most reverence at Stonehenge."

"You're such a pagan," he joked while hugging me tightly.

We felt out of sync all Sunday in Bath, but coped with the nagging feeling anyway, thinking it was because we were in a country where words, familiar to us, were used in unfamiliar ways. Not until we sat down to tea in a converted house near Prince Charlie's Highgrove were we informed by a fellow tea drinker that, during the night, England had leaped forward to Daylight Savings Time. No wonder our waiter at breakfast had been surly when we sat down five minutes before the kitchen was scheduled to close. That neighborly tea drinker also politely urged us to try clotted cream after she overheard my asking Christopher if he thought it could be like haggis.

For the most part, our days in England drifted into a tangle of pleasant memories layered upon the area's peaceful, greening, rolling countryside. Painswick's churchyard had yews pruned to match trees I had seen in a cartoon version of Alice's Wonderland. Near that picturesque village we dined in a genial roadhouse where armored knights, famished after a day of jousting, clanked while they ate and their ladies, attired in jewel-toned medieval costumes, fluttered between tables. During the following days, we made up deliciously obscene limericks to pass the miles we drove.

The towns we discovered had imaginative names, such as Snowshill, Burton-on-the-Water, Morton-on-the-Marsh, Guiting Power, Stow-on-the-Wold, Upper Slaughter and Lower Slaughter. In those small villages, the cottages were constructed of local stone. Most had slate roofs. Some were crowned with thick thatched roofs and guarded by fences made from saplings snugly laced together. Mosses and ferns draped nonchalantly over ancient, dry-stacked rock walls. Early spring flowers, in shades of bashful blue, peeked out of low grasses along the narrow lanes we traveled. Everywhere, the wonderfully majestic English oaks spread their strong branches.

Unlike the land we drove through after we left Gatwick that reminded me of Kentucky's Bluegrass Region, the Cotswolds' countryside looked as if Laura Ashley had her hand in its design and decoration. Adding to her quintessential British country home look, unfamiliar breeds of long-haired cows and sheep with dred-locks dotting lush pastures brought to mind overstuffed, slipcovered furniture. In the typically refined English manner, country road-kill was pheasants, not the 'possums I found back home. Magpies flew instead of cardinals.

Shaped stones placed atop one another combined to form rock mushrooms called staddles, a word I had first used while solving crossword puzzles in the comfort of my living room. Instead of protecting granaries from marauding rodents, these days they adorned cottage gardens. And each garden we passed was a glorious jungle of blooms and greenery that only the one who tended them could point out their original design.

We frequented pubs with the locals where my adventuresome travel companion sampled indigenous beers and I stayed safe drinking white wines. Some evenings, we observed games of skittles and darts. We dined at the inn where King Charles stayed before the Roundheads arrested him. That historic pub had a fireplace so large I could stand inside it with my arms outstretched, still not touching its stone surround. The rich, golden sheen of long-polished brass and the soft, gray patina of real lead pewter displayed there made the recreated pub we visited at Epcot too touristy, too pasteurized and too new.

If we had been married in the church ruins near Beaufort, England assumed the destination for our belated honeymoon. Each night, I slept warm and safe within Christopher's arms. Each morning, I awoke early to watch his resting face in the filtered light just before dawn, filing my memories for future reference. We shared every sunset we could and made love two and three times a day. Each day as we packed up to start our wandering, I removed shriveled, faded flowers from my golden bouquet, wrapped damp paper around the remaining stems and nestled them inside a plastic bag to carry with us.

Some afternoons we hiked, drinking in the calmness of the land. Our walks took us down country lanes and through farm pastures where footpaths remained, by law, public domain. Some had once been Roman roads. Some pathways predated even those. We found daffodils blooming everywhere, wild in the fields or crowded in ancient, hewn-stone watering troughs. Once, we came upon a nodding cluster of them peeking from inside the bowl of an abandoned, modern, porcelain commode leaning outside a kitchen door.

Sauntering through the countryside was easier for Christopher and his long legs. The sloping pastures were not my major problem. I stayed up with him fairly well on the flats and down hills. It was those mean fence crossovers that slowed my pace. Since my straddle was about one inch too short, more than a few crossings became so intimate that I felt we should have been on a first name basis before I attempted to clamber over.

One day, while exploring Warwick Castle, Christopher surprised me by assisting some obviously lost French students in near-perfect

French. Another evening, I was astounded when he enjoyed a cigar with his beer. And during one lunch, I was grateful when he was not bold enough to order a hot spotted dick for dessert.

I stopped whooping in alarm whenever he ventured too close to my edge of the pavement. Whenever we had to pass oncoming traffic on narrow country lanes, I found it much easier to shut my eyes and pretend to trust his driving skills, a very Southern Lady attitude for me to take. Mom would have been so proud.

Each day, I waited for the announcement that he considered our relationship changed and that it no longer excited him. Afraid that time would come for him. Afraid that time would not come for me. While our relationship remained constant, the fickle March weather vacillated between spring-warm, sunny days to winter-cold, snowy days to English-soggy, rainy days. Each night, we stayed in a bed-and-breakfast in a different village. Each morning, there was a smaller bouquet to carry out to the car.

I luxuriated in having his warm body next to mine while I slept. My body became accustomed to having its desire for sex sated. I held his hand whenever I had that need. Yet time passed too quickly, and I felt the dread of our parting creeping closer. We had not yet kissed good-bye, and I had already started to wonder when would I see him again.

At breakfast on the day before we were to return to Gatwick, Christopher pointed to a lone man who had been seated at a tiny table, his place setting was such that he faced the wall, whereas the larger tables held couples and faced windows.

Taking my hand in his, he said, "Rachael, I want to thank you for being here with me this trip." His tone was earnest and sincere. "Because, if you weren't here, that man would be me. I would be sitting alone, facing the wall and eating a lonely breakfast. I'm most grateful." He brought my hand to his lips and kissed it most gallantly.

Well now, if that won't warm the cockles of your heart.

He released my hand. "Do you feel up to another hike today?"

"Honey, I would follow you anywhere," I answered grandly.

After packing our belongings, we headed in the direction of London, stopping at a village where the Ordnance Map indicated a loop trail nearby. The sun was bright hot when we began our seven-mile, last jaunt. We soon left the farmlands and started uphill. Christopher walked his normal faster pace. I walked my usual slow one. Under the burning sun, I trudged up the dirt road that now passed through a dense wood. I glanced at my watch. He had been gone from sight for over ten minutes. I had no idea where I was because he had the map. Not only was I hot and sweaty and mad but frightened because hidden guns were being fired in the hillsides looming around me.

I muttered to myself, "I should have walked more this past winter. I can't keep up with him. Had I known English food was goin' to be this good, I would have lost weight before startin' this trip." Pains in my right leg that had bothered me the last few days began to hurt in earnest and portions of my right foot felt numb, and I could no longer ignore the tightness encircling my lower back. "My back feels funny. If I had the keys, I would turn around and high tail it right back to the damn car and wait for him to finish this forced march. Where in the hell is he, anyway? I thought we were goin' to see England together? This hike is just like our relationship. Together, but apart. Both suck. Damn, but my lower back hurts."

"Rachael!" I heard Christopher's voice wafting through the trees from far above me. "Keep on coming!" he encouraged.

The ridiculousness of the situation hit me. I yelled furiously up the hill, "What choice do I have?"

"Damn, this hill is steep. I'll never see Christopher again," I muttered aloud to no one. "He'll make it back to the car and to America without me."

Another gunshot went off. I jumped in response.

"My body will be found weeks from now in the woods," I continued my lonely tirade, "killed by an errant bullet from a mad Englishman who had been in the sun too long."

Panting hard, I moved slowly up the hill. I was out of shape. My lower back ached, even raising my legs each step was an effort. The trees finally thinned out, exposing a lane beside a grassy pasture. I saw Christopher beside a fence reading the map and gazing about for the next yellow dot to walk toward.

When I reached where he stood, he apologized, "Rachael, I can't walk as slow as you."

"I know," I answered, "and I can't walk as fast as you. My legs aren't as long as yours." I purposely did not mention how badly my back hurt or the numbness in my right foot because I was embarrassed to be in such sad shape for hiking.

"Can you read this map? I can't locate the next dot," he explained, "and I'm not sure which way we're supposed to go."

We both studied the map before deciding to head toward the left over a slight rise in the land. While we were still walking close, Christopher said, "Rachael, I'll stop whenever there's a turn to make certain you see which way to follow before I head on. Is that all right for you?"

"That'll work," I agreed. Perversely I added, "I know you won't lose me. You'll find me before bedtime because I am the best piece of ass you've ever had."

Christopher stopped to tenderly brush back the strands of hair that had escaped my bun and stuck to my sweaty face. Taking the time, he kissed my mouth sweetly. "You're right, but that's not the only reason I won't lose you."

We hiked the rest of our last day in the Cotswolds in that manner. It did work. If the man had trouble following the trail, he waited for my assistance. If the yellow dots marking the trail were plainly visible, Christopher whistled and pointed to the direction I was to follow, waiting for my wave indicating that I understood before he walked on.

Why can't we reach a solution, I thought, for our hike through life as easily as we did on this hike through the Cotswolds? Why does his life remain in California and mine in Tennessee? What a bitch of a situation!

Damn, Rachael, are you a member of the slow group or what? We've had this conversation before. You know the answer. The man wants it this way. The only choice you have is: You meet him or you don't meet him. He doesn't need to make a life with you. He already has one that you can never share.

But I can't give him up.

Well, at least you're consistent. Accept your choice and quit grousing.

❦

After thoroughly surveying the toilet fixtures at our last inn, I announced, "Honey, there's a bidet in here." I picked out the remaining three freshest daffodils and went to the sink for water. "How do I use it?"

Christopher marched into the bath to gaze upon the pink porcelain throne. "I don't know. I've always washed my socks in them." Turning, he walked back to the bed.

"You're no help," I called after him. "I thought you would know about these things since you know French."

Our last supper together started out as an elegant affair in the formal dining room at our inn, except that Christopher drank too much. He tipped his glass during the first course, spilling red wine on the white table linen. I had never seen him like this. As our meal progressed, we replayed highlights from our past travels, and we recalled favorite episodes from this trip. The more he drank wine, the more I drank water, granting Christopher his turn to overindulge since I had been the drunk at Cocoa Beach.

After dessert, he stumbled up the stairs to our room. We undressed down to our skivvies. Lying across the bed, we again listed the English towns we had visited and discussed the sights we had seen. Afterwards, Christopher insisted we floss our teeth, after which, he passed out on top of the covers, too soused to make love.

I looked upon his limp body before staring at the ceiling. I reported to the contents of the mute bedroom, "This is not at all what I had in mind for our last night together."

After tugging at the blankets until he was covered, I snuggled up to the curve of his back, our bodies fitting together like two stacked spoons. At least, I thought, I learned tonight that he's a pleasant drunk.

The following morning, Christopher touched my shoulder to wake me. "I'm going for a walk while you get your things together."

Sitting up in bed, I noticed his packed suitcases by the door and that Christopher wore the same clothes he had on when he met me at Gatwick. Mentally, he was already on the plane, returning to his Californian existence; however, I was not yet ready for our time together to be over.

I reached my hand toward him. "Come back to bed. Let's make love one last time."

He firmly shook his head. "No, we can't. I've got to pretend when I arrive home that I haven't had sex for two weeks."

Damn, Christopher, that was more than I needed to know!

Staring in his direction, I felt the blood drain from my face. Since I did not have my glasses on and the man was too far away for me to read his expression without them, all I saw was a blurred figure turning away, leaving me in bed alone.

Thirteen

Refreshed from a stay on Mount LeConte, I returned home Saturday afternoon ready for anything, come what may, but my hike could have in no way prepared me for what I found Monday morning. My life had been normal only a half hour before in the cool morning, selecting fresh produce at the wholesalers. In shocked disbelief, I watched the scene unfolding. All I could do was stand helplessly by and out of the way until the fire was brought under control.

While leaning against the side of my car staring at chugging fire engines and flashing lights, I felt ineffective and small as men, garishly garbed in yellow protective gear, swarmed over my flame-engulfed restaurant. I waited impatiently to get into the building because I needed to see the devastation up close before I could begin to accept the hard fact that everything was gone.

I knew that desire was morbid, yet I could not help myself. I personally had to view the remains to comprehend the loss, just as I had needed to touch Aunt Maurie's stiff, makeup-covered hands to verify her death when her embalmed body rested inside a massive, gunmetal gray casket with heavy chrome trim that gleamed as brightly as a freshly detailed, 1950s Buick's front bumper.

Be careful what you wish for. Be careful what you wish for. Be careful what—

I interrupted the other's calloused singsong. Sweet Jesus, I'd only wanted work to slow down some! I didn't mean for it to go up in smoke.

I watched Liz and Margaret rush to where I stood. They did not need to speak. Their expressions spoke volumes. I studied their concerned faces before saying, "I don't know anything. I drove up the same time the trucks came roarin' in." Wordlessly, they joined me in staring at the seductive flames flickering through the windows.

Because they frequently dropped by for carry-outs, the firemen from the neighboring fire halls knew us. After the blaze was put out, they allowed only me, as the sole owner, to enter the dining area when they deemed the building safe. Ironically, they warned me to stay out of the kitchen.

Walking stiffly from the shock caused by the fire as much as from the sore muscles left over from my hike, I picked my way through the charred, acrid mess of what had been my livelihood. Even with my untrained eyes, I could tell what contents that were not burned were so smoke and water damaged as to be unusable.

At the door to my kitchen, I leaned over in order to look through the hole in the ceiling above where the stove stood. Disgustingly cheery blue skies greeted me.

"Damn them!" I muttered before stepping backwards, nearly tripping over a chair leg. I twisted awkwardly to keep from completely falling and felt a strong pull followed by a dull pain in my lower back. Landing on my right hand, I managed to keep my butt from touching the sopping-wet, sooty-black floor.

"Be careful! I think I'd better get you out of here."

I turned my head in the direction of the voice. Will's face had no soot smudges, whereas my livelihood was covered with the nasty stuff. That fact did not seem fair to me.

Upon first seeing him this morning, I had felt better with Will Sharpe being part of the shift responding to the fire because we had graduated high school together back in 1964. The tenuousness of that relationship had eased some of the horror associated with the impersonal flames. Although reluctant for me to enter the building, Will had come along to keep me out of harm's way. He had stayed close, just not close enough to catch me when I tripped.

He extended his right arm to me.

"I think you're right." I agreed. Begrudgingly, I caught hold of his hand and allowed him to pull me to my feet. The ache in my back quickly overshadowed any discomfort from tight leg muscles. I ignored them both. After a final, long look at the smoldering kitchen, I turned to the tall man at my side. "Oh, Will, this is terrible."

We left the rubble through the blistered, once beautiful doors that Hugh Ed had painted going to where Liz and Margaret waited next to the nearest fire truck. Behind them I noticed Joey, my long time busboy, leaning his bicycle against a distant tree. After reaching my friends, all I could do was slowly shake my head in disbelief. The girls solemnly enclosed me and my defeated spirit in the circle of their arms. We clung together, exactly as we had done after sunset at Cliff Top only two nights ago.

"Funny," I finally said, pulling away from their embrace, "this was a lot more fun Friday night." It was a meager attempt on my part to lighten the morning. And a wasted effort at that.

Practical as ever, Margaret suggested, "Well, we can't do anything about this right now. Let's go home and come back later. Liz and I'll call the customers who have catered orders."

"What in hell happened!" Joey shouted as he rushed to us from the parking area. "I was on my way to the gym and saw the fire trucks."

I had no desire to recap the morning's events for him. "Liz," I said, wanting her to take his question.

Liz cleared her throat to begin the telling. "Rachael was here when Margaret and I drove up. She said the firemen pulled in about the same time she did."

The stunned boy asked, "What caused it?"

"Don't know yet," Liz answered. "They're waitin' on the arson investigator now."

"What's she goin' to do?" He looked at Liz and then to Margaret. "I have to work. I've got bills to pay." Joey's angular, teenaged face looked confused, worried by this abrupt upheaval of his world. He had questions for which there were no quick answers.

I was aware that my voice sounded far away as I suggested, "I guess, Joey, you can apply for unemployment until we get reopened. Don't know when that will be, but it'll be as soon as I can because I've got bills, too." Distracted by the growing pain in my back, I added, "I've got to lie down. I'm goin' home. I can't do anything here."

❦

When I awoke from my nap, I found myself enveloped by a raging pain centered in my lower back. I could hardly breathe and realized I must have twisted something bad when I stumbled at the restaurant. I needed to pee, but the back ache was so intense that I foolishly debated with my bladder for some time as to whether we really, really needed to get to the toilet. Rolling off the bed to stand, my spine felt like a dull blade had severed it. When I tried to hold myself erect, my upper body listed like a sailboat with a broken keel board. As wave after wave of searing pain swept over me, I feared I would fall out before reaching the bathroom.

"This can't be good," I told myself as I gingerly lowered to my hands and knees, crawling slowly into the bath.

With that necessity concluded, I carefully made my way to the top of the stairs leading to the front hall. As I pulled myself erect, tears began to flow in miserable anticipation of the agonizing journey to come. Leaning heavily upon the banister, I descended the flight of steps sideways, each tread more torturous than the last. Once that goal was reached, I rested with my knees bent and my back flat on the floor to recover from the brutally sharp spasms before tackling the next obstacle on my course to my car parked in the basement. Entering the kitchen, I glanced once at the wall phone before deciding that reaching it was out of the question and drove, without calling ahead, to my doctor.

Back home, I rested uneasily atop my bed with Sybyl and Beatrice huddled nearby. They sensed something was wrong and were uncharacteristically quiet. For no apparent reason, the sisters sprang to their feet. Immediately, the hairs down their backs bristled and their tails fluffed. They stepped cautiously to the foot of our bed and faced the open bedroom door. The girls began growling before I heard a key turn in the front door. I calculated the effort required to roll over to the bedside table drawer where I kept my loaded pistol, dreading the increase in discomfort that movement would certainly create. My mind flashed to an early Lash LaRue western where the bad guys surrounded the encircling wagons.

After the front door opened, I heard Mom call, "Rachael, Darlin', it's just me!"

With the arrival of reinforcements, my mind relinquished some control, knowing that now I would not have to go it alone.

Sybyl jumped stiff-legged onto the floor and raced to the top of the steps, all the while telling the day's events as she knew them. My mother's words were nearly drowned out by Sybyl's strident, Siamese cat voice.

"I had Margaret come and get me," she continued from the downstairs hall, closing the door. "Liz is bringin' your prescriptions as soon as they're filled. Honey, I'm so glad you had Dr. Speer's nurse call before you left her office."

Next, I heard Sybyl's feet thudding down the staircase to exchange a proper greeting with my guests at the door.

Always the perfect feline hostess, I mused.

With the possibility of an unwanted intruder over, Beatrice relaxed her guard and lowered her hair follicles. She returned to hunker down protectively near my shoulder.

Mom entered my room, cradling a limp Sybyl in her arms. "What did the doctor say?" she asked.

When she deemed the distance within range, Sybyl leaped to rejoin her sister on the bed. I grimaced from the jolt of her weight landing on the mattress.

"A ruptured disc. Doc says it would be better to let it heal on its own and not do surgery. She said if I could stand the pain, my back would be better off in the long run." I repeated, "If I can stand the pain . . ." I wanted to laugh, but my heart was not in it.

As she came up the steps, I heard Margaret asking, "Mrs. Taite, where do you want your bags? What did the doctor say?"

I listened as Mom repeated what I had told her.

"Oh, hell," Margaret swore quietly as she came to my bedside. "Rachael, that Will guy went back into your office and got out the caterin' book. Mrs. Marshall was the only name down for today. When I called her, Clyda said she needed the cake for her bridge club this afternoon. I told her about the fire and suggested your special almond cake since it doesn't take long to whip up. I carried it to her house in time. So, she's one happy camper."

"Clyda? Since when did you and Mrs. Marshall go to first names?"

Margaret slyly smiled. "Well, since I plan to marry her nephew," she explained, "we'll soon be family. I'm just gettin' a head start."

"Damn, Margaret," I sharply reminded her, "the man hasn't shed his current wife!" Getting back to the catered order, I added in a kinder tone, "Thanks for doin' the skillet cake. That was too good of you." Knowing my friend as well as I did, I knew the delivery was primarily intended to keep her in Miss Clyda's good graces until she and the nephew were formally introduced. I inquired archly, "And just when do we meet her nephew?"

"Well now," Margaret began, "we have hit a slight snag with him. It seems that the fool has taken back that cheatin' wife of his. Clyda told me today that the girl told him she was sorry and begged forgiveness. Now they're off to some island for a second damn honeymoon."

The nephew and his wife on a reconciliatory holiday would definitely slow down the Carolina juggernaut, but my money remained on Margaret. Because I understood the nephew's behavior, I nodded but not in agreement with Margaret's assessment of the yet-to-be-met attorney. "When you love someone," I explained to my friend, "you grant them do-overs."

Unannounced, Liz appeared in the doorway. She carried a glass of water and two small containers. "Just what the doctor ordered," Liz joked.

I took the glass and read over the paperwork accompanying the plastic vials. Dr. Speer had done right by me with her prescriptions.

"Thanks," I told Liz.

As I swallowed the medications, Liz reported, "Margaret and I have decided that we can do the special orders that are down on the book. We'd hate to disappoint all our loyal customers."

"We'll cook at home," Margaret added. "I figure the food police won't find out that we've been caterin' out of our kitchens until it's too late."

I nodded. "Our people have been awfully good to us. Just don't take on any new orders. I don't want the food police too mad. Take out expenses and your cuts from what you collect."

Liz broke in quickly, "We'll discuss that later."

Although I wanted to clear the matter now, my heavy eyelids fell closed and my drugged mind floated elsewhere.

During my initial appointment on the day of the fire, Doc Speer had instructed me to schedule my next office visit in two weeks. Her directions said to take the medications every four hours as needed for pain. Although during those first few days, every three hours would have better suited, I waited the prescribed two hundred and forty minutes between doses, hating every second of that last hour.

While I knew it was going to be a long recovery, I just had no idea how long. I dreaded the not knowing, especially since the muscle relaxers and scheduled narcotics only dulled my mind while the pain never really left my body.

Over the following days Liz and Margaret worked off the special orders, never asking for a date when I would be ready to reopen the restaurant. They called daily to check on my progress, running errands as Mom said they were needed. My four-legged girls stayed close enough to keep me company, yet never crowded against me into our customary cat sandwich. Mom made herself at home in the guest room across the hall from my bedroom.

Keeping the world at bay, Mom created a protective environment in which I healed. Always organized, she quickly imposed her personal regime upon my household. She prepared meals and carried them upstairs on a big tray for me to eat in bed. She opened cans of salmon for the girls to share in the kitchen. She cleaned out their litter boxes. She screened my calls and each evening read back the messages she had taken that day. She washed dishes and clothes. She made out grocery lists containing foods she remembered to be my favorites and that Liz and Margaret took turns filling. Mom would softly smooth back my hair every time she refilled the tall water glass I kept on my bedside table, making certain the shorter glass for the girls had spring water, too. Mom assured me every day everything was going to be just fine, and I wanted to believe her.

On the Friday after the fire, I lay on my bed in a drugged stupor, praying for stronger pills for the pain. I wished it were the previous Friday when Liz, Margaret and I were atop the mountain and my life had been one great adventure. I wanted Christopher to call.

Earlier that afternoon Mom had come upstairs to report that the fire department's expert had decided the fire was not arson, but something having to do with a bad ballast in a ceiling light fixture. Nobody's fault, but the restaurant was out of business.

Nobody's fault. Damn, I wanted someone to be held accountable.

I had turned my body awkwardly while picking my way through the rubble that had been my livelihood, rupturing a disc, and that Dr. Speer explained had something to do with an existing bulge in my lower back. Again, nobody's fault, but I was unable to work.

Nobody's fault. Double damn, that was the hand I was dealt. Those were the cards I had to play.

Now having some concrete information, I wanted to share my sorry lot with Christopher. Since he had not called, I decided to call him.

Lifting the phone off its cradle, I slowly picked out his private number on the push buttons. Thanks to my nearly nonexistent coordination, I struggled through several attempts before my fingers finally landed on the correct numbers in the proper sequence.

He answered on the second ring.

"Hey, Honey." My slurred greeting sounded slow to my ears.

He immediately asked, "What's wrong?"

I felt his concern come over the connection, washing over me.

"Everything. There's been a fire, and I've ruptured a disc." I began sobbing like a brokenhearted woman on a bad drunk in a cheap roadhouse alongside a poorly maintained county road. All that was lacking was Willie Nelson singing in the background. "The restaurant's a total loss, and I hurt bad."

"Oh, Rachael, I wish there was something I could do."

"Me, too."

Although the wagons were circled, the cavalry remained back at the fort and would not be riding out in neat orderly columns. It never crossed my mind that Christopher would travel to Knoxville to be with me, I had called only to ease my burden. As a companionable silence spanned the distance between us, I felt less isolated simply by knowing he shared my woe.

Finally he said, "I was going to call the cabin tonight. I'm so glad you called when you did because I would've hated to wait any longer to hear from you. Is your Mom there with you?"

"Yes."

"Then I won't worry too much about you. I'll call in a couple of days to check on you. Call me whenever you need to talk."

"OK." The pills that I had taken before I dialed kicked in. "I need to go now."

"Bye, Rachael. Get better soon. I miss you."

※

Leaning heavily upon my right forearm that rested on the padded armrest, I drove home from Speer's office. Steering my Olds with my left arm and working the pedals with my right foot, I made the journey both ways without incident, staying on the Pike with its lower speed limit and less crowded lanes, reasoning that route would be safer than the interstate.

Even though I had delayed medication for the day until after my early morning appointment, Mom had argued for Liz or Margaret to drive me. Wanting to manage the visit myself, I had refused. Wishing to be less of a burden to anyone than I already was, I despised my dependency for I found it demeaning.

It seemed another lifetime ago that Christopher and I tramped through England. That trip had been taken by a happier someone, not by the me who cried every night because she could do so little for herself. Too much had happened since the fire. My days revolved around nothing except my damn pain and that damn fire. My life in Knoxville had been literally reduced to ashes. I could not stand, I could not sit, I could not even turn in bed without excruciating pain.

I should have had more insurance. What was I to do? The business account contained enough money to cover payroll taxes for the last weeks the restaurant was in operation. I was grateful for that small favor.

The beautiful restaurant I had created, however, was no longer there to support me. Sweet Jesus, not even my back could support me. I could not provide support for my employees. Telling those good people I had to let them go hurt the worse. At least, they could draw unemployment, whereas I could not.

Margaret had assured me she was glad for a break in the action because she wanted to visit her family in South Carolina and do some traveling. Liz had reported she had some renovations to supervise and not to worry about her. Their offer to honor the pre-fire catering orders brought in money, helping to keep food on my table, sand in the litter boxes and my utility bills covered. Every time I suggested they take their cut from their work, both acted offended and refused. When they finally protested that was what friends were for, I cried.

What would become of me? I would have to sell everything I owned. What savings I had would not cover all my growing debts. Mom was helping out with both my house payments.

Christopher had said he would always be there for me. I needed him now. Where was he?

Rachael, he said he would be 'there,' not 'here' for you. He didn't lie.

"You bitch," I muttered to my twin as I aimed my car into the basement garage, "who needs your sarcasm at a time like this!"

As soon as the engine was cut off, I quickly flipped the lever lowering the back of my seat. I needed to lie flat until the searing pain became manageable again so I could get myself up the stairs to bed.

Mom walked over to the driver's door and opened it. "Darlin', how did it go at the doctor's office?"

"Fine." If I said 'fine' enough times, maybe I could believe that everything really would be fine. "She said again, if I could tolerate the pain, my back would heal without surgery and be much stronger in the future without any invasive procedures. Doc said she would make sure I had enough pills to deal with the pain, except that she calls it 'discomfort.' She thought I should start some type of therapy next week."

"Good. Do you want some help gettin' upstairs?"

"No thanks, Mom. I'll be ready to move in a minute or two." Waiting out the pain, I shut my eyes.

"I'll get back to the laundry then. By the way, one of your customers called. You know, the one who teaches yoga."

Although I had no idea to whom she referred, I nodded to indicate I did. That response with her was always simpler.

Mom went on, "She said she does something that could help you. I told her to drop by this afternoon. That'll be OK, won't it?"

"Yes, Mom." I was extremely tired. I needed drugs and my bed, and all that was far above me. I knew if I never got better, I would have to sell my sweet house with its two flights of stairs, whether I was able to make the mortgage payments or not, and probably my cabin on Little River. Without my house and my cabin, I would again feel homeless.

If I can tolerate the pain, I silently chanted my new mantra before tackling the steps.

Mom called to me over the sound of the filling washing machine, "And your landlord called this mornin'. Said to tell you not to worry about anything. Just said to rent from him when you're ready to go back to work."

Claudia Youngblood arrived late in the day, looking as a yoga instructor should look. Her body was lithe and trim, and her face was kind and serene. I vaguely remember seating her a few times at my restaurant.

Saying that the technique she had studied in California worked with the soft tissues in guided assistance, she told me its correct name, which I promptly forgot. She explained the principles by which it worked, which sounded, frankly, like hocus-pocus to me. Had I not been under the influence of heavy drugs, I might have refused to allow the woman to practice her magic but within five minutes of guiding my right arm through the air, the elbow that I had rested heavily on while driving no longer ached.

"Well," she asked hesitantly, "what do you think?"

"I think you're a godsend. Thank you so very much. Dr. Speer said

I could start therapy next week. Can you fit me in?"

She smiled a wide, bright smile. I noticed she had large teeth for a petite woman and thought her smile must be a match to her generous heart.

"Yes, I've got some time next Thursday afternoon. I don't usually work with patients in acute pain, but since your medical doctor wants you to begin treatment, we'll go just as slow as your body wants to go."

Purposely misunderstanding her description of my condition, I laughed sarcastically. "Let me tell you something, Claudia, there's nothing 'cute' about the pain I'm in. I just want it over."

Dr. Speer returned my call later that evening. After saying I did not want to see a conventional physical therapist, I told her about Claudia and about an acquaintance of mine who was a chiropractor. We agreed on the conservative treatment I was to follow. When the call ended, I felt like I had taken back some control of my life.

As long as I could tolerate the pain . . .

I drove to my friendly chiropractor five blocks away from my house for palliative treatments three times a week. Claudia came by my house once a week. After four weeks passed with no decrease in my level of pain, I felt discouraged. Had I been capable of standing, I would have imitated my favorite Southern heroine angrily raising her fist in protest because I definitely refused to continue this passive acceptance of my pain any longer.

One morning while watching my companion cats stretch and flex their backs as they arose from their naps, I decided Sybyl and Beatrice were on to something. I tried a modified cobra and cat-backs that I remembered from yoga lessons I had taken some years ago. Miraculously, during the third day while I was going through the cobra, something subtly changed along my spine. Instantly, the ever-present pain vanished. I had actually forgotten how wonderful my body felt when it was not smothered with pain. Amazingly enough, the pain stayed away until later that morning when I left my bed to list to the bathroom.

I could tolerate the pain as long as I knew I was getting better. But most importantly, I had discovered an off switch.

※

After my world crashed, I could find nothing on which to anchor my future. My days became consumed with healing, and those days drifted into months. Christopher called often to check on my progress and to tell me the best jokes he had heard since we last talked.

After my injury became a manageable entity, the only consistency remaining in my life was my longing for him. That ache was painfully familiar.

During those weeks when I was incapacitated, inertia overtook me. Although I had plenty of time to plan my future, I lacked the energy to make even the simplest decisions. Mom attempted to persuade me that my apathy was merely a side effect from all the drugs I had taken. I slowly began to believe her, yet I had no desire to jump back into a kettle of boiling water that big ever again.

Although I loved my cats and my mother, I needed time away from their constant presence and hovering care. As soon as I quit requiring heavy pain medication and felt up to driving any distance, I headed to my cabin near Sunshine for a night of blessed solitude.

At a convenience store along the way, I purchased two bags of potato chips in celebration of my first night alone since the fire. I wanted the coming evening to be the turning point in my recovery. I wanted to create a master plan for the rest of my life. I wanted satisfyingly long lists of actions to follow.

Staring at the blank, top page on the legal-sized pad of yellow paper, I was down to broken pieces of potato chips at the bottom of the bowl with nothing to show for my efforts except greasy fingers and salty lips. The rotary phone rang. Hoping that the caller would be Christopher, I picked up the receiver.

"Darlin'?"

Although the call was not from the one I wanted to hear, I tried to keep the disappointment from my voice. "Yes, Mom."

"What do you think about us flyin' out to San Francisco?" she asked. "I've got enough money set aside that we both can go."

"I don't know, Mom."

What is that woman thinking? Here we are, broke as the Ten Commandments, at the cabin trying to think about how to make money now that you can again stand, and your Mom wants us to travel as if we have no financial worries. Sweet Jesus!

"You're not tied down with the restaurant right now." Supporting the defense of her argument, she concluded, "This would be a good time to go before you get tangled up in some new venture."

I considered her offer. I really did not have any desire to travel, but since she and Daddy had never gone to San Francisco when he was alive, the least I could do was accompany her now. I could not see how I could refuse my mother this trip.

I tentatively ventured into her snare when I asked, "How long do you want to stay?"

"A couple of weeks," she answered. "Rachael, Darlin', maybe Christopher could meet us for lunch one day while we're out there." Mom smoothly jerked the string, closing the trap's door.

"Wonder if he would do that?" I mused aloud. I could be persuaded to fly to California for a few days if I could see Christopher for a few hours.

"Why don't you call him, Darlin'?" She finished with her customary *coup de grâce,* and I had not seen it coming. As usual.

❦

Mom and I arrived at the designated location five minutes before the appointed time. My hands were cold. My heart pounded with anticipation. With Christopher the only item on my mind, I was so tense that I had hardly spoken to Mom all morning. After giving our names to the hostess, I followed Mom into the bar on the right where we sat on a plush bench to wait for my beloved's arrival.

Our being together was wrong for so many reasons, but as I marked time to see him just once more, I could not imagine what those reasons could be. All I knew was that the days we had spent together were too precious and too few. While those confoundedly long minutes ticked off, I concluded that if I applied the moral codes which Mom had dutifully taught, I followed some badly flawed logic because being with that man felt so right on so many levels. So, sitting quietly beside my mother in a restaurant near Union Square, I cast aside those old rules that confined my heart and breathed Christopher in freely, amazed by the ease the old established regime had toppled.

I might never tell him about the visions I had seen of our past lives because he might not believe in such possibilities. I decided that was all right because Christopher did not have to be aware of our pasts. On the other hand, I was curious as to how this time around would affect us, and I waited patiently to watch it play itself out to its natural conclusion.

The subtly lit bar in which we waited was decorated with shiny chrome and shades of charcoal. Its austere atmosphere reeked of power meetings and influential people and big money. However, we were pastorally dressed in two-piece, fall-weight, knit dresses and walking shoes with white cotton socks. Had the room been crowded with its usual denizens, Mom and I would have stuck out like sore thumbs. With the place empty, except for the bartender smartly dressed in black, we were only mildly inappropriate as schoolgirls dressed in red plaid dresses and black patent leather Mary Janes requesting vanilla malts in a biker bar.

During the flight to the West Coast, Mom and I had gone over how her presence at lunch would work well for Christopher because we were meeting on his turf. Mom, being the designated *duenna*, defused the situation should we be seen by anyone he knew. I just could not imagine how any person could think he was doing anything illegal or immoral while my sweet, petite, gray-haired mother was present. Although I found that a comforting thought, I was still amazed that we were meeting in his hometown.

As much as I wanted to be with him, I did not want my presence to upset his apple cart, but having The Velvet Hammer along would keep up appearances for propriety's sake. We Southern women are big on propriety. Hats, gloves and stockings, for example, must be worn to teas. And widows must wait one year before marrying, although they could date as soon as the body was in the grave. I knew a woman who drove around Miami one entire vacation with the windows on her car rolled up because she refused to let anyone know she could not afford a vehicle equipped with air conditioning. Maybe we Southern women were just big on keeping up pretenses.

Christopher strolled through the doors dressed in a three-piece charcoal gray suit. His clothing was appropriate for the starkness of the bar and, from my perspective, he certainly looked like he was from around here. As he came to where we sat, his presence seemed to fill the room.

For propriety's sake I rose and extended my hand to shake his as I felt this was not an environment where people hugged in greeting.

I observed the manner in which Mom and Christopher addressed each other. While I felt as awkward as a three-legged stool with one leg cut short, she chatted graciously. It had been years since they last saw one another, yet both talked as easily as if it had been yesterday.

"Come this way, ladies," he invited when their chitchatting stalled, "the restaurant is downstairs."

We left the bar, walking down two wide steps to a transitional area containing squat, padded chairs upholstered in somber colors and low, round tables. After we crossed that section, the dining room appeared. Its colors were bright, and light streamed through the floor-to-ceiling, two-story glass wall that faced us. The room felt happy and cheerful. Except for our white walking shoes and socks, Mom and I blended well with this space's warm palette of colors.

We moved down the airy, metallic and wooden staircase to the restaurant's floor where we were immediately met and shown to a booth. To keep up the pretense, Christopher settled on the bench across from Mom and me. Watching as his face relaxed when he slid to center himself, I decided he must not have seen anyone he knew as we walked down the stairs.

Since I was unable to dampen my smile whenever I looked in his direction, I stopped trying. I felt my heart keeping time to happy rhythms, my blood bouncing through my veins. We would be together at lunch for a few hours. That would be enough for me for now. Maybe.

Mom and I read through the chef's inspired offerings for today's lunch while Christopher selected a wine for us to share. There were three listings for appetizers, three for entrées and three for desserts. Since every choice sounded too good, we ordered all nine.

When our waiter re-appeared with the appetizers, he asked, "Who gets the pumpkin soup?"

Christopher replied, "It doesn't matter. Just put them down anywhere. We're sharing."

From there, our meal proceeded leisurely with animated conversation. Without saying anything to one another, Christopher and I stealthily removed our shoes and touched toes under the table. During lunch, Mom drank two glasses of wine, which was one more than her usual limit, and he and I shared a second bottle of wine. Enjoying a progressive dinner of sorts, each of us ate one-third of the selection placed in front of us before passing the entire plate to our left.

Before dessert was presented, Christopher excused himself to leave the table. As he walked away, I noticed he had replaced his shoes. Before I could say anything to Mom, I felt a soft tap on my shoulder. When I turned, the woman behind me in the next booth asked, "Where's home for you?"

I answered, "Tennessee."

She smiled. "I thought so. Looks like you three are having a good time."

Mom turned and chimed in, "Yes, we are."

"Everyone in this room would like to be sitting with you," the woman added.

Oh, Sweet Mother, we're drawing attention to ourselves. Not what I wanted to do. How would Christopher react if he heard? Politely, I asked the woman, "Oh, dear, are we bein' too loud?"

"No," she quickly assured me, "there's a happy glow coming from your table."

Turning to look into each other's eyes, Mom and I shared conspiratorial smiles.

Soon after Christopher returned to our booth, Mom asked directions to the ladies' room and left us alone. I waited until she was out of my sight before speaking.

"Hey, Honey," I greeted him softly, hoping to exclude the woman sitting in the next booth from our conversation.

"Hello," he answered as both his stockinged feet searched out mine. "Do you think your mother would mind if you left her alone for a while this afternoon?"

Hot damn! As my heart speeded up, I answered calmly, "No, I don't think so."

Mom returned to the table. "Gracious," she announced after she melted back into the booth, "I shouldn't have had that second glass of wine."

"Are you all right?" Christopher and I asked simultaneously.

She rolled her eyes to the heavens for assistance. "I'm goin' to have to take to my bed," she paused before continuing, "but after dessert." Mom looked back to her cleared place setting and then across the table to Christopher. "This has been a wonderful lunch. Thank you for includin' me."

My mother was a piece of work. As if the entire trip leading to this lunch had not been her idea, she nodded graciously.

She was one sly vixen. I could not help but smile.

"We'll walk you back to the hotel whenever you're ready," Christopher offered.

"How's about some coffee?" I suggested.

Our waiter appeared with three desserts. He caught the tail end of my question. "Coffee? Who wants coffee?"

"Mom does." I realized then that I had never before seen my mother intoxicated.

The desserts were to die for. After sampling all three, I turned to the same lady still sitting behind me. "Save room so you can order the chocolate," I suggested.

After Christopher had taken care of our tab, we walked the few blocks to our hotel. While on the way there, I offered to accompany Mom up to our room. She graciously refused my assistance. Christopher insisted that I go with her and assured us that he would wait until I got her settled. Mom, always the Velvet Hammer, overruled us. After saying her good-byes at the front door, she crossed the lobby with an ageless dignity. Christopher and I stood a few feet apart as we waited patiently outside the hotel until the elevator door closed and Mom was out of sight.

As soon as the two sides glided together, he said, "Let's go."

He strode out ahead on his long legs in the direction of Market Street with me trotting behind in a struggle to keep within ten feet of his coattails. During lunch, Christopher had not divulged his plans for the remainder of the afternoon, leaving me no idea where we were headed. I watched him duck down the BART entrance. As I followed quickly to where he stood near the tracks, I noticed that he seemed to be looking for any one he might recognize. When he took my hand to wait for the approaching train, I decided the area must feel secure to him.

After boarding, he led me back to the rear of the car before indicating a bench for us to share. Sitting ever so close during the subway ride, I snugged into his side while his right arm over my shoulder held me tight. We did not attempt to speak over the noise of the train, but occasionally I felt soft kisses grace my temple. I rested my left hand on the inside of his right thigh. Feeling protected and at home while sitting nestled against my heart's desire, I had little need for conversation.

Some time later, he whispered into my ear, "The next stop is ours." His lips tantalizingly brushed my ear.

Holding hands, we hurried off the train and ran up the steps leading into the bright sunshine.

"I couldn't hold your hand back at Union Square," Christopher explained, "because my company has clients near the financial district."

As he walked briskly to wherever it was he wanted to go, I stumbled slightly, trying to match his stride. Unlike in Washington, I did not fall.

"Then that restaurant wasn't a good place to meet," I commented, wondering why he had selected such a dangerous location for lunch.

"No," he answered, "it really wasn't, but I knew you would like it so I took a chance that we could meet and not be seen." He stopped to point to a high hill. "From up there, you can see the whole city."

"I know," I replied, happy to be given a chance to catch my breath. "We were up there yesterday with a tour."

"Good." He looked around us while we waited for the light to change. "Now, where is that place?"

I looked, too, as if I knew the precise location for which he searched. "What place, Honey?"

But Christopher was a man on a mission and did not answer me. We crossed the wide avenue and walked a few minutes more before he proudly announced, "Here it is."

After he pulled open a side door in an unadorned concrete-block building, we looked down a gaping, narrow stairway. My nose was immediately assaulted by high humidity and a stout odor of chlorine that rushed to the outside. Those sensations reminded me of the indoor swimming pool in the basement of the Knoxville YWCA where I learned to swim as a child.

I would follow this man anywhere, I thought, but where am I? Surely, we can't be going for a swim.

Christopher bounced quickly down the steps to disappear around a corner. While crossing the lobby of the establishment, I saw him at the counter, conversing with an Oriental man. Hesitating, I hung back and failed to hear what was being said. After the attendant handed over a key and a stack of towels, Christopher motioned that I was to follow him down the hallway.

Stopping at a wide-planked door, he unlocked it. When I peered beyond the open door, I discovered a room lined in redwood with an enormous hot tub squatting in the far corner.

Walking into the spacious area, I muttered my first thought, "Oh, great, I'll get a vaginal infection for certain!"

I slowly spun around to check out our surroundings. The air was dense with moisture. A showerhead hung from the wall near the right of the door. The concrete floor had a round drain cover positioned under the shower. Empty brass hooks were on the wall to the left of the closed door. Tucked into an alcove near the hooks was a long wide bench. The ceiling was covered in the same wood as the walls and the bench.

"The bathrooms are outside to your right. Are you interested?" Christopher asked.

After I shook my head in the negative, he locked the door before crossing the room to turn on the hot tub. The noise from its motorized water jets and swirling, bubbling water immediately filled the room.

Over the muffling sounds, he went on to explain where we were. "These places have sprung up recently because of all the Japanese businessmen who come to the Bay Area. They're accustomed to having them available. You rent them by the hour." Christopher placed the towels on the bench.

"OK," I commented deliberately as I made a second, slower turn, checking out the stark room more thoroughly. I laughed nervously. "Rented by the hour, you don't say." OK, now I really feel like a whore.

He walked up to me and cupped my face between his hands, searching my eyes before gently offering me an out. "Rachael, we don't have to stay. We can leave if you're not comfortable."

I centered my gaze on his concerned expression. Sweet Mother, I thought, this place is awful but, if I focus on his face, I won't see the room.

"I'll be fine," I assured him as much as I assured myself. "I love you and want to be with you." I turned my head in order to kiss the palm of his right hand before adding, "The where doesn't matter. We have an hour?"

"Yes."

"That'll work." I began to pull my knit dress over my head.

Undressing in silence, we hung our garments on the provided hooks. Christopher took my hand, leading me to the bench that he quickly covered with towels. Reclining there, we touched and kissed and shared bodies, but it was not the same for me because the man was quiet when he climaxed. As that was the first time he had ever failed to call out my name, I found the omission unsettling.

For that matter, she snipped, *he could have been screwing her.*

Feeling moistness ooze out of me, I asked, "How come anything so much fun is so messy?" My first question did not deserve an answer and did not get one. My second question required one immediately. "Why didn't you say my name?"

"I was trying to be quiet." He handed me a towel.

I snipped, "Oh?" I waited before allowing the next sentence to rush out. "As if that man didn't know what we were goin' to do when you closed the door." My voice was calmer when I added, "I never thought you could be quiet while lovin' me. I missed havin' you call out my name."

"I'll do better next time," he assured me.

Accepting that he would do just that, I spooned my body against his. With my lover's arm resting over my side and his hand cupping my breast, we talked over subjects we had purposely avoided in the restaurant.

"Did I tell you that Carl left Idaho and is now working in Oakland?"

"I didn't know he'd left California. How is the ol' boy? Has he married?"

He replied, "I thought I told you. He's fine and no, he hasn't."

"How's the family?" I asked.

"Victoria, as always, is perfect. Vinnie has had his moments, but has scraped together enough classes to be considered a sophomore." He paused.

I dreaded that his next sentence would be about his wife.

"We have a cat now. A stray adopted us this spring." Quickly he changed the subject. "Your mother looks wonderful. How old is she now?"

I counted up. "About seventy-five. She is beautiful, isn't she?"

He removed his hand from my breast to stroke my face. "You'll look that way when you're her age. Hope I'll be there to see it. What will you do now that the restaurant has burned?"

"I have no earthly idea." I answered his query honestly.

"How's your back?"

I sighed deeply. "Much better, but it still aches when I walk or stand too long." I was not sure how much time we had left on our hour. "What about the hot tub? We don't want any part of this room to go to waste."

We eased into the bubbling water and sat next to each other. Christopher raised his arm to allow his fingers to twist the short hairs at the nape of my neck into curls. That had been one of his favorite pastimes when we were in England.

I allowed my muscles to go limp in the massaging, frothy, hot water. "Honey, have I ever told you how to cook a frog?"

"Is this a trick question?"

"No," I answered, "it was a scientific experiment."

He closed his eyes and was quiet for some time. "Something about the temperature of the water the frog is put into?"

"You got it." I was becoming too, too relaxed. "Good food. Good wine. Good company. Good sex. Honey, if we stay in here too much longer, I'm goin' to melt into a puddle of unrelated cells."

Christopher's eyes remained closed while he murmured sarcastically, "Poor baby."

Pushing against the currents pummeling my body, I moved to straddle Christopher. Sitting facing him, I kissed both his lowered eyelids before nibbling at the smiling corners of his mouth. We kissed deeply. I closed my eyes to better concentrate on kissing him. Our tongues touched and teased, expressing all our wanting for the other.

Even as my mouth responded to his, my ever-active mind raced ahead. When would I grow tired of this man? Would my heart ever cry 'Enough!' and I would leave? Is that how we would end? With me walking away?

He pulled my body closer. A thrill rocketed up my spinal column and burst against the base of my skull like a single firework exploding during a hot July night.

Sweet Mother, I'll never be over him or my wanting him close. Between nibbles on his lips, I said, "I love you."

"I know that," Christopher commented rather smugly.

I punctuated my next words with light kisses scattered about his face. "That's not the three little words I wanted to hear." I pulled my head back, staring at closed lids until he opened his eyes. Looking deep into them, I murmured, "Let's try that again." I kissed his mouth deeply before repeating, "I love you."

I felt his penis grow hard between my legs. He pulled my face close to his and showered me with kisses before he stopped his tender assault. He said passionately, "I've missed you, Rachael Taite."

I was taken aback by the wealth of emotion in his voice. Again, I pulled my head away from his in order to focus on his face.

"I've missed you, too, Darlin'," I replied, searching for what truth was associated with his tone. I saw it, almost hidden but not quite, peeking out from behind the fire burning within his sparkling, blue eyes.

"I love you," I repeated, coaxing the words from him, willing him to voice his feelings toward me. Not asking as a needy beggar, I merely uttered the words as a teaching example.

With his hands, Christopher brought my face closer to his. His forceful kisses overwhelmed me with his desire. Again I pulled my face away from his. He leaned forward. I felt teeth clamp onto the flesh of the left side on my neck. I held still, knowing should he bite harder, vital blood vessels would be severed. Yet, at the same time I instinctively realized the seemingly aggressive action was a ritualistic display of dominance and possession. The choice for the next move in this ages-old, non-verbal communication was mine. Relaxing my neck muscles, I willingly remained under his control, responding in a primitive display of submission, allowing him free access to my defenseless throat, aware somehow that those who had celebrated the Ancient Ways would have approved.

During the following long pause, we gasped for breath. Next, Christopher's mouth blazed a passionate trek across my extended neck. I felt the words 'I love you' vibrate against my skin rather than heard them.

Moments later, he said huskily, "Let's get out of this damn tub."

We rose, leaving the water. We touched and kissed, dripping our way again to the bench. He was as hot and hard inside me as if this was the first time, not the second time in less than thirty minutes, that we had made love.

"Rachael Taite!" Forcefully, he whispered his words in my ear as he came.

"Christopher Saracini, I love you," I whispered as soon as I had caught my breath.

No matter what, I adored this man. That we had not made love that last morning in England was a moot point in my feelings for him because he had taken risks to make it possible for us to be together today.

Frou-frou is better than no frou at all, I thought.

Leaving the basement spa before our hour was up, we had roses in our cheeks, twinkles in our eyes and springs in our steps. The moisture in the air, combined with the heat from my body, made all the hair not caught up in my tightly twisted bun into kiss curls that haloed my face. We did not discuss that he would be leaving soon to return to his other life, but that fact followed us like a shadow on a sunny day.

Walking back toward the main street, he suggested, "We'll catch a bus back. It will take longer."

I nodded in agreement as a bus rounded the corner where we waited.

"Damn," Christopher reached into his trousers' pocket for bus fare, "this one's ours."

On the ride back to Union Square, I watched passengers stepping on and off the bus on their commute from work to home. Gloating, I wanted to shout triumphantly at them that 'I've just fucked my brains out this afternoon, and y'all haven't!' but I restrained myself. My kiss curls were statement enough.

We left the bus a block from my hotel. Because of the change back from Daylight Savings Time the previous weekend, the hour seemed much later than my watch indicated. Twilight was tiptoeing in, and the coming night seemed strangely too near. Now that regular business hours were over for the day, deserted Market Street was quiet.

Too soon our day would end. I stood a short distance from Christopher, tears in my eyes, needing to look at him for as long as possible, afraid to reach for his hand for fear we would be seen by someone who should not see. While I steeled myself for his final good-bye, he glanced at the watch on his wrist.

"Rachael, I've time before I must leave. Let me show you something I think you'll find interesting."

We walked quickly side-by-side a few blocks before turning down a side street and into the impressive, secondary entrance to a massive hotel complex. Walking through graceful, Victorian-age arches, we came upon a long, oval dining area where many tiers of rooms overlooked the waiting tables.

"This was here before the big earthquake," Christopher explained. "Carriages would drive under the arches behind us and pull up right to the check-in desk inside the hotel. This," his arms grandly pointed to the dining room, "was the old lobby. I've read that back then guests whose rooms opened onto the lobby would complain about the smells coming from the manure."

Omitting the odorous piles of horse apples and annoying flies, I imagined how the area must have looked when filled with fancy carriages and beautiful horses. "How excitin' this place must have been," I exclaimed. Since we were alone inside this wing of the hotel, I reached for his hand.

He pulled me closer before continuing, "When the hotel was rebuilt after the quake, they moved the front desk to its present location and had the carriages stop outside on the street to unload passengers."

"I'm glad you showed me this." Leaning against his comforting body, I kept a tight hold to his hand. "It's really beautiful in here."

"I thought you'd like seeing it."

Once more, I braced to hear it was time for him to leave me. Instead, Christopher said, "There's another place I want you to see."

We turned to leave the stately relic. At the doors we let go of each other's hand before exiting the hotel. The natural light outside had become early evening dark. As we crossed the deserted street, he gave a brief background sketch of our next destination. "This next place is near the Hearst Building. Until recently, it was a men-only bar."

When we arrived at the site, Christopher opened the door to reveal a very masculine environment. The cavernous room was dimly lit, and its walls were richly paneled in dark wood. Hairy animals' massive, antlered heads hung high in a line around the room. The air smelled sharp from stale tobacco and sweet from spilt alcohol.

Separated by an expanse of bar stools, two solitary men sat near either end of the long bar. Under the aligned, big game heads, booths along the walls were empty. The tables crowding in the middle of the space were vacant as well.

OK, now that I've seen this bar, I thought, he will say it is time to leave me.

Instead, I heard him ask, "How about one drink before I go?"

Relief washed over me, I had been granted a reprieve. "I'd like that," I agreed before asking, "Where do you want to sit?"

"Not at a booth or a table."

Quickly grasping that he felt sitting alone at those places would appear too intimate should we be seen, I rephrased my question. "Where at the bar do you want to sit?"

"The far end."

We wove a path through the tangle of tables to the last two stools on the right. We sat together, but not too close. Because this was his hometown, we were wary that someone he knew could walk in at any time.

After ordering two wines, Christopher asked, "What do you plan to do to earn a living?"

Before I could frame a reply, the man sitting to my left leaned forward and looked in our direction. He called out, "Chris, my man!"

"Lawton," Christopher answered back.

The man inquired across my face, "How you doing, buddy?"

Looking straight ahead into the smoky glass of the mirror behind the bar, the reflection of the middle-aged woman I saw matched the glassy, frozen stare of the mounted trophy heads on the encircling walls. She had been caught in blinding headlights and was fair game.

Sweet Mother, they know each other. Only two other customers in this joint, and we sit beside the one who knows Christopher. Oh, double damn, where's Mom now that we really need her!

The men continued their friendly banter around me. I turned my head in the direction of whichever man was speaking at the time, quickly becoming a caricature of an engrossed spectator at a tennis match, following the bouncing ball. I heard sounds, not comprehending words, until I heard Christopher speak my name and the man to my left say, "Nice to meet you."

I smiled, uttering the proper response, "Nice to meet you, too."

However, my heart was not in my greeting. I had not wanted to share our last remaining minutes with another living soul, but I do not always get what I want. Settling for what I had been given, I jumped into their conversation as if there were no tomorrow and as if I had a legitimate reason for being in this bar in San Francisco, sitting next to Christopher Saracini, with my Southern accent and with kiss curls surrounding my face. After we finished our drinks, Lawton came out with us into the night.

Strolling along the sidewalk, I was glad there would be no pop quiz following that lengthy exchange because I could not remember a single topic that had been discussed. After stopping at the entry to a towering building, Lawton explained, "I'm meeting my date at her office. We're going to dinner. Care to join us?"

Christopher graciously lied for us. "Thank you. Another time, maybe."

"Another time, then." His friend sounded genuinely disappointed. "Rachael, have a good visit while you're at your conference and a safe flight home." In parting, I shook his hand.

"Chris, see you around the club." After the men shook hands, Lawton pulled open the massive door and was gone.

Having been discovered in the bar, Christopher and I were both concerned that there might be others lurking about who also knew him. Keeping a wide distance between us, we completed the remaining block beside Market before arriving at the street for my hotel. At the corner, we stood two feet apart. We could not kiss. We dared not hug.

"I refuse to shake your hand good-bye," I told him before laughing nervously in a foolish attempt to ease the pain of our coming separation.

The wind coming off the Bay and up Market was chilly. We shivered separately in its cold.

"We'll be together soon." He looked at my mouth. "I promise."

Staring at his lips, I nodded, all the while longing to taste his sweet kisses, wishing he again held me in his sheltering embrace. I could wait. Besides, he had just said that we would be together soon. Secure in the knowledge that Christopher was in my future, I would wait.

Leaves newly emerged from the soil basking in spring's warm sunlight immediately came to mind. Comparing myself to a trillium, I felt I also came to life whenever my sun appeared. Maybe at long last I had acquired the patience innate in a solitary bulb nestled against the mountainside. Smiling as that train of thought passed, I watched Christopher lift his hand to touch my face in farewell. Catching himself, he paused with hand in mid air and almost smiled. After dropping his arm to his side, he shrugged his shoulders in silent resignation.

The last second of our time together was over. The visit had ended. He said softly, "I'll stand here and watch you safely to the door."

I nodded, unable to reply. Although reluctant to leave, I turned away, feeling strangely like a deserter. As soon as I realized this was the first time since Nashville that he had watched me depart, lifting my feet to walk atop concrete required the same effort necessary to slog through thick mud while on a rainy hike in the Smokies.

Under the canopy at the entrance to my hotel, I stopped. The smiling doorman pulled the door open. One last time, I looked back to the corner to see him raise his right arm. Only after I waved farewell did Christopher move toward the subway entrance. Lowering my head to keep the doorman from seeing my tears, I quickly crossed the lobby.

The other attempted to comfort me as we rode alone in the elevator to the floor leading to our room. *Rachael,* she said, *it's just as well that we live in Tennessee and he lives in California. It would be pure hell living in the same town with Christopher and not sharing the same house. Maybe we are granted a small kindness by the distance that keeps us apart.*

Fourteen

After Mom settled onto the passenger seat of our rental car and adjusted her sun visor, I handed over a thick envelope that had my name and address sprawled in Christopher's bold handwriting across its plain manila front. It contained his proposed itinerary, based on the sights I thought she would like to see during her long-awaited California vacation. Mom smiled delightedly when she peered into the packet.

"Is this what I think it is?" she inquired, correctly assuming what the clasp envelope held.

Nodding in the affirmative, I reminded her, "Buckle up. Then hold onto your hat. We've got a lot to see and do in the next few days."

After silently assuring myself that driving through San Francisco's crowded streets could not be nearly as confusing as driving in England, I steered north toward the Golden Gate Bridge. From there I followed the yellow lines Christopher had marked on the accompanying map: from Marin County's rugged coastline and lofty redwoods, through Napa's lush vineyards to Sacramento's urban skyline, up steep mountain flanks to a welcome center near the Nevada state line where overly ripe pomegranates still hung like forgotten Halloween decorations on outside shrubbery, on to old Silver City's frontier-width streets, down to the moonscape starkness of Mono Lake, over serrated mountain ridges on a roadbed originally carved out by Chinese laborers, into Yosemite's deep pockets of wilderness, across the fertile valley to Monterey's craggy coast and its nearby monarch butterfly winter retreat, into the forested solitude of Big Sur and back again to the bustling, foggy Bay Area. During those ten days, Mom and I plotted my future against the ever-changing, incredibly beautiful scenery.

I was fifty-one years of age. Whatever I chose to do needed to keep me occupied, as well as entertained, for the next sixty-odd years. Growing up, Mom had always preached that a person should plan to live to be a hundred-and-twenty so that everything a body was supposed to do got done in one lifetime. She always ended that particular homily with Mammy's sage observation: You don't want to have to lick that calf twice.

I decided that I must be a slow learner because, if I had gone through all those past lives with Christopher but had to keep coming back, what lesson could I not get through my thick skull? Perhaps if I knew which course was giving me trouble, I could make cosmic flash cards to help with my studies. The obvious truth was I would rather spend the rest of my life with that man. Unfortunately, during this lifetime, that would neither make my house payments nor put salmon in the girls' bowls at mealtimes.

Where did I want to live these next half-dozen or so decades? After running into Lawton, I voted against California. Too much opportunity for misery there. I would just stay hidden in my Tennessee hills, working at something I liked that left me free to cut away and meet the man I loved. Simply because he said we would be together soon, I would fashion a career that allowed for such opportunities.

Maybe that was really the only reason I kept returning to this earth, solely for the chance to share space with that other being. Now, I knew if the Southern Baptist Church ever found out about that line of reasoning, my letter of baptism would certainly get hunted out and burned.

Before Mom and I boarded our plane home, we had formulated a plan. My future would hold a restaurant, but on a less grand scale. For the new establishment to be successful, I knew its groundwork depended on the kindnesses of friends and business acquaintances, and time alone would tell if they could be relied upon.

"It's comin' together nicely," I told Christopher during one of what had become his bi-monthly telephone calls. "My accountant went with me to the bank today. I got my loan approved, and it wasn't the humiliation that gettin' my house had been."

"What happened when you applied to finance your house?" he asked.

"Oh, Christopher, Honey, it was just plain awful." The entire process still irked me. "I had a good job, but because I didn't have a husband, my parents had to cosign my loan."

"You're kidding, aren't you?"

"No, I told you things are different for women down here." I did not want to waste any more time reciting the past because I was so excited about the prospects that were coming together for my future.

"Anyway, I had my accountant with me. We were prepared to use the cabin as collateral for the loan, but the banker knew me. She asked if I was goin' to have my seven-layer salad on the new menu. I said 'Of course' and she said 'Good' and I got the money on just my signature alone."

"That's wonderful." His voice sounded as delighted as mine.

"And Liz and Margaret will help out." I continued filling in the details for my new endeavor. "They said they still didn't have enough quarters paid in for coverage, and since I was thinkin' small, they wanted in."

"Great."

I laughed. "I think they just lied about the quarters."

Christopher began a related topic. "How's this going to affect your back?"

"I'll be able to rest on the floor whenever I need to," I replied. My back remained weak and occasionally became a problem whenever I stood or leaned over for any length of time. I had questions about its holding up, too, but had decided to cross that bridge when and if I had to.

"Rachael, I think you should start exercising and consider losing that weight you've put on."

My shoulders slumped. I leaned against the desk holding my phone as I prepared myself for the coming lecture. In an attempt to beat him to the punch, I said, "I know. All I've done since we met is get fatter."

"No, Rachael," he cut in before I could utter my next sentence, "my concern is for your health. To me, you are perfect no matter what you weigh. I want you to start an exercise program and lose weight to help your back."

You silver-tongued devil.

Taking a deep breath, I stood erect again. "Thank you for sayin' I'm perfect. There's a gym next to the new site. I'll check into it."

"Be sure to get a trainer to start you out on the right track," he advised. I heard his hand cover the phone. He spoke to someone in his office before he said, "Rachael, I've got to go."

"OK, Honey. Love you."

"Me, too."

My following days were unbelievably busy with every detail needed to have Rachael's To Go ready for a January opening. I never made it to the gym. However, I did begin walking by the river on Cherokee Boulevard in the afternoons five to six times a week. I was too embarrassed to tell anyone I could hardly manage a tenth of a mile each time that first week.

With the new place about three blocks from its burned predecessor, I anticipated great things for the downsized endeavor. Hugh Ed brought in his handy sons and reliable trades buddies to remodel the space my former landlord had available. I purposely kept the concept small so that three could easily handle the customers. Mom apologized that she felt her age too much to do more than provide moral support and decorating advice. Hell, I knew I was lucky to have her around, period.

The Brickyard location I chose was much too compact for any interior tables where customers could sit and lounge. Since the kitchen equipment I purchased was limited in size and variety as well, there was no possible way we could continue catering large parties off premises as we had in the past. Every selection underlined my intent to provide carry-out service only. Still, during the entire time the space was being prepared, I worried that the smaller scale would be financially unable to support me, leaving me no choice but to be open six days a week.

Despite miserable January weather, prospects of again tasting my signature salads, my like-mother-used-to-bake desserts, my hearty sandwiches, my rich soups and thick slabs of my savory quiches soon brought back our old customers in droves. We did not bother advertising, word of mouth alone kept us busy. Within four short months, I had paid off the start-up loans and, surprisingly, had attained the personal milestone of walking two miles at a stretch. Life was sweet again, and I realized I could comfortably exist with an establishment this size.

Whenever my back pained me, I quickly retreated to the kitchen to lie flat on the floor where our loyal customers could not see me. During those occasions, Margaret and Liz simply stepped over me any time they needed to get food out of the back.

It was after four, Friday afternoon. With June already this hot, I anticipated summer would be worse. As it was too muggy to weed the yard, I had invited Mom over home while I tested a new recipe.

Standing over a batch of banana-nut muffins, steaming hot right out of the oven, I complained, "I never can decide about these things. They're just never pretty lookin' enough." My critical eyes picked apart the brown, roughly textured muffins. "How could anyone want to eat anything this homely?"

"Pretty is as pretty does," Mom answered in a cryptic, motherly-wise way.

She sat in a director's chair by my kitchen table. My four-legged girls hunkered just inside the doorway leading to the dining room, safely supervising our culinary efforts without actually being under foot.

I picked up a cooling muffin from the first baking. "Taste this one." It was almost too hot to hold, but I was impatient to hear her opinion. "What do you think? Good enough to add to the menu?" I held out the hot item for her to sample.

Leaning over to bite into the muffin, Mom vigorously nodded as she chewed and inhaled air, at the same time trying to taste and cool the proposed addition to my current menu. The kitchen wall phone rang the very instant the long-ring timer loudly went off. Unnerved, I jumped, throwing the muffin straight up in the air. As if in unison, the startled cats scurried under the dining room table while Mom whooped and jumped from her chair, but managed to catch the falling muffin by instantly extending the skirt of her apron before picking up the phone.

I quickly moved to the oven, grabbing nearby hot pads off the counter top. As I took the second pan of muffins from the oven, Mom held the telephone receiver to my ear with her free hand. Although preoccupied as I was with the hot pan, I managed to say, "Hey."

"Baltimore."

"Baltimore?" I questioned, happily recognizing the voice. "Why Baltimore?" I rested the muffin tin on top of the stove, motioning for Mom to take over my duties as I took possession of the phone.

"Because," Christopher replied, "I'll be consulting there after I return from France. What do you want to see around there?"

"Baltimore?" I repeated, picking up the atlas kept on top of the kitchen hutch in anticipation of this very reason, and thumbed through the pages, searching for Maryland. Upon finding the proper page, I studied the map before suggesting, "We could go on up to Pennsylvania and explore the Amish country."

"OK," he slowly answered. I recognized he was deep in thought. Next I heard the rustling of papers and imagined him getting into the maps he kept at his desk. Seconds passed before he suggested, "And we could drive over to Gettysburg."

"Gettysburg?" Yuck, I thought, another ghastly, ghostly battlefield to suffer through. It had to be a man thing. I changed the subject. "Hey, guess what."

"What?"

"I joined a gym. Aren't you proud of me?"

"Rachael, I'm always proud of you."

⁂

Walking through the Baltimore-Washington airport and getting into a cab and riding to the hotel took an effortless and mindless twenty minutes. I needed 'mindless' after the events of the past few days. If only I could have talked with him, if only I could have shared what I had been through, if only he had not been in France for the last two weeks, but all the comfort I had received had been a brief message on my answer machine this morning that gave a Baltimore hotel's name and a room number.

Upon entering the busy lobby, a fire alarm shrieked. I was too exhausted to bother jumping when the siren suddenly sounded near my head. All inside were shooed outside, leaving me no choice but to be swept along. Surrounded by uncaring strangers, I stood alone on the sidewalk, knowing I had almost made it to Christopher and safety.

So close, yet so far away.

Sweet Mother, I don't think I can manage another major crisis right now. Just let me get inside and to his arms. Just let him hold me while I catch my breath. After that, You can throw something else at me. I'll be able to handle anything then.

After a few minutes under the hot sun, a uniformed hotel employee permitted the crowd into the hotel lobby. I overheard a clerk behind the front desk say something about a false alarm as I walked into an elevator where I rode directly to his room. Outside the door, I hesitated, thinking I really should have called ahead on the house phone as I normally did. While mentally debating over returning to the lobby to make that call, I decided I lacked the strength to do that and get back upstairs.

I knocked. There was no immediate answer.

Maybe, I thought, he'd left the building when the alarm first went off and hadn't yet returned. I knocked harder and waited. Maybe he was lying inside, like Margaret had been when I found her, dead from a ruptured aneurysm. Frantically, I pounded on the door.

The other sobbed, *Christopher, where are you? We need you.*

I was frantically beating on the door when it opened. Christopher smiled, a tiny dollop of toothpaste at the left corner of his mouth.

"You're early. I was just brushing my teeth. Come in."

Almost knocking him aside, I bolted inside. I saw a spacious room with windows making up most of the outer walls. I saw a king-sized bed and a pair of overstuffed chairs around the obligatory round table placed in the far corner. I saw only clearly enough to keep from stumbling into any furniture, yet little registered. Abruptly I stopped in the center of the sunlit room, my right hand still tightly gripping my roll-along luggage. I had made it to safety, but I had reached my limits and could move no further.

After Christopher came to stand in front of me, I noticed a concerned frown upon his face. Placing both hands gently on my shoulders, he asked, "Rachael, what's wrong?"

I shut my eyes before bringing myself to say, "Margaret's dead."

"Oh, Rachael." He gathered me against his warm body and held me. His kind voice offering condolences as he continued, "I'm so sorry about Margaret."

Opening my eyes, I stared at the interlocking threads making up the fabric of his white shirt. I started wondering what had caused our lives to be intertwined before my thoughts went blank.

My body and my mind had been drained, sucked dry after all the grief I had endured. I had been a rock for Margaret's family. Everyone had said so. Now, I was with Christopher and did not have to be strong any longer. I knew he would watch over me. I knew I would be safe with him. My body shuddered as if someone were walking on my grave.

I looked up into his eyes to see the sadness and concern for me there. No longer able to control those unshed tears that I had held in abeyance for days, I felt my chin trembling and saw his face slowly become distorted by my tears.

He carefully pried my fingers away from the pull-bar on my luggage and led me over to one of the chairs. He sat down and tenderly drew me onto his lap. "Now, my sweet Rachael, tell me all about it," he gently coaxed, removing my glasses from my face.

I sat rigidly in Christopher's lap, recalling that horrific morning and the ensuing, blurred-together days. After wiping the toothpaste from his mouth, I heard myself relating the tragic events in a detached, flat tone. "Margaret didn't show up for work the other Thursday. She didn't answer her phone when Liz dialed her number. Once we got everything baked fresh for the day, I drove to her place to check on her."

Had we been younger, I would have bet money that Margaret had been partying the night before and was too drunk to make it to work on time, or perhaps she had discovered a hot, new lover and was too exhausted to answer the phone. Liz and I had even joked about those possibilities as we scurried about the kitchen, having to do the work of three.

Leaving Liz to open the restaurant, I drove Scenic Drive toward The Village to check on our absent cohort. Since HIV hit the scene years earlier, all my single friends had become very circumspect in their recreational choices, and I grew to fear something terrible must have happened. When I parked next to her black Mustang convertible in front of The Commons, a cold dread crept over my body. It held my heart prisoner by the time I let myself inside her condo, using the key my friend had given me years ago.

Calling her name, I searched through strangely quiet rooms until I found her body in bed, where she must have died in her sleep. She looked so peaceful, so natural except for the swelling on the left side of her neck. I lay beside my dear friend on the bed, holding her almost-warm, pale hand, saying my good-byes. After calling 911, I wiped away the saliva spilling from the left corner of her mouth. Margaret always hated that she drooled sometimes when she slept, and I did not want strangers seeing her this way, with spit running down her chin. Finally, I sat with my legs crossed in the lotus position on the floor by her bed and held her lifeless hand, noticing her blue fingertips for the first time and waited, wondering why she had to die alone.

Relying upon all my inner strength, I willed myself to endure the necessary actions of the emergency medical personnel and the detective who later came in response to their call. I recalled the weight of a man's strong hand resting on my shoulder. Raising my head, I found Will Sharpe, who had arrived on the fire truck with the other First Responders, standing beside me. When asked, I told them to call McPhaille's because I remembered Margaret saying she liked how they had taken care of my Daddy. I held her stiffening, cool hand until the mortuary's attendants came to carry her away and I was not allowed to stay with her anymore.

Days later, I remembered nodding that I understood when I was given the explanation that a weakness within the Circle of Willis had ruptured, but I failed to comprehend why one of Margaret's arteries inside her head could fail when she always looked so healthy.

When the time came, I followed her body across the mountains to her parent's home outside Swansea. There, in South Carolina's humid heat, I stood brave and strong alongside Margaret's grieving family, comforting them through the receiving of friends, the graveside service and following the interment.

I relived all those scenes vividly, wanting to describe them in detail, but what came out instead was an out-of-sequence jumble of phrases and sobs. "Friends since sixty-six . . . never touched a newly dead person before . . . had to be strong, had to be brave . . . had just given her a new backpack for her birthday . . . her skin felt so . . . everyone was looking to me for what to do next . . . what will I do without her?"

I cried until there were no more tears left inside me. They were all on his shirt. My face stuck to the dampness on his collar where I had pressed my face into the comforting, warm curve of Christopher's neck.

I had started my tale of woe emotionally cold and rigidly upright and falsely brave. When I ended, I found myself emotionally wasted, my body slumped and defenseless. Suddenly I was ashamed of exposing my soft underbelly. Christopher thought I was perfect and strong, not this mass of quivering helplessness. Instinctively, I knew the weak were eaten alive and, at the very least, I must appear as if I could defend myself. As I struggled to stand in order to show I was no easy prey, I became aware I could no longer breathe through my nose.

Once more, I tried to pull away, using the excuse, "I need a tissue." Upon seeing the wet circle on his shirt, like a child I repeated the first thought that entered my mind, "I've got tears and snot all over you."

What a dumb thing to say, Rachael, she scolded.

He pulled me closer, brushing his lips to my forehead. "Don't worry, my sweet Rachael. It's just a shirt. Let me hold you a little longer."

My shoulders stiffened against his embrace as I recalled once hearing Mom telling a friend I was a hard child to rock because I wiggled about so much. Ironically, I could only remember a childhood in which I was never rocked enough. I remembered trying to get comfortable against her chest, but having to move about because my arms would go to sleep whenever Mom held me. I waited for the arm now caught between my body and Christopher's to get that familiar, uneasy needles-and-pins tingling. When those niggling sensations failed to appear, I relaxed into him, basking in the luxury of being firmly held as I had always hungered to be held.

When was the last time a man held me on his lap, not wanting a sexual favor from me? When was the last time I was held by a man without having prepaid for that embrace with my body? I could not even remember my parents cuddling me when I was hurting as a child. Maybe they did, and I had forgotten.

I could remember Daddy's angry yelling at night when he was stationed at Warner-Robbins, and I could remember Mom coming into my bedroom, ordering me to be a big girl and begging me to stay in my room and pleading with me to be quiet, with the unspoken terror that underscored her words alerting me to the uncontrolled, dangerous emotions erupting in the next room. And I could remember standing on my narrow bed in my shadow-filled room, being scared and crying as quietly as I could into my pillow, trying not to bring attention to my existence.

I could remember running to Mom some months later after I had fallen hard on my elbow and being slapped across the face to stop my screams of pain. I could remember that, after determining nothing was broken, Mom fashioned a colorful scarf into a sling for my arm, saying that would make it all better.

I could remember the bleak night when Doug and I had gone on a date after Daddy was hospitalized that last time. Mistakenly thinking I had found a shoulder to cry on, I had gotten drunk and was date raped.

After that last remembrance, I found myself dispassionately examining an age-old tenet that I had always found puzzling. Why did people euphemistically accuse a girl of losing her virginity as if she had casually misplaced it while, simultaneously, slyly congratulating the male for taking it? Being a woman, I knew a girl could lose an earring through carelessness, but she would never mislay her virginity. Maybe some day I would search out Doug to take back what was rightfully mine.

I had never before allowed those raggedy memories the light of day. Since I did not chase them away now as I always had in the past, those thoughts easily floated about my mind. While I gingerly watched those tragic vignettes unfold from the safety of Christopher's embrace, I saw them for what they were, harmless pictures from long ago that no longer wielded power to cower me. Afterwards, I watched them slowly drift to settle in their rightful place, where they belonged, with other memories from my childhood.

While I sat securely enthroned on Christopher's lap, an empowering idea gradually evolved. I decided that good and bad were concepts based on subjective judgment and that I had been trained to assign my experiences into one of those two opposing factions. If I accepted that events simply were events, I reasoned I could place all past happenings into a single category with no positive or negative sub-listings.

The idea dawned on me that although I was not an omnipotent being, I had arbitrarily defined 'goodness' and 'evil.' So, who died and made me God? Upon reaching the conclusion that I no longer wanted that job, I then realized that while I had little power over what had happened to me as a child, I held power as to how I, as an adult, viewed those events. I had held it all along, but had not known it.

The implications quickly followed that evil cannot exist without its complementary pairing with goodness and what was deemed to be right and what was chosen to be wrong had been modified over the centuries and had always been subject to interpretation. Intuitively, it came to me that those moral concepts were society's version of nature's lichen and were unable to exist without the other. After internalizing that final comparison, all manner of chains snapped and fell away. And I was immediately set free.

Drawing upon Christopher's strength while he cradled my body, I put aside the fundamentalist need to personally judge morality. I reached the conclusion that the Wicca manual, resting on that well-used card table in my cabin, was correct in its single, simple commandment that one should live in such a manner as to do no harm.

Sweet Mother! Of course, I thought, a world governed by just one law that was not at the mercy of personal bias but elemental in its purity and simplicity. What perfectly good sense!

What came next was a deeply felt peace and belonging. Within the stillness that followed, I noticed that every cell in my body resonated with the knowledge of how much this man cared for me. I realized, too, our strong mutual attraction had nothing to do with sexuality. Sex was just the icing on our cake.

So this is how secure feels, a child's voice inside me whispered in awe.

Upon hearing that thought, I felt pieces parts inside me joining together. I recognized most, but some were merely shadows. Finally, I heard an extraordinary sound. Inside my head, all was quiet. There were no more chattering voices. There was nothing but silence. Beautiful, glorious silence.

Yes, this is how secure feels, I thought. And felt astonishment because I heard only the one voice. She spoke my thoughts, and she was I.

I drew a very deep breath, held it for as long as I was comfortably able before slowly releasing the spent air. After that, my breathing returned to normal. I felt confident in my abilities. I felt whole in spirit. I felt fully prepared to take my rightful place in whatever era I found myself.

After climbing out of the protecting shelter of my healer's arms, I retrieved tissues from the bath. Returning to Christopher and for the first time since entering the room, I noticed the bouquet of red roses and the welcoming bottle of wine chilling on the dresser. My eyes stung as if they could cry again but there was no moisture available, even for happy tears.

With amazement clearly evident in my tone, I exclaimed, "Roses. You got me roses." My voice was thick and raspy from my recent crying. "You never forget."

As he came toward the dresser, he asked, "Ready for a drink now? I have a sparkling white. I know you don't care for red." His voice sounded as drained as I felt energized.

I answered quickly, "Yeah, I think I'm ready." Speaking slowly with absolute conviction, I immediately repeated, "Yes, I am ready. Thank you."

I watched him pop the cork and pour wine into two plastic cups. After taking the offered drink and going to the windows to gaze out on rooftops, I heard his footsteps heading toward the bath and its door closing.

Alone at the window, I considered the amazing chain of events that had occurred since I entered this room. Emotionally, I had been in splinters, yet he had created a space that gave me the opportunity to heal. Maybe I had been splintered for a long time, even before Margaret's death, but now I sported only smooth edges. As a result of the melding, I knew I was greater and stronger than the sum of my parts. I did not care that years earlier Christopher had disagreed with me, for this afternoon, I had come to know the man for the magician he truly was.

The images of the city I viewed through the glass were strangely more distinct, their colors brighter, than when I had entered. I could almost see around the margins of every object, like scenes in the slides for Martha Carol's old stereoscope Mom had inherited. The surroundings appeared clearer, yet I was no longer a mere observer because I now truly belonged in this world about me.

I realized that a most eerie transformation had transpired, one that I would be hard pressed to explain. Deep inside, I felt newly born. If Athena had arrived on earth via Zeus's head, this afternoon I had sprung full-grown from Christopher's heart. Unlike those fleeting feelings I had experienced the night we first met on LeConte, I owned this new awareness. I sensed that whatever happened here, and I was not really sure what had happened, was greater than the healing of the wound caused by Margaret's sudden death. I knew I would be eternally grateful for this most special gift, this rarest of all, he presented alongside the roses and wine.

I heard Christopher crossing the carpet behind me. "Where's the harbor?" I questioned as I looked for any trace of water through the window. "I thought you said your hotel was on the water."

"It's several blocks away," he answered. His voice sounded refreshed.

"Then why did they name the place 'on-the-water' if it's blocks away from the water? That's not logical. Whatever happened to truth in advertisin'?"

"You've got me."

Purposely misunderstanding the context of his last remark, I said, "Yes, I've got you. Now, what am I goin' to do with you?"

He stopped behind my back. "Hold this," he requested, handing me his wine.

Not being given a chance to refuse, I took his glass in my free hand. Still behind me, Christopher gently nibbled at the nape of my neck. Relaxing my body against his, I suggested, "You can do that all day."

When I attempted to turn to face him, his firm hand on my shoulder prevented me.

"No, Rachael," he whispered in my left ear, "this one's for you."

I smiled. "That's what I usually tell you, isn't it?"

He whispered his next tease in my right ear. "You can't use your hands, but I can use mine."

His was a good directive while it lasted, but I soon disobeyed. Not being one for following directions, my guiding principle throughout life had always been: When all else fails, read the directions. Happily, Christopher had never complained.

⁂

Touring Baltimore by way of a water taxi was proving to be faster and much better for my mending spinal column than pounding the town's hard sidewalks. While the launch motored around the harbor, I studied Christopher while he sat, engrossed in an ever-present map.

His hair was almost silver, and it curled about his ears and his collar. Noticing that its length was much longer than usual, I decided it must be because of the time spent out of the country and away from his customary barber. If a laurel wreath were placed on his head this very minute, his profile would become the perfect model for a Roman coin. His body had grown sinewy with the passing years. He wore faded khaki pants and a pastel pink knit shirt and dark brown Sebago's. I could not recall one instance when the man had worn blue jeans, and the only times I had seen him in T-shirts were when we hiked.

While he studied the map, his shoulders slumped as his eyes squinted periodically, intently focusing on the paper in front of him. The man was not movie star handsome, but the years of living rested easily on him. He had ordinary features and the kindest blue eyes. The lines on his face were deeper than when we first met. His hair was thinner and his hairline higher. There was nothing about the man that would strike me as remarkable and make me look twice if I did not already love him, but he could eat crackers in my bed anytime, and I would never kick him out.

Enjoying the wind combing my hair back from my face, I allowed my attention to follow the urban skyline around the harbor before next mentally exploring my newly obtained sense of security. I felt at fifty-one years of age it was about damn time I had it. It was not that my parents did not love me when I was a child. They simply had loved each other more. I had never felt a part of the whole because they had never needed me to be complete. Maybe acquiring security was like any teachable moment. All the elements must be present, including the willing teacher and the receptive pupil, or else the idea was fumbled and dropped during the handoff between teacher and pupil.

Rachael, I scolded myself, you're mixing metaphors.

Thanks for sharing, I silently responded.

Christopher spent his time in California while I continued residing in Tennessee. Ours could be considered a functioning dysfunctional relationship. All we had were occasional days together. Must be something, too, about quality and not quantity of time. While slumped in his arms this afternoon, every cell in my body had become permanently imprinted with how that elusive feeling of security felt. If being with this man taught me nothing else, then these last nine years had been worth all the tears. Somewhere along the line, he had become my emotional hidey-hole, but I still was unable to pinpoint exactly what it was about being with him that made it so. I simply knew that when I was with him, I was at home and I was at peace and I was safe and I was whole and I was where I was supposed to be.

Suddenly a wave of tenderness and thankfulness swept through me. I patted his closer knee. When he glanced up, I said, "Thank you."

Interrupted from his map study, Christopher looked at me. Puzzled, he asked, "For what?"

"For simply bein' you."

As if he understood my oblique reference, he smiled before sharing his ideas for dinner. For appetizers, we would have steamed mussels in a well known bar located in historic Fell's Point. Afterwards, we would catch a water taxi back to Baltimore proper to dine on whole crabs.

※

Early the following morning, we waited with other departing hotel guests for transportation to the airport and access to our rental car. We stood in the general vicinity of each other, but not close enough that a casual observer could assume we were traveling together.

A van pulled up, and its driver called out, "All for Baltimore-Washington!"

We gathered up our luggage, as did a thin woman who had been standing in front of us. From the rear, I judged her to be a business traveler in her late forties or early fifties before dismissing her from my mind. Christopher, ever the gentleman, helped me and the other passenger with our suitcases. Entering the van after the woman, I took a bench seat on the opposite side of the aisle, just to the front of her. I watched as he walked toward me, then past me, to take the seat behind hers.

I overheard him ask, "Aren't you with Smith, Tatum and Taylor?"

I heard her answer, "Yes. Aren't you Chris Samson?"

"Saracini," he politely corrected.

Well, I'll be damned. Can't we go anywhere without running into someone he knows? You'd think this was a bigger country than that. Perhaps, in the future, we should just stick to meeting in foreign lands.

I stared out the window, shaking my head in disbelief as I listened to them chat about computers the entire trip back to the airport.

In our rental car, we crisscrossed the narrow lanes through the Amish countryside. Land there was carefully tilled, stock well tended, houses properly prim and barns enormous, but the countryside was not the Cotswolds with its postcard perfect vistas at every turn. I was vaguely disappointed.

For our first evening in Pennsylvania, we opted for a stone farmhouse that had recently become a bed-and-breakfast. The house dated back to the early 1700s, and each of its many rooms was decorated with the family's carefully collected, museum-quality antiques. Since the house was not air-conditioned, we opened the windows in our bedroom on the second floor to allow cool breezes to sieve through screens before we left to continue our exploring.

We found choices for our evening's entertainment to be limited. That afternoon we had driven all the available paved roads within thirty miles, we had eaten in a barn of a restaurant designed for busloads of tourists at mealtimes, and we had seen the local vineyard. When we drove past a cow auction, we seized the opportunity to watch the proceedings.

Overcome by the fear in their soft eyes, I cringed with each new animal herded in. These cows had been tenderly cared for by their Amish masters, raised with gentle hands and voices. Under the bright lights and the loud auctioneer's magnified, harsh, singsong chant, they did not know what was required of them or what was to become of them. I sat rigidly while one lot of milk cows was sold, wishing I knew how to comfort them.

I needed to leave this sad, frightening place. After the gavel dropped for the last cow and she was prodded out of the pen, I whispered, "Honey, I'm afraid to scratch my nose for fear I'll end up with a cow to take back to Knoxville."

"Ready?" he asked.

"Yes." Oh, Sweet Mother, yes! Let me out of here before I buy all these cows and take them safely home with me.

❦

Back in the quiet darkness of our room, I listened to horse-drawn buggies as the Amish clip-clopped back and forth on the highway in front of our inn. The sweat from our recent lovemaking cooled on my shoulders.

"I love you, Christopher Saracini," I whispered.

"I know, Rachael Taite," he whispered back.

After my healing yesterday, I no longer needed to hear him say in return that he loved me. For me, it was now enough that we were together. "This has been a good day."

"Yes," he sighed sleepily.

I relaxed back into the strangeness of the mattress under my body and listened to the country noises outside our windows. Crickets and tree frogs chorused loudly, but this Amish setting was nearly too rural. My ears missed the distant, soft purr from the interstate and the muffled clackity-clack of the long freight trains near my house. The night creatures at the cabin were not this loud, or perhaps I was too tired when I got to the cabin to lie awake and hear them, or perhaps the cabin's air conditioner droned them out. I considered that nature's night sounds must have been much like this before civilization had encroached, eons ago, back when Christopher and I first roamed the earth.

I heard him take one deep, soft breath. Thinking he wanted to talk, I asked, "What is it, Love?"

When he did not answer, I listened more closely to his breathing. I had been mistaken. He was asleep. After I nestled closer into the curve of his body, his arm blindly reached backward until his hand rested on the rise of my hip. Without moving, I wallowed in my newly acquired secureness, like a robin taking a dust bath, still amazed how this deliciously new sensation had permanently changed everything for me.

Come morning, I made a mental note, I must search the floor to find whatever object it was that had fallen off the bed's frame while we were making love. In keeping with the concept of doing no harm, I hoped we had not done permanent damage to the antique rope bed.

On the drive out of town the next morning, Christopher grandly announced, "I've always wanted to say I had intercourse in Intercourse!"

"So that's why we stayed there last night." I leaned over to pat his head. "It takes so little to make you happy. Speakin' of intercourse, did I tell you that Hugh Ed'll soon be a grandfather? Travis married that girl he went to England with. It seems odd that someone younger than me is goin' to be a grandparent. Sometimes I think I'm caught in a time warp. Everyone about me gets older, but I stay in my twenties."

"You certainly don't look much older than twenty," he said.

Laughingly, I answered his compliment. "Spoken like a man in love. By the way, have I ever told you about this paintin' of me that I have hidden back home?"

On our way west across Pennsylvania, we stopped to try our hand at forming dough knots in the first pretzel bakery in North America. After a few short hours in that muggy establishment, I was happy that my compact kitchen at work was air-conditioned. I could not help wondering how my ancestors near the Black Forest had dealt with the heat from their ovens those centuries ago.

When we arrived in Gettysburg, we located a bed-and-breakfast near the battlefield. The original structure of the recently remodeled inn had been a farmhouse that had done duty as a field hospital during the conflict. Dreading the next day, all evening long I steeled myself against the onslaught of emotions I knew I would have to tolerate.

We set out early the next morning to experience the area's place in American history. The enormity of the slaughter hit home as I watched the lights flash on and off on the mock-up of the battlefield inside the visitors' center. Later, I drove our car while Christopher read over the guidebook and we listened to the auto cassette. At some of the sites, we parked the car in order to walk the contested grounds. We learned that over seventy thousand horses and mules were destroyed in that battle.

Early in the afternoon, as we stood on a rocky rise overlooking a peaceful meadow where countless lives had been lost, I could only shake my head at the waste. "Wars should be fought only by old men. It wasn't bad enough they killed all those young men on both sides. Hell, those horses and mules didn't have a dog in the fight, and they died, too."

After that outlandish statement, Christopher turned to me in amazement.

Undaunted, I marched steadily onward. "The War Between the

States should have never happened. Our Foundin' Fathers should have dealt with the slavery issue back when the Constitution was first conceived. If this country was founded on freedom, why were blacks kept as slaves and white women not allowed the right to vote? Both were considered property. That's hardly 'liberty and justice for all.' Originally, the Proclamation of Emancipation only applied to the slaves held in the states that seceded. Was it proper then to keep slaves in the North? And those people in the North were too busy pointin' their fingers southward to see the inhumane workin' conditions in their own damn factories. The Yankee pot callin' the Rebel kettle black!" Before continuing, I paused to catch my breath.

"Honey, did you know that the IRS audits southern returns more than they audit returns from any other region? Hell, reconstruction is alive and well today!" If I got any more worked up, I fully expected steam to pour out both of my ears.

"No," he answered.

"It was in the newspaper recently." That aside finished, I returned to my take on last century's bloody conflict. "Husbands, fathers, brothers, uncles, nephews were lost on both sides. The land in the South was raped. The cost was too dear, I'm a-thinkin'. Over one hundred years later and civil rights discrimination continues to be an issue. Non-WASP men and most women are not quite equal with those free men described in our Constitution who were 'born with certain inalienable rights.' And it all could have been so very, very different!"

"Honey," I stormed, "have I ever told you how much I hate Civil War battlefields?"

"Not until now."

He had listened to my philosophical tirade without volunteering a comment. I figured he had offered no reply because, coming from California, he was too far removed from the passions swirling about the War. During our previous travels, I had become acquainted with his fascination with the strategies and the whims of war, any war, which he merely regarded as a deadly form of chess. The remainder of the tour while I gazed out over now calm green fields with tears in my eyes and an empty ache in my heart for all those lives lost more than thirteen decades ago, Christopher, deeply entrenched in his study of the maps and literature provided, searched out the locations of the two armies and the directions of their bloody charges.

It's got to be a man thing, I thought.

On our way to Annapolis, we passed through rural towns that were scattered over the countryside like so many handmade glass beads from a broken antique necklace. Their well-maintained frame houses sat on manicured lawns facing shaded, tree-lined streets, reminding me of small-town America as depicted in television's Mayberry.

Swapping turns driving, Christopher never once mentioned that my name did not appear on the rental contract. He never commented on the speed I drove or how I changed lanes. After he told me I was one of the few people he felt comfortable riding with, I teased that he must be keeping his eyes closed when he was not concentrating on his maps.

The heart of the Maryland capital was a wonderful tangle of narrow streets and old buildings, abutting on close sidewalks. Its layout made the English traffic circles reasonable in comparison. I found it similar to driving in Winchester or in the City of Wells, except for the fact that I was on the proper side of the road in an adult-sized car.

We explored the harbor and walkways near the Naval Academy. For supper, we found a small steak house close by. Christopher requested a booth, and we were soon seated in a wood-lined corner nook for two.

After settling into our intimate surroundings, I asked, "Honey, is this how bein' inside a confessional feels like?"

"No," he protested, "this is just cozy." After more carefully regarding the compact, paneled booth, he shrugged his shoulders. "Well, no, not quite," he corrected himself before returning to his study of the menus.

Reading over my menu, I was surprised to learn the type of meat used exclusively by the restaurant. "Oh, Christopher, we're goin' to be eatin' a 4-H-raised cow. I don't know whether I can eat someone's pet."

"Force yourself," he absent-mindedly teased. He was currently lost reading the wine selections provided by the restaurant.

"I may want seafood." Still mentally debating my order, I changed the subject. "I've done a better job keepin' up with you walkin' this trip, haven't I?"

Murmuring in agreement, he again referred to the food selections.

I continued, "My back isn't as bad as it was. I was really hurtin' when we were in England. That was the main reason I couldn't keep up when we hiked in the Cotswolds."

Our waiter soon approached with a bottle of red wine to accompany steak and a glass of white wine for me, since I had not firmly decided against fish. After they went through the ritualistic dance of presenting and tasting the sample of wine, Christopher said, "If you order red meat, I think you'll like this wine."

"OK," I reluctantly agreed, "I'll order Daisy."

"Daisy?" Puzzled, he put down his menu to look at me.

To clear up my mysterious reference, I explained, "That was the name that Grandmother Taite gave every milk cow she owned."

The waiter left with our orders. In an uncharacteristically pensive mood, we began retracing our trips, each of us detailing personal highlights. It was our favorite pastime, except we usually waited until dessert was served to begin.

Christopher was silent a long while before saying softly, "You'll be leaving me soon."

What the hell does he know!

I heard myself answering in a heated, angry voice, "Don't be tellin' me what I'm goin' to do!"

I stared at the stunned look on Christopher's face. The sharpness of my tone had shocked even me because this was not the first time he had voiced the thought of my leaving. Amazed at my reaction, I looked to him for possible explanations, but he offered none.

Taking a deep breath to calm myself, I silently asked, Where did that sharp reply come from?

I checked the almost full wineglass by my hand. It was my first of the evening. I took time to do a full body scan.

No, I wasn't drunk. That wasn't the alcohol talking, that was me.

After further consideration, I decided that I had not yet learned to control the new power unleashed within me. It was the only plausible reason I could find to explain my outburst.

I looked again at Christopher before continuing in a softer, more composed voice. "I cannot imagine my life without you in it. I will not. You must not understand how important you are to me or you wouldn't say that I would leave you. I love you. You are what makes livin' every day possible."

Before he responded, our waiter brought our meal and another rounded glass for me. After pouring the red wine into my new glass, Christopher cut into his steak and placed the first bite in his mouth.

Chewing, he nodded his head.

"What do you think?" I asked before tasting my steak.

"Very good."

The forkful of cooked flesh I placed in my mouth was the juiciest, most tender cut of beef I had ever enjoyed. "Too good," I agreed, still finding something almost cannibalistic about eating a child's hand-raised pet. Dispensing with that topic, we discussed comfortable, nothing-things while we ate. After many years of practice, we were fluent in nothing talk.

While making love on the king-sized bed in our motel room, we were slow and careful in our movements. As we changed positions, we covered the entire surface area afforded by that spacious bed.

He was a tender lover at times. Other times, he nipped playfully. Wet, warm kisses graced the dimples at the small of my back, then trailed slowly down the backs of my thighs, all the way to the bends of my knees. The pleasurable sensations this man created were a form of near torture. As his hands guided me or teased me or commanded me, I followed wherever they directed. There were no thoughts in my brain, only tactile sensations rushing in from my peripheral nerves until we climaxed together.

"Rachael Taite!" he called out at last.

I was unable to speak. My body felt hotter than the hinges of hell. My heart pounded without rhythm. My breathing came in ragged gasps. My entire body was bathed in sweat. My limbs felt totally disconnected from my torso. At that instant, if my life depended on my ability to roll to one side to escape danger, I would be dead. I was absolutely drained and totally amazed that my partner had the ability left to yell my name with such energy.

His fingers traced my profile with a touch that felt as soft as eider down. "I love you, Rachael Taite," he said gently. In the darkness of our room, his words were as light on my ears as his fingertips were on my face.

Sweet Mother, this man actually admitted, without any prompting from me, that he loves me. I must have died and gone to heaven.

Inexplicably, I drifted away to sleep before I could answer back that I loved him.

Fifteen

I hated leg day.

Finishing my second set of walking lunges with a final set of ten to complete, I collapsed on the nearest bench, my heart pounding. Gasping for air, I stared at the gray, industrial strength carpeting.

I also hated upper body day and abs day, but exercising at the gym had become something I loved to hate. My bosoms no longer hid in either armpit when I lay on my back. My butt did not dangle and jiggle above the backs of my knees in the late afternoons when I walked my two miles along Cherokee Boulevard. Now that I was in my early fifties, I was in better shape than I had ever been in my thirties. I could hardly wait to share my newly reconditioned body with Christopher.

As much as I hated the workouts, the gym itself had proven to be worth the price of membership in sheer entertainment value alone. The establishment was tucked off Kingston Pike behind Parker's in a sun-faded, metal building that was as banged up as any punch-drunk sparring partner who has taken one glove too many to the head. Looking as a serious gym should look, its tattered exterior matched its worn interior. The equipment's white paint had aged to a chipped cream and the heavy, black plastic on its padded sections had been patched. The walls were gray and scuffed. Elsewhere, the floor-to-ceiling mirrors shined. Although ceiling fans and floor fans stirred the air year round, the interior seemed too hot in the summer, too cold in the winter. It was a no-nonsense sort of place. From the first day I joined, I felt comfortably at home in my torn, faded T-shirts and baggy scrub pants and heavily scuffed sneakers.

This place attracted only hard-core enthusiasts. No one showed up in matching designer outfits, waiting to be discovered by a modeling talent scout. Knoxville had other gyms that catered to those fluffy types. With no segregation here, members of both sexes came to sweat and grunt to the driving beat blaring from a hard rock radio station. Although males would gallantly hold open an exterior door for a woman, once inside she had to lift her own weights to the machines. Now, if she asked, a man would spot for her.

In this rarefied environment, should a naked woman sashay around doing her circuits, the men might glance up once as she casually bounced by. But let that same female, fully clothed, attempt a front-facing, one-handed pull-up and those same guys would crowd about, wildly cheering her on.

I liked the place. It had character.

Working out here was like having sex with an experienced partner you trusted to know what would make you feel good without him needing to ask you first. I had yet to walk out these doors unsatisfied. Exhausted maybe, but never disappointed in the time spent inside.

Picking up one ten-pound free weight in each hand, I gathered strength to complete the set.

"Miz Rachael, is that you?" a voice behind me called.

I turned to find Joey standing there, attired in workout sweats. His face had lost its boyish angles, and under his loose-fitting garments, his body was thicker with more muscles than I remembered him having. "Hey, Joey. Yep, it's me. How's it goin' with you?"

"Just fine. I've been workin' nights down at Belle's Tavern since your fire. Saw where you opened up again."

I smiled. "Yeah, my back finally got better. So, what's all new with you?"

He knelt to my level. "I've been takin' classes at Pellissippi State." His face brightened. "You won't believe who I saw down there last semester."

"Who?"

"That painter, Hugh Ed."

Since Liz had not said anything about Hugh Ed recently, I wondered if she knew. "Really?" I responded.

"Oh, yeah." Joey was silent before saying, "I was sorry to hear about Miz Margaret."

I nodded, but could not comment more as tears quickly flooded my eyes. I missed Margaret and her the-world-revolves-around-only-me attitude something fierce, even more than I could have imagined.

Embarrassed for having caused tears, he cleared his throat. "Did you hear that Lightnin' went to New York City? His ol' lady got herself a recordin' contract." He cleared his throat once again. "Say, I was wonderin' if you and Miz Liz could use some help in th' back? I could pick up and keep dishes washed for you'ns."

"That might work. We've been strugglin' to take up the slack since

Margaret's death." With the amount of work proving too much for just Liz and me, I had begun looking forward more to Saturday afternoons than to the start of the workweek.

Joey went on, suggesting, "I could start at th' beginnin' of next term. The classes I need are only bein' offered at night, and Belle's is closed durin' the day."

With my tears retreating, I stood up, ready to complete the lunges. "We need more than just a busboy or a dishwasher, Joey. Think you could chop and dice and put together orders?"

His face immediately glowed with excitement. "Yes'm. I'll tell them at Belle's, and I'll see you in a couple of weeks." He walked toward the water fountain. On his way to the racks holding free weights, he passed me again. "Miz Rachael," he said, "I've missed workin' with you. It'll be good to get back home."

"Thanks, Joey. We've missed you, too."

The next morning when Liz walked through the back door into the kitchen, I said, "Saw Joey down at the gym yesterday. He asked if we needed help."

"What did you say?"

"I said we did, and he's comin' to work in a couple of weeks. Can we make do until then?"

She nodded.

"Joey said he saw Hugh Ed at Pellissippi." I watched closely for any reaction.

Liz did not look at me as she put away her purse. She responded casually, "Really?"

"Is he paintin' down there?" I asked just as casually.

She still had not looked in my direction. "No, I think he's takin' a class or two."

"Oh?" While waiting for more information, I removed chicken breasts from the stockpot. Above my steam-fogged glasses, I watched her go to the radio and turn it on before she busied herself wrapping cooled muffins. After the colander's contents had drained and I had removed the meat from the first five breasts, I demanded, "OK, Lizzie-Lou, when were you goin' to tell me the rest?"

I watched a blush creep up the back of her neck.

"There isn't much to tell. Hugh Ed decided to take some college classes after he passed his GED last fall."

"This sounds serious. Would you tell me if it was serious?"

She answered briskly, "No, it isn't, and maybe yes."

"So, the two of you are still not datin'." I laughed at my close-mouthed friend. "Liz, you really should work for the CIA because you sure know how to keep a secret. Next time you talk with Hugh Ed, ask him to drop by. I've been thinkin' that Margaret was right. We need to make the front more attractive."

Happy that I had changed the subject, she quickly suggested, "What do you think about havin' cards and little nothin' gifts to sell? So many times I've had customers ask for enclosure cards. I could look into that for us."

"Sounds good. I'll do the decoratin'. You can do the buyin' of what-nots."

"I'll call Hugh Ed right now and have him drop in this mornin' before he goes by the Westwood house for me. By the way, Travis's baby's here. They had a little boy and named him after Travis." She walked to the wall phone near the kitchen's back door.

I turned to Liz, demanding, "Tell me they're not goin' to call the child Junior."

"No, he and Holly are dreamin' up a special nickname for the baby."

Later, after listening to Liz's side of the conversation while she was on the phone to Hugh Ed, I decided that their relationship was much farther along than just his helping with her properties. Even her voice softened when she spoke to him. Besides, any man who would go back to school at Hugh Ed's age had to be in love.

Revisiting events of the last few months, I realized that I had been too wrapped up in everything else that had been going on to notice that she seemed happier than usual. I had also failed to notice how close Hugh Ed had stood by her when they had come to my house that first afternoon after Margaret had passed. I then concluded my powers of observation must be slipping in my old age.

The new interior of Rachael's was a big improvement over the plain vanilla walls and stark, utilitarian glass display counter we had opened with last January. Not wanting to press my luck, I planned not to allot much money on decorating, in case the new shop could not become self-sustaining.

Margaret had never been one for generic white walls. She would have liked working here now and maybe, soon, would I.

My formerly bare bones establishment now looked as good as it had always smelled. Dark green walls peeked from behind white lattice panels. Natural wicker display shelves held candles, cookbooks, inspirational books and personalized stationery. Cards filled a rack just inside the front door. Artificial ivy trailed realistically up the staircase to the storage area and was entwined within the latticework on the walls. Stained-glass sun catchers, for sale of course, glimmered in windows. Boston and asparagus ferns hung from the ceiling in graceful, feathery bundles. Individually wrapped muffins crowded in a wicker basket on the counter. Liz had taken to tying narrow curling ribbon on each, dragging the loose ends across a single scissor edge to leave two dangling, Shirley Temple-tight curls per muffin.

Hugh Ed, Liz, Joey and I toiled hard all Sunday getting the place ready. I was tired, but it was a satisfying tired. I welcomed the changes because with Margaret gone, cooking for the restaurant had begun to seem like a job. Joey's presence had made the hours easier, but he could not add the sparkle that Margaret once brought to my days.

I felt almost as if I were walking into my garden when I stepped through the kitchen doorway when opening up Monday morning, except we were minus those striped, blood-sucking mosquitoes, whose existence in the world I could not quite justify. I was not surprised to find Clyda Marshall waiting on the outside. Before unlocking the front door, I took a deep breath in preparation for dealing with the little dynamo. Miss Clyda always seemed to pull energy away from me, like a sump pump sucking up water.

"Good mornin', Miss Clyda. Is that another new car?"

"Rachael, this is just too lovely!" She breezed by me. "I really do like the changes." Unescorted, she completed her grand tour while I took my position behind the counter and picked up paper and pencil, ready to jot down her order.

"Thank you very much, Miss Clyda. I think we're goin' to like the new look."

She came to lean against the glass. "You know, Rachael, you need to think about franchisin'. I'll have my nephew, Jackson, talk to you."

Sweet Mother, franchising! I don't think so. "Thank you, but I—"

"Now, Honey, don't say no just yet. Let my Jackson tell you how to go about it right."

Simply from having seen her name emblazoned across that first check she had presented me nearly a decade ago, I knew Clyda Baptiste Marshall to be a woman accustomed to having her way. A lot of older women who lived near The Village were like that. They were from old money and old families. They took cruises in the winter until the chance for snow in East Tennessee became minimal. They played bridge, they golfed, they gardened, they planned charity events to while away the rest of their time.

She was a chunky woman, nearly as short as me, with silvered hair that was set weekly, and her perfectly almond-shaped nails were painted fresh with pearlized white polish at the same time. I would swear she traded a car as soon as the odometer rolled around for its first oil change. Each factory-new purchase was a loaded, white-on-white Cadillac. Her carefully coordinated clothes were dry cleaners crisp, and her shoes matched whatever outfit she wore. Margaret had used the same cleaners as Miss Clyda and had confided the woman even had her undies cleaned professionally.

The woman belonged to the generation that rigidly wore matching sweater sets and wool skirts in winter, linen pastels in spring, white shoes only between Easter Sunday and Labor Day and dark cotton plaids in the fall. No matter the season, Miss Clyda always sported a single strand of graduated, creamy pearls, whether she was grocery shopping or playing tennis or going to church. I wanted to ask if she wore them while gardening, but had never worked up the nerve to do so.

Despite her manner being heavier handed than Mom's, I knew that like my mother, she had good intentions. Bless her heart. On the other hand, I would dread less talking with Miss Clyda if only her manner was not so overtly demanding.

"Yes, Honey, that's my new car. Don't you just hate it when they lose that new car smell? I won't have a car that doesn't smell fresh. I just wish I could have gotten my nephew and Margaret together." Before embarking on her next sentence, she sighed deeply. "But I guess it wasn't meant to be. Are you available? I just don't know how much longer he will stay with that woman he married." Women of Miss Clyda's ilk talked fast and often changed subjects without signaling. "What's the soup today? And I need a whole hummin'bird sheet cake to go."

"Tomato bisque. What else do you want to go with the cake?"

"Just a quart of the soup." She patted her rounded stomach. "I'm tryin' to lose weight. You're lookin' good. How much have you dropped?"

"Oh, not that much weight," I answered. "Since I've started workin' out, I've lost fat while puttin' on muscle. "

Her sparkling black eyes narrowed as she considered my response. "I might try that. Which gym?"

"The one around the corner," I replied.

She shook her head. "Oooh, no, I couldn't go there. Jackson says only body builders go there. I wish Pascal's hadn't closed. It was for women only, you know. I don't think men need to know that women, you know," Miss Clyda wrinkled her regal nose before whispering the distasteful word, ". . . sweat. What's the quiche?"

Because I lagged one subject behind in our conversation, I had to think a second before answering her. "Bacon and spinach."

"Benton bacon?"

"Nothin' but."

"I'll have two slices, then."

❦

I pushed against the porch's flooring to get the swing going. The four-legged girls and I had snuck up to the cabin early Friday afternoon to unwind and get away from the city's heat. Debating whether to stay the night and get up early to drive back Saturday morning, I halfway hoped that someone or something would make that decision for me. Today had been almost too hot to think.

This month was starting out to be a typical East Tennessee September in that the days burned with summer's shimmering, white-heat while the nights' chill hinted of coming autumn. Having celebrated another birthday this week, I sipped a Bloody Mary and considered these yearly milestones were becoming millstones about my neck. I craned my head to the window at my back. My four-legged girls quietly stood sentry duty at the kitchen screen waiting for their squirrel nemesis. I knew that brazen rodent would not come onto the porch as long as I was here.

Disappointed by his absence, Sybyl barked a curse before moving away from the screen. After that display of feline temper, I heard a heavy thud when she landed on the floor. Persevering Beatrice remained silhouetted against the lightness of the refrigerator's bulk.

Later, as I sipped and watched the shimmering surface of Little River, I decided that bourbon and scotch were for forgetting and wine was for making memories, but a stout Bloody Mary remained the best accompaniment for daydreaming. The chains supporting the swing sang overhead as I replayed the memory of Christopher's only night at the cabin. A strong shudder ran through my body when I recalled how we had kissed, for what seemed to be forever, there on the couch.

Sweet Mother, it had been wonderful.

Recalling our last night in Maryland when he actually acknowledged he loved me, I laughed aloud with the pure joy for having heard, without any prompting on my part, those three little words. Although I had known for some time the man loved me, I could have sworn there had been an accompanying heavenly chorus when that sentence appeared unsolicited.

So, Christopher Saracini loves this little ol' hillbilly. About damn time he admitted it aloud to me and to himself.

I wondered how much longer our relationship could continue. As it was, if Christopher and I kept meeting, we would both soon qualify for senior citizens' discounts and would require airport personnel to roll our aged, infirm bodies to and from airplanes in wheelchairs. What if one of us died while we were together? I remembered hearing that Miss Clyda's husband had died on the golf course with his girlfriend of some thirty-five years. Now that funeral had to have been awkward for all parties involved.

Rachael, I heard myself say, don't even go there. Not even in a flight of fancy.

Although I wanted our meetings to go on forever, I was well aware that could never happen. Being a realist, I would settle for our time together to last as long as it could.

I checked my wristwatch. It was almost seven on Friday evening and his usual time to call. Listening for the phone, I stopped the swing. As I stood, I could almost feel him thinking about me. I went to the screen door and pulled it open just as the black rotary phone rang.

As soon as I had the receiver to my ear, I heard him say, "Rachael, here you are! I just tried your house and got your answer machine. Can you leave for Washington in two weeks?"

"Of course," I replied, "no trouble."

"Sorry about the short notice." He continued, "I don't want to stay in the Capital. We've already done that. What else would you want to do in the area?"

"Have you seen Williamsburg?"

"No."

"Well, we could drive down the Blue Ridge Parkway. Check out Jefferson's Poplar Forest outside Lynchburg. See Appomattox before headin' over to Williamsburg." I was familiar with that region of the country and had no need of an atlas to plan our next weekend.

His voice sounded drained. "I don't want to drive as much as we have. Besides, we'll have only two nights before I fly back. I can't get away for any more time than that."

The thought of only a short weekend together was disappointing, but I agreeably said, "Fine. No problem. We can drive directly to Williamsburg from Washington." Over the phone lines, I heard paper rustling. I took a long sip of my tangy drink while waiting for his response.

Checking the map, he suggested slowly, "We could drive some of the Parkway, then cut east."

"We must eat seafood at Yorktown. You'll like that place. I've got friends in Portsmouth. I'll call Patti and Rick and ask them to meet us for supper."

"No," Christopher said emphatically before he explained, "Rachael, I don't want to share you with anyone."

After our conversation ended, I calculated this coming trip would make the third time in less than eleven months that we had met. That was a record for us. Maybe he needed me more than I thought. Recalling his reaction to my contacting my friends, I was both surprised and amused that the man did not want to share our hours with outsiders. I never would have imagined he would so jealously guard our time alone. I could have just as easily thought that after almost ten years the man had grown tired of me and looked forward to having new conversationalists to share one meal.

I would enjoy showing Christopher around Colonial Williamsburg as much as he had enjoyed showing me the redwoods above Eureka. That historical city had become one of my favorite destinations after Daddy carried us there for vacation the summer of 1960. Touring Virginia had been the best and last family vacation we took. Saying he had traveled all he cared to during World War II, Daddy was happiest at home.

Surprisingly, the downsized Rachael's was not easier for Liz and

Mom to handle the weekend I flew into Baltimore. As it happened, they ran out of my signature yellow cake with caramel frosting early Friday afternoon. That was doubly unfortunate for me when I returned because following their words of condolences for Margaret, the disappointed customers let me know about the cake calamity for days afterwards. To prevent that disaster from happening again, I planned to be in the kitchen double-time for two days, making up cakes. Even with Mom handling phone orders as Liz and Joey worked the kitchen and counter, it would be hectic for them but well worth the trade-off for me to have time with Christopher.

Sweet Mother! I stared in disbelief at the airline clerk.

I exclaimed, "Do what!"

She patiently repeated her same words, "Your flight to Washington, D. C., has been canceled due to mechanical problems."

Calmly yet firmly I explained, "No, you don't understand. My sweet darlin' is meetin' me at that airport. I have to be there by noon. And there's no way I can contact him if my arrival time changes."

This could not be happening. Outwardly, I acted more serene than I felt.

The uniformed clerk consulted her computer for several minutes. Finally, she suggested an alternative, by saying, "There's space available on an earlier flight that leaves Knoxville in ten minutes, goin' through Cincinnati, that will get you to D.C. at 12:05."

"That'll work." I breathed easier, feeling a near-disaster had been averted. I silently promised never again to complain about the airlines' request that passengers arrive at least an hour before their scheduled departure. After receiving boarding passes for my new flight, I turned from the counter, hurriedly walking toward the security check.

I made it through the scanning gate, but my luggage did not pass x-ray inspection.

I'm jinxed. The gods aren't smiling on me or on this trip. I can't get out of town, I thought. Hell, I can't even seem to get out of the airport.

A bored security guard dragged herself off a swivel stool to step toward my suitcase at the end of the scanning machine. She asked formally, "M'am, you'll need to open your suitcase."

I unzipped my luggage, pulling back the side as she requested, but the guard was not satisfied with the items I initially exposed. Politely, she insisted, "M'am, you'll need to move your things around so I can have a better view."

I complied, all the time praying that her delays would not keep me from making my rescheduled departure. I moved my weekend supply of clothes and makeup, revealing the rest of my suitcase's contents. She pointed to an aluminum foil-wrapped bottle, indicating by flicking her long, blood-red fingernails that I should pull back the foil.

"Frank," she called to her partner who stood facing the viewing screen, "you won't believe what all this lady has in here."

"What have you found?" he asked, slipping his hand over his holstered sidearm in preparation. He quickly came to inspect the contraband his co-worker had discovered.

I stared into my once orderly belongings as she itemized my cache.

"Well," the woman began, "she has packed a bottle of wine, two wine glasses, a round of cheese, a box of crackers, one small china plate, one corkscrew, a cuttin' board and one fancy cheese knife." She chuckled. "It has a cute, little, wooden duck head for a handle."

Disappointed that his cohort had not found concealed illicit drugs, Frank slowly returned, without comment, to his post.

"Where's the blanket?" she asked me.

Smiling, I replied archly, "The man's supposed to bring somethin'."

The woman's stern mouth broke into a delighted grin in anticipation of my coming repast. "Have a good time," she chuckled, shaking her head.

After rewrapping the wine in the aluminum foil to keep it chilled, I said, "Just think, when you're havin' your afternoon break here, I'll be on top of the Blue Ridge Parkway, sharin' this with my sweet darlin'." Zipping my case shut, I smiled a smile as broad as hers. "Wonder which one of us will be havin' more fun?"

Automobiles, vans, urbanized four-by-fours and taxis all streamed in front of me, lanes deep. Intent on their personal agendas, people paced by me, getting on to where they were going. I stood alone, an isolated island of stillness in an ocean of activity.

The last time we spoke, Christopher had said to be outside the Washington airport at a quarter after noon. My plane had landed on time, at five after twelve. Renovations to the Washington terminal had been completed since the last time I flew here, which made the walk from my arrival gate to the outside into an easy five-minute stroll.

As trusting as a blind cat posed on an inside windowsill patiently awaiting her owner's return, I knew Christopher would meet me, simply because he had never failed to meet me. While I stood outside the terminal, I found the exhaust fumes to be overwhelming. Having no clue as to the type of vehicle he would be driving, I searched each oncoming car for his dear face.

I got here, I thought, so where is he?

Twelve-thirty arrived, but he had not. I wondered what I should do if he ever failed to show up. The reality would be that I would simply board the next available flight home, unless I was found dead from carbon monoxide inhalation at the curb of the Washington airport.

Knowing that dealing with why he failed to keep our appointment would be the rat's nest, I held onto my faith that the man would be where he said he would be. I trusted, without a single question clouding my mind, he would appear soon. Like that blind cat, I assured myself, all I needed to do was wait.

A squat, olive-green car eased to a stop. As its driver leaned to open the passenger-side door, I bent down, peering inside to find Christopher. I hurriedly tossed my single suitcase onto the backseat before settling into the vehicle. My weekend could now officially begin.

Christopher talked a mile a minute, hardly allowing time to breathe between sentences. "I can't believe this traffic. Have you been waiting long? I stopped to get flowers, and the woman took forever. You'll need to help me read the signs to get us out of here."

Not even attempting to get a word in edgewise, I checked the long, narrow box in the back seat. After removing the lid of the cardboard container, I discovered twelve of the most elegantly beautiful, long-stemmed red roses with each perfect petal so lush and with coloring so three-dimensional that the still-budded blossoms appeared to have been created from the plushest silk velvet. Every stem had been carefully inserted into individual, green, transparent plastic vials to prolong their ethereal beauty for as long as humanly possible.

"Christopher, these are the most perfect roses you have ever given me!" I was awed by their sheer beauty.

"Quick, Rachael! Tell me which turn to take!" His tense voice fairly brimmed with urgency.

I did as he requested and was able to decipher the overhead interstate sign only moments before we drove under it. "Bear right."

He followed the exit, and we took the Beltway around the nation's capital with Christopher continuing his fast-paced, one-sided conversation and with me concentrating on his phrasing so I could understand what he said. I had never seen the man so distracted by heavy traffic. In comparison, he had been laid back that first day he had driven in England.

"I left in plenty of time to meet you, but I was driving past this florist and stopped to get your flowers. The owner insisted that she had to put those little plastic things on each stem. I thought I would never get away from her. Now, which way?"

"Keep right," I directed.

Clogged with traffic heavy in the middle of lunch hour, the Beltway was as little fun as Atlanta's paved maze. His being ill at ease, of course, made me ill at ease. As he negotiated the small car through the crowded lanes, we chitchatted, barely keeping our individual nervousness at bay.

"Victoria finished her MBA. That son of mine, when he does bother to sign up for classes! . . . " He pounded the steering wheel once.

It was unclear if the blow was due to the traffic conditions or to Vincent languishing in the backwaters of a community college. I had no problem recognizing the frustrations in Christopher's voice, whichever the cause.

"Sophia's well. Just getting over a cold."

Sophia? Who the hell is Sophia? Is that the cat?

Fortunately, he soon added, "And that damn cat presented us with a litter of seven kittens before I could get her to the vet to get fixed. Sophia and my children had trouble finding them homes."

Amused, I looked out my window, not allowing him to see my smile. I was grateful that I had not blurted out my confusion between his wife, whose name I had never heard prior to today, and the family cat. Not caring to make that mistake again, I inquired, "What's the cat's name?"

"Nancy, of course. *Momma mia* said all male cats are Toms and all female cats are Nancies."

Quickly associating his cat with the woman, last seen at the Super

Bowl Party, who had cattily confronted me when we both were interested in Old What's-his-name, I knew I would have no difficulty remembering the feline's name.

Changing the subject, I volunteered, "Mom's doin' well. Agin' gracefully as ever. I'd swear she just gets prettier every year."

"My business has expanded since we ventured overseas. I'll be hiring more people as soon as I get back. My secretary has three days of interviews set up."

"Honey, isn't it strange how your business is growin' now that I've scaled mine back?"

"Speaking of your place, how do the changes look?" he asked. "Are you liking it better now?"

I placed my left hand on his right thigh for the comfort I could draw by simply touching his body. "Oh, I don't know," I finally sighed. I gathered my thoughts before adding, "It's just not the same without Margaret. Somehow, all the joy is gone. One of my customers thinks I ought to franchise."

"How do you feel about that?"

While considering how to reply, I looked at his profile for several moments without answering.

"Rachael," he chuckled, "that isn't a trick question."

"I know." More time ticked off before I replied, "This third reincarnation is bustlin'. Even with Joey comin' back, Liz and I are far too busy. And I am as unhappy as hell." I turned to watch the scenery outside my window. "I don't think I want to look into franchisin'. Now, if you and I were together, it would be a different story. I just don't want to have to face that hassle all by myself."

The next miles were traveled in silence. Since we both understood the reasons for my wanting him with me and his for not being with me, we did not waste words by repeating them again.

"Did I tell you that Carl moved back to Oakland?"

"Yes," I reminded him, "you told me when I saw you in San Francisco."

"I met him for lunch two weeks ago."

More miles rolled by. Christopher's words and voice became less frantic as we wove through the suburbs and entered the Virginia countryside. We repeated our newest, tactless, politically-incorrect jokes, each of us groaning when the other presented the punch line.

Driving past Harper's Ferry, he suggested, "Rachael, why don't you remove your panties?"

"Why?"

"Why not?"

Climbing the incline of the northern terminus for the Blue Ridge Parkway, we became surrounded by fall's explosion of color. The higher we drove, the richer the colors became. With the heat from the early afternoon sun seductively warm through our clothes, but not hot enough to need the car's air conditioning, we rolled down the four side windows and drew deeply into our lungs the fresh, clean, earthy smells of the enveloping wilderness. Except for the occasional vehicle going in the opposite direction, we had the road to ourselves.

I watched all the creatures I could clearly see and distinctly felt all the creatures I could not see watching me. As the pavement snaked along the ridges, scattered deer families gracefully bounded across the road in front of our car. Turkey buzzards idly glided the cloudless skies over head. Later, a small chevron of Canadian geese hightailed eastward toward the coast on their migration southward. Their formation heralded the coming of cold weather, and I instinctively longed to accompany them away from the approaching winter's famine.

During the drive on the Parkway, I reflected on my life since our last meeting. My existence had not been the same since Baltimore. Amazingly, I had continued feeling whole and complete away from him. I smiled as I remembered how I had worried when I first returned to Knoxville that the peace and security would be temporary conditions and that I would wake up one morning naked without them. That loss had yet to happen, and I now tentatively accepted the sensations would never leave.

Despite no longer receiving pleasure from my work, my living had remained effortless. I had gradually grown aware of one subtle, yet major, difference: My essence, that intangible which made this physical body me, had become joined to every living creature. My connection to life's components deepened daily. So much so that I had stopped stepping on spiders and now ushered them outside on paper toweling. In addition, I found myself only taking what I needed for my maintenance from the bounty before me for, with my current acceptance of my place in the food chain, I cared not to waste the lives of the plants and animals with which I shared the planet. From my newfound place within the universe, my energy soared with the birds and my toes gripped deeply into the soil with the trees.

What a priceless, precious gift Christopher had given me that afternoon when he comforted me after Margaret's death. Now, I worried how I could ever cover the debt I owed him.

Out of the corner of my right eye, a swirling dark mass as thick as any strangle of flying gnats caught my attention. I turned to watch hundreds of large birds, belonging to some predatory species, flying in a pulsating glob. Sorting through my mental files, I knew I had seen that phenomenon somewhere before.

"What the hell?" Christopher swore reverently, slowing down the car when he noticed the birds.

"I think they're migratin' broad-winged hawks," I said slowly, dredging information from a televised nature program I had seen a few years back before sharing an interesting tidbit. "Native Americans believe a hawk is sent by the Spirit World to alert humans of an important incomin' message, some comin' vital event or an unveilin' of something profound."

He said firmly, "Judging by the size of that flock, it must be something pretty big. How do you know that?"

"I saw it on public television." I laughed softly aloud before adding, "I'm a veritable fountain of obscure information."

He patted the inside of my bare thigh. "Yes, and I bet you are great with small talk at cocktail parties."

After we pulled into a deserted parking area, I rummaged through my suitcase, gathering together lunch provisions before we walked down the steep embankment to a grouping of picnic tables.

"Well, it looks like we're alone here," he announced. Pointing to a specific tree-shaded picnic table and benches, he asked, "Does this one meet with your approval?"

I nodded, following him to the table. "It'll do. Alone, you don't say. I think we thought we were alone in a park once before."

Affecting a French accent, he sang from a musical, "*Ah, yes, I remember it well.*" While reaching for the corkscrew and wine bottle, he leaned to nip my neck before he went on ahead.

After opening the cheese and crackers, I hopped atop the short end of the weathered table. He handed me a glass of wine. We clicked the mismatched glasses I had supplied before we sipped their contents.

I watched him swish the liquid in his mouth before swallowing. He smiled his approval.

"Good wine, my dear." He held his glass up to the light.

"Do you recognize that glass?" I asked. "It's one of the two you carried to Eureka."

"I thought it looked familiar." Sitting on the bench near me, he added, "I liked them so well that I purchased ten so I would have a set at the house to match the two I gave you."

Jolted upon learning he owned similar stemware that he used at home on a regular basis, I changed the subject. "This will be a wonderful weekend. You know, Honey, it doesn't matter what we do as long as we're together." I thought for a moment before saying, "But then they've all been wonderful weekends."

While solitary birds called to one another from separate trees, we munched in silence until we had our fill. Popping the last of a wheat cracker in my mouth, I announced, "That should hold body and soul together until we reach Yorktown."

Christopher came to stand in front of me, and I held out my arms to welcome him closer. After opening my knees to allow him nearer, he leaned into my embrace. He kissed my mouth ever so softly before brushing a loose strand of hair away from my face. A thrill shivered through my body when I detected a mischievous twinkle in his eyes.

"Did I ever tell you how good your hair smells?"

I smiled, nodding that he had. "On numerous occasions."

"Put your glass down," he said huskily.

We placed our glasses on each side of my hips. Again, we kissed tenderly once. Shortly after our kisses had become deeper and more demanding, he looked over my head to the parking area above us as he unzipped his trousers.

"Come closer, Rachael."

I complied, wanting him inside me as much as he wanted to be inside me.

Well, I thought, why not?

The table was the correct height, my panties were tucked away in my purse back on the floorboard of the car, my jeans skirt conveniently buttoned in the front, we were alone and, as Big Momma had always said, 'Where there's a will, there's a way.'

"Rachael Taite!" he called to the surrounding trees.

I tightly held him to me. My pounding heart and our ragged breathing were the only sounds I heard. The erotic spirit of this adventuresome man had never yet failed to take me by surprise. Gradually, I became aware that my shouted name had silenced the birds.

"Honey," I began innocently enough, "does this mean that even though we haven't had unsanctioned sex in every state as yet, we're goin' to start chalkin' up the national park system, too?"

He laughed, delighted at the prospects. "I'll sure give it a try."

Although I held the man's body against mine, I felt him shrinking out of mine. "But, Darlin'," I protested, "I'm not ready for you to leave me yet."

Christopher pulled away from me and the table, putting himself back together. He had climaxed. I almost had. That was a moot point because I knew that score would be evened out later in Williamsburg.

Feeling an immediate urge that needed attention, I complained, "Man, oh, man, I thought I was packin' everything we would need for a picnic, but I forgot napkins and I sure could use one right now." I dreaded my coming damp ride across Virginia.

He chuckled that wonderfully obscene chuckle of his. Offering little condolence, he said, "Poor baby."

I attempted one of my patented if-looks-could-kill expressions, but I was too happy to maintain the pretense for more than a second. Coyly, I asked, "You wouldn't happen to have a handkerchief handy, would you?"

Gathering up the remains of our light meal, he shook his head in the negative.

❧

After crossing the middle of Virginia by interstate, we both breathed a sigh of relief when we exited onto quiet, scenic Highway 5. As the day faded into an early fall evening, we passed along the rear entrances for some of the James River plantations, peacefully weaving between dark green shadows of the heavily forested roadsides and brilliant golden shafts of light spilling through breaks in the foliage. Although the hour was much too late for any house tours, I directed Christopher into the drives for Shirley and Berkeley so that he could view these two magnificent historical homes.

While gazing at the numerous restorations as we wound around the outskirts of Colonial Williamsburg, Christopher announced, "I think I'm going to like this place."

Having sat uncomfortably upon my folded panties since the Blue Ridge Parkway, I not so subtly reminded him of my predicament by commenting. "I think I'm goin' to like a shower."

Those interminable miles this long afternoon had underscored the wisdom of my mother. I squirmed against the car seat. "Years ago, Mom told me never to date a man who didn't carry a handkerchief. Now I know there is at least one thing she was right about."

He glanced briefly in my direction. "I don't remember you complaining after we left the redwoods."

I thought about his remark before theorizing, "I must have worn cotton drawers back then. Cotton, you know, is a bit more absorbent than these little, pink, nylon skivvies I put on this morning. Besides, I didn't know you well enough to complain ten years ago."

He laughed. "What a difference ten years make."

***

"So, what do you think?"

I watched Christopher take in Yorktown's famed restaurant's eclectic collection of life-sized marble statues, massively embellished gilt-framed mirrors and gloriously mismatched ornate crystal chandeliers. Waitresses, all dressed in white blouses and gathered skirts with colorful Greek vests and pill-box hats, glided swanlike from kitchen to table. The waiters wore formal attire and moved as easily as professional skaters on ice.

I explained, "Rumor has it that our maitre d' was very high up in the Vietnamese army before the war ended. On a crowded night, you ought to see all the waitin' customers snap to when he orders them to get in a straight line."

He changed his focus to concentrate on the food laid out on the neighboring tables. Thoughtfully, he said, "This could be interesting. What's good here?"

"I can't get past the lobster casserole and the seafood kebobs," I answered truthfully. "I usually alternate between the two each visit." We returned to study our menus before I put mine down. I did not know why I even bothered to look because this was the kebobs trip. Next Friday, when I carried Mom up for the Fall Pilgrimage Weekend, I would order the casserole.

I looked up to find him staring at me.

"Rachael, my dear, sweet Rachael," he said as he reached for my hand, then stopped, saying nothing more.

I waited for him to continue. When he did not, I prodded, "Yes, Darlin'?"

"I've been doing a lot of thinking lately."

"And what have you come up with?"

A cryptic smile crossed his lips. He announced, "I've decided that love is forever."

I studied his face, wondering if now would be a good time to relate what I understood about our past lives together. "What brought that profound thought on?"

He was quiet for several seconds before answering, "I'm simply growing older and wiser." Our waitress appeared to take our orders, and we never returned to that conversational tack the rest of the evening.

Come morning we boarded the first bus leaving the visitors' center to step back in time to Colonial Williamsburg. We admired the detailed craftsmanship used to reconstruct the buildings, finding it difficult for our untrained eyes to detect which buildings were recreated and which were restored. Christopher did not care to explore the interior of any of the houses, saying he was much more interested in the public buildings. That worked for me since next weekend Mom and I would spend one entire day going through the interiors of old houses in Charles City County.

Awaiting the start of our Williamsburg recreated retreat into the colonial experience, we sat on benches in the cool morning air in front of the rebuilt capitol. In no time at all, the yard filled with milling tourists. After a short wait, a woman dressed in traditional costume skimmed toward us.

"A good morrow to all," she greeted. "I'm Mistress Anne. I bid you welcome to Williamsburg, the second Capital for His Majesty's Colony of Virginia. Once inside the building, we shall attend a mock trial. For that event, I shall choose, from among you gathered here, four to portray the parties involved." Looking over the motley-attired tourists before her, she smiled as if she were party to a great conspiracy.

After immediately selecting Christopher, she took only seconds to point out two stout men attired in Bermuda shorts and T-shirts stretched over their protruding bellies. She methodically searched over the group a final time before staring into my eyes. "And you." Her attitude implied she expected no protestations from those selected, and she received none.

"Now, ladies and gentlemen, please follow me. But you four remain close by as you will enter the Court's chamber after everyone else is inside."

Dutifully, we waited with Mistress Anne for the rest of our group to file silently into the reconstructed courtroom. She called ahead to the people entering, "Leave that chair on the left free." Turning to Christopher, she instructed, "You'll sit there. You are the Accuser."

After he had taken his seat, Mistress Anne handed each burly man a halberd, instructing them to guard me, the Accused, and not to enter the Court until she, as the Presiding Judge, ordered us to do so. She positioned a guard on either side of me with their ceremonial spears crossed in front of my body, each gripping one of my arms with his free hand.

She sternly admonished, "You soldiers, do not allow this prisoner to escape." As if not to allow that to happen and then have to incur her wrath, both men tightened their hold on me.

Before she boldly strode across the courtroom floor, the costumed re-enactress brought together the massive double doors behind us, their hollow thuds sealing off my last chance to flee.

After all were in their rightful positions, her imperial voice rang out, "Bring the Accused forward!"

I was led to trial.

Fall's golden sunlight streamed through the room's large, oval windows; however, the paneling in the Court's chamber was so dark and the space so large that its brightness was softened and dimmed, except for rigid shafts of strong bright light coming through the distorting panes of old glass. Illuminated dust motes slowly bobbed in the wedges that the sun's rays created in the still air within the courtroom. As the bodies ahead of me became smudged in the darkened recesses, shapeless figures from a long-past century and a faraway country sifted through the thick walls to gather in the chamber, joining the group of tourists within the deep shadows.

While standing there, a startling concept slammed into my twenty-first century consciousness with the force of a meteor striking the earth. I sensed that I had been here before and what had happened before was about to occur again, and I could do nothing to prevent it.

I could almost smell the stench of the newcomers' unwashed bodies, but I was vaguely grateful to be away from the damp, crowded cell where I had been held. My guards led me slowly forward until I came to stand alone, spotlighted in the natural sunlight.

"Prisoner, turn that you may face your Accuser!" the Judge sternly ordered.

Blinded by the sun's rays and frozen by the stunning awareness that centuries could peel away as easily as I could pull leaves from a head of lettuce, I was unable to move when ordered.

"Guards!"

I felt my body forcibly being turned to face directly into the light and toward Christopher. I squinted my eyes and turned my head slightly, but was only able to make out the silhouette of a carved chair.

Encased in a swirling vortex composed of disjointed segments of eras and places, I heard, from high above, the charge levied against me.

"This previously released indentured maid comes before this Court accused of thievery. She was caught, while fleeing under the cover of darkness, with a silver cup cunningly concealed in her bundle of possessions."

I felt a sudden jolt of panic as adrenaline pumped through my body. I had felt it before. I wanted to flee but, like the last time I had appeared before this Court, I had no safe place to go. As I had done centuries earlier, I panicked. I dared not give out too many details for, if I told the truth, I would be stoned as an adulteress. I knew I was no common thief because my master had given the cup as a bribe. When my indentured time had been fully served, I departed with only my pitiful few possessions and his growing seed in my belly.

I looked in the direction of my former master. With the sun's rays backlighting his chair, I was unable to see his face. As my heart furiously pounded beneath my ribs, I feared the entire assemblage could see the coarse twine that closed my chemise throbbing as clearly as I felt it, and I determinedly fought against scratching the recently acquired lice roaming my body. Although I was unable to make out his face, I felt the man's blue eyes boring into me as I stood isolated within a shaft of strong sunlight. I stared in his direction, pleading with my eyes, hoping to will my thoughts into his mind, praying he would speak only enough truth to set me free.

Let me go free, I silently begged. Tell them the truth. Tell the Court I stole nothing. Tell them the cup was a reward for good service, not that you bought my body with it. Please.

"What say you!" the Judge's cold, hard voice pierced the silent court room.

I jumped at the sound. My mouth was dry, but I managed to say, "The master . . . he . . .," I hesitated, all the while praying: He cannot fail me. He will speak truthfully, for I served him well. I swallowed hard before being able to compose my simple defense. "My master gave the cup to me. I am no thief."

"Does the maid speak the truth?" the Judge asked of my Accuser.

"No!" he shouted out. His one-syllable condemnation echoed inside my skull and throughout the courtroom and down through the centuries.

My mind was overwhelmed as past visions came and went in violent flashes. First, I saw my back beaten with whips. I watched as the letter beginning the word 'thief' was branded into the flesh of my right palm. I next saw myself, with my hands bound in front, tethered by a rough leather strap that twisted around my master's right fist and being spat upon as he led me away from the village. Later stumbling alongside his horse, I felt my stubborn pride growing because I had not fainted or vomited or cried out when my unmerited punishment had been meted out. Finally, after the last jeering villager was far from sight, I watched him carefully lift my bloodied body onto his fine steed. To shield my wounds from the tormenting swarms of hungry, biting flies, he placed his luxurious cloak over my shoulders. Completing our long journey deeper into the Black Forest, he took me to a woodsman's crude hut in a secret corner of his inherited ancestral fiefdom.

Quickly returning to the present time, I shook my muddled head to clear away the haunting visions.

You sonofabitch, my mind screamed, you've done it to me again! You could have sided with me and let me go free, but you chose to lie and keep me in bondage.

Stunned that my sweet darling would allow me to be found guilty and sentenced by the Court, my body felt cold and my mind was numb. As Mistress Anne calmly completed her commentary on colonial law, my erstwhile guards and I stood apart from the others while I rubbed my arms to knock down the chill bumps that had first appeared when he called out my guilt.

Thinking over the visions I had seen, I knew, as that young girl, I had left under the cover of darkness because Christopher, then my master, had inadvertently learned from another servant that I was with child. Aware that he would never allow me to leave with his child, I had attempted to run away so that my offspring would be born free. But, because I had been caught and returned to bondage by the Court's Decree, that had not been allowed. And I—as her—had loathed and despised him for his lie.

Soon after the exercise in colonial justice ended, our group milled out of the chamber and was directed to the exact same room where Patrick Henry would have given his impassioned speech of liberty versus death had the original colonial building not been destroyed. Christopher made his way through the tangle of tourists to my side.

"Rachael, I'm sorry," he apologized, "but the guide told me what to say after I walked into the courtroom."

I studied his concerned face. Part of the present-day me refused to accept such a lame excuse at this late date. During my life's cycling as that young servant, I had suffered the Court's punishment and those scars were still raw after all those centuries. Some part of me forgave him because Christopher, then my master, had tenderly cared for my wounds, binding them with his own hands, all the while crooning that he needed me too much and that he would never allow me to leave. Yet another part rebelled against staying in the household of this married man who professed to love me. All the while knowing I would never again leave him because, despite everything, the punished servant, who was me, loved him, but had been too proud in her lifetime to grant him forgiveness for his lie.

As confusing as the jumble of thoughts combining the separate centuries and events were, I understood the serving girl's dilemma too well. Having no face-saving solution available to her, my mind effortlessly postulated the two lovers must have existed in an age before the concept of do-over was invented.

Do-overs, of all things! I quickly chided myself, These flashes of a former existence, Rachael, are weird. Just too, too weird!

I waited until the entire group had walked on before responding to my betrayer. "Honey, you didn't have to say what that guide told you to say. You could've stood up for me." My tone conveyed her hurt, as well as my hurt, at the man's lack of integrity.

Considering that if I told him, right now, we had lived through that trial before and he had lied to make me guilty then, too, I did not think he would accept my extraordinarily fanciful explanation as truth. I chuckled aloud to myself. Hell, I did not understand how I knew it either, but deep inside my bones and beyond any doubt whatsoever, I knew it had happened.

At the sound of my ironic laughter, his expression changed from contrition to confusion.

"That's OK, Love, we forgive you," I said, instantly feeling the burden of a centuries-held resentment fall away. Taking his hand, I silently wondered at my unconscious choice of 'we.'

After completing the tour's segment for the impressive chamber holding the legislative portion of Colonial Williamsburg, we lunched at a reconstructed colonial tavern. Halving a bowl of Brunswick stew and an oyster sandwich, we planned on leaving space in our tummies for a shared piece of peanut pie. I enjoyed stew while Christopher ate half the sandwich before we swapped plates.

"Honey, when you asked yesterday about my restaurant, I was slow in answerin' you because I've been toyin' with the idea of doin' something different."

"Like what?" He asked before tasting his half of the stew.

"Like sellin' the business and doin' like Liz, manage property. I'm tired of conjurin' up potions—Damn, where did that phrase come from?" I asked myself aloud, not expecting an answer from either Christopher or me. I continued, "What I meant to say was that I'm tired of all that cookin' every day. Since Margaret's death, even with the redecoratin' and Joey comin' to help out, it's no picnic anymore. I could almost hate my life, except for you." To soften my words, I tenderly laid my hand atop his nearer thigh.

He considered my career change before asking, "What do you know about managing real estate?"

"Absolutely nothin'," I breezily replied, "but what I don't know, Liz can teach me. Hugh Ed would help, too. I know he would."

Again he was thoughtful before he said, "Well, if you're not happy, you need to do something about it."

Considering that exchange over, I changed the subject. "What do you think about headin' down to Carter's Grove this afternoon? They have recently unearthed one of the oldest English settlements right down from the big house." After that suggestion, I bit into my remaining portion of our sandwich to discover a hard object in with my bite.

Oops! There's something foreign in my mouth, I thought, and it's not bread and not oyster meat. Damn, I thought, I must have broken a tooth or lost a filling.

The expression on my face stopped Christopher in mid-thought. "What's wrong?" he asked.

I mumbled, "I think I broke somethin'." To isolate the offending object, my tongue searched through the bolus of food, taking a considerable amount of time and unlady-like effort. Although I had been schooled that it is not proper to look at offending objects that one retrieves from one's mouth at the dinner table, 'curiosity killed the cat.' Besides, I wanted to know if I needed to contact a dentist any time soon. I quickly popped a small white sphere the size of a peppercorn from my mouth into my palm.

Holding the offender between my fingers for closer examination, I exclaimed, "Now, would you look at that!"

The tiny, misshapen orb was not one of Mother Nature's best efforts at gem making, but it was still a pearl.

Taking sole credit, as if he were responsible for its appearance in my half of the oyster sandwich, Christopher stated matter-of-factly, "I hope this makes up for sending you to jail this morning. I didn't think roses could possibly get me out of the doghouse this time."

Upon hearing his offhand reference to our experience in Court this morning, I decided this might just be the time to tell about our past lives together. Clutching the small gem in the palm of my hand, I looked into his eyes before taking a deep breath.

Drawing strength from the mysterious appearance of the pearl, I began. "Honey, do you believe in reincarnation? And what would you say if I told you that you and I have been together before?"

He took a long sip of wine from his colonial reproduction stemware. After precisely placing the now-drained, sturdy shrub glass on the bare wood tabletop near his plate, he turned to face me. "I believe the concept is possible."

With that bit of encouragement, I slowly began to unravel what I knew of our history, starting with the information I gleaned at mother's family reunion and ending with the visions I had during this morning's mock trial. I spoke almost in a whisper. Christopher listened intently, making no comment. I paused in my telling only when our waiter made an appearance at our table. By the time I had finished, our empty dishes had been removed, and we faced two forks and one serving of pie.

"Well?" I cut into the dessert with my fork, awaiting his opinion of my recital.

"Rachael," he finally spoke, after swallowing his second forkful of pie, "there are events and things in this world I don't understand, and I will never understand." He continued slowly, "Our relationship being the major one. What you've just told me could be possible. I believe you consider it a reasonable explanation, and I believe that love is forever." Christopher placed the final piece of dessert on his fork. "What I do know for a fact, my dear Rachael, is that I look forward to being with you until my dying day." With that said, he ate the last of the pie.

Later, outside the palace walls, we strolled a side street that led to a recreated lumberyard. A heavy carriage clip-clopped past us. The speed of the matched Belgian bays was much slower than those Amish buggies that had trotted outside our bedroom windows that night not so long ago in Pennsylvania.

"Doesn't that remind you of Intercourse?" I asked in all innocence, referring to the town where we had stayed.

Suddenly, he swooped me up in a bear hug and swung me around in the street. "That's all I've been thinking about since this morning. Let's hurry back to our room."

That's not the 'intercourse' I had reference to, I thought, but it'll work.

⚜

I lay abed wondering: Why is making love in the afternoon so decadent? It's like one spangle too many on a singing cowboy's sequined jacket. Like one rose more than a dozen. Like chocolate syrup poured over two brownies sandwiched around a chocolate mousse center. Almost too rich. Almost too much. Almost too gaudy. Almost too sinful. Almost, but not quite.

I listened to Christopher happily singing in the shower. I would join him shortly. First, I needed to search out the remote control because I had to know how the pivotal game in Tennessee's football season was unfolding. I clicked on the television, surfing the unfamiliar channels until the correct school colors appeared on screen. The jovial broadcasters played at not playing favorites for our opponent. After much friendly banter that they, themselves, found amusing, one man announced the lopsided score.

"Damn," I muttered, "double damn."

After snapping off the set, I stomped into the bath and stepped into the shower.

"Honey," I said, grabbing the soap from him and vigorously lathering his back, "I'm glad I'm here with you in Virginia and not home havin' to watch us play Florida on national TV."

He commented wryly, "By the way you're scrubbing my back, I take it your team is losing."

"Big time." Working my way down to the back of his knees, I added, "That coach of theirs has our coach's number, just like you have mine."

※

I became aware of his warm body beside mine before opening my eyes to the gray light of a new dawn. This time of day was lovely because there were no brightly contrasting hues, only soft shades of gray. In just minutes, the sun would pop above the horizon. While thinking that this trip had been extraordinary, and, possibly, even the best yet, I shut my eyes and snuggled closer to Christopher.

Still half asleep, I gently reminded myself, I say that each time. I'm not ready for him to be gone. And I think that each time, too. Maybe, if I just lie here and don't move, the hands on the clock won't move either.

With that last thought, I drifted peacefully to sleep.

※

Awakened by his lips gently brushing my shoulder, I whispered, "Good morning, Love." I smiled blindly in his direction, unwilling to open my eyes.

As if he had always known where to touch and how to touch, Christopher ran his hands over my body, and my body responded to his commands as compliantly as a devoted slave to her lord and master. While making love this one last time, I could swear I heard time stand still.

"Rachael Taite!" he called out when we climaxed.

Afterwards, he lay quiet and exhausted while little thrills ran repeatedly throughout my body. He was still inside me when my body was rocked by one final wave of shudders.

"Sweet Mother," I exclaimed, "I feel like a car that needs its idle or somethin' adjusted."

"It's called dieseling," he explained.

He lazily reached across my body to turn the face of the clock radio toward him. "Damn, look at the time!" Christopher jumped out of bed, throwing clothes haphazardly into his suitcase. "We must leave now to reach Washington in time to catch my plane."

After checking both pieces of luggage with our carrier, we sped on foot through the Washington airport. Conveniently, our flights left from the same gate with my departure scheduled an hour after his. Arriving with only minutes available for one final drink together, we sat in the bar nearest our gate.

After checking our surroundings, I said, "Honey, I do believe this is the same bar we sat in the last time we flew out of here."

"Really?" After a brief look around, he said in agreement, "This does look familiar."

Before our drinks were presented, we went into our patented, safe nothing-talk.

"How's about Seattle, come May?" Christopher suddenly sprang the destination of our next meeting.

I nodded. "I've never been there. Sounds—"

After first call for his flight's boarding interrupted me, I realized how quickly time had flown since leaving our rumpled bed in Williamsburg. Ignoring that he must soon leave, he downed his beer and ordered another round each although I had a half glass of wine remaining. Even as tears filled my eyes, I willed them to stay put while I listened to him listing the highlights of our most recent trip. Before he mentioned the pearl episode, his flight's final boarding call was given, forcing Christopher to quickly finish his second beer.

"I'll be back," I called to the bartender. "Don't take away my wines."

Feeling like the condemned trodding their final steps, we headed to the doorway leading to his plane. Tenderly cupping my face between the palms of his hands, he passionately kissed me farewell. Too quickly, he was gone.

Puzzling as to the reason Christopher had publicly kissed me before boarding his flight, I stumbled back onto my barstool to finish the remaining wine in my first glass.

The attentive bartender walked over to me to remove my empty glass. Stopping to examine my face closely, he asked, "Weren't you two here a few years ago?"

After looking at him for a moment, I vaguely recalled his face and nodded. I sadly informed him, "Goodbyes haven't gotten any easier." My tears flowed as we chatted until new, thirsty travelers arrived, needing his services.

Left alone, I sat in that bar in that far away airport, wondering how Christopher and I, who try so hard to be anonymous, could be so easily remembered. Perhaps that woman, dining long ago in that San Francisco restaurant, was not the only outsider who sensed an aura about us whenever we were together.

Sixteen

Despite dreading the time now spent at Rachael's To Go, my days quickly settled into a comfortable rhythm when I returned from Williamsburg. Mondays through Saturdays I rushed between the kitchen and the counter. Come Sundays, I relaxed within the cabin. Life was not what I had once thought it would be. Given my options, on the other hand, life had been good. When I had the time to reflect, Christopher Saracini still remained my heart's most favorite desire.

Mementos from our travels were tucked discreetly in plain view at my house and cabin. Yet, without a map, no item especially stood out. An ornate, wooden box holding his cards and notes stayed under a stack of books on the night table by my bed. His first roses stood in the antique milk glass vase residing in a dark recess of the bookshelf in my living room. His toothbrush hung alongside mine in the cabin's bathroom in the off chance that he would return some day to use it. Residing on the cabin's coffee table, treasured knickyknacks were nestled together in a basket woven from Charleston sweet grass.

Even an early picture of Christopher, framed by a hazardous tangle of special orders, grinned from the bulletin board at work.

Lying in bed one night, I considered how the past ten years had glided by at the speed of a silk top sheet sliding off a rumpled bed. I quickly calculated we had six more years before he retired from his job and from me. Only three, if he took early retirement.

Sweet Mother, don't let him take early retirement.

✻

"Mom, quick! Turn to Channel 20."

I had seen the offbeat western, starring Charles Bronson and Jill Ireland, years earlier while channel surfing during a long, sleep-chasing night. I needed Mom to catch the unfolding storyline so that we could discuss it later.

We often watched TV together on separate sets in different houses.

Not wanting to miss any more of the movie than I already had, I hastily hung up the phone.

From Noon Till Three was not an epic of titanic proportions, but a priceless, satirical ditty pointing out the differences between male and female attitudes toward unsanctioned sex. For the hero, intercourse had been merely a biological itch that needed scratching. The heroine, perversely, had romanticized their three-hour relationship into a bodice-ripping novel, a nationally popular song, numerous trite souvenirs and an accompanying theme park. Even the most obtuse viewer could see that her embroidered memories, the basis for the heroine's hugely successful financial empire, were so much greater than what their physical couplings had been.

When the film's credits rolled, I was left with a troubled mind. If a movie happened to be made about Christopher and me, would I be like Jill Ireland's character, failing to recognize my lover when he finally returned because he was not as tall or as handsome in real life as my mind had him pictured? And upon seeing my sweet darling again, would the identification of that singular member of his anatomy that my body unerringly recognized lead to a similar ending?

Immediately, my phone rang. Knowing the caller would be Mom, I answered by asking, "What did you think?"

"What a delicious story!" Mom continued, "Wasn't that scene with the judge when Bronson was dressed like the dentist just too hilarious?"

"Yes," I snorted in agreement. "Didn't that banner with Graham Dorsey holdin' Amanda Starbuck in a passionate embrace remind you a little of that Rhett and Scarlett coffee cup I have?"

Mother and I chortled gleefully. A moment later, she softly commented, "But, Rachael, that story's not at all like you and Christopher. I saw how he looked at you over lunch in San Francisco."

Soberly, I replied, "Thanks, Mom, I needed to hear that."

Although I had never considered that we were simply fuck-buddies, my heart was reassured that neither had Mom.

♦

Passionately, I ranted to the kitchen ceiling, "Take me now!" before muttering a menacing, "If I ever have to make another caramel cake . . . "

Dicing celery, Joey stopped his knife in mid-stroke to look in my direction.

A wide-eyed Liz leaned through the gaping, chest-high opening connecting the counter in front to the kitchen in back where Joey and I toiled. Staring at me, she said nothing at first before scolding, "Rachael, it's a good thing no one is here but me and Joey to hear you."

I stormed, "Oh, Liz, Joey, I can't do this any longer. I've tried. Sweet Mother, how I have tried, but it's just no fun anymore."

Putting his knife down, Joey started undoing his bib-apron in preparation to leave.

Seeing him taking my outburst so literally, I forced a laugh. "No, Joey, stay. I won't be closin' down immediately. We'll keep goin' until I find some profitable way out, and you and Liz are taken care of."

"Don't worry about me," Liz replied indignantly. "I'm fine. My properties keep me and Hugh Ed much too busy. I'll be happy to leave whenever you're ready to cut out. Although right now, after that outburst, I could become worried about you."

After hearing her sentiments, I smiled my gratitude while Joey busied his hands by retying his apron strings.

"Glad to hear that, Miz Rachael. Thank you," he added, "I'll stay on, too." He went back to the celery as if my outcry had never happened.

"Just what are you thinkin' about doin'?" Liz questioned firmly.

Before I could answer, the bell on the front door tinkled, announcing a customer, and Liz returned to the front counter. Soon afterwards, a steady jingling of the little bell accompanied the lunch rush. Joey and I worked speedily to fill the orders as rapidly as Liz placed them up.

Just another typical day in the mundane world of Rachael JubelleLee Taite, I ruefully mused, while she pines for the Romance of her life.

Later in the afternoon, just before our three o'clock closing, Liz called, "Rachael, can you come out front? There's someone askin' for you."

I dried my hands before pushing loose hair back to place behind my ears. When I came through the doorway, I found an older, slightly thicker Joe Bill standing by the plastic-wrapped pumpkin muffins. Seeing the changes that had taken place in his physique since 1989, I was reminded of the subtle alterations to body mass that age and hormones create in a tomcat as that feline matures.

"Well, hey," I greeted him. "How are you?"

As he smiled, his wonderful green eyes crinkled in greeting. I was pleased they had not changed with the years.

"Hi, Rachael. I'm good. And you?"

"Fine. What brings you to town?" I asked as another customer walked in the door. I nodded toward Liz. "Liz?"

She responded, "I'll take care of her."

Joe Bill said, "My dad is having some minor heart surgery in the morning. I'll be here a few days. How about I'll call and we'll have dinner later?"

"I'd like that. What hospital will your dad be in?"

"University Hospital."

"Have you had lunch yet?"

"Yes. My folks sent me here to get a half of a hummingbird cake to bring home for supper," he chuckled before adding, "if I wanted back into the house."

"Joey," I called over my shoulder to the kitchen, "cut that fresh hummer and wrap half of it to go out now."

While Joey prepared the carry-out order and Joe Bill and I chatted, I noticed that the last customer through the door leaned against the counter, waiting patiently. Liz was missing from the front. Hearing footsteps overhead, I decided she must have gone upstairs to replenish our stash of carry-out cake boxes in the kitchen.

After Joe Bill walked away with his boxed cake in hand, I turned to the petite young woman to ask, "Is Liz gettin' you taken care of?"

"No, Miss Rachael, she isn't. I really came to talk with you."

She had a little girl's soft, shy voice that was charming. But jaded by experience, I wondered what this stranger was selling. Dressed in expensive clothing, her hair artfully salon-streaked and casually styled, and wearing enough square-cut diamonds on her wedding finger to discourage all but the most ardent unsuitable suitors, the petite woman was a studied example of fine, Southern, feminine eye candy. If she were dressed that well to make a business call, I decided in advance we could not afford what she was rep-ing.

"OK," I addressed the young woman, waiting for her to start her spiel, "you've got my undivided attention."

To jumpstart herself, she cleared her throat once. "I'm Jackson's wife. You know, Miss Clyda's nephew."

I nodded that I knew who she was, even though I had never met Jackson face-to-face. As fragile as the young woman appeared, I wondered how she stood up to Miss Clyda and immediately understood why any man would allow her a do-over, no matter her transgression.

"I overheard Miss Clyda tellin' Jackson that you might be interested in franchisin'. I wanted to make sure to let you know, in person, that I want that first franchise." Even though her statement sounded well rehearsed, she was tentative in her delivery.

"Honey," I started, but changed the direction of my conversation. "By the way, what is your name?" The young woman had dutifully listed her pedigree, a time-honored Southern requirement, but I still had no idea as to her given name.

"Sydney," she answered quietly, almost whispering.

"Well, Sydney, I've no plans to franchise. I'm thinkin' more about sellin' outright."

I watched as the girl drew in a deep breath and stepped up to the plate to proclaim in one breath, "Well then, Miss Rachael, I'll buy you out." Taken aback by her own sudden boldness, she exhaled, looking surprised. Regaining her composure, she said more slowly, "You and Jackson can figure out the details and the price later."

"Sydney, Honey, you don't know what you're gettin' yourself into." I attempted to dissuade her.

"Miss Rachael," she explained patiently, "my husband is a very busy man. Some days, he doesn't have enough time for me, and I get bored too easily." Ever so slightly, she leaned over to me, confiding solemnly, "If I get bored, I get into trouble." She straightened up to complete her presentation. "I figure a place like this would keep me occupied enough to keep me out of trouble."

She sounded most sincere pleading her case, but knowing what I knew about Christopher and me, I hooted, "Baby Girl, you'll have to keep your own self out of trouble! But, if you want this place and if Jackson and I can work out the details, it's yours. You'll need Joey to help run the place for you. Liz and I will be around should you need us."

We smiled at each other. With both of us knowing the transfer of ownership was a done deal, we hugged. Whereas gentlemen firmly shake hands to seal business dealings, women who were properly schooled in Southern ways prefer to hug chastely.

◈

Christopher had just finished his telephone family update and I was about to give mine, when he interrupted by saying, "Rachael, I've been thinking about what you said about past lives."

"Oh?" My curiosity was piqued.

"I won't rule out that possibility." He paused for several seconds before continuing, "I must love you enough that it takes more than one lifetime to show you how much."

A continent separated us, yet the distance was not great enough to prevent my hearing the slight break in his voice when he spoke that last sentence. "Sweet Mother," I whispered, realizing he now accepted the depth of our relationship. Tender emotions swept through me, and tears streamed uncontrollably down my cheeks. With my throat tightening, I managed to say, "Christopher, did I ever thank you for what you did for me in Baltimore after Margaret died? By holdin' me in your arms, you made me feel I finally belonged. You made me whole."

"My dear, sweet Rachael, no one can make you feel like you belong or make you whole," he earnestly protested.

While thinking over his comments, I realized his voice had sounded tired from the very onset of our conversation. "Are you feelin' OK, Honey?" I asked, changing the subject. "You don't sound like your usual self."

"I've not felt like running the last couple of mornings. I don't seem to have as much energy as usual, but I'm fine, I guess," he off-handedly answered.

"Take care of yourself, Love. I need you with me always." Returning to our previous topic, I said, "You're right. I control me but," purposely dragging out that one-syllable word into two as only a

Southerner can, I added, "figuratively speakin' you held me in a safe place, allowin' me the space to heal. I want you to know how very different, how very much better, my life has been because of you."

"OK, you're welcome."

"Blood, Sweat And Tears got it right when they sang: *I'm so glad you came into my life.* I couldn't have gotten my pieces parts together without you."

His tone shifted, signaling our conversation was ending. "Speaking of people coming into your life, I have a call waiting. Give us a kiss. I'll be with you soon."

<hr />

On the plane to Seattle, I sat passively while the miles and minutes flew by. Even with all the time and distance that had to tick off until we were together, I felt Christopher close by my side. I could hardly wait to tell the good news about an office building on Concord Street that had recently come up for sale. I glanced down at my watch. With his knowledgeable eye, Hugh Ed was looking the structure over for me this very hour. When I returned to the restaurant on Monday, he would bring his recommendations and he, Liz and I would then discuss if this building would become the ticket to my new future.

After deplaning, I had over an hour to kill before Christopher's scheduled arrival. I walked the concourses, exercising my legs after my long, cross-country sit, before settling down with a cup of hot chocolate to reread Keyes' *Senator Marlowe's Daughter.* For some reason, stories with ill-fated romances attracted me.

Phrases of an announcement floated into my consciousness, ". . . service desk. Passenger Rachael Taite, please come to—"

Damn, now what all could that be about?

Gathering my few possessions, I rolled my luggage over to the airline's nearest passenger assistance desk. When the jacketed agent glanced away from his computer, I said, "I'm Rachael Taite. I was just paged."

"Yes, Mrs. Taite. Just a minute while I look it up." He efficiently tapped a few keys on the keyboard in front of him.

I watched his impassive, squared face. I hated when someone assumed that because I was over fifty, I was a married woman. What if I were a physician? I would be truly indignant if, after having spent all that time and all that money, people called me 'Mrs.' instead of 'Dr.' Upon remembering the bastardized greeting used by some in my part of the country, I realized his greeting could have been worse. He could have addressed me as 'Miz-riz Taite.' Considering things could always be worse, I smiled.

As I waited for a response to his electronic inquiry, I watched his dark eyes dart over the screen.

"You need to call your mother," the agent finally informed me.

I frowned, wondering why she would call. Could something have happened to the restaurant or to the girls?

"Where's the nearest phone?"

Not wasting words on verbal directions, the agent pointed to a bank of telephones lined in readiness against the far wall. I rolled my suitcase to the nearest phone. After dialing my home, I needed to wait only one ring before Mom answered. Instantly, I knew she must have been sitting by the phone for my call.

"Hey, Mom, what's goin' on?" I asked cheerfully, wanting to pretend nothing could spoil my coming weekend.

"Oh, Rachael." Her greeting was not her usual 'Rachael, Darlin,' and her voice sounded strained. "Honey, a man called and said you needed to call him."

I heard her words. At the same time, I was acutely aware there was something she was not telling me. "Was it Christopher?" I asked.

"He didn't say. He just gave this number." Her voice remained oddly tight, not its usual lilting, enticing drawl.

"What's wrong, Mom?"

She was insistent. "Rachael, I'm fine, but you must call this number." She began dictating, "Area code—"

"Wait! Hold your horses!" I fumbled with the zippers on my fanny pack to retrieve the items I needed. "Let me get a pen and something to write on." I easily found my Cross ballpoint. When paper eluded me, I removed the folder holding my return plane ticket. "OK, I'm ready." I copied down the number, asking her to repeat it a second time. I recognized the area code as Christopher's. Needing Mom's assurance that everything back home was fine, despite the sound of her voice, I chatted a bit longer before we hung up.

Reluctantly, I dialed the scribbled down number. After ten unanswered rings, I was about ready to terminate the call. With the eleventh ring, someone picked up the phone.

"Hello?" The accent was similar, but it was not my beloved's voice I heard. I felt relieved momentarily.

"Hey," I answered quickly. "I was told to call this number."

"Rachael?"

"Yes," I responded hesitantly. Still unable to place the male voice even though it sounded vaguely familiar, I felt dread, like a heavy mountain mist, closing in on me.

"Do you remember me? We met years ago on LeContie. I'm Carl."

"Oh, Mother God, no!" I breathed out softly, leaning against the telephone's unforgiving cold metal shape, seeking some needed support.

Intuitively I knew, without any additional words, the reason for his call. Needing only one question answered, I managed to ask, "Was he alone? Was Christopher alone when it happened?"

"No," he replied, "Sophia was with him. She had just . . ."

I did not hear much else he said. His words entered my skull through my left ear, but they got caught up in some neural eddy, swirling inside my head, before my brain was able to process their sounds into a decipherable awareness. Something about a massive heart attack this morning. Something about a promise he had made to Christopher on the flight back from Tennessee.

As my knees slowly buckled and gave way, I silently offered up my appreciation, Thank you, Mother, he was not alone.

Gut-punched by the enormity of the terrible news, I crumpled the remaining distance to the carpeting.

Sweet Mother, I must have known somehow back in Nashville that this call would be necessary.

With every cell in my body screaming with anguish at our loss, the emotional pain I felt was so much worse than the physical pain I had experienced with the ruptured disc.

A horrific picture of a once homeless cat, now trapped in a laboratory cage, with wires attached to her shaved head came to mind. As divorced from the sufferings displayed by my subject as any researcher methodically studying pain perception in humans by stimulating electrodes implanted in feline brains, I measured my body's response elicited by the news of Christopher's death. Scientifically intrigued, I dispassionately discovered that, in dealing with this exquisite form of torture, my mind had escaped to some safe plane, leaving my poor, defenseless body no way to flee.

I next focused my concentration on masculine, black leather shoes and cuffed black twill trousers that mysteriously appeared within my sight. After noticing the heavy shoes appeared freshly polished, I decided the man owned no pets because there were no stray hairs adorning the dark fabric of his pants. Critically, I judged the creases down the front of his pant legs to be nowhere as crisp as those in Hugh Ed's jeans.

"Mrs. Taite! Mrs. Taite!"

Faintly, I heard a familiar name being called, the sound coming from far above my head. My eyes followed the inferior crease-line up the left trouser leg to an outstretched male hand. I slowly looked farther to discover the anxious face of the airline's customer service rep who had me call to get my bad tidings. While wondering if he had any idea of the pain he had helped cause, I considered which guard I would order to kill the bearer of such terrible news. I watched his mouth move and considered telling the man he should purchase a bleaching kit for his stained teeth. Seconds later, the meanings associated with his vocalizations reached my brain.

"Mrs. Taite, are you all right? Can you stand? What can I do?"

Why doesn't Mom answer his questions? Decisions, decisions, Sweet Mother, how I hate decisions. I don't care what he does. I don't want to do anything.

I heard Christopher lovingly instruct, "The only thing you have to do, my dear Rachael, is breathe."

Taking a deep breath that seemed to be my first in some time, I placed the folder containing my tickets in the opened hand before me. Through the darkness of my misery, I begged in a frightened child's voice, "Home. Please, I want to go home."

After taking my tickets, the agent placed the dangling receiver to his ear. "Yes." He paused to listen. "Yes." He waited again. "Yes, I'll tell her."

I watched the stocky man return the phone to its cradle before he laboriously lowered his bulk to kneel in front of me. "Mrs. Taite, Carl said to tell you that Christopher simply stood up and then dropped to the floor, dead. He wanted you to know that Christopher didn't suffer."

I nodded that I had heard his words. My response seemed to relieve him, yet I felt little comforted by them.

※

I, who trusted only one man, had to rely on the kindnesses of strangers, like Tennessee Williams' poor Blanche, on my flight home. The return trip seemed the longest of my life. It also seemed the shortest. Surrounded by the aroma of leather and the cushioned comfort of first class, I sat while whispering flight attendants hovered nearby, supplying me with tissues and protecting me, as much as possible, from the stares of passing passengers.

Averting my gaze into the nothingness view provided by cottony gray clouds through which the plane flew, I attempted to sort out my thoughts and drank Virgin Marys, fighting hard to hold myself together. This was a future I had never anticipated encountering. Me, living out my life in Tennessee and Christopher's body, decaying away in California. His children would never know their father was not a stodgy old man. I would have continued sharing him with his family and his work. I had never demanded all or nothing. Now, we all had nothing.

Sighing, I gingerly blew my now raw nose while musing, What a bitch of an ending. So, why had all these years and trips happened? I'll never have the chance to hold him again.

Countering, my mind reasoned, I was offered the opportunity. I ran with it and made the most of the time we had.

Those two sentences sounded as generically genuine as those of a beaten football coach, giving an interview after losing the SEC championship game. I would have snorted in disgust at the triteness of my response, but my nose was clogged.

Oh, great! That means the sum of my years on this earth can be distilled into only thirty-five days. What about all those one hundred and twenty years Mom always talks about? I should have never gone to Nashville. I should have stuck with my resolve in Ogunquit and left him there.

But had it ended then, an alternative line of reasoning offered, I would have never learned how it felt to be secure and safe.

But, the argument within my head continued, I hurt too much now. I want more time with Christopher.

This is all you got, this time around. Now, Baby Girl, deal with it!

❦

During a short layover in Atlanta, I phoned ahead to tell Mom the time of my arrival in Knoxville later that evening. Before ending my call, I added, almost as an afterthought, "Oh, Mom, I hurt all over."

I knew she understood. Having lost the love of her life, she knew firsthand the smoldering devastation that remains in death's aftermath and through which survivors must sift.

"I know, Darlin'," she said. "I hurt for you. Carl told me what had happened, but I could not bring myself to be the bearer of bad news." She changed the subject before we both became too overcome with emotion. "When you're safely home, I'll tuck you into bed."

When I sleepwalked off the plane into Mom and Liz's outstretched arms, I momentarily regretted not telling Mom I had planned to drive to the cabin as soon as I collected my suitcase. Just as quickly, however, I became deeply grateful for their protection.

Allowing them to assume charge of my care, I relinquished all decision making to the two women I knew well. Staying as close as human shields protecting a head of state from possible snipers, they steered me toward the area to retrieve my single piece of luggage. After wondering for the hundredth time how my hurt-swollen heart would ever heal, I shut my eyes during the drive along Alcoa Highway north to Knoxville, finally able to will my mind to be silent.

Mom and Liz followed me upstairs to my bedroom. Softly mewing their unusually reserved greetings, Sybyl and Beatrice sat expectantly on my bed.

I stripped, leaving clothes in a heap on the floor beside my customary far side of the mattress. Pulling back the bedcovers, I collapsed onto the bed. Before rolling over onto my right side, I covered my entire body with the top sheet.

"Liz, you can go on home now," Mom said. "I'll stay the night here."

I felt a paw tapping near my hidden head, insisting that I raise the sheet to make room for a companion. After I elevated the fabric with my left elbow to provide an opening, two cats slinked under my raised arm to nestle their warm bodies against mine.

Touching my shoulder, Mom said, "Rachael, Darlin'."

I peeked from my hidey-hole. She removed my glasses before tenderly brushing back my long hair from around my face. Not giving name to the cause, we searched deep into each other's eyes, wordlessly sharing each other's grief.

"I'll just rest over here on the faintin' couch," she said at last.

I retreated once more into the cocoon of bedding. Through the covers, I listened as she picked up my clothes to put them away. When I heard her finally relax upon the recliner near my bed, I mumbled, "Thanks, Mom."

"You don't need to be alone these first few hours." She continued, "Darlin', I remember how you stayed with me that first night after your daddy died."

Afterwards, as I lay awake with agonizing thoughts, Mom maintained sentry duty until she fell asleep. I decided I would never go to California to mourn. Since I had never driven by his residence while he was alive, I saw no reason to seek out his grave now that he was dead. Long ago I had accepted it was not just the 'tween-the-sheets attraction that kept me wanting Christopher near, because if we had been only sex-mates, our relationship would have never lasted much beyond Eureka. Now, with him gone, where will be my Romance? Who would make me smile?

Wallowing in my pain and loss, I wanted to rant, beating my arms and legs against the mattress, but neither did I want to wake up my mother nor disturb my cats. No one slept well my first night home. Surrounded by maternal and feline snoring, I dozed fitfully. At dawn, I was awakened by muffled mews as my cats talked in their restless sleep.

Whereas Miss Scarlett had her Tara in the Georgian countryside, I had my cabin in the foothills near Townsend. After breakfast Saturday, I took the girls to search for sanctuary there.

Of all the places where Christopher and I had shared time, this was the only one close. Here, I could touch the items he had touched. Outside was the swing where we had sat. Over there was the radio to whose music we had danced. We had kissed and explored each other's bodies on this couch. I could hold the toothbrush he once used.

The Charleston sweet grass basket he gave me usually sat beside the couch, but all morning I sat cross-legged on the floor, silently mourning and cradling the plunder that it held. Sybyl and Beatrice perched on the couch's arm near my bowed head.

A rock I picked up at that New England quarry. A small piece of driftwood he had handed me as we strolled along the beach above

Arcata. A brass hedgehog he bought me in the Cotswolds. A shell shard gathered from sands at Daytona Beach. Each item verified that he had truly been with me. I held the basket close for the small comfort it afforded.

In the afternoon I went outside to the porch, devoting more time to the nurturing of the anguish caused by his death. Remaining at attention behind the kitchen window, the girls watched over me while I sat on the swing, staring at the glistening water rushing by but finding no beauty there.

Later, when maddened by grief I paced through the cabin's interior, my four-legged girls kept clear of me, padding behind at a respectful distance, yet never allowing me out of their sight. To silence the audible signs of my pain, I screamed into a pillow because true Southern women do not care to disturb neighbors with their loud keening. My furry companions crouched close by when finally I slumped, pitiful and spent, to the floor.

Hours later when I lay on Christopher's side of the mattress, staring at the ceiling to search for answers that never materialized, the girls padded into the bedroom, joining me on the bed. Posing as Siamese sphinxes to protect me, their wise blue eyes never closed. With their chests rumbling with purrs, Sybyl and Beatrice sang to me all the ancient songs of comfort they knew.

Mom called several times but otherwise left me alone to grieve. She had been there and had faced some of the demons I battled, but not all. Aware that I would honor all he had done for me after Margaret's death, I fought hard to keep my pieces parts together. When the worst came and slowly passed, I discovered I had succeeded in maintaining the whole.

<hr>

As Sunday morning dawned, I found I had not perished but had, in fact, survived the black night only to face another long day. Thinking that the return flight from the Coast had been easy by comparison, because then I had remained stunned by the suddenness of the news, I now sported raw sores, leaking primitive emotions. After my initial numbness had worn off, the ooze had seemingly increased in intensity each passing hour. I was left wondering how the wounds would ever close.

Being a dutiful daughter, I phoned Mom. "Hey," I said when she answered. "Sorry if I woke you."

"No, Darlin'," she lied. I knew she lied by the thick sound of her sleepy voice. "I was awake. What time is it, anyway?"

I walked around the low bookcase until I saw the clock on the kitchen wall. "About five. I'm goin' for a hike after I feed the girls. Maybe I can think better on the trail. Call Liz and tell her I'll see her at work Monday."

"Liz said for you not to worry about the restaurant," she quickly reminded me. "She and Joey can take care of things. I don't like that you'll be hikin' alone."

I brushed aside her parental concerns. "I'll be fine. I'm just goin' up to the Bluff. It's Sunday. The trail will be crawlin' with day hikers."

The phone line was crowded with unsaid words between us. At long last, she said, "OK, but be careful. Don't talk to strange men."

"Don't worry, I won't. Remember that's what got me into this mess, Mom," I joked, tears accompanying my bitter laugh, leaving me to wonder how it was possible I had any tears left to shed.

"I'm sorry, Rachael. I shouldn't have said that. Darlin', just be careful. Don't let anything bad happen to you. I love you."

"I love you, too, Mom."

I drove the winding road from Sunshine to the crowded, double parking lots for Alum Bluff Trail. Once there, I could not bring myself to open my door. Waiting thirty minutes inside the car after shutting off the engine, I reluctantly cranked the motor, returning to the cabin to find the girls asleep on my bed where I had left them that morning.

"All right, ladies, it's time to get on with our lives," I announced, gathering a limp body on each shoulder to carry them to the waiting car.

Standing in front of my bathroom mirror Sunday night, I examined my face for an outward sign of my grief. Except for frog-eyes and a mouth that had forgotten how to smile, I looked no different from how I had Thursday morning before Christopher's death.

"This won't do," I muttered before marching downstairs to the kitchen.

Upon resuming my stance in the bathroom, I placed the current year's Williamsburg dishtowel calendar over the sink and used kitchen shears to lop off my long hair. Recalling how he had loved running his fingers through my hair and twisting kiss curls in the short tendrils that always escaped being caught up into a bun, I had decided not to allow another the opportunity to participate in that pastime. Staring into the mirror, I surveyed the disastrous results, musing that a blind hairdresser, strung out on bad drugs, would have done a neater job. Still, I did not care because now I looked the part, joining the ranks of the Ancients mourning the loss of their men.

Folding the linen so as not to lose a single strand of hair, I returned to the kitchen and took down a certain wine flute that rested in the back of my cabinet, carefully placing it within the folds of linen. After locating a shovel in the basement, I carried the gathered items outside. Walking the yard, I searched for a special place before stopping in front of a gangly, spindly native shrub.

"This is it," I announced aloud, gently putting the folded towel aside.

I began digging. When the dimensions of the shallow hole met with my approval, I placed the special bundle reverently against the dark, rich soil before stepping firmly on the cloth packet, enjoying the oddly satisfying sound of the fragile glass shattering under my weight. After lifting shovelfuls of soil back to place, I tamped the ground, covering the fresh scar with old leaf litter.

Feeling the proper rituals had now been observed, I turned my back on the hearts-abustin'-with-love bush, going inside to bathe my body for the first time since Wednesday night. In my wake, the night creatures were silent.

❦

Monday morning found me at work mixing batter for lemon squares, simply because I did not know any other way to heal except by performing mundane tasks. Life was supposed to go on. As a matter of fact, life was going to go on whether I joined it or not.

Liz entered the kitchen through the back door. Not expecting to find me so far into preps this early nor anticipating the change in my appearance, she dropped her purse onto the floor at the shock of seeing me.

"Oh . . . my . . . God!" she gasped. "Your hair!"

Looking away from the contents in the mixer, I glared at her defiantly. "I don't want long hair anymore!" I barked out.

Saying nothing in response, she left the kitchen for the front of the restaurant. In a few minutes, she returned. After retrieving her dropped purse, she inquired softly, "What do you want me to tell the customers when they ask about the door?"

She referred to the three white roses on a bed of fern fronds, bound by black ribbon tied in a simple bow, that I had cobbled together at Kroger's and hung across the glass of our front entry as soon as I had gotten to work.

I snapped loudly, "Tell them I died!"

Taking a just-done cake out of the oven, I allowed the door to slam shut. The sound matched my mood. Liz patiently waited for a more reasonable answer to her question while I rested the hot rectangular pan on a large cooling rack.

Since she was not the cause of my pain, I felt remorse for my unreasonable outbursts to her reasonable questions. My voice was kinder when I next spoke.

"No, just tell them there's been a death in the family."

Joey breezed through the back door. He stopped in mid-stride when he saw my head. "Good God! Who had aholt of those scissors?"

Liz shook her head, hoping to warn him not to tread any closer to the subject. Catching her signal, he said no more. She walked to him. Lifting the baseball cap from his head, she firmly pushed it down on mine.

"There." Liz kindly suggested, "Now keep this on and stay in the kitchen. You'll scare our customers otherwise. I'll call my hairdresser as soon as his shop opens."

After pulling the uncomfortable cap off my head, I regarded it closely. "Liz, I can't wear this thing."

"And why not?" she asked.

Joey was indignant. "Miz Rachael, I don't have no head cooties!"

I stared at him before looking in her direction. I again studied the cap before replying, "It won't fit. My head is bigger than Joey's."

She jerked the cap from my hands and gave it back to Joey. "Here, fix the damn thing!"

As he fiddled with the back strap on his baseball cap, I said, "I still can't wear it."

"And why not this time?" Liz demanded, having lost her patience with me.

Although I was close to stepping on her last nerve, I could not stop myself. "Damn, Liz, look at the thing. It says 'Gators' on the front." I pointed to the obvious. "You can't expect me to wear a cap that says 'Gators.'"

Ripping the offending cap out of Joey's hands before he had completed his task, Liz crammed it on my head, pulling the cap downward until it covered my face and precariously hung from my forehead. She stormed, "Play pretty or I won't call Roy's shop at all!"

I remained motionless until gravity pulled the cap from my face, revealing a half-smile. Upon seeing my expression, their strained faces broke into smiles, too.

"Oh, Rachael, for a while there I was beginning to think your sense of humor had died, too. I know this has been a bad weekend, but it will get better." She walked over to hug me.

"What happened?" Joey asked. "I'm out of the loop here."

Making no effort to respond to his question, I waited for Liz to answer.

"Why do I always have to tell the bad stories?" she half-heartedly complained, when she realized I would not answer.

"Because," I truthfully explained, "if you tell them for me, Lizzie-Lou, then it's like they happened to someone else. Not to me."

Releasing me, she sighed, accepting her undesired role as narrator. "Joey, come help me out front while I fill you in. Rachael has already lived this once."

❦

One of the many advantages of no longer being a teenager is being able to tell your mother you are going somewhere with a friend and she does not ask for minute details, such as who is the friend, who are their parents, what does their daddy do for a living, where do they live and what exactly will the two of you be doing, before she informs you what time you will be back.

I enjoyed that benefit once more when the third weekend of May rolled around for my annual hike up LeConte, and I did not want company. Lying, I told Mom that Liz was coming along. After I asked Liz not to answer her phone until late Saturday afternoon, in case Mom called her by mistake or to check up on my whereabouts, Liz handed me her cell phone, suggesting I call if an emergency arose.

That Friday morning, I began my customary preparations for the hike. Even with a few minor revisions in The Ritual, such as having no hiking buddy and packing one battery-operated phone, the number of beads in the amended Rosary almost totaled the same.

Except for a shadowy figure that strode out ahead, barely out of my sight, I enjoyed a solitary march to the Lodge. Really, I found it not that much different from our last hike in the Cotswolds. Whenever I stopped along the trail to share the views, I continued the litany of our times together, conversing aloud with the man who was not there, but who was always there with me.

At Gracie's Pulpit, I rested, snacking on roasted, salted sunflower seeds. While gazing toward the brow of the mountain that I knew to be Cliff Top, I felt a cool breeze run through my short hair, bringing with it the cherished memory of fingers playing with kiss curls.

My eyes prickled with tears as I told my absent companion, "Christopher, Honey, we had a damn good ride. Better than most people could ever dream of having. I wouldn't have missed knowing you for the world. But Sweet Mother, it's just no fun without you."

Sadly, I recalled reading the heart-wrenching ending for Sally Hemmings and her secret lover. She had the misfortune to watch her virile Thomas waste away, becoming a dotty, senile, old man.

My mind conjured up pathetic images of poor Sally gently wiping foamy spittle from the creased corner of Jefferson's slack mouth and kindly suggesting a change of trousers when careless urine spots dampened the front of the pair he currently wore. Aching with the emptiness of my sorrow and at the same time laughing at those pitiful scenarios my imagination had painted, I wept quietly, knowing full well that Christopher and I would never share similar, unfortunate situations. We would never grow old. He was dead, and I teased about a nonexistent oil painting, tucked away in a closet that aged for me. Allowing tears to dry on my face, I continued my lonely journey to the top of LeConte, holding on to the comforting thought that cabin number four and hot chocolate awaited my arrival.

That evening while sitting off to myself amidst swirling, heavy clouds that never parted during sunset at Cliff Top, I became even more desolate because in three hours, one less pair of blue eyes in California would be watching the same sun go down. I stayed on the mountain's peak until the clouds cleared and the moon rose before making my solitary return to the Lodge.

That night as I slept fitfully, cradled inside the snug walls of the rustic cabin, Christopher came to me in a dream.

Passing under a thick canopy of Frazier firs, together we walked the old way to Cliff Top. Our boots made no noise against the slate gray stones and the wind, blowing up from the deep valleys in Carolina, made no sound as it moved through the rhododendrons and fir boughs. Only his voice supplied my dream with sound.

"Rachael," Christopher told me as we walked, "we will be together again."

Later, sitting on the rocky ledge with our feet dangling over into the vast openness below, I felt his fingers run through my cropped hair yet my body did not feel the cold sharp stone I sat upon. Leaning against each other's body for support, we shared the most dazzling show of colors any sunset could provide.

As the blue of the sky ignited to burn yellow-orange above distant mountain ridges, the sun became a huge sphere, the color of the flesh of a blood orange, before easing below the horizon. When at last the day's dying glow faded and our pinpoint position on the earth inched degrees to the east, away from the light-giving sun, mists settled over the ridges below us changing the emerald greens to mauves, slate blues and smoky navy blues. The juncture, where the earth and the heavens met, gradually became a mossy green that blended to turquoise overhead, then became a rich, dark teal blue to contrast with the risen silvery moon.

"This time of day, the very moment the sky becomes green, reminds me of your eyes," Christopher said. Moments later, he chuckled. Pulling me closer to kiss the top of my head, he teased, "You may change your hair, but you can't alter your changeable eyes. I've always loved watching them go from blue to green when we kiss. I noticed that change our first night at your cabin."

In my dream, I did not waste our precious time together by arguing that my eyes were blue.

With the sun rising over the eastern-most peak of the mountain, I awoke with a renewed feeling of peace. As the brilliant dawn's rosy-golden light spilled into the cabin, I felt the length of Christopher's body resting next to mine and realized this man had never failed me.

Even though he never physically arrived in Seattle, his intent was to be there. He simply had no control over the timing of his death.

I recalled that during our last telephone conversation, he had said we would be together again, and so we had. I felt him near in the plane as I flew west that morning, and he was at my side when I learned of his passing. He was here with me now, and I, who had trusted no man but him, would continue trusting in him.

Luxuriating in the intoxicating sensation that my lover's body was once again close to mine, I was afraid to move for fear of losing his nearness. Minutes passed before the thought came to me that Christopher would never leave me as long as I needed him. At the very instant that my heart acknowledged that truth, I felt too greedy, almost embarrassed by the weakness shown by my strong desire to keep him with me. Compelled by a wellspring of emotion deeper than my childish wish to keep my love close, I accepted the time had come to grant him leave to go.

"Christopher," I directed my words to the coolness nestled against my back, "if you are stayin' because you think I can't make it without you, please, my love, don't worry. You mentored me well. I will be fine."

Mere moments passed before I felt only the smooth cotton sheeting resting upon my back. Realizing I was now alone in the small cabin, I was truly fine because we had shared the last, best sunset together.

I locked the front door of the restaurant for the final time as its owner. Come Monday, the business would legally belong to Sydney, and when I came to work that next week, it would be as a consultant helping with the transition. I slowly wandered back to the kitchen where Liz busily wrapped up the few items that had not sold, divvying them up into three stacks. I heard Joey plundering overhead through the stored, non-perishable foodstuffs. I went to put the keys by my purse, but it was nowhere in sight.

"Liz, this has been a day full of surprises," I announced to my faithful friend. "I could hardly wait for the last customer to leave. You won't believe who came by! My dentist strolled in with this pretty-young-thang and when we were introduced, I naturally assumed the girl had just graduated from dental school and would be comin' to practice with Alice. But no, the PYT isn't Alice's new dental partner! She's her new life companion. Damn, why don't people clue me in on such things before I go and make an ass out of myself?"

Liz said matter-of-factly, "I thought you knew Alice enjoyed an alternate life style."

"Well, no. I just thought she liked wearin' tailored suits and bossin' people, tellin' them how to floss." Finished with that tidbit, I sprinted off on another subject. "Then, just when I had decided the datin' pool had dried up, it started rainin' men."

"How so?" she asked.

Hunting around the kitchen for my missing purse, I explained, "First, Will Sharpe drops by for quiche and asks me to supper when he is off duty this weekend. So, we're goin' out tomorrow night. He's goin' to cook for me. Imagine that. Somebody cookin' for me. Then Rob, who I've not seen since he left for Korea better than thirty years ago, comes by. Seems that he has retired from the military and moved back to Knoxville. Says I'm the only girl whose name he remembers from when he lived here and wonders if we could go out sometime."

"That is flatterin'. What did you say to him?" Liz put our wrapped food in three plastic grocery bags.

"Say to who?" Joey asked when he breezed into the kitchen to grab his stash of food.

Liz answered for me. "An old boyfriend of Rachael's."

"Oh." He sounded disappointed with our choice of topics. "Gotta go work out. See y'all Monday morning. I'm outta here," he called, pushing open the back door.

"Don't let that door slam!" I yelled after him, but I was too late to prevent the inevitable. I looked towards Liz. "Must be a Joey thing," I commented. "You know, there'll be a lot of things I'll miss about this place, but that slammin' door won't be one of them."

"Right." She nodded her agreement. "So, what did you say to Rob?"

Continuing my search, I replied, "How could I refuse a retired general who just left the Pentagon? I told him I thought it would be kinda nice to catch up. Have you seen my purse anywhere?"

"I think I saw it on the other side of the fridge. I'll just put your sack over by the door so you'll see it on your way out."

"Better put it inside the fridge because Joe Bill is comin' by to take me for a ride over the mountain to Fontana. Can you believe that?"

She laughed. "You're right. It is rainin' men. Whatever happened to his wife?"

Not wanting to repeat all the details related to me this morning in his call, I shortened the tragedy to a few sentences. "He said she came down with some mean form of mouth cancer and was dead within six months. And didn't even smoke. Some surgeon friend of his tried removin' the cancer, but she hardly made it through the recovery before things started goin' south."

"Damn," she whispered sympathetically. Her voice brightened as she quoted, "Well, when one door shuts, another one opens."

I looked at her over the frames of my glasses. "Lizzie-Lou, you're soundin' like a mother. In my case, however, there's three openin' doors."

We both jumped upon hearing a knock on the back door. Joe Bill pushed the door open. "Hi. Are you ready?"

"As soon as I put my hands on my purse." Having just said that, I found my blue leather bag where someone other than me had stacked empty boxes in front of it. "Dang that Joey! Here it is."

"You might want to bring just your keys," Joe Bill suggested, "because I thought we would take my bike. OK by you?"

"OK by me."

I retrieved my keys before returning my purse to its new hidey-hole. After verifying that the door would lock, I followed Liz through the doorway, walking by Joe Bill's muscular body on my way toward a waiting sleek, black Harley. After waving our goodbyes to Liz, he handed me a massive helmet. I considered the strange object in my hands, not knowing exactly how to place the heavily padded protection on my head.

"Here, let me help you," Joe Bill offered, taking the shiny helmet and placing it on my head. He snapped the strap in place, snugly under my chin.

I watched him swing his right leg over the saddle before securing a matching helmet firmly on his head. Next I heard a crackle before a distant male voice in my head said distinctly, "Be careful as you get on."

Puzzled by that never-before-heard voice, I looked skyward. Normally, whenever I got on a bike, my mind replayed Mom's dire warning that I would soon wreck and scar my face.

Damn, I thought, not again! I haven't heard voices since Baltimore. I turned, vainly searching for the source of that caution before I heard that same male voice laugh.

"Rachael, I've got the intercom on so we can talk while we ride without having to shout to be heard."

"Oh, Joe Bill," I sighed gratefully, "I thought I had lost my grip and was hearin' things!"

Seventeen

Dressed in an apricot, two-piece outfit crocheted last winter and with hair brushed and makeup freshly applied, Rachael appeared nearly ready for the coming proceedings. Startled to find herself in front of the cheval mirror, she jumped slightly as her reflection registered for the first time this afternoon. So engrossed in her old memories, she had been unaware of time passing or the steps required for being this far into her preparations.

Now more collected, she turned sideways, drew her stomach in and patted her taut belly. Admiring how well the dress draped over her body's generous curves, she reminded herself to hold those muscles tight and to stand as erect as five-feet-one-and-a-half inches would allow.

Frowning slightly at the effort required to keep her stomach flat, Rachael realized, no matter how hard she worked abs at the gym, that little fat pad had never quite gone away. After relaxing her stomach muscles, the slight paunch quickly reappeared under the lacy garment.

"Oh, what the hell," she muttered, "I'm no spring chicken and neither is he."

Once more, she turned to check the straightness of her seamed hosiery. Turning again to face her reflection, she made one final appraisal before checking off the time-honored requirements.

Something old. Her hands strayed to her ears to touch the dangling sapphire and gold ear bobs first worn by Greatgranny Jubelle Lee. A cousin in New Orleans, who had inherited the earrings from her mother, Rachael's Aunt Maurie, had sent them by registered mail with a note wishing they might bring better luck for this coming marriage than Rachael had enjoyed on her two previous trips to the altar. The glint bouncing off the antique gold blended well with the rich apricot tone of her dress.

Something blue. She had splurged for new undies in the palest blue trimmed with white lace. Even the garter belt holding up her ecru stockings matched.

Something borrowed. Her right hand moved to the delicate gold chain that carried a misshapen pearl enclosed in a gold mounting. Its links had been precisely cut so that the special jewel came to rest inside the hollow at the base of her throat. Caressing the petite pearl discovered at Williamsburg, she honored the memory of the man the gem represented.

Whereas some people might be living on borrowed time, Rachael felt she was marrying on borrowed love and had pondered long and hard before accepting this unexpected proposal. After Christopher's death, she had never intended to marry again. Indeed, she thought she would never again have enough love inside her to share with another man.

Pleased with her overall reflection, she leaned forward to better check her makeup. From across her bedroom, a song played on the radio. Stepping back from the mirror, she listened to Mick and the Stones, unconsciously joining in the line, '*you just might find you get what you need.*'

She turned to face her ever-faithful companions on the bed. With their once dark, sable points now silvered with age, the elderly sisters rested more these days than they played.

Still sleek Sybyl lay on her side, stretched out long and languidly near the foot, her head hanging limp over the mattress's edge. A heftier Beatrice contentedly hunkered atop a pillow at the head, comfortable as any setting hen.

"Ladies, what do you think? Do I pass muster?" she questioned them.

Sybyl raised her eyes to the woman who asked so earnestly. Beatrice turned her head only slightly in the speaker's direction. Signaling their approval, both slowly blinked their sapphire blue eyes once.

Placing her glasses upon her nose and adjusting her hair behind the earpieces, Rachael walked to the bedroom window overlooking the back gardens where the ceremony was to take place. Gently separating two of the blind's wooden slats, she peered down into the backyard. Upon hearing the living room clock chime the quarter hour, she knew by the single run of the Westminster chimes that in fifteen minutes she would need to have her sandals strapped on and be out the front door and on her way to where her assembling friends awaited.

"But . . . am I really ready for this?"

She had grave concerns if she was prepared for any commitment, legal or otherwise. She had only known her groom-to-be since the 1960s, whereas she had been with Christopher for centuries.

The movement of her mother's snowy white hair caught Rachael's attention. Dressed in a flowing jersey gown, the color recalling the delicate blooms of Grandmother Taite's heirloom double lilac, her mother sat on the weathered-to-gray teak bench, talking with Liz and nodding her head in agreement with something the younger woman said. By the forward tilt of her mother's body, Rachael recognized that she was deeply involved in whatever they were discussing.

Hugh Ed towered nearby as if guarding his new bride whom he had toiled so long to earn. Only the biblical Jacob, laboring for his second wife who was his heart's desire, could have invested as much effort. She counted up the years he had indentured himself in school while painting houses and working on Liz's properties in his spare time. Hugh Ed now efficiently managed all of his wife's real estate holdings, sold real estate on the side and oversaw the maintenance of their properties as well as Rachael's recently acquired office building. The only painting she was aware of that he did these days was loving portraits of his wife and their adopted child. With the ever-present chain to his wallet sparkling in the bright sunlight, Hugh Ed had dressed for her special day by adding a silvery gray, silk vest atop his starched white shirt and freshly pressed blue jeans whose distinct creases were visible even from Rachael's distant vantage point.

Liz wore the same gauzy, pale yellow, ankle-length, flowery dress that she had worn to her own wedding in April. Draped easily across her cocked left hip, Deuce sported navy shorts and a white shirt topped by a red bow tie. His childish ringlets, caught in the sun's rays, reflected back new-gold glints. Long-legged and lanky even as a two-year-old, the mark of the Dalton clan was obvious even to the most casual observer's eyes. Held instinctively close to Liz's heart, the handsome toddler was Travis and Holly's child, too soon orphaned when his parents died in a crushing automobile accident on a rain slick road before winter solstice.

After Hugh Ed took his grandson to rear, Liz had lost her heart to both Dalton men and quit running from his advances. Rachael smiled, amused by the knowledge that had Margaret been present, their missing friend would have commented that Liz had cast her lure into the dating pool patiently as any skilled angler casts into a rushing mountain stream for a brookie, until Lizzie-Lou caught what she wanted.

A stocky figure purposefully striding down the drive to the first crossover for the wet weather creek next captured Rachael's attention. From the shock of silvery, thick hair, Rachael knew who had arrived and nodded her approval of his attire. As a former priest, Michael Thomas Stooksbury impressively looked the part with black, pleated trousers and the narrow clerical band of white at his throat atop a black, short-sleeved shirt. As a notary, he would make the proceedings legal; however, only because his religious views matched hers had she entrusted him to officiate at the approaching ceremony.

Her thoughts drifted away to the afternoon when she first met the cleric.

※

Two springs before . . .

After renting her beloved cabin to a man who had arrived from out of state to supervise Knoxville airport's remodeling, Rachael had been reduced to short hikes in the mountains whenever she needed to escape. The extra money, which would pad her cash flow over the next four years, did little to reimburse her for the loss of not being able to retreat to her cozy hidey-hole.

She had gone alone to the mountains on the day of the new moon. Hoping the showy red and gold native columbine and the shy, wild blue phlox blooming among the emerging grasses would refresh her spirits in preparation for the lunar rite, she had opted for the beauty of White Oak Sink.

Coming toward her amid the isolated meadow's solitude, a hiker had appeared, slowly strolling through ankle-deep, young grass. She had immediately admired his proud bearing which was in strong contrast to the backdrop of soft, spring-growth green covering the small cove's steep walls. Having seen no one else during the hike into the center of the sink, she had quickly assumed the stranger must have followed another trail into the secluded area.

Drawing closer, she had stopped, in uncharacteristic boldness, to share with him the beauty surrounding them. Feeling the warmth from his direct gaze and hearing the appreciation of nature he expressed as their conversation continued, Rachael had sensed the man to be at peace within himself and with his place in the world.

Talking easily with the stranger, she had inadvertently used the expression 'the beauty that Mother had provided.' With that one phrase, their eyes had instantly locked in recognition of kindred souls.

Retracing her steps, they had continued in deep discussion, to the slender, sparse waterfall that cooled one corner of the secreted cove before disappearing into a deep crevice. Against the soothing background their Mother had created, the two had spent the remainder of the pleasant afternoon sharing their similar philosophies of life.

The irony behind their chance meeting was underlined by the unspoken care she and Michael Thomas circumspectly observed, quietly staying below the Bible Belt's religious radar. Even now, the circumstances surrounding their initial meeting continued to mystify her.

❧

She remained looking through her bedroom window down to her family of friends gathering below as the former minister was warmly greeted by the others. Soon her gaze was drawn to focus on Deuce.

Waiting for the grownups to do something entertaining, the fidgeting youngster had grown tired of Liz's confining arms and tried to push himself free. She watched as Michael Thomas reached to take the fussy child. He next touched the toddler's forehead, using a secret blessing that Rachael, now a recent convert into the Ancient Ways, recognized. Her smile widened as Deuce leaned forward, gently patting the older man's face in return. After being returned to his adoptive mother, little Deuce settled himself onto Liz's side, contentedly placing his head against the curve of her shoulder.

During the past year, Rachael had often seen restless souls of all ages responding alike to the priest's calming manner.

Coming across a neighboring driveway, her Intended appeared, seemingly out of nowhere. Observing his measured approach through the garden's back entry, her heart skipped a beat.

Damn, that man was almost too handsome. She felt a twinge of regret that her genetic pool had dried up some time back. Had she been younger, they could have created beautiful offspring.

Don't even go there, Rachael gently chided herself. Be happy with what you've got. This is the hand you were dealt, play it out.

She returned her attention to the man she was to marry. Though not as tall as Hugh Ed, he had a more massive figure. There was a strong sense of stability to him that Rachael found deeply comforting. With shoulders held proudly, he carried himself well as he patiently shepherded his mother to where the others waited.

Holding a clear acrylic cane in her left hand to aid her balance, the tall woman walked splendidly upright, as regally as her son. Upon reaching the small gathering, she took a seat next to her counterpart on the teak bench, her dusty rose suit contrasting well with Rachael's mother's soft bluish-purple.

Rachael remembered a piece of advice heard too many times from childhood: Watch closely how a man treats the women of his family for that is how he will treat you. She hoped that singular piece of motherly wisdom was correct. For having observed how her groom-to-be cared for his widowed mother, she knew she would be as well attended in the future as she had been these last few months. If it were true.

After assisting his mother, Rachael's new love placed a portable disc player on the brick terrace. As they had planned, he would start the music at half past the hour when she was scheduled to leave her house.

Her thoughts immediately went to the memory-laden hours they had spent arranging and recording tunes for today. Starting with her pet, Debussy's "Reverie," they had compiled a blend of old Carolina shag songs, some K. T. Oslin, a little rock and roll, a touch of blue grass, a few more classical pieces and ending with his favorite, Ivory Joe Hunter's "Since I Met You, Baby." Their amassed musical selections, as eclectic as their lives had been leading to this day, meshed together surprisingly well.

Her groom positioned himself near both mothers, feet firmly planted and his hands clasped behind his back. His stance brought to her mind a seasoned soldier at parade rest.

She recalled yesterday when he had asked for assistance selecting the summer-weight suit he now wore. Since his muscular body was so perfectly formed, the suit had merely required the pants being hemmed for a fit that appeared custom-made, a fact Rachael found totally intriguing since she had such difficulty buying clothes off the rack.

From her vantage point in the house, his suit's rich navy background overpowered the light-blue pinstripe she knew the fabric to have. His red and blue, boldly striped tie lent a colorful accent. Upon noticing the sprig of variegated ivy pinned to his lapel, Rachael reminded herself not to forget her own flower spray.

He turned, enabling her to see the back of his head. She heartily approved of the minuscule, circular bald spot resting amid his perfectly styled, salt-and-pepper hair. With his inherited tonsorial flaw so obvious to the heavens above, Rachael hoped, as the early Romans had once believed, that envious Immortals would not be tempted to take this precious man from her.

He's a good man, she thought. We'll make a matched pair, complementing each other's strengths, shoring up each other's weaknesses. He'll guard my back.

We do make a good team, she assured herself, now sounding less than sure.

I think he is a good man, she told herself once more, yet feeling less certain in her decision to marry.

While her husband-to-be stood confidently waiting for their marriage to take place, Rachael questioned how he could appear so sure of himself while she was quaking with doubts. A feral sensation rose from deep within her, pulsing in time with her now racing heart. Immediately needing to use her arms for a comforting self-hug, she let the slats fall and tightly held her body as if to shore up her weakening resolve.

With her view of the garden now blocked, she cried out, "There's no way I can do this!"

After taking several deep breaths for encouragement, Rachael said aloud, hoping to instill confidence in herself, "I can do this. I can do this. I can."

With each declaration, her voice grew lower until the sentences echoed in her skull. Dropping her arms to her sides, she mentally continued, obediently repeating her new mantra: I can do this, I can do this.

"Well, at least," she said aloud, "I think I can do this."

Padding in stockingfeet to the closet to retrieve dress sandals from her horde of Charleston-purchased footwear, she once more became grossly unsure of her decision to wed. Breathing deeply in an attempt to rein in her stampeding fears, Rachael slipped her feet under the soft straps of the cream-colored leather.

After slowly inhaling more deep breaths and praying that she would be able to scrape together her crumbling courage, she again firmly muttered aloud, "I can do this. I can do this. I can do this."

With each affirmation, her panicked voice lowered until the words again became faint echoes inside her head. Unaware of tightly clutching the stems as if clinging to a life preserver, she removed her delicate bouquet from its box on the dresser and left her bedroom.

Rachael abruptly stopped at the head of the staircase, a death grip upon the stems in her clenched fists. With morbid fascination, she looked past the three pale, peachy-pink calla lilies cradled against graceful strands of variegated ivy and bound together by narrow streamers of softly knotted, silk ribbon in hues harmonizing with her dress and flowers. She found herself studying her skirt as it vibrated atop her trembling knees.

"You know, ladies, there's simply no way on this earth that I can possibly go through with this," Rachael abruptly announced to her feline companions.

While her brain desperately raced about looking for an excuse, any excuse, to cancel the pending nuptials, her legs became leaden. She watched her toes curl downward, bending the sandal's thin leather soles, in an attempt to firmly grip the oak flooring at the head of the stairs.

"Oh, Sweet Mother, what have I agreed to do?"

From behind her, Rachael heard a confident voice say, "Yes, you can do this, dear Rachael."

As a slight chill enveloped her arms and shoulders, she felt immediately comforted. Sensing that shawl of cool air was an embrace, she breathed in deeply, drawing sorely needed strength from his second visit of the day.

His familiar voice continued, "That's a fine man, Rachael. You've chosen well. Don't you see, my sweet Rachael, now you won't be lonely until we can meet again."

Recalling their original conversation, she softly laughed because that sentiment sounded just as audacious to her today as it had years ago. Still, she was not completely convinced that this pending ritual was one in which she could participate.

"But I can't go downstairs alone, I'm . . ." She faltered, before finally protesting, "I can't walk all the way out there all by myself."

It was fright that immobilized her but she would not allow herself to use the word 'afraid.' Having no fear of the man she could not see, she simply feared the unknown of her future.

Christopher continued, "I'm here. You aren't alone. I'll walk with you. Then when we reach the garden, I'll proudly give you away. Marry with my blessings, and always remember, my sweet Rachael, love is forever."

She found his rich voice comforting. His soothing words came softly into her ears, calming her as one would a frightened animal. As her breathing gradually became normal, her heart rate also slowed.

Although no vents existed in the upstairs hall to direct airflow from the still-winterized unit, Rachael was unperturbed when her body became engulfed by a moving mass of cold air. As if standing in a strong draft, she felt the damp coolness smoothing the ends of her hair before slowly moving to lovingly adjust the tiny pearl resting in the pulsating hollow of her throat.

Determinedly pulling in Christopher's abiding strength, she took time to make it her own. Finally, taking one last deep breath, she gathered herself. Accepting that her friends and the remainder of her life awaited just on the other side of the glass security door, Rachael confidently stepped down each stair tread toward the locked front entry.

Hesitating at the doorway, she concentrated on her hand that now grasped the key beneath the doorknob. Needing only to unlock the latch and walk out into the sunshine, Rachael smiled as she softly reminded herself, "No trouble. Just no trouble at all."

Photograph by Gordon Hodge
www.gordonhodge.com

Nancy Melinda Hunley is a retired dentist living in Knoxville, Tennessee. Although having written for personal amusement since grammar school, *This Time Around* is her first publication. Like Rachael, she shares her house with two cats and enjoys hiking in the Smokies. She is currently at work on a second novel, *The Edisto Games*.

Available soon are *Love in the Middle Ages*, a collection of poetry appealing to the unrequited angst in those of us who remember when Aretha Franklin, the queen of soul, was merely a lady in waiting and *Southern Graces*, a tongue-in-cheek guide to approved feminine behavior.

Check her web site at www.nmhunley.com for updates.

The Edisto Games

To whet your appetite for *The Edisto Games,* here is a taste from its prologue:

"On the map, the Edisto River links the interior of South Carolina with the Atlantic. Its thin blue line meanders roughly ninety miles from near Aiken on down to Beaufort on the coast. On its banks, you can see no more than a few inches into its murky depths. That fact alone makes the Edisto unique because the world possesses only a handful of black water rivers.

"Where the Edisto runs through the public rose gardens in the community of Snowshill, its waters are cold and dark. Just like the heart of Hamp Sellars."